Tears ran down he[...]
Colum, and in her he[...]
for ever. Anguish tore her at the mental vision of him
lying bleeding. But she knew that no matter how she
might grieve for the loss of her lover, the bond of union
she shared with her brother would always be paramount. Dermot and she were one soul and could never
be spiritually divided.

Other travellers in the waiting room looked at the
weeping woman with sympathetic eyes, but refrained
from intruding upon her distress. Weeping women were
an all too common sight in the railway stations of this
vast metropolis.

Montague's Whore

SARA FRASER

WARNER BOOKS

A *Warner* Book

First published in Great Britain in 1997
by Little, Brown and Company
This edition published by Warner Books in 1998

A CIP catalogue record for this book
is available from the British Library.

ISBN 0 7515 2430 1

Typeset in Times New Roman by M Rules
Printed and bound in Great Britain by
Mackays of Chatham PLC, Chatham, Kent

Warner Books
A Division of
Little, Brown and Company (UK)
Brettenham House
Lancaster Place
London WC2E 7EN

Montague's
Whore

Chapter One

London, 1859

The men crammed close around the table in the small room had been haggling and disputing for hours, and the air was hot and foul with rank-smelling tobacco smoke.

The light from the guttering oil lamp hanging from the low beam above the table glinted in Dermot Calatrava's dark angry eyes and glistened the sweat on his high forehead as he suddenly rose to his feet and slammed his fist down upon the dirty wooden boards.

'You talk and talk and talk, and do nothing,' he hissed with contempt. 'You're just as bad as those posturing fools in America, with all their bunkum and bluster.'

A tall, lantern-jawed man wearing the scarlet and blue uniform of the British Army jumped to his feet and, pointing at the long ragged scar which ran from his left eye to his chin, shouted, 'I got this at the storming of the Redan. Call me coward, and I'll break your dammed head for you.'

Calatrava, although physically smaller than his challenger, was unafraid of the threatened violence. 'Got that scar in the Crimea, did you? Then count it as the badge of a fool who has shed his blood fighting for the enemies of his own nation.'

'Sit down, Sergeant Slavin.'

The grey-bearded, bald-headed man who had been sitting silently in a deep-shadowed corner of the room now rose and came to stand at Calatrava's side. Although as short in stature as the younger man, he was more thickset, and his manner radiated authority.

The soldier, still glaring resentfully at his opponent, reluctantly resumed his seat, and the grey-bearded man addressed the gathering at large.

'I summoned you here tonight so that this gentleman could tell you of his plan. He is unknown to you, but I can vouch for him, so I want you to listen carefully to what he has to say. He has only just come back from America, and so has first-hand experience of what's going on there. We can all learn from him.'

He stepped back into the shadows, and Calatrava began to speak.

'To begin with there are a few things that you people should know about the Irish Americans . . .' The biting edge of sarcasm entered his tone. 'At midnight, full of drink, they are all ready to die for Erin. They are true Sons of the Gael. No sacrifice of their own money and effort, or blood is too much for them to make. They're positively screaming for the chance to take ship back to the Holy Ground and drive the English into the sea.' His full lips, almost feminine in their shapeliness, curled with contempt. 'But at eight o'clock the next morning Erin is forgotten, and all our American brethren can think about is grubbing for the almighty dollar to line their own pockets with.'

A neatly dressed, bespectacled man with the stooping shoulders and pasty complexion of someone who spent his days crouched over ledgers in a sunless counting

4

house, lifted his hand in timid plea for notice.

'Yes, sir?' Calatrava invited.

The clerk coughed nervously, then asked, 'If, as you tell us, sir, our brethren in America are all bunkum and bluster, then to whom can we turn for help?'

'To ourselves alone. There are more than sufficient numbers of true Irish patriots.'

More confidently now the clerk argued, 'But we haven't got the resources to equip an army. We need the Americans to supply us with the necessary arms and equipment and money to fight a war against England.'

An elderly, irascibly scowling man sitting at the far end of the table lifted his hand, and Calatrava nodded.

The aged voice was weak and querulous, the words lisped through long blackened teeth. 'I've come here tonight on the understanding that you were going to tell us how we could strike a blow for our freedom. So let's be hearing your plan, and waste no more time talking about things we already know too well.'

'Very well, sir. You shall hear it. My plan is very simple. We must provoke the English Government into once more taking measures of harsh repression against the people of Ireland.'

Instantly doubt clouded several faces and there sounded exclamations of protest.

Calatrava openly sneered at his audience. 'Ahh now, how else can you get people to rise in rebellion unless they are brutally treated? And how else will we be able to shame the Irish Americans into helping us, unless they can see their own kith and kin being once more crushed down under John Bull's boot?'

'How can you justify bringing sorrow upon our own people? Haven't they suffered enough?' the old man challenged.

'Most of them deserve to suffer, for being such servile lickspittles to their English masters,' Calatrava spat back fiercely. 'You all know that I speak only the truth. Just consider our people now. At this time they are completely disunited. The upper classes have no interest in creating a separate nation, they're the same breed as their high-born English friends. The tenant farmers are only interested in their better harvests. The owners of property and land are only interested in getting their rents. The respectable people of the towns are quite indifferent, even hostile to the idea of an Irish nation. It's only among the sons of peasants, among the labourers and small tradesmen that there is any disaffection with the English Government . . .'

From the shadows Terence McCulloch interjected. 'Tell us how you intend to provoke the Government to carry out a fresh repression against our people?'

Calatrava's epicene features wore a rapt expression, and his dark eyes were glazed, as if he were contemplating some inner vision. His voice dropped so that his listeners strained to hear him. 'I intend to strike at the very heart of the English ruling class. I intend to strike at their Royal Family.'

For some moments there was complete silence as his listeners absorbed what he had said. Then a hubbub of voices filled the air.

McCulloch came to stand facing Calatrava, and gestured for silence. The noise stilled, and McCulloch demanded: 'Strike at the Royal Family, is it? Do you mean kill them?'

Calatrava's full lips curved in a grim smile, disclosing small white even teeth. 'But of course. What else could I mean? The destruction of the Royal Family will strike terror into the hearts of Ireland's enemies. The news of it will resound throughout the world . . . And the English Government will be forced into acts of repression, because we shall make it clear that it is Irish patriots who are killing their precious Royalty.'

His dark eyes swiftly scanned the upturned faces around him, and he experienced a savage contempt for the varying degrees of shock and alarm that those faces displayed.

'Well now, gentlemen,' he baited sneeringly. 'What do you think of my plan? You all look as if it excites you.' He chuckled with sardonic amusement. 'I thought that bold rebels like yourselves would jump at a chance to destroy our nation's oppressors.'

By now his listeners were fast recovering from their initial shock, and it was the soldier, Slavin, who first spoke out.

'I've no great love for the Royalty, but I've worn the Queen's coat for nigh on twenty years, and I'll have no part of murdering her or her family.'

A loud chorus of agreement sounded from around the table.

Terence McCulloch stroked his full beard reflectively, his gaze flickering from man to man, before meeting the questioning stare of Dermot Calatrava. He gave him a barely perceptible wink, and then said, 'Your proposal has given us much to think about, sir. What I suggest is that you leave us now, and we can discuss it further among ourselves.'

Calatrava bowed in courteous acquiescence. 'I'll bid

you goodnight then, Mr McCulloch, and yourselves, gentlemen.'

'I'll see you out,' McCulloch offered. He lifted a candle from the battered dresser behind him, lit it at the lamp, then led the way out of the attic room and down several flights of stairs to the ground floor of the house. In the entrance lobby he took a top hat, gloves and cane from the hall stand.

'These are yours, I think.'

'Thank you.' Calatrava adjusted his sleeved, knee-length cloak, and straightened his silk cravat, then accepted the other articles from his companion, and clapped the top hat onto his pomaded black hair. He presented a dapper, affluent figure, and his erect stance compensated for his lack of physical height.

McCulloch moved to open the street door and stood to one side of it with the air of a manservant waiting for a distinguished guest to leave.

Calatrava halted midway through the open doorway and stated accusingly, 'Your people are not what you represented them to be, McCulloch. They appear to be sadly lacking in spirit and courage.'

The older man grimaced and spread his arms in a placatory gesture. 'They didn't react in the way I'd hoped, I confess. But I'm sure that once they become accustomed to the idea, they'll do all that is required of them.'

Calatrava's dark eyes were cold, and his voice tinged with a hint of menace.

'I hope that it will not take them too long to accustom themselves to the idea. I have placed a great deal of trust in you, Mr McCulloch. I would not like to find that my trust had been misplaced.'

The older man bridled instantly. 'What do you mean by that?'

'Exactly what I say,' Calatrava snapped and passed on through the door to be swallowed in the misty darkness, only the diminishing echoes of his boot heels as they struck the cobbles signalling his progress.

McCulloch stood in the open doorway until the last echoes of footsteps died away, and not for the first time experienced an uneasy uncertainty about Dermot Calatrava.

The laborious climb back up the steep flights of stairs to the attic room caused McCulloch's diseased heart to thud painfully and he was panting wheezily as he rejoined the other men.

Even before he could seat himself at the table voices remonstrated angrily.

'That fella is a madman! He'll bring ruin on all of us if we listen to him.'

'It's true, Mr McCulloch.'

'That's right!'

'We can't go killing the Queen of England. They'd hunt us down like rats if we did!'

'Yes, there's none of us would escape being hung.'

Grey-faced and sweating, McCulloch drew in rapid gulps of the hot, foul air in an effort to slow the rapid, painful thudding of his heart, and his thoughts were sour: Hark to them whining and yapping. They sound like cur dogs. Calatrava is right, they are cowards.

His heartbeat gradually slowed and his breathing eased, and he was able to snap curtly, 'Will you hold your noise, and give me chance to speak. Remember who commands here.'

They subsided into grudging, sullen silence.

McCulloch stared grimly for some seconds then, satisfied that he had quelled them, went on. 'I can't help but think that there is some substance to the gentleman's plan. The assassination of the Royal Family could well have the effect he claims it will. And, if nothing else, it will demonstrate that no one, not even the highest in this land, is safe from us, and prove to our brethren in America that we're a force to be reckoned with.'

'I'm a soldier, not a bloody assassin!' Sergeant Slavin roared in furious indignation. 'I don't make war on women and children, and I'm surprised that you should even be considering that man's plan, Mr McCulloch.'

'None of us wants to make war on women and children, Sergeant Slavin. We're all men of honour here,' McCulloch answered levelly, but resentment lurked in his eyes.

'Then let us act like men of honour, and not as assassins,' Slavin retorted heatedly. 'When the time is right then let us fight like soldiers and meet the English army in open battle.'

There sounded a general acclamation for his words, and McCulloch accepted that nothing more could be achieved by prolonging this particular meeting.

'Let us take a vote on the gentleman's proposal. Those in favour, signify.'

No hands rose.

'Those against, signify.'

Every hand rose with one exception.

McCulloch stared curiously at the bespectacled clerk. 'Have you no opinion to voice, Mr Docherty? You've not voted either way.'

Thomas Docherty's eyes, grotesquely enlarged behind

the bulbous lenses of his spectacles, blinked rapidly with nervous tension. He coughed twice, then muttered, 'I'm undecided, Mr McCulloch.'

Angered by the voting, McCulloch brought the meeting to a close and, as was customary, those present left at intervals by ones and twos so as not to draw undue attention to themselves by a mass exodus.

Soon only he and Thomas Docherty were left in the room, and Docherty rose to leave also. There was something in the clerk's manner that aroused McCulloch's sharp-honed wariness, and he requested, 'Wait, Mr Docherty, sit down again. I'd like to talk to you.'

The man reseated himself.

'Is something troubling you, Mr Docherty?'

The man's sense of unease was now palpable, and McCulloch frowned slightly, but spoke softly. 'What is it, Mr Docherty? You can confide in me.'

Docherty's enlarged eyes blinked rapidly behind the bulbous lenses, and the soft white-skinned hands clasped and entwined upon the black-clad knees. He spoke diffidently. 'The young gentleman from America, Mr McCulloch? How well do you know him?'

'Well enough,' McCulloch informed him curtly. Then he demanded, 'Come now, Mr Docherty, speak plainly. I can see that something is troubling you.'

'Very well, Mr McCulloch.' The clerk's manner hardened perceptibly. 'In my opinion the young gentleman is like a keg of gunpowder which needs only a single spark to explode it. Tonight we have voted against following his plan. But what is to stop him from acting without us? And if he does so, then he will stir up a hornet's nest. We shall all of us be placed in grave jeopardy.'

McCulloch scowled. 'I can trust my own judgement,

11

Mr Docherty. He won't act without my consent.'

'To be sure, your judgement has always proven excellent, Mr McCulloch.' Docherty hastened to mollify the older man. 'And I know that you're not a man to be fooled by anyone. But again, I must ask you, how well do you know this young gentleman? I formed the impression that he is somewhat unstable in his mind.'

Unpalatable though it was, McCulloch was forced to accept that he shared his companion's opinion concerning Calatrava's instability. To hide his own misgivings he forced himself to chuckle and joke bluffly.

'Sure now, Mr Docherty, aren't we all unstable in our minds? Stable men don't get involved in rebellions, do they?' He clapped the other man on the back. 'Don't you worry about a thing, Mr Docherty. I've got the young gentleman under control. Good night to you now. Have a safe journey home.'

Chapter Two

Rosaleen Calatrava slipped the robe off her shoulders and let it fall slowly to the floor, then stood motionless. The soft lamplight fell across her body and the naked old man drew long shuddering breaths as he hungrily stared at her full breasts, rising and falling in cadence with her breathing.

She beckoned with the riding crop she was holding in her right hand, and ordered harshly, 'Come here, you dirty little boy.'

He moved jerkily, sweat sheening his wrinkled face and withered neck.

'You can touch me.' She laid the shaft of the riding crop against his cheek in warning. 'But take care you don't hurt me.'

His trembling fingers gently stroked the firm warm flesh of her rounded shoulders, then travelled downwards to cup and caress the full breasts. He bent forwards, his lips sucking the dark, jutting nipples in turn, then clumsily knelt before her and buried his face in the curly black triangle of hair between her thighs while his hands clutched and kneaded her smooth shapely buttocks. She raised the riding crop high and brought it slashing down onto his scrawny shoulders, and muffled moans sounded from deep in his throat as the riding crop bit mercilessly into his flesh again and again.

The reddened weals were thick upon his skin when he finally shuddered and cried out sharply, then releasing his grip, slumped onto hands and knees, his mouth gaping wide as he gasped and wheezed.

She remained standing above him, her dark eyes contemptuous. Then she ordered, 'Come now, get up.'

She helped him to rise to his feet and he clung to her, and she could not repress a faint grimace of distaste as she felt his shrivelled flabby sweatiness pressing against her.

She led him to the bed and helped him onto its silken coverlets.

'Rest now,' she told him, then spoke more sharply as he voiced a whimpering protest, and attempted to pull her down beside him. 'No, you must rest. I'll join you later.'

He pouted, and for a moment resembled a petulant, ancient baby, and she grimaced then slapped his cheek lightly and, taking her gown, left the room.

In her own bedroom she tugged the silken cord of the bell pull and when a tall, raw-boned, middle-aged woman came in answer to the summons, ordered, 'Get my bath ready, Theresa.'

'I'm thinking that you'll not be taking your bath for a while.' The woman's accent was of the Dublin slums. 'Your brother's come to see you. He says it's urgent business he's come on, and he must see you straight away.'

Concern shadowed the younger woman's eyes. 'How long has he been here?'

'About an hour, more or less. I told him you was busy, so he waited,' Theresa answered off-handedly. 'So I'll wait with the bath, shall I?'

Momentary irritation caused the younger woman to

snap curtly, 'No, you won't wait with the bath. You'll get it prepared for me this instant.'

The woman snorted indignantly, but made no answer and after a brief moment bustled away.

In the opulently furnished drawing room Dermot Calatrava was seated on one of the plush velvet armchairs smoking a cheroot when his twin sister came to him.

He rose and bowed gallantly to her. 'Rosaleen, as ever you look beautiful.'

He regarded her admiringly, for she was indeed a very beautiful woman. Her long black hair hung in shining coils down her back, her lustrous brown eyes were almond shaped, giving her an almost oriental appearance, and even the voluminous folds of her silken gown could not hide the voluptuous curves of her shapely body.

She crossed to the screen-shielded fireplace and stared into the large mirror that hung above it. He came to stand behind her, peering over her shoulder at their joint images.

Side by side like this, of equal height, sharing the dark colouring inherited from their Spanish ancestor, they bore an uncanny resemblance to each other, the man's good looks a masculine reflection of her beauty.

'How did it go tonight?' she asked.

'Aggghhh!' he exclaimed in disgust. 'They're useless!'

He went on to give her a full account of everything that had occurred at McCulloch's house.

She frowned angrily. 'Dear God above! Isn't it always the same. Promises and more promises, but never any action.'

As her anger fuelled upon itself a trace of Irish

15

brogue had entered her speech, overlaying her cultured English accent.

She moved away from the fireplace and seated herself upon one of the over-stuffed chairs, and bent her head as if deep in thought. The man remained standing, dragging the smoke of his cheroot deep into his lungs.

As the minutes lengthened, and his sister maintained her silence, the man finally pressed her. 'Well, Rosie. What shall we do?'

She considered briefly, then told him. 'If McCulloch isn't ready to help us, then be damned to him! We'll have to make plans to do the business ourselves. I want you to keep watching the she-shirt, and to try to find out when he'll be in a suitable place for us to make contact with him.'

'Do you want me to approach him?' he questioned, and she shook her head.

'No, I'll do that.'

'What if he kicks up rough?'

She smiled mirthlessly. 'I don't think he's the kick-up-rough type. And anyway, I'll take Thomas with me.'

She opened the drawer of the small table at the side of her chair and took out a silver box which contained cheroots and some lucifer matches. She selected a cheroot and lit it, then leaned back in her chair, drawing the fragrant smoke deep into her body and exhaling it in a long thin grey stream. Again she appeared deep in thought, and the young man waited patiently until she should speak. When she did so, it was as if she were talking to herself, and her voice was so soft and low that he had to strain to hear what she said.

'The ideal target would be the brood mare herself, but I doubt that we'll be able to get at her at present.

16

Her husband might be a better possibility. But his death wouldn't rouse the Government or the people to much anger. He's not that well liked. So, I think we'll concentrate on the Prince. If he's still at the Lodge at Richmond he'll be more vulnerable.'

She lapsed into silence once more, and the long streamers of grey smoke wreathed the air before her. Then she nodded, as if satisfied, and told her companion, 'The Prince it is. We'll go for him.'

Dermot Calatrava nodded. 'Very well. And afterwards, what then?'

'We lie low until the fuss dies down. Then we strike again.'

The young man scowled, and demanded in a surprised tone, 'You'll be staying here?'

She frowned at his tone. 'It's my home. Where else should I go?'

'But I thought that you'd be glad to get away from here. You've money enough salted away for us both to go to America. We could establish ourselves there, and organise for the rebellion. Why must you stay here?'

Anger entered her eyes and she reminded him sharply, 'Are you forgetting where the money for your fine clothes and easy living comes from?'

'No, I'm not forgetting.' There was bitterness and disgust in his voice and expression. 'But I'd have thought that once we've done the job, then you'd be only too happy to leave this life behind you. It's a torment to me having my own sister an old man's paid whore.'

Her face blanched with a terrible fury and before her brother could move she sprang from her chair and her hands whiplashed across his face.

17

'A torment, is it?' she almost shrieked. 'A torment, is it? Well, it doesn't stop you from using my money, does it? It doesn't stop you from living off what I earn. From living off a whore's wages!'

Dismayed by her reaction, he cowered back from her, shielding his head with raised arms.

'No, Rosie! No! I didn't mean it the way you think! No, Rosie. Don't do this. Stop. Please, Rosie. Stop this.'

At last her fury spent itself, and she let her arms fall to her side. Her breasts rose and fell rapidly as she took breath and she jerked her head. 'Get out.'

Still shaken by her savage assault, he silently obeyed her command.

She sank down into a chair, her emotions a maelstrom raging within her. Remorse at having attacked her brother forced itself into the ascendancy, and she muttered aloud. 'Why do you have to say such things to me, Dermot? Why? Isn't my own shame enough for me to bear?'

She began to cry, the sobs tearing from her throat. 'Why, Dermot? Why do you have to be so cruel? Why?'

The bond between sister and brother was close and intense, forged by many years of shared hardship and bitter experience. And yet there were times, such as today, when they would savagely wound each other's deepest feelings. Wounds made harder to bear by the sheer depth of their attachment to each other. An attachment so strong that sometimes Rosaleen would wonder if they did not indeed share a common soul.

When she had calmed she tugged the bell pull, and almost instantly Theresa appeared.

Rosaleen scowled, and challenged. 'Behind the door again, were you? Listening to what doesn't concern you?'

The woman's bony features remained impassive, and she stated calmly, 'Your bath's gone cold by now, I shouldn't wonder.'

'Then put some more hot water into it, you fool,' Rosaleen snapped.

The woman stayed where she was, and Rosaleen demanded, 'Well?'

'America,' Theresa stated baldly.

'What about it?'

'Wouldn't we be safer going there after it's done?'

'Getting frightened now, are you?' Rosaleen jeered.

Once again Theresa's features remained impassive, and she answered in an expressionless monotone. 'Haven't you learned yet, girl, that when you kick the English, they kick you back? If we kill their prince, they'll not rest until they have us dangling from a gallows. Dead heroes are not what Ireland needs. Only living beings can go on fighting for her. If we get away to America, then we'll be able to go on fighting. If we stay here, then chances are that they'll lay us by the heels and choke the life from us.'

'I'll bear that in mind,' Rosaleen promised ironically. 'Now will you get my bath ready.'

Theresa nodded, and walked ponderously away.

Alone, Rosaleen turned and once more stood staring into the mirror, but it was not her own features that she saw reflected there. Pallid images shimmered before her eyes. Faces that were gaunt and wasted with suffering. Faces that were long dead.

'Soon,' she whispered to them. 'Soon, it will be done. Soon, I swear to you . . . Soon.'

Chapter Three

The afternoon sun was beginning to cast longer shadows across the greensward of the Regent's Park. Swarms of noisy, excited children played their games of battledore and shuttlecock, Prisoner's Base and tag, running, gambolling, skipping across the grass, shrieking and laughing, their faces flushed and rosy, while their neatly uniformed nursemaids gathered in clusters to exchange gossip and to flirt with the numerous scarlet-coated soldiers and young loungers who thronged the park in company with the ragged beggars and homeless wanderers.

A road encircled the park and at this hour it also was crowded with carriages carrying crinolined ladies with gay bonnets and frivolous parasols, escorted by horsemen and horsewomen.

Rosaleen owned a smart carriage and pair, but today she preferred to walk in the park, fashionably elegant in her blue, bell-shaped crinoline skirts and long green shawl-mantle, her close-fitting bonnet creating a dainty framework for her heart-shaped face, at which many men's eyes stared longingly. But the warning scowl of her brown-liveried footman, following three paces behind her, was sufficient to deter anyone from approaching her.

Thomas Quinn, Theresa's husband, was huge in

stature, his scarred face a fearsome testimony to his old profession of prize-fighter.

A bouncing ball would have cannoned into Rosaleen's skirts, but she moved with graceful swiftness to catch it in her hands. The small boy intent on its pursuit halted and stood staring warily at her, as if fearful of reprimand. She smiled and tossed the ball to him, and he laughed with delight and scampered away, hooting in pleasure. For a brief instant her heart was sick within her as she remembered the boy child she had lost and wondered if he would have grown to resemble this mischievous, rosy-cheeked urchin.

Then she furiously castigated herself for her own weakness. Your child is dead, and you can never bear another one, so don't waste time in futile regrets. Concentrate only on gaining revenge.

Bitterness welled up within her, suppressing all the softer emotions which had been permeating her heart as she walked among these children.

She passed a soldier who was laughing and flirting with a pert little nursemaid, and her ears caught the lilting tones of his Irish brogue. Sudden fury against him surged through her, and she inwardly berated him. Why do you and thousands like you fight and die for the British Empire? Why can't you fight to liberate your own country?

The pert nursemaid frowned at her, and for a brief moment Rosaleen feared that she had unconsciously voiced her angry thoughts aloud. Then she saw that the young soldier was staring at her with open admiration, and she realised that the nursemaid was merely displaying jealousy.

She walked a further fifty yards, and saw the man she

had come here to meet. He was grey-haired, of medium height, his clothing shabby, his face patterned with deep-etched lines of hardship and deprivation.

She signalled Thomas Quinn to halt, and went on alone.

'You're late,' the man assailed her angrily. 'You know well the risk I'm taking hanging about here waiting for you.'

She reacted indignantly. 'And you know well the risk I'm taking, Sean Gallagher. I could get hung for it as well as you.'

She extracted a small paper-wrapped package from her skirt pocket and slipped it to him.

He became apologetic as he secreted the package. 'Jasus, I'm sorry for barking at you, Rosaleen. It's just that me nerves are all in pieces. I'm scared that some bloody Peeler will recognise me.'

She shook her head. 'It's the least risk, Sean. After ten years it's not very likely that any Peeler will know you, is it? We'd best part now. It wouldn't do for anyone who might recognise me to see us together.'

There came a sudden tumult of shouts, screams and movement further across the park, closer to the wild beasts' enclosures, and Sean Gallagher jerked with fright like a startled animal.

Rosaleen stared across the intervening distance, shielding her eyes against the sun. 'It's just some men brawling,' she said. 'I expect they've been on the drink.'

Neither of them noticed the ragged youth who came swiftly and silently behind them.

Rosaleen felt a sudden tug at her wrist, as the youth slashed the strap of her purse with his knife, and then he was fleeing.

'Stop! Stop thief!' she shouted involuntarily.

Other voices instantly took up the cry. 'Stop thief! Stop thief! Stop thief!' and several passers-by went in chase.

'Oh, Jasus! What shall we do?' Gallagher was white with fear.

'You go now, and quickly,' Rosaleen told him, and he scurried away.

Rosaleen looked again at the fleeing youth and saw that he was distancing his pursuers.

He's going to get away, she thought, and despite her anger at being robbed, paradoxically she found that she was experiencing some sympathy for the hunted thief. She could well imagine the terror that was pulsing through him as he fled with the noisy crowd baying for his blood.

Then from behind her there sounded the thudding of hooves on the grass and a horseman burst past, so close that the small clods of turf flung up by the horse's hooves struck Rosaleen's skirts. The horseman's top hat was bouncing on its retaining cord behind his back and the sun struck golden glints from his fair hair as he pounded on, angling across the fleeing youth's line of flight.

The thief saw the danger and altered direction, but the fair-haired man switched his own angle of pursuit and quickly overhauled his quarry. He closed on the youth and rode him down to send him sprawling, then hurled himself from the saddle. There was a brief, violent struggle and the thief was pinned helplessly.

Impelled by curiosity to see both the thief and the man who had captured him, Rosaleen began to walk in their direction. Now other pursuers were reaching the couple and surrounding them with noisy excitement. A top-hatted, blue-uniformed police constable ran past her, sweating and panting, and Rosaleen came to an abrupt halt. Policemen meant magistrates' courts. Magistrates' courts meant newspaper reporters seeking colourful stories. If she witnessed against the captured thief it could mean her name in the newspapers, and questions as to whom she had been talking to in the park when the thief had struck.

She rapidly made a mental inventory of the contents of her purse. A few sovereigns, a few small items of toilette – nothing in it that could be traced back to her. She turned on her heels and walked quickly away in the opposite direction. She saw Thomas Quinn walking towards the perimeter road and was glad that he had instinctively followed her example.

She risked a quick glance behind her, and saw that the constable was dragging the prisoner towards the zoo enclosure and the crowd was accompanying the pair, chattering and laughing and hurling insults and threats at the captured thief.

She walked in a wide circle across the greensward and turned in the direction of St John's Wood where her villa was situated. Then, as she neared the perimeter road over which she must cross to leave the park, a top-hatted horseman came cantering in her wake. She quickened her pace, but he rapidly overtook her, and she saw that it was the fair-haired man who had captured the thief.

He brought his mount to a halt some distance in front of her, then dismounted and came towards her on foot, removing his hat and bowing, and she was forced to come to a reluctant standstill.

'I do crave your pardon, ma'am.' He smiled at her, displaying fine white teeth. 'Pray don't be alarmed at my accosting you in this way, but are you not the lady whom that scoundrel robbed?'

She was surprised by the unfamiliar accent, and after a brief moment realised that the young man spoke like an American.

She shook her head, and answered curtly, 'No, sir.'

He frowned in puzzlement. 'I beg your pardon, ma'am, but I could have sworn that it was you. I actually saw that young fella creep up behind you and snatch your purse. You were in company with a gentleman.'

Again she shook her head in denial, and now his pleasant, fresh-complexioned features betrayed a hint of irritation, as well as puzzlement.

'I've no wish to appear ill-mannered, ma'am, or to offer you any disrespect, but I have to repeat that I saw that fella rob you. I confess I am mystified by your denial of that fact. My friends over there will bear witness to what I claim because I immediately drew their attention to the robbery also. It was remarked upon when the gentleman you were with made no effort to go after the thief.'

For the first time Rosaleen became aware that a trio of stationary horsemen were intently watching the exchange between herself and this man.

Although the horsemen were at some distance, something about one of them seemed familiar to Rosaleen, and after a brief instant she recognised the man. Inwardly she cursed her bad luck, and her agile brain instinctively reacted to minimise the damage.

'Alas, sir, this is a grave embarrassment to me.' She allowed an expression of distress to cross her features, and noted with gratification the American's instant look of concern. 'I must throw myself on your mercy, sir.' She lowered her head as if unable to meet his gaze, and continued in a hesitant, nervous manner, 'I am betrothed, sir, to a gentleman who is extremely protective of me. Because of the recent series of robberies in this park, he has expressly requested that I do not walk here.' She paused, and glanced up from beneath her long thick lashes into the blue eyes of the American, well aware of the effect this gesture always had on susceptible men. 'Just think, sir, how distressed my betrothed would be were he to discover that my selfish disregard of his wishes had resulted in the very thing that he most feared. I feel so ashamed, sir, and am very concerned that it would cause him much anguish were he to find me out in this matter. It is for this reason, sir, that I would beg you to forget that you have ever encountered me here, and to cast my role in this unhappy incident from your mind. It would make me very happy, sir, if I could rely on your discretion.' She smiled with just a hint of roguishness. 'Incidentally, the man who was with me was once a servant of my family, whom I'd encountered quite by chance. He's far too old to chase after sneak thieves, I fear.'

Utterly charmed by her, Dirk van Riesdal bowed low. 'Forgive my intrusion upon you, ma'am. I see now that you are not the unfortunate lady who was robbed.'

She smiled radiantly at him, and bowed her head in demure acknowledgement, then continued on her way.

He stood watching her moving away, the fragrant scent of her still in his nostrils, the vivid memory of her heart-shaped face and black eyes imprinted on his brain. Then he remounted and rejoined his waiting companions.

'How have you fared, Dirk?'

'What did she say?'

'Are you to call on her?'

They hurled questions even as his horse came to a sliding, stamping halt.

Grinning ruefully, he shook his head, and they good-naturedly crowed with delight at his failure, and ribbed him.

'There you were, mooning after her as soon as you set eyes on her, and presented with a heaven-sent opportunity to make her acquaintance, and she just does not wish to know you.'

'She quite obviously doesn't find you irresistible, Dirk.'

'Yes, but I think Old Montague's money might be blinding her to our Dirk's Yankee charms, don't you know.' The speaker was a sun-bronzed man with luxuriant cavalry whiskers, slightly older than his youthful companions.

'Then why didn't you tell her that you had expectations of your own, Dirk?'

'Because she didn't give him time to tell her. She brushed him aside in mere seconds.'

'Perhaps we should ride after her, and tell her about Dirk's expectations? Surely the handsome younger son of one of New York's most prominent families is to be preferred to an ugly old Jew?'

'That's just where you're mistaken, my boy. Rich old age is what all the girls prefer, rather than handsome young expectations. It's the old story of the bird in hand, don't you know.' The sun-bronzed man chuckled.

'There might be truth in that old story, Henry, because she told me that she is betrothed to the gentleman,' Dirk informed them.

Henry Winstanley, the sun-bronzed man, whistled through his teeth. 'Betrothed to her, is he, and his wife not dead these twelve months! I find it hard to credit.'

'I can't blame him for it, Henry.' The youngest man laughed. 'She's a stunner to look at, ain't she? Where is she from? What's her family?'

The older man shrugged. 'She's a mystery woman, Rupert. It was only by sheerest chance that I discovered she was Montague's fancy piece. The cunning old devil has kept her existence the deepest secret. I had to see him on some extremely urgent business, and his office directed me to a house in St John's Wood. The maid who answered the door insisted that her mistress knew no one named Montague. I persisted and eventually that lady came to speak to me herself. Old Montague put in an appearance then, and hustled me off with him. He appeared quite upset that I'd seen her, and he didn't offer to make any introduction. Naturally, I put two and two together. Of course, his wife was still living then so he needed to be discreet about his fancy piece. I've spotted her occasionally since then when she's been out and about, but she's never acknowledged me, nor I her.'

'I'll wager Old Montague is afraid that some other younger Johnny might steal her away from him, eh, Henry?' the third member of the group put in.

'I'd steal her, given half a chance,' Dirk asserted firmly. 'She's truly beautiful, and very charming with it. I think she's from a good family, she has the manners and speech of a lady.'

28

'She spends like a fine lady also, judging from the way she dresses,' Winstanley observed cynically. 'She must cost Old Montague a pretty penny. She's got a pair of matching bays in her stable that are worth a cool thousand.'

'You seem to know a great deal about her affairs, Henry. I thought you said she was a mystery woman?' the American challenged.

'And so she is, my boy,' the older man assured him. 'I've only been able to find out a very little about her.'

'What made you so curious?' Dirk pressed. 'It cannot be that you're smitten with her yourself, can it?'

'I'm always curious about a beautiful woman, Dirk. But, sadly, I couldn't afford her. I'm a poverty-stricken English cavalry officer, not a stinking rich Jew money-broker.' Winstanley appeared to lose interest in the subject. 'Come now, let's head back to town. I have to dine in the mess tonight. You'll be my guest, won't you, Dirk?'

'With pleasure, Henry,' the young American accepted cheerfully.

The four men cantered across the greensward towards the smoking chimneys of the city, and Dirk van Riesdal tried to dismiss the meeting with the beautiful woman from his thoughts. But try as he might, the image of her black eyes and heart-shaped face persisted in his memory, and already the intention of attempting to get to know her was hardening in his subconscious mind.

Thomas Quinn was waiting for Rosaleen at the park gates and he fell in behind her without any exchange of words. As she walked through the tree-shaded streets of opulent houses and villas, Rosaleen thought about her meeting with the American, and about his companion whom she had recognised, Henry Winstanley, a cavalry officer with whom her protector, Solomon Montague, often had financial dealings. She frowned in annoyance. She thought it very likely that Winstanley had recognised her. She was vain enough of her beauty to expect that any man who had made her acquaintance would remember her.

I don't doubt that Winstanley's already informed his friends that I'm Solomon's paid whore, she thought then smiled sardonically and corrected herself. No, I'm not the paid whore any longer, am I? I'm now Solomon's betrothed.

It was true, what she had told the young American. She was in fact betrothed to the old man. He had asked her to marry him some weeks previously, and she had accepted his proposal. They would marry as soon as the customary year of mourning for his dead wife was completed. The hypocrisy of this convention gave her some ironic amusement. Solomon Montague and his deceased wife had hated each other for almost their entire married life. By his account she had been an unpleasant termagant, but now she was dead she was elevated to the role of a dutiful and adored wife.

The bitter hardships and tragedies which had marred her life had served to make Rosaleen a cynical realist where men and love were concerned, and she accepted that this proposal of marriage was a stroke of rare good fortune. Solomon Montague was old and feeble, and she had become the dominant partner in their relationship. Marriage would make her financially able to devote more resources to the achievement of her all-

consuming ambition. It was not so much the freedom of
Ireland that she wanted, as revenge upon a people and a
nation that she blamed for what had happened to herself and her family. For Rosaleen Calatrava it was a
personal crusade of vengeance that she was embarked
upon. Rosaleen felt no qualms at the prospect of
becoming the old man's wife. She had been his mistress
for nearly four years now, and he had always treated
her with kindness and generosity. His sexual tastes had
at first caused her disgust, but she had hardened herself,
and now she catered to his needs with a tolerant
contempt.

When she reached the secluded villa that was her
home, Theresa Quinn opened the door to tell her,
'Young Emma's here. I've put her in the kitchen.'

Rosaleen's eyebrows lifted in silent question, and the
other woman nodded grimly. 'That bad bastard's given
her another hiding.'

Rosaleen scowled angrily, and Theresa demanded,
'Why won't you let Thomas give that dirty scut what he
deserves?'

Rosaleen shook her head dismissively. 'All in good
time. Now fetch Emma to the drawing room.'

Emma Carr was a petite, delicately featured, blonde-
haired girl, and the bleeding bruises swelling around her
blue eyes were brutally stark against her pallid, translu-
cent skin.

'Sit here, honey.' Rosaleen patted the cushions by her
side on the chaise longue, and anger hardened her voice.
'When are you going to get some sense?'

'Don't start, Rosie, please!' the young girl pleaded,
and tears fell down her cheeks.

'Oh, all right! I'll say nothing.' Rosaleen sighed

31

impatiently. 'But you're a fool, Emma. You're a pitiful fool. No man's worth it.'

'It's not his fault, Rosie. He just gets so angry and frustrated, and then he drinks, and then he doesn't really know what he's doing. He's always ever so sorry afterwards.' Her voice was soft, its tone gentling the strident cockney accent.

Rosaleen's impatience spilled over. 'Sorry? That animal is sorry, is he? Let me tell you, girl, Billy Gilligan is only sorry because when he's battered you like this he knows that you can't earn good money for him. The rich punters won't pay for damaged goods.'

'Oh no, Rosie. He really doesn't like me to go with men. He tells me all the time that if he could get work he wouldn't let me set foot on the streets.'

'If he could get work?' Rosaleen could not help scoffing contemptuously. 'He's big and ugly enough to swing a pick and lift a shovel, isn't he? If you weren't such a fool, you'd leave him.'

The girl only buried her face in her small hands and wept piteously, her thin shoulders heaving. Rosaleen's heart welled with pity, and she cradled the girl in her arms.

'There now, honey, don't cry,' she crooned. 'Don't cry. I'm not angry with you.'

Silently she promised herself, Just as soon as you've done what I want, Billy Gilligan, you'll get what you deserve.

When the girl's sobs had quietened Rosaleen told her, 'I've got the clothes for you, Emma. And I'll give you enough money to keep that animal happy until you can work again. How's the baby?'

'She's lovely, Rosie. I've got a real nice woman

looking after her when I work. Ever so clean and careful she is. I don't have to worry about my Sophy at all when she's with Mrs Jenks.'

'That's something to be grateful for.' Rosaleen nodded, then urged, 'Listen, Emma, leave Billy Gilligan. I'll look after you and the baby if you do. I'll find you somewhere to live, and I'll give you money enough for both of you.'

'But I can't leave Billy,' the girl answered plaintively. 'I love him too much. I'd die if I ever lost him.'

You'll die if you stay with him because he'll kill you one day, the way he beats you, Rosaleen thought, but knowing the futility of argument said nothing aloud and only hugged the frail body.

After a while, Emma recovered and was able to smile brightly when Rosaleen handed her some coins.

'Take this, Emma, and now go and see Theresa in the kitchen. She'll give you the clothes I've put by for you. And tell that rotten man of yours that he'll be needed very shortly, so he must keep sober and behave himself.'

Alone once more, Rosaleen took one of the long thin cheroots from the silver box and lit it. She lay back on the chaise longue and watched the grey smoke spiralling above her head. Her thoughts wandered aimlessly, mental images appeared and disappeared, memories, some happy, some unhappy, mingled pain and pleasure, succeeded one another, until finally she laid aside the fragrant cheroot and drifted into sleep.

Chapter Four

Dirk van Riesdal always enjoyed dining in the Officers'
Mess of the Duchess of Connaught's Own, the 19th
Light Dragoons, the regiment of his close friend, Major
Henry Winstanley. The martial portraits on the walls,
the flags, the weapons, the splendid table centrepieces of
regimental silver, all redolent of battles and desperately
won glory, appealed to his romantic fantasies of the military life, and there were many times when he envied his
friend to the bottom of his heart for being a part of
such glorious tradition.

Not that the young man was entirely devoid of military experience himself. He was a captain in the New
York Seventh Regiment, the New York Greys. But to his
secret shame his regiment was a part-time National
Guard regiment composed of civilians, and he was convinced that despite the kind comments about it made by
his friends of the 19th Light Dragoons, in their secret
hearts they despised the New York Greys as being
merely militia.

He enjoyed above all else the times in the Light
Dragoons' Mess when the meal had been eaten, and the
fine old port wine was circulating, and the assembled
officers and their guests exchanged reminiscences about
the arduous campaigns and bloody actions they had
taken part in.

On this evening there were few officers present, and Dirk was the only guest. The conversation during dinner was desultory, and there were long periods of silence broken only by the sounds of eating and drinking.

When the port was being passed and the diners lit up their cheroots, Henry Winstanley apologised to his friend.

'I'm sorry for being such a dull dog tonight, Dirk. Only I've had some unwelcome news.'

Dirk frowned with concern. 'Is it anything I can be of help to you with?'

Winstanley chuckled wryly, and shook his head. 'I fear not, Dirk, unless you've a mind to become a nurse-maid.'

This statement attracted an immediate outburst of catcalls and jeering laughter from the other officers at table, and Dirk stared in amazement.

Winstanley chuckled with genuine amusement at his friend's expression, and hastened to explain. 'I've been selected to act as nursemaid to the "Teutonic Brat", Dirk. The glad tidings were given to me on my return this afternoon.'

'Bully for you, Henry!' a grey-whiskered old veteran chortled.

'What an honour for the regiment!' another young man laughed.

'They'll have to give us another title now, won't they? How about the "Royal Nursemaids"?'

'No, I think the "Arse Wipers" would be more appropriate.'

'The "Royal Arse Wipers", if you please, Rupert!'

Other suggestions, becoming increasingly obscene,

were bandied around the table, and roars of laughter greeted each sally.

Dirk was nonplussed and, although caught up by the infectious gaiety, was laughing without really understanding the point of the joke.

Henry Winstanley finally explained. 'The "Teutonic Brat" is our name for the Prince of Wales, Dirk. And for my sins I have been selected by the Prince Consort to help make the Prince of Wales not merely a gentleman, but the first gentleman in the country in respect of outward deportment and manners. It appears that he wishes above all else to become a soldier, but the Queen is determined that he shall never serve in the army. However, his father is prepared to allow young Bertie to sit a military examination, and to play soldiers for a short while.'

'To call him the "Teutonic Brat" seems rather an unkind description of the boy,' the American remarked, and the grey-whiskered veteran broke in on the conversation to exclaim, 'It's dammed well merited, in my opinion. He's a stupid, bad-tempered, lazy young dog. Apparently he treats his valet and his other servants contemptibly. Especially the valet. He torments that poor fellow in every way possible: he raps him on the nose, continually complains and berates him, pours wax and other nuisances onto his livery, throws water on his linen, tears his ties. If I were the valet I'd give the young hound a thorough licking.'

'His mamma loves her precious Bertie though,' another officer offered. 'Although he is such a disappointment to her. She always compares him with her beloved husband, don't you know. And of course there is not a man in the whole of Christendom who can match our dearest Albert, the paragon of all the virtues.'

Dirk's surprise at these displays of apparent disloyalty to the Royal Family showed clearly in his expression, and Winstanley chuckled. 'I see that our opinions shock you, Dirk. I can assure you that we are all loyal subjects of Her Majesty, but like many other gentlemen in this country, we feel that Royalty should set an example to their subjects, and treat even the meanest of those subjects with respect. In fairness to the Prince Consort, and to Her Majesty, they are amiable enough, but Bertie is quite a different kettle of fish. I fear that my colleagues and I will have a difficult time of it.'

'Are there to be others helping you then?' Dirk asked.

'Yes, Chris Teesdale, young Loyd-Lindsay and Lord Valletort and I are each to serve as a kind of equerry to the "Brat" in monthly rotations. We're to live at the White Lodge in Richmond Park where he's presently residing with his tutors, Gibbs and the Reverend Tarver – a couple of sanctimonious bores. Fortunately, Chris Teesdale and Loyd-Lindsay are both good fellows. They each won the Victoria Cross in the Crimea, and they're majors. Valletort is not known to me.'

'When do you commence your duties?' Dirk asked.

'Next month. So we've still got ample time to enjoy ourselves before you return to America.'

Dirk lowered his voice and broached a subject which had been increasingly preoccupying him.

'Henry, I want to meet Montague's woman again. Is there any way you could arrange for that?'

The other man stared quizzically, but said nothing, and after some moments Dirk felt driven to justify his request. 'She's very beautiful, Henry. She's made a strong impression on me.'

'She's a kept woman, Dirk. To put it bluntly, she's his paid whore. What do you hope to get from her that you couldn't buy from a hundred other women who are just as beautiful?'

To his own surprise the young American found himself resenting his friend's blunt words. 'You can't call her a paid whore, Henry. She's betrothed to the man.'

Winstanley scoffed at this. 'I'll believe that when I see them married, and not before. Every kept piece of tail that I've ever known has claimed betrothal. It makes them feel better about themselves.'

Dirk's first impulse was to protest against his friend's scathing dismissal, but he was reluctant to risk precipitating any disagreement, and so he merely repeated, 'Is there any way you could arrange for me to meet her again?'

The older man pursed his lips and reflected. He did not like Solomon Montague, and the idea of scoring off the old man appealed greatly to his sardonic sense of humour. After some reflection he smiled at his friend. 'Yes, it might be possible to arrange another meeting. Let me think about it.'

And with that Dirk had to rest content . . .

Chapter Five

The day was warm and sunny, and Dirk van Riesdal enjoyed the ride from Windsor to Ascot Heath in company with Henry Winstanley. The previous evening the two friends had stayed at the Castle Hotel in Windsor, and today they were going to a race meeting at Ascot. Dirk was not a racing enthusiast, but he was keenly anticipating the day ahead because his friend had arranged to present him formally to Solomon Montague and Montague's woman.

'I've told Montague that you're looking to invest some funds in this country, Dirk, and he scents some advantages for himself if he can persuade you to let him act for you in the matter. Of course, I haven't committed you to anything but, truth to tell, he's a shrewd old devil when it comes to investments, and you could do worse than let him act for you if you've any floating cash.'

'But how did you persuade him to bring his woman to meet me?' Dirk wanted to know. 'I thought you said that he kept her a secret?'

Henry Winstanley chuckled wryly. 'My judgement was faulty. It appears that the lady was speaking the truth when she told you of her betrothment. The old devil suggested bringing her along himself. It seems he now wants the world to see what a beauty he's going to wed. He's as cock-a-hoop as a dog with two dicks.'

Winstanley chuckled again. 'There's really nothing better than sweet fresh meat to perk up old peckers, is there?'

Dirk made no answer. Instead he pleasurably pictured the black eyes and heart-shaped face of Montague's woman, and told himself, There's no fair play in love or war. Given the chance I'd take her away from that old man and make her my own mistress.

As they passed through the wooded parklands the road became increasingly thronged with fellow travellers making their way towards the race meeting.

There was a veritable procession of both open and closed, four-wheeled and two-wheeled vehicles. Stately town carriages with liveried, cockaded footmen and coachmen trundled along in company with dashing curricles and phaetons. Huge flat-bodied farm carts drawn by massive shire horses, loaded with noisy gangs of half-drunk clerks and artisans, vied for right of way with tiny, single-ponied gigs. The garishly decorated vardos of Romanies ran side by side with the canvas-barrelled hoops of tinker vans. Young bloods in elegant array rode fine horseflesh. Off-duty soldiers from the Windsor barracks presented a martial spectacle of scarlet and blue. Navvies and labourers in broad-brimmed hats and red flannel shirts, great hobnailed boots and yorked velveteens trudged in tough, aggressive phalanxes, their shawled, wild-haired women raucously singing as they followed their menfolk. A party of clergymen, crammed side by side in a charabanc, surreptitiously shared supplies of Madeira wine, and left a trail of emptied bottles on the roadway behind them, which ragged tramps rushed to pick up, only to curse and hurl them aside when they found them drained.

Far ahead of Dirk van Riesdal and Henry Winstanley a closed carriage with a liveried driver and footman bore Solomon Montague and Rosaleen Calatrava towards the racecourse.

Rosaleen was busy with her own thoughts as the iron-rimmed wheels crunched over the gravelled road, and the colourful noisy throng through which she was passing held no interest for her. She sat with downcast eyes, while the old man sitting opposite to her dozed fitfully, breath snorting, his wattled jaw gaping open to display ill-fitting porcelain teeth.

At first, when Montague had proposed that she accompany him to the races to appear in public for the first time as his betrothed, she had been uncertain whether or not to accede to his wishes. The course of action that she was set upon made her reluctant to mix in society. She wished to preserve her anonymity. But after some reflection she realised that the respectability which this marriage would confer upon her, and the undoubted power of Montague's money, would serve to place her above suspicion of any sort of wrongdoing. To become widely known as Solomon Montague's intended wife was the best possible concealment for her nefarious activities.

She was reasonably content with the progress of her plans, but had considerable reservations about one element, namely, Billy Gilligan. Because of McCulloch's failure to help, she had been forced to let Dermot recruit the man. Gilligan would serve his purpose, of that she had no doubts. The problem was that she knew he had no loyalty to her, or to the cause she served.

Gilligan is criminal scum. A common thug. He'd betray us all if he was offered more money than we've promised him. The mental image of Emma Carr's bruised features rose before Rosaleen's eyes, and her full lips tightened angrily. He's an animal. A mad dog. Then she reassured herself. Well, I know how to deal with mad dogs, don't I?

The carriage lurched to a halt, and after a moment Thomas Quinn's face appeared at the door.

'Where now, ma'am?'

Rosaleen reached out to shake the old man's bony knee. 'Solomon. Solomon, we've arrived. Where do you want the carriage placed?'

Montague awoke, spluttering and coughing, his bleared eyes staring wildly about him. Rosaleen gave him some moments to collect his senses, then asked again.

'Where do you wish the carriage to be situated?'

He tried to speak, and his porcelain false teeth slipped alarmingly, so that he was forced to use both hands to click them back into position before he could tell her, 'Overlooking the north end of the promenade, my dear. I've arranged to meet Henry Winstanley and his American friend there.'

The information came as a shock to her, and the reaction showed fleetingly in her expression, causing the old man to stare at her curiously.

'Does that disturb you, my dear? Meeting Winstanley and his friend?'

She recovered herself almost instantly. 'Why no, of course it doesn't disturb me, Solomon. Only I had not expected that we would be joining with others today. I thought it was to be just you and myself.'

He smiled dotingly at her. 'While Clara lived I was forced to keep our relationship a private thing, my love.

42

But now the need for that privacy has disappeared I want all my acquaintances to meet the future Mrs Montague. I shall enjoy being the object of their envy.'

As the carriage moved slowly onwards, the bustle and excitement of the racecourse enveloped them and, to give herself time to think, Rosaleen affected a great interest in the scene around her and stared out of the windows. Winstanley's American friend must be that same young man she had encountered in the park. She wondered if he would betray the fact that he had met her before then, after a few moments, accepted that she could only wait and deal with whatever might happen, as and when it happened.

As the carriages rolled onto the course the hordes of male and female touts and card sellers and augurs swarmed to sell their wares, which were the inside tips, the sure winners, the latest information on the jockeys and their mounts, the trainers and their stables.

Solomon Montague livened up considerably, and began to point out the various characters to Rosaleen. 'See there, my dear, that's Black Jemmy.'

This was a negro dressed in a startling green cutaway coat, a huge tam o'shanter on his head, and a great flowing tartan cravat around his neck.

'And there's Sailor Jack. Just look at him, will you, wearing a man o' war's rig, and he's never seen the sea in his life. Here comes Billy Priest. See his bare feet. He's never worn shoes in his life, and he can still run fifty miles a day after the fox hounds.'

The hoarse, raucous shouts of the touts and card sellers filled the air.

'I have a winner, my lords and ladies. I have a winner!'

'I gave you Lanercost, I gave you Topsail, I gave you

Gasporonii, I gave you Millipede, I gave you all the winners.'

'Who was it tipped Voltigeur when all the others gave Shillelagh? It was me, my good sirs. It was old honest Sailor Jack, the knowingest cove that ever sailed the stormy oceans.'

'I've got a horse today whose odds cannot be bettered, my lords. Whose odds are as long as a mile-long rope.' This was a handsome, dark-haired woman, whom Montague identified as 'Fair Helen', the self-styled 'Queen of the Female Augurs'.

Mingling with these colourful characters were the travelling acrobats, the ballad singers, the wax baby vendors, the ginger snap women, the lemonade men, the coffee stallers, the roast potato sellers.

Rosaleen laughed out loud as she saw the grotesquely fat old soldier known as 'Crimea Billy', dressed in a soiled scarlet uniform, and performing his trick of picking up needles from the ground with his eyelids, shouting all the while as he did so.

'I used to go at the Rooshians in the Crimea like a hungry dog goes at his dinner, and their bloody bayonets never bothered me, and these bloody needles don't bother me neither.'

Above all the tumult Rosaleen suddenly heard a tremendous braying noise, as if some giant donkey were on the loose. Solomon Montague chuckled at her surprise and told her, 'That's only "Donkey John", my dear. Charges sixpence a bray. Look, there, he's coming this way.'

She stared in amazement at the oncoming tall, skeletal figure dressed in a woman's ragged gown, with a long blonde wig topping his drink-purpled face. His nose was the longest and biggest red excrescence that she had ever seen.

'Here, Donkey John, give us a sample, if you please.' Solomon Montague tossed a silver shilling to the man, who caught it deftly, then bowed and came up to the carriage.

'You'd best beware your ears, my lady,' he warned Rosaleen, and then proceeded to trumpet an ear-splitting bray through his nose.

She laughed, covering her ears with her hands, and then begged, 'For pity's sake, go away before you deafen me.'

'Give us another, Donkey John,' some youths shouted, and he looked down his long nose in scorn.

'I only brays for the carriage trade, not for low-born mawkins like you lot be.'

The carriage came to a standstill overlooking the north end of the promenade, and a gang of ragged, barefoot, curly-headed gypsy children came clamorously begging for pennies.

Rosaleen instantly felt in her purse.

'Don't give them anything, my dear,' Montague warned. 'They'll not give you a moment's peace if you do. The word will spread and we'll have all the tribes of Egypt pestering us.'

She laughed gaily. 'Don't worry about that, Solomon. Thomas will chase them away if they become too wearisome.'

She pitched a handful of coins high in the air and, cheering and whooping, the children scrambled to catch them.

Bookmakers' runners came to wheedle, 'Will you wager with Honest Joe Baldock, my lord?' 'Bet with Tommy Smout, my lady, he gives the best odds to pretty ladies like yourself.' 'Can I take your bets, sir? The highest born in the land always places their bets with Peerless Jem Tompkins. Can I take your bets, sir?'

'Look there, Dirk.' Henry Winstanley pointed. 'There's old Montague's coach.'

The American experienced a frisson of excitement at being so close to meeting Montague's woman once more. Then, remembering the brief exchange he had had with her, told his friend, 'Don't make any mention of my meeting with her in the park, Henry. I promised her my discretion.'

The older man chuckled. 'Now I'd say that this is a good omen for an illicit liaison between you and she. You're already sharing a secret with her.'

'I live in hope of sharing something more than that, Henry,' Dirk quipped.

As the two horsemen neared the coach Rosaleen saw them first and said to Montague, 'Is that not Major Winstanley, Solomon?'

'So it is, and that will be his American friend, no doubt.' The bleared old eyes shrewdly evaluated the quality of Dirk's clothes and horseflesh. 'Hmmm, he looks to be warm enough.'

'So he should be, he's fully dressed, and the weather's fine,' Rosaleen observed artlessly, and Montague laughed fondly.

'What an innocent you are of the financial world, my dear. If we say that a man looks warm, we mean that he appears to be well supplied with money.'

'D'you want a horse-holder, my lords?' A ragged man swept off his cap and tugged his lank forelock, ducking his head in rapid sequence.

Winstanley and Dirk dismounted and the man took the reins from their hands. 'Thank you, my lords, thank you. They'll be well with me, my lords. I'll walk 'em up there a ways so as not to discommodious you, my lords.'

The pair walked up to the carriage door, taking off their top hats and bowing courteously. Dirk's eyes met the glowing eyes of Montague's woman, and his heartbeat momentarily quickened as he saw how truly beautiful she was; even more beautiful than he had remembered.

With pride throbbing in his voice Montague made the introductions, and Dirk removed his gloves and felt the touch of her silken-gloved hand upon his fingers, and again his heartbeat quickened, and he inwardly jeered at himself for reacting like an infatuated schoolboy to her smile.

Once the introductions were completed Montague invited the two men to take refreshment, and all four of them seated themselves on camp stools around a small table which Thomas Quinn had set up, and they feasted on cold hams, roasted game birds, savouries and meat pies, jellies and sweet dishes, and fine wines, taken from the several hampers carried on the back of the carriage.

Rosaleen made a charming hostess, joining easily in the general conversation, yet not attempting to centre attention on herself; serving the men with delicacies, but devoid of affectations of manner as she did so.

As the picnic went on Dirk found his envy of Solomon Montague for possessing such a woman mounting to an uncomfortable intensity. Indeed, he admitted to himself, envy was too weak a word to describe his emotional state of mind. Jealousy, and acute jealousy at that, was a more fitting adjective.

Rosaleen was enjoying the picnic immensely. During the introductions she had been apprehensive that by some unguarded word one or other of the two men would betray the fact that she had been in the park in company with Sean Gallagher. But now she felt relaxed, and at ease in their company, and took pleasure from their conversation. For the first time in years she was again acting in the role to which as a young girl she had been accustomed. She was once more a gentlewoman entertaining gentlefolk. She felt that she had regained her rightful place in society, and that the years of personal shame and degradation were finally behind her. Being here, openly acknowledged as the intended bride of a wealthy gentleman, engendered in her an emotion that she had feared she would never again experience: a sense of belonging; a sense of acceptance as an honoured and respected member of good society. Her birthright had been restored to her. She was, once more in the world's eyes, an honourable woman.

An added fillip to her enjoyment was the recognition that Dirk van Riesdal was infatuated with her. Although he made no attempt to monopolise her conversation, and was behaving with the utmost circumspection, she knew with complete certainty how he felt. The fleeting, unguarded moments when his eyes shone in admiration as he looked at her, told her all. Although she was faithful to her protector, and intended to remain so, she admitted to herself that she found the American very attractive physically, and charming in his manner. She could not resist the impulsion to bestow upon him her most beguiling smiles.

Then, abruptly, all her newfound emotional wellbeing was stripped from her by Winstanley's news. He informed Montague and herself that he was to take up a position within the household of the Prince of Wales.

Her instant reaction upon hearing this was the thought, Then you are a potential obstacle, Winstanley. And might have to be removed.

A shock of dismay assailed her as she realised, Dear God, I was deluding myself in thinking I could ever belong to decent society again.

Sudden depression overwhelmed her, and she saw the American staring at her curiously.

'Are you all right, ma'am?' he queried. 'You appear as if something has perturbed you?'

Montague and Winstanley were also staring at her now, and Montague questioned anxiously, 'Are you unwell, my dear?'

She struggled to regain her equilibrium, but an overwhelming compulsion to escape from her present company was more than she was able to control and she pleaded, 'Please, would you all excuse me. A sudden terrible headache has come upon me. I feel as if my head is bursting.'

All three men were instantly solicitous, but when she inadvertently glanced at Dirk van Riesdal she saw the disappointment in his expressive eyes and, much to her own surprise, experienced a moment of guilt. Then angrily she berated herself, Don't be so ridiculous. You owe him nothing. It's not your fault that he has feelings for you.

The picnic came to an end with protestations of regret and expressions of sympathy, and the company went their different ways.

During the journey back to St John's Wood Rosaleen remained silent and withdrawn, and Solomon

49

Montague, thinking that she was unwell, considerately made no attempt to talk.

Back at the villa Rosaleen told him gently that she wished to be alone that night to allow her headache to wear itself out, and the old man returned to his own home in central London.

Rosaleen remained in a troubled mood. The memory of her reaction to Winstanley's news constantly returned to her, causing her considerable disquiet. She had found the man to be pleasant company, and had begun to like him. The knowledge that he had now become a potential target was causing her to re-examine her own motivations for her present course of action.

Deliberately, she forced herself to recall the terrible events of her youth, the famine years in Ireland that had destroyed her family and so many of her people, torturing herself with visualising the suffering faces, the gaunt, wasted bodies, the pitiful corpses. Slowly her mind hardened once more, until she was able to thrust aside the softening emotion that had threatened to weaken her resolution.

By the time she went to her bed to sleep, she had succeeded in once more dedicating herself, heart and soul, to taking the vengeance that she believed was her birthright.

Late the following morning a letter was delivered by hand to her villa, addressed for her personal and private attention.

It was from Dirk van Riesdal, and contained wishes for her recovery from her headache. It also contained expressions of his great pleasure at having made her acquaintance, his deepest and sincerest regrets that an unexpected development in his family affairs forced his immediate return to New York, and his profound wishes that they might someday meet again. He ended by entreating her to visit him at his home in New York, and telling her that if ever she was in need of a friend, for whatever reason, he would be honoured to be that friend.

Rosaleen read the letter several times then, very thoughtfully, folded it up and placed it with other documents that she treasured, in a hiding place known only to herself.

Chapter Six

Dermot Calatrava left his lodgings in the late evening and walked quickly through the quiet, dark side streets, continually checking that he was not being followed. He reached the bustling Euston rail terminus, and from there he took a cab to Pall Mall. Alighting, he wandered along with apparent aimlessness, but always carefully observing the passing traffic and pedestrians. Satisfied that no one was following him, he turned off the main road and again walked quickly along quiet side streets until he reached his destination. A tall house in a secluded square. Going to the tradesmen's entrance at the side of the building he rapped the door panels with his cane in a staccato signal. The door was opened almost immediately by a motherly looking, middle-aged woman wearing black widow's weeds.

'It's your own self, sir,' she welcomed smilingly, and Calatrava frowned irritably.

'Were you expecting someone else?'

'Of course not, that's how I knew it was youse that had come.' Her nasal accents betrayed her Liverpool origins. 'And you're very welcome, sir.'

'Don't gammon me, woman,' he snapped. 'It's my money that's welcome.'

'That, too, of course,' she agreed equably, lifting her hand in expectation.

He held a gold sovereign before her eyes. 'What do you have for me?'

'Those that you're interested in has been here again,' she told him. 'Twice this week. Last Monday night, and then on the Tuesday as well.'

He allowed her to take the coin from his fingers, and it disappeared into the bulging bodice of her gown.

'When are they likely to come again?'

'How should I know that?' she demanded indignantly. 'The customers don't confide their social calendars to me that much in advance.'

He smiled grimly. 'I've told you before, woman, don't gammon me. Now tell me, when are they coming again?'

She pouted and complained, 'You're not the most generous gentleman I've ever met.'

Gusting a sigh of exasperation he took another coin from his pocket and watched it also disappear.

'They're here now. Up in the third floor back.' A speculative gleam entered her bloodshot eyes. 'It's going to cost you more to watch them tonight. Because I'm going to have to turn away another gentleman who is coming later if you want to stay.'

Wordlessly he gave her yet another coin, and she stowed it with the others, then smiled, laying her finger across her lips.

'Follow me close, and not a sound now. When we go upstairs you'll need to hold onto the back of me skirts. I can't risk a light.'

She led him along a musty-smelling, bare corridor, dimly lit by a hanging lamp, then through a recessed door and up several flights of narrow stairs. In almost pitch darkness, holding with one hand to her skirts, his other hand feeling along the rough damp brickwork,

Calatrava experienced an uncomfortable sense of vulnerability, and was relieved when she came to a standstill and, turning back to clasp his arm, guided him alongside her and put her lips next to his ear.

'Place your feet very careful now. You must move as quiet as a mouse. A bit higher to go and then you'll hear them through the wall.'

Her breath reeked of stale gin, meat and onions, and he had to fight against the urge to jerk his head away.

Four steps upwards and Calatrava heard faint sounds of voices and laughter. The narrow staircase widened abruptly and with each step the voices were louder. Another few steps and the couple reached a flat stretch of flooring.

Calatrava could now hear quite clearly the conversation and laughter, even the clinking of glasses from the room.

'Oh, Susanna, you're nothing but a shameless Dollymop!'

There came an indignant cry of protest, and another voice declared laughingly, 'Stella's quite right in what she says, Susanna. You're a trollop. A cheap trollop!'

'Now look here, Alicia, Dollymop I may be; trollop I may be. But don't you dare to call me cheap! If you persist in insulting me I shall tell my husband.'

Shrieks of high-pitched laughter greeted this threat.

The woman's dress rustled faintly as she fumbled in the pitch darkness, and a tiny circle of light suddenly appeared in the wall, level with Calatrava's head. Her hands guided him and he cautiously pressed his eye to the tiny aperture to peer through into the room beyond the wall.

It was well lit by a myriad candles, its walls hung with

richly coloured tapestries, its wide floor furnished with several low tables and divans and plentifully bestrewn with large cushions.

Three people were lounging upon divans and Calatrava grimaced contemptuously as he studied them. They were obviously male, but were dressed in low-cut ballgowns, profusely bejewelled and wearing elaborately curled and ringleted wigs. Their faces were heavily rouged, black kohl darkened their eyes, their lips were scarlet slashes.

For some time Calatrava patiently watched and listened as the three men fluttered and preened, chattered and giggled, sipping daintily at their glasses of champagne. He paid particular attention to the one named as Susanna. This man was large and obese, with hanging jowls and goitred eyes, and the corset he wore had pushed up his fat chest so that in grotesque parody of a woman's breasts rounded globes of flabby flesh spilled over the décolletage of his ornate gown. Susanna was more extreme than his companions in his exaggerated femininity. He flounced, and pouted, and fluttered his kohled eyes. His laughter shrieked more hysterically and his voice was shriller.

The conversation turned to sex, and the trio began exchanging anecdotes and intimacies, their language coarse and their descriptions graphic. Names and places were mentioned, and the unseen observer took note of these names and the other details, carefully committing them to memory.

From somewhere out of Calatrava's limited range of view there came a knocking on wooden panels, and a gruff voice called, 'Susanna, come on now, I'm ready.'

Susanna simpered. 'That's my husband. Come to

claim his conjugal rights again. He can't get enough of me.'

'What's he like, Susanna? Is he good?' Stella questioned eagerly. 'I've always wondered how a black prick feels.'

The fat man rolled his goitred eyes and lifted both hands. 'Darling, once you've had a nigger prick inside you, everything else is an anticlimax. He's hung like a stallion. The first time he had me I thought I was going to be split in two.'

'He must be simply huge then, dear.' Alicia's tone dripped acid. 'If you could feel him so distinctly.'

Susanna bridled and arched his back, demanding venomously, 'What exactly do you mean to imply by that remark?'

Alicia's expression displayed spiteful pleasure. 'Well, my dear, I'm told that you've had so many pricks up your arse that a company of guards could probably march through it wearing their bearskins.'

Susanna's rosebud lips opened wide and she shrieked in outrage, 'You're just jealous of me, you horrid bitch.'

Stella hastened to soothe them both. 'Don't quarrel. Be friends again. We're here to enjoy ourselves and you're spoiling everything.'

The knocking sounded louder, and the gruff voice was impatient. 'Will you come now, Susanna?'

The fat man rose and flounced out of Calatrava's view, and the sound of his voice as he declaimed indignantly to the newcomer became faint and muffled. There came the impact of another door being opened and slammed shut, and Susanna could no longer be heard.

Satisfied with what he had seen and learned Calatrava

touched the woman's arm, and she moved to close the aperture, then put her lips against his ear to whisper, 'They're using the Green Room. We'll go there now.'

In his turn he whispered, 'No, I'm leaving.'

She preceded him down the stairs to the bottom of the house and when they reached the kitchen she asked him curiously, 'Why don't you want to watch them having each other tonight? You've paid the extra for it.'

Calatrava had been coming to this house for three weeks now. The woman's business partner, Terence McCulloch, had introduced him and vouchsafed that he was to be trusted, and initially she had accepted that he was just another anonymous voyeur, who achieved sexual satisfaction by secretly spying on the various perversions practised in her rooms. There were several such regular visitors to the house, and she made a useful extra income from them. But she had quickly realised that this quietly spoken, taciturn man was not this type of pervert, and her curiosity about him had increased until it had become a torment to her.

Now he shook his head. 'No, there's no need. I've seen enough of that fat scum and his buck nigger performing.'

She huffed pettishly. 'Suit yourself . . . When do you want to come again?'

He shook his head. 'I won't be.'

The woman could not resist asking, 'Why were you so interested in those three in particular? You're not a she-shirt, I can tell.'

He frowned warningly at her. 'You should know better than to ask me questions.'

'Do you know that there's a good market for the type of information that I can sell?' she remarked with

57

apparent casualness, and then lied, 'I get to know everything about everybody who comes to this house. And I mean, everybody.'

Her statement appeared to make him nervous. 'Does Mr McCulloch know that you get to know everything about everybody?'

She was pleased at his apparent discomfiture, and bluffed confidently, 'Of course Mr McCulloch knows. He's my business partner, isn't he? We share everything.'

Calatrava made no reply, and shuffled his feet as if eager to leave, his eyes shiftily flitting around the room.

She scented success, and was happy at the ease with which she had obtained it.

'I'm sure that you know that a generous gentleman like yourself can always rely on my absolute discretion though. What I mean to say is, that if anyone was to come round here asking questions about yourself, well you can rely on my discretion. Generous gentlemen can always rely on my discretion.'

'What about the ones who aren't generous?' he enquired.

She chuckled. 'Then it's their own funeral, if you see what I mean. But I'm sure that you intend to be very generous towards me tonight, don't you, sir? Mr McCulloch told me that you was very generous.'

'Does Mr McCulloch share in this extra money you're asking for?' he asked, and she chuckled with amusement.

'Let's just say that he doesn't object to me making a little bit of extra for the house.'

'Then I suppose I have no real choice in the matter,' he said quietly, and again she chuckled amusedly.

'But you'll have no cause for concern either, will you, sir. You'll have peace of mind.'

He bobbed his head as if in gratitude. 'I'm relieved to hear that.'

'Oh yes, I can be as silent as the grave, if a gentleman is generous to me. As silent as the grave.'

She held up her hand and rubbed her fingers and thumb together meaningly.

The next instant she was flat on her back, half-stunned by the impact of her head smashing upon the stone flagged floor. His left hand clamped painfully upon her mouth, smothering her cries of protest, his knees pinned her shoulders, his right hand pointed a long-barrelled Colt revolver down at her terrified eyes.

'Stupid bitch! Don't you know that you'll be in your grave if you ever breathe a single word about me?' he hissed, and she knew that death was only a finger's pressure away.

Her shock and terror were such that she lost control of her bladder and hot urine flooded beneath her buttocks.

'You don't know my face. I have never been in this house,' he snarled. 'You have never set eyes on me in your life. Remember that, and you'll live. Forget it for one instant, and you'll die.'

The hand on her mouth increased its pressure, and his fingernails dug into her flesh until muffled moans of agony tore from her throat.

He suddenly raised the revolver and brought it slashing down against the side of her head, bruising and cutting her flesh. Then he was gone, leaving her writhing and groaning on the floor.

Chapter Seven

'Look what he did to me. He's a bloody madman, so he is.' Kitty Wainright wept angrily as she showed Terence McCulloch the injuries that Dermot Calatrava had inflicted on her.

The man stroked his grey beard, his hand moving jerkily, betraying his inner tension. 'You must have done something to provoke him.'

'I did not!' She indignantly rejected the accusation. 'I did nothing to him.'

'Tell me again what happened,' McCulloch demanded, and his eyes were troubled.

'Oh, Jasus! Haven't I already told you a dozen times what happened!'

Now he showed a flash of temper, and his voice rose. 'Tell me again.'

With a bad grace she obeyed and related what had occurred up to the point immediately prior to the assault on her. She said nothing about her attempt to blackmail Calatrava.

'. . . he hit me for nothing. I thought he was going to kill me. He's a bloody madman, he is,' she finished, and again shrilly demanded that McCulloch should punish Calatrava.

'I'll deal with him,' he told her and gave her some money. 'Here, take this and keep your mouth shut about what happened. Leave it to me to deal with that man.'

He ushered her, still shrilly protesting and complaining, from his house and slammed the door against her grating voice.

For some time he remained motionless, standing with his back to the door, deep in thought. He was now strongly doubting the wisdom of having introduced Dermot Calatrava into his sectors of interest. It seemed that the man was much more volatile, unstable and dangerous than he, McCulloch, had anticipated.

Now he gave thought also to the fact that he knew virtually nothing of Calatrava's antecedents. He had appeared in McCulloch's life about a month previously, bringing with him a letter of recommendation from John O'Mahoney, a long-time friend and fellow conspirator of McCulloch from the days of the abortive 'Young Ireland' rebellion of 1848. O'Mahoney, in concert with the famed rebel James Stephens, had very recently organised an embryo revolutionary movement in America known as the Fenian Brotherhood. In the letter of introduction O'Mahoney had recommended Calatrava to McCulloch as a trusted member of that brotherhood, and had entreated McCulloch to give the young man any aid that was in his, McCulloch's, power to give. But apart from that letter, Calatrava was a mystery. McCulloch did not even know where the man was staying in London, or with whom.

McCulloch pondered deeply for some considerable time the problem that the young newcomer was beginning to present. You seem too much of a loose cannon for my peace of mind, Calatrava, he thought. I'm not sure just how much of a risk you might prove to be to my own safety.

61

Uneasy though this made him, after further ponderings, McCulloch decided. I'll let him run for a while longer. I just hope to God that I don't live to regret it . . .

Chapter Eight

The Reverend Alban Augustus Smyth-Prescott enjoyed telling any new acquaintances that he was named after a Christian saint and a Roman emperor, because prior to his birth his mother had experienced a vivid dream in which the Lord Jesus had appeared to her and told her that the child she bore in her womb was destined to become a ruler of the church. For this reason she had named him thus. One noted wag to whom the Reverend had told this story afterwards suggested that the Lord Jesus should have instructed the woman to add two further names, Gluttonus Bacchus, because the Reverend Smyth-Prescott possessed an awe-inspiring capacity for eating and drinking to excess.

Now it was midday, and the Reverend Smyth-Prescott was sitting at his favourite table in his favourite Chop House in the Strand, demolishing with great gusto a large platterful of broiled beefsteaks topped with oysters. Each succeeding mouthful was washed down with copious draughts of claret wine. His goitred eyes were bloodshot, and his fat face with its hanging jowls was hot and sweaty from the effects of the rich food and drink. As he chewed he smacked his greasy thick lips, grunted constantly, and periodically belched.

At intervals he would lean back in his chair and tug with his fingers at the constrictions of his high clerical stock and cravat and his vast belly would strain against the fine black cloth of his clerical waistcoat.

The Chop House was full of sombrely coated men of business and banks and counting houses talking, eating, bargaining, drinking, while perspiring waiters in long white aprons and black dress coats rushed around with trays of steaming meats and vegetables, tankards of ale and cider, bottles of claret and port, brandy and gin. The air was thick with the scents of food, the smoke of pipes and cheroots, the fumes of cooking wafting in from the adjoining kitchens.

'Pardon me, sir.' A waiter hovered obsequiously at Smyth-Prescott's elbow.

'Dammit all, man, I'm eating!' the cleric pouted irritably. 'I want no interruptions.'

'I beg pardon, sir, but the lady said it was most urgent that I give you this. She said it were a matter of life and death, sir.'

He proffered a silver tray on which lay a folded and sealed sheet of notepaper.

Smyth-Prescott grunted sourly and leaned back in his chair. 'What lady?'

'She's a widow lady, sir. She's waiting outside in her carriage for your reply, sir.'

Smyth-Prescott squinted towards the nearest window, but its panes of glass were made opaque by condensation of the steamy air in the room, and he could not distinguish anything in the street beyond except meaningless blurs of passing shapes.

'Dammit!' the cleric exclaimed in annoyance, then ordered the waiter, 'You can bring me another bottle. I want the fifty-three, mind. Not that new muck you've been trying to foist off on me.'

'Very good, sir. Thank you, sir. Thank you.' The man scurried away.

Smyth-Prescott broke the seal and smoothed out the sheet of notepaper, briefly scanning what was written upon it.

'Oh my God!' His face blanched and his heart pounded painfully with shock and terror. He felt that he was choking, and tore at his high stock to loosen it so that he might more easily draw air into his straining lungs.

As the first terrible wave of shock receded he shot fearful glances around him, but no one was observing him. They were all intent upon their own food and company. He tried to pull his scattered senses together, and to think rationally. Hiding the notepaper with his arms, he bent low over it, reading the printed words over and over again. The message was brief:

'Susanna, you are in mortal danger of discovery. I must speak to you immediately. A Friend.'

By the time the waiter had returned with the fresh bottle of claret, Smyth-Prescott had regained some semblance of control over his shock and terror. But he could not stop the trembling of his hands and body.

'The lady who gave you this, where is she?'

'She said to tell you that she'd be waiting in her carriage outside, sir.'

Smyth-Prescott drew in long, shuddering breaths as he rose to leave, and fumbled in his pockets for some coins which he dropped onto the table.

'Are you all right, sir?' The waiter stared at the cleric in amazement at this early departure. 'Is the meat not to your liking, sir?'

Smyth-Prescott ignored the man.

The old woman attending the cloakroom stared curiously at the tremulous, white-faced cleric as she handed over his top hat, gloves and topcoat.

'Are you quite well, sir? Do you need any assistance?'

Smyth-Prescott shook his head in abrupt refusal, and went out into the bustling street.

Even as he stepped through the doorway and onto the pavement a big man wearing a coachman's livery and cockaded top hat accosted him.

'My mistress is just down there, sir.' He indicated a closed carriage with two matching bay horses some little distance further along the street.

Smyth-Prescott felt both terrified and bemused, and could not bring himself to move.

As if sensing what the fat man was feeling, the big coachman told him reassuringly, 'You're perfectly safe, sir. My mistress only wants to help you.'

Battling with his fear the cleric reluctantly waddled after the big coachman.

The man opened the carriage door, and Smyth-Prescott hesitantly approached and peered inside.

The woman was dressed in deepest mourning, her face concealed by a thick black veil. 'I'm so happy that you've come to see me, Susanna. I want to help you.' Her voice was husky and low-pitched. 'Please seat yourself inside. This will only take a short while.'

The fat man experienced an overwhelming impulse to take flight, but now the big coachman crowded close behind him, urging him in a voice which contained a latent threat, 'Do as my mistress asks you to, sir. It'll be the best for you.'

Gasping with the effort, he lifted his large body into

66

the coach and sagged down on the seat opposite the woman.

The coachman closed the door, plunging the curtained interior into gloomy shadow.

'We'll drive around while we talk, Susanna,' the woman said, and the next instant the carriage lurched into motion.

Smyth-Prescott, feeling a sense of utter helplessness, closed his eyes and let his fear whelm over him.

The carriage swayed on its springs, rocking its passengers with the sway, and Smyth-Prescott began to feel giddy and nauseous.

'Now, Susanna, listen to me very carefully.' The woman's low-pitched voice held a soothing quality. 'I am going to tell you what I know about you . . .' She went on to give him every sordid detail of his doings in the male brothel. Names, dates, accounts of the various perversions he practised flowed from her lips, and he cringed and whimpered as he listened, realising that she could ruin him utterly and completely if she so chose.

At last she fell silent, and allowed him to tearfully beg and plead with her to be merciful. After a while she ordered curtly, 'Stop snivelling. Your secret is safe with me, just so long as you do what I ask of you. No one shall ever know what passes here between us. All I want from you is a little harmless information.'

'But what information could I possess that would be of any service to you, madam?' the cleric questioned pathetically. 'I'm a person of little importance.'

'You are one of the appointed chaplains to the Royal Family, are you not, sir?'

'I am, yes, but what can . . .'

'Hold your tongue and listen to me,' she commanded

sharply, and the abrupt hardening of her tone again sent shafts of fear quivering through the fat man.

She waited a moment, then went on, 'The Prince of Wales is presently staying at the White Lodge in Richmond Park, is he not?'

'Yes, he is,' Smyth-Prescott confirmed quaveringly.

'You yourself attend upon him there twice or thrice weekly, do you not?'

'I do, yes, madam. I impart religious instruction to His Royal Highness.'

'Very well. I want you now to give me the fullest account you can of the Prince's daily routines. I want also to know everything that you can tell me about the interior and grounds of the White Lodge, about its occupants, its servants, its daily routines.'

She paused for a moment to let him digest what she had said, and then told him, 'If you do this to my satisfaction, then this will be the last time you will ever see me or hear from me. It shall be as if I have never entered your life. And no one will ever come to know from me the terrible secrets that we share.'

He wept with relief, and the woman allowed him some time to vent his emotions. Then she ordered, 'Now, tell me what I wish to know.'

He began to speak rapidly, almost gabbling the words, so eager to please her that he talked on and on without pause, repeating himself continually, jumbling his sentences, saliva flecking his thick lips, and Rosaleen Calatrava sat in complete silence as she listened and absorbed what she was hearing.

Chapter Nine

The Royal Park at Richmond covered two thousand, two hundred and fifty-three acres and was some eight miles in circuit. Since the coming of the South-Western Railway to Richmond Town the park had attracted Londoners seeking the peace and beauty and clean air of the countryside. Now, as the knowledge of the presence of the Prince of Wales at the White Lodge had spread, so the numbers of people coming to the Richmond Park had increased sharply. Family groups and individuals were to be seen walking, on horseback, riding in carriages, all hoping to encounter the heir to the throne. It had been widely reported that each day, at varying times, the Prince, who was a keen horseman, would ride in the park, accompanied by an equerry and a couple of attendants.

The information that the Reverend Smyth-Prescott had given Rosaleen Calatrava had caused her to decide against any attempt to assassinate the prince within the confines of the White Lodge itself. The building and its grounds were constantly patrolled by watchmen, arms were kept in the house, and several of the servants had been trained to use those weapons against intruders. Rosaleen decided that the attack would be made during the prince's daily ride, and she instructed her brother accordingly.

Dermot Calatrava welcomed the presence in the park of so many would-be royal viewers, and was happy to be taken for one of their number as he carefully reconnoitred on horseback and on foot the undulating ground with its plentifully scattered plantations, copses and wooded hillocks.

From his personal observations, and from casual conversations with other visitors to the park, he was able to establish that the prince's party usually left and returned to the White Lodge by the same bridle way, before branching out in varying directions for their ride.

Each evening he would go to his sister's villa and would discuss the day's findings with her. On several occasions she herself travelled to the park, and viewed the various locations in company with her brother.

Several carriage roads criss-crossed the park, and Rosaleen spent many hours traversing the roads she considered might be utilised. After much consideration she finalised her plans and told her brother, 'Sunday. We'll do it this coming Sunday.'

Chapter Ten

'Good afternoon, your Highness.' Henry Winstanley stood to attention and bowed his head to the youth lounging in the vast armchair.

'Ahh, here you are at last, Winstanley.' The slender youth's soft, effeminate features mirrored the petulance in his voice, and his protuberant blue eyes were sparkling with temper. 'Why have you kept me waiting for so long? The afternoon is all but gone.'

Winstanley suppressed the urge to answer sharply, and apologised quietly. 'I'm sorry, sir, but I was unavoidably detained at the barracks. There was some regimental business needing my attention.'

'Business?' The youth sneered openly. 'Business? You begin to sound like a tradesman, Winstanley.'

Anger flickered in Winstanley's eyes, and he snapped curtly, 'But I *am* a tradesman, sir. My trade is war. And war must be treated as a business. It does not do to expend men and material without return of profit.'

The youth considered the older man's answer for a couple of moments, then clapped his hands, laughing like a pleased child, and applauded. 'Bravo, Winstanley, bravo. I do wish that Mamma and Papa would allow me to enter your regiment. You could teach me much.' Now he entreated the man, 'Do you think that you might urge Papa to let me enter the army? I'm sure he would give weight to your opinions.'

A grim smile touched Winstanley's lips. He was neither surprised nor disconcerted by the Prince's lightning mood change. During his short sojourn here at the White Lodge he had swiftly become accustomed to the vagaries of the Prince's moods. The youth was capable of displaying temper, spite, greed, generosity, kindness, cruelty, affection, enthusiasm, boredom, energy and laziness all within the space of an hour. Winstanley considered that Albert Edward, Prince of Wales, fully deserved his nickname; he was truly a spoiled brat.

The Prince jumped to his feet. 'Will you speak to Papa about it, Winstanley? I'd make a very fine soldier, you know. I've the gift of leadership. When I give commands men jump to obey me.'

'I shall speak to your father at the earliest opportunity, sir,' Winstanley promised, and added ironically, 'I'm sure that your gift for leadership will prove to be an asset to the army; jumping is such good exercise for the men.'

'Come, let's go riding.' The youth was all eager energy now, in contrast to his bored slothfulness of the minute before. 'I feel like a good long gallop.'

Outside, on the gravelled forecourt before the house, two mounted orderlies from Winstanley's regiment were waiting with two ready-saddled mounts for the Prince and Winstanley. The orderlies were uniformed in blue shell jackets, white overalls and pillbox forage caps, but the Prince and Winstanley both wore civilian riding dress, and top hats.

Frederick Waymouth Gibbs, the principal tutor to the Prince, was also waiting on the forecourt. He was a sombre man who disapproved of any levity. He did not approve of the daily riding excursions of the Prince either, considering that his pupil would be better employed in study. Young Albert Edward was not noticeably intellectual, and in his secret soul Frederick Waymouth Gibbs was forced to acknowledge that had the Prince not been of the Blood Royal, then he would have been justly described as scholastically stupid. But in their own best interests, his tutors could only report to the Queen and her Consort that their eldest son was reluctant to apply his high intelligence to his lessons.

'Major Winstanley,' Gibbs addressed himself to the soldier, 'I do implore you to keep His Royal Highness from endangering himself by wild riding.'

Winstanley cordially disliked the pompous tutor, and his dislike showed as he frowned and snapped, 'Of course, Mr Gibbs. Do I not always do so?'

The tutor sniffed with disdain, and countered, 'Regrettably, I consider that you do not do so, Major Winstanley.'

'Do come along, Winstanley.' The prince was already mounted and eager to be off. 'Time's wasting.'

As the four horsemen trotted towards the great ornate gates of the Lodge grounds, the Prince and Winstanley in the lead, the two orderlies some four lengths behind, Frederick Waymouth Gibbs stood scowling after them until they were gone from his view.

The closed carriage moved at a fair pace, and in its curtained interior Rosaleen Calatrava sat upright, swaying slightly from side to side with the vehicle's roll. She was wearing widow's weeds, and a heavily veiled bonnet. Her nervous tension was betrayed by her hands, gripped so tightly together on her lap that the blood was squeezed from the finger ends.

Thomas Quinn was driving the carriage, and he also was tense and nervous, his eyes constantly searching the ground around him.

Although the day had earlier been clear and sunny, the skies had gradually darkened with clouds and now, in the late afternoon, a drizzle of fine rain had begun to fall, and the crowds who had come to the park for their Sabbath outing were heading homewards, thronging the carriage roads that led to the different gates. The road along which Rosaleen's carriage was travelling reached deep into the park, and now was empty. For some hundreds of yards it paralleled within a quarter-mile distance the bridle path along which the royal riding party exited from the environs of the White Lodge, but the undulating terrain and the various copses and plantations rendered travellers on the two roadways invisible to each other.

Hidden in the thick undergrowth of a hillock above the bridle path, Dermot Calatrava kept watch along its length, using a small brass telescope. Concealed in a clump of bushes some feet below him, Billy Gilligan and Sean Gallagher lay side by side. All three men wore the rough clothing and heavy boots of labourers, and wide-brimmed hats pulled low on their heads.

When the rain began to fall Gilligan cursed sibilantly. He was in his middle twenties, with a muscular body and brutal good looks, his black curly hair and long sideburns giving him the look of a gypsy. Both he and Gallagher were armed with muzzle-loading, percussion-cap Enfield rifles.

'Never mind swearing,' Sean Gallagher remonstrated

hoarsely. 'Just make sure you keep your cartridges dry.'

Gilligan turned fiercely on the older man. 'Don't try telling me me business, you wee scut.'

'Shut up, the pair of you,' Dermot Calatrava hissed, still staring through his telescope, and Gilligan glared up at him, but fell silent.

'There they are.' Dermot Calatrava snapped his telescope shut and pushed it into his pocket. 'Make ready now,' he ordered. 'And give fire when I tell you to, and not before.'

Sean Gallagher squinted short-sightedly along the bridle way where, in the far distance, four horsemen were approaching at an easy trot.

'Which one is himself?'

'The one wearing the fuckin' crown, you stupid wee bastard,' Gilligan gibed, and once more Dermot Calatrava angrily ordered, 'Shut your mouth, will you, Gilligan. I'll not warn you again.'

To Gallagher he said, 'Your target is the one on the chestnut, Sean. I'll tell you when to fire.'

On the bridle path the Prince was becoming impatient. 'I want to gallop, Winstanley. Let's all of us have a race.'

Winstanley looked down at the ground, which at this spot was intersected by small rivulets and covered with rapidly spreading puddles of rainwater, turning the surface to slippery mud.

'The going is too treacherous along here, sir. There's no point in risking the horses. Let's travel a little further before we race. See there, where the ground rises, that should be firmer going.'

He pointed to an area which lay around a thickly wooded hillock.

The rainfall suddenly intensified and the wind began gusting. And on the hillock Sean Gallagher wiped his eyes, and silently bewailed his failing sight – a condition he had kept hidden from the Calatravas.

Dermot Calatrava checked his own weapon, a six-shot, percussion-capped, muzzle-loading Colt revolver, then slipped it back into his pocket, and ordered, 'Make ready, both of you. And wait for my command.'

The men beneath him came to a crouch in the thick bushes, loaded their rifles and, as the four horsemen drew nearer, assumed the aiming stance.

'Surely this will do well enough, Winstanley?' The Prince challenged excitedly.

The cavalryman assessed the ground, and his trained eyes mentally traced out a route, which he pointed out to the youth. 'We'll go along there as far as the solitary tree, sir, then left up to the nearest point of that plantation, and then straight back here.'

He pulled a handkerchief from his pocket and, leaning down from his saddle, tied it to the branches of a small shrub growing at the side of the bridle way. 'Whoever takes this has won the race.'

The Prince laughed delightedly. 'Bravo!' and told the orderlies, 'If one of you takes it, I'll give you a guinea.'

Both men grinned in delight and saluted.

'Thank you, your 'Ighness.'

'And now, Winstanley, a small wager between ourselves. Shall we say ten guineas?'

'Done, sir.'

'Hurrah!' the youth shouted and suddenly slashed his whip down across his mount's croup. The beast bolted forwards and, almost simultaneously, there sounded two sharp reports, and one of the orderlies' horses emitted a high-pitched whinny of agony and reared high as a small black hole appeared on its flank.

'We're being shot at!' Winstanley shouted and, rising in his stirrups, searched the surrounding area. He spotted a faint wisp of smoke in the undergrowth of the hillock.

Completely unaware of what had taken place behind him, shouting and hallooing, the Prince went galloping on, and Winstanley shouted to the orderlies, 'Corporal Wilson, go after his Highness, get him back to the Lodge. Private Tibbs, follow me.'

And instantly he spurred his mount towards the hillock, his free hand scrabbling in his saddlebag for the loaded double-barrelled percussion pistol he always kept there.

'You've missed him, blast you!' Dermot Calatrava bellowed in fury. 'Reload and fire again. Quickly, damn you!'

Frantically, the two men tried to obey, but the wet weapons were slippery in the grip, and Sean Gallagher fumbled and dropped his ramrod and cartridge.

'Goddamn it!' Dermot Calatrava howled in frustration and, scorning any attempt at concealment, hurled himself downwards and snatched the rifle from Gallagher's hands. With frantic haste he loaded, ramrodded and fitted the percussion cap.

Billy Gilligan's weapon roared, and smoke jetted from its muzzle. But the distant figure of the galloping prince kept going.

Dermot Calatrava took aim and fired, but even as the recoil bruised his shoulder he had the sickening awareness that he also had missed his target.

'Jasus! Watch out for your man there!' Sean Gallagher shouted in warning, and Calatrava saw that the Prince's civilian-clad companion was already urging his mount up the lower slope of the hillock, and the uniformed soldier was close behind him.

Both men dismounted now and the soldier snatched a carbine from his saddlebucket, but as he ran forwards his foot twisted and he fell, tried to rise, shouted in pain and fell again.

'Are you all right, Tibbs?' Winstanley shouted.

'It's me ankle, sir, I've broke it, I think.'

'Are you still able to shoot?' Winstanley asked him, and the man nodded grimly, then propped himself into a sitting position, took aim and fired.

Sean Gallagher screamed and toppled, his body jerking, his hands scrabbling at the bloody wreckage of his chest.

The top-hatted civilian was again crashing upwards through the undergrowth. Billy Gilligan shouted, 'Fuck this!' He hurled his empty rifle aside and took to his heels up and over the crest of the hillock.

The injured soldier fired again, and the ball whipped through the branches only inches above Dermot Calatrava's head.

'He's a good shot,' Calatrava realised. 'He won't miss next time.'

He turned to flee, and tore through the clinging brambles and over the crest, but as he plunged downwards he could hear the crashing pursuit of the civilian behind him.

Calatrava pulled his revolver from his pocket and, still running, tried to look back at his pursuer. His foot snagged on a fallen branch and he tripped and fell headlong, cannoning into a tree trunk, momentarily stunning himself and losing his grip on his weapon, which spun away into the undergrowth.

Terror gripped him and gave him the strength to push himself upright and run on, reeling with giddiness, still half-stunned. Winstanley, in pursuit, experienced a surge of elation as he narrowed the gap between them.

Calatrava reached the carriage road and began to run along it, and Winstanley pounded after him, and found to his dismay that now his quarry appeared to be getting further away from him. He lifted his pistol and fired wildly, but the ball whistled wide. A few more paces and Winstanley came to an abrupt halt, then, fighting to steady his heavy panting, used both hands to grip and aim the pistol.

The ball struck the fleeing man's leg and brought him down.

Winstanley ran onwards, and saw a carriage and pair come hurtling dangerously fast around the bend further along the roadway.

The fallen man was trying desperately to scrabble along the ground, dragging his useless injured leg behind him. Winstanley came up alongside him and, shouting in triumph, grabbed his quarry and slammed him face downwards onto the muddy roadway. Clubbing his prey with his empty pistol, he used his knees to trap the squirming man, as he shrieked with the agony of his wounds.

Winstanley heard the carriage coming to a skidding, juddering halt, and lifted his head to shout for help. His eyes widened in shock as he saw the black-clad woman leap from the carriage and run towards him, her crinoline skirts billowing about her. She came to a halt in front of him, and, with one hand, lifted the thick veil from her face.

'By God!' Winstanley exclaimed in disbelief. 'What do you do here?'

And disbelief still gripped him in its thrall as the woman lifted the pistol she held in her other hand, aimed it directly between his eyes, and pulled the trigger.

Thomas Quinn bodily lifted the groaning Dermot Calatrava and, with Rosaleen's help, bundled him inside the carriage. Within seconds the carriage went hurtling on, leaving Winstanley where he had fallen, blood oozing from his head and snaking sinuously over the mud to form a widening pool into which the raindrops fell, splashing and spattering minute scarlet flecks.

Chapter Eleven

The carriage had covered three miles and was crossing Barnes Common. In its dark interior Rosaleen Calatrava fought to stem the loss of blood from the wound on her brother's thigh. She ripped strips from her petticoats and bandaged the torn flesh, but still the blood spurted. Desperately she clamped her hands upon the bloodsoaked cloth in a futile attempt to stem the bleeding, but the lurching and jolting of the fast-moving vehicle over the uneven road surface threw her helplessly off balance, rendering it almost impossible for her to maintain any pressure. In desperation she hammered with her fists upon the front panels and shouted to Thomas Quinn to halt the carriage.

He quickly joined her, his battered features grim as he regarded the waxen pallor of Dermot Calatrava's face. The young man was slipping in and out of consciousness, eyes rolling and unfocused.

'He looks bad,' Quinn grunted.

Rosaleen was shaking with shock and fear. 'Do something, Thomas,' she begged. 'For the love of God, do something!'

Quinn unbuttoned his coat and took his leather belt off. 'We'll have to risk the gangrene, ma'am, if he loses much more blood he'll be gone,' he told Rosaleen, and used the belt as a tourniquet high up on the wounded man's thigh, grunting with effort as he pulled it tight, and the blood loss lessened visibly.

She put her head close to her brother's ear. 'Don't die, my darling!' she pleaded tearfully. 'Don't die. Don't die.'

'We've got to get him to a surgeon. The arteries need to be tied off, and the wound cauterised. If the tourniquet stays on too long he'll get the gangrene in his leg.'

Despite her distress Rosaleen's shrewd brain still functioned. 'The hunt will be on for us now. What if the surgeon gives us up? What's the use of saving Dermot, only to lose him to the hangman?'

Quinn thought briefly. 'There's somebody lives near here who might help us. I knew him well when I was prizefighting. He's a drunken old rogue, but he was a good surgeon in his day.' The battered features suddenly looked doubtful. 'But he might be dead by now. He was drinking himself into the grave fast when I knew him, and that was years since.'

'Let's try to find him,' Rosaleen entreated desperately, and cradled her brother in her arms as the coach lurched onwards once more.

Barnes village lay along the banks of the Thames, a straggling haphazardly interspersed collection of ancient tumbledown cottages and tenements and newly built villas and terraces.

Quinn drove the carriage through the village to its opposite outskirts and halted the coach in front of a ramshackle old house, its windows broken and rag-stuffed, the garden a wilderness of overgrown bushes and weeds.

Quinn came to the carriage door and Rosaleen peered anxiously at the seemingly deserted building.

'It looks empty,' she observed despondently.

Quinn stared briefly at the now deeply unconscious Dermot, whose breathing was ragged and shallow, his face a pinched, deathlike grey.

'If it's empty, then your brother's doomed, ma'am. So pray to God that the old man is still here.'

He turned and hurried through the garden and hammered on the cracked, warped panels of the front door, and while he hammered Rosaleen prayed tearfully.

'Dear God, let the man be here. Please, please, let him be here. Let him be here.'

Time seemed to stretch interminably as Quinn hammered, the impact of his blows shaking the door until it appeared that it would fly from its hinges.

Then, at last, it creaked ajar, a wrinkled old face appeared in the narrow opening and a toothless mouth spewed out a torrent of abuse.

Quinn's hands raised high, opened in supplication, and he talked rapidly. Then he hurried back to Rosaleen. 'Quick, ma'am, give me all the money you've got, and anything else that's valuable.'

She gave him her purse, and tore the rings from her fingers, the bracelets from her wrists, the necklace from her throat, the jewelled watch from its pocket-fob.

Quinn ran back to the old man and, after a few moments' haggling, returned again to the carriage. He lifted the limp body of Dermot in his arms and carried him into the house like a sleeping child, head hanging back, arms and legs dangling, with Rosaleen following, hardly daring to hope that her beloved brother might be saved.

The cold stench of the house enfolded her like a rancid shroud, and she gagged and retched and tasted the sourness of bile in her mouth.

The room's high ceiling, intricately patterned with the plaster designs of long-dead master craftsmen, had long black tendrils of dust-filled spider's webs hanging from it, and more webs curtaining the damp-stained walls. The furnishings were broken, the floor littered with filth, rotting food and excrement, and dozens of empty bottles.

'Put him on there,' the old man instructed in a wheezing voice, and Quinn told Rosaleen to sweep the grease-thick table top clear of the stinking rubbish that covered every inch of its surface.

With a sinking heart she obeyed, all hope fast leaving her as, for the first time, she looked fully at the old man.

His head rocked on his scrawny, withered neck as if from a palsy, and his clawlike hands with their blackened, taloned nails were jerking fitfully as if he had lost any muscular control. Ancient dirt was deep engrained into his skin, and his rheumed eyes were watering and heavily bloodshot.

He lifted a leather bag, green with age, from a chest in the corner of the room, and took rusty surgical instruments from it, dusty rolls of bandage and small jars of medications. Then he ordered Thomas Quinn, 'Light that candle, and hold it close to his leg. My eyes aren't as good as they used to be.'

He used a knife with a long curved blade to cut away the bloodsoaked trousers and then bent low to peer at the copiously bleeding wound.

'It's a gunshot, I see,' he muttered, and grinned toothlessly at Rosaleen. 'This is going to cost you a pretty penny, young woman. Silence don't come cheap.'

Then he ordered Quinn, 'Hold the candle there, and keep it still.'

His long-taloned fingers spread wide upon the wound and, laying aside the knife, he lifted a long metal probe and inserted it into the wound, feeling for the bullet. After a few moments he grunted with satisfaction. 'There it is. I'll reach it with the first incision.'

Leaving the probe *in situ*, he took up the knife and slashed down with the curved blade, slicing deep into the flesh. Blood spurted and Rosaleen screamed, then blackness overwhelmed her sight.

The old man swore at Thomas Quinn as the big man turned and the candle he was holding guttered. 'Keep the light still, you damned fool. She's only fainted.'

He bent close to the wide, bleeding gash, rubbing his watery eyes with the back of his hand, then dug into the red flesh with his fingers and extracted a flattened lump of lead. He cackled in triumph. 'There, I haven't lost my skills, have I? Pass me that hook.'

Quinn handed him the thin metal rod with the hooked end, and the old man used it to draw out the blood-spurting artery and tie it off.

Stepping away from the unconscious man he ignited a spirit lamp, and heated the point of a knife blade to red heat, then used it to cauterise the cut veins, causing the flesh to sizzle and smoke. Then, with needle and waxed threads, he sewed up the wound, and finished by expertly bandaging the thigh.

Dermot Calatrava had other wounds on the back of his head where Winstanley had clubbed him with the pistol, and the old man briefly examined these, then dismissed them as needing no treatment.

Finally, he told Quinn, 'I've done all I can for him.'

Quinn stared at the deathlike mask of Dermot

Calatrava's face, and questioned doubtfully, 'Will he live?'

The old man cackled with laughter, and retorted, 'I think it's fair to say that the operation has been a success. But whether he survives it is up to God. Speaking for myself, I wouldn't give him too much of a chance. Now get him out of here.'

He rummaged in the same chest from which he had taken his leather bag, and straightened up with a bottle clutched in his hands. He pulled the cork and drank straight from the mouth of the bottle. Gasping with satisfaction, he offered, 'Will you take a mouthful? It's best French brandy.'

At their feet Rosaleen stirred and moaned, and Quinn took the proffered bottle and knelt beside her.

'Take a sip of this, ma'am. It'll clear your senses.'

The fiery liquid burned Rosaleen's throat and brought her, coughing and choking, to full awareness.

'Dermot?' she begged to know, and Quinn nodded and assured her with a confidence he was far from feeling.

'He'll be all right.'

She wept with relief and Quinn allowed her to lean against him until she had recovered herself.

Outside the wind was gusting strongly, hurling the falling rain across the sodden ground, and Rosaleen blessed the storm for keeping curious eyes indoors.

As Quinn carefully carried the comatose man to the carriage, Rosaleen began to express her gratitude to the old man, but he rudely cut short her protestations.

'Just remember what I told you. Silence is costly to buy. I know your face, and the man's face. And I know Thomas Quinn. You'll send me two hundred guineas before the Sabbath day comes again, or I'll be asking the authorities if they are seeking a man who was shot on this day.'

Paradoxically, this blackmail did not anger Rosaleen. She was too grateful for the life of her beloved brother to worry about the old man's extortionate demands. No amount of money would be too much for her to pay to save her brother's life.

'Don't worry, you'll have your money, and welcome.'

She left the house and returned to the carriage.

Once she was settled, cradling her brother in her arms, she told Quinn, 'Drive home carefully, Thomas.'

Quinn remained standing at the door, his battered face showing doubt.

'What is it?' she asked and, drawing the wrong conclusion, reassured him, 'There's no need to be worried about Mr Montague. He's gone to the Midlands on business. He'll not be back for at least a week.'

'It's not Mr Montague I'm worried about, ma'am.' Quinn jerked his head in the direction of the house. 'It's him. I'm not sure that he's to be trusted.'

His doubt raised an echoing doubt in Rosaleen's mind and, seeing her expression, Quinn offered, 'I can make sure he'll keep silent, ma'am. It'll take me only a moment.'

For a brief instant Rosaleen almost gave in to the temptation of allowing him to silence the old man for ever. But then her conscience berated her. 'You owe Dermot's life to that old man. You can't let Thomas kill him. Not after he's just saved Dermot's life.'

She shook her head. 'No, leave the old man be. I'll pay him enough to ensure he stays silent.'

Still doubtful, Quinn grudgingly acceded to her wish

and, remounting the driving seat, gathered the reins in his massive hands.

'Walk on,' he commanded, and the horses, dripping wet, stepped off.

It was some time before Rosaleen gave thought to the man that she had killed. She found that she felt no remorse for what she had done.

'He was trying to kill my Dermot. He deserved to die. I'll kill anyone who tries to hurt my Dermot.'

Gazing anxiously down at her brother's pallid face she whispered, 'I love you, honey. I love you more than my life. Don't die. Please don't die.'

Chapter Twelve

Although Conrad Cumlinson Esquire was a permanent Government official of the Home Office, he was very rarely seen in the environs of Whitehall or any other seat of political power and influence. His departmental offices were at number 50 Harley Street, a prosperous but not particularly fashionable section of London's West End. The house bore no visible signs to proclaim it a department of the Government, and no brass name-plates to identify its occupants, only small, black-painted numerals on the left-hand pillar of its entrance.

Cumlinson himself was of a retiring nature. He was an unobtrusive man, slightly above medium height, who dressed always in sombre black, and attracted no interest in a crowd. His immediate office staff numbered only two elderly clerks who, like their superior, were quiet men who passed unnoticed through their daily lives. Three burly, dour-mannered, ex-senior NCOs of the Foot Guards acted in the capacity of general factotums and security staff, and also prepared food and drink in the basement kitchen when required to do so.

Cumlinson's department had initially been embodied to monitor and counter the activities of anti-Government agitators and potential revolutionaries such as the Chartists. Following the Young Ireland rebellion of 1848, the department had also been tasked with monitoring and countering the activities of militant Irish Nationalists. In the quiet rooms of number 50 Harley Street, Cumlinson and his two assistants received and evaluated information from a network of agents and informants. The assistants acted as filters, taking decisions as to what information was valuable enough to pass through to their superior. Cumlinson in his turn studied and evaluated that filtered information, and decided what action he should take concerning it. For the physical means to carry out that action Cumlinson was empowered if necessary to call upon the aid of any branch of Her Majesty's military and civilian services. He also employed a small group of agents directly answerable to himself.

Over the years Conrad Cumlinson had so enhanced his reputation for sagacious judgement that the politicians who succeeded each other as Home Secretary virtually allowed him *carte blanche* to act in their name and take whatever action he considered to be necessary. So that now, in this twenty-first year of Queen Victoria's reign, his covert power and influence were considerable.

Only scant hours after the attempted assassination of the Prince of Wales, Conrad Cumlinson received an urgent summons from the Home Secretary's office at Whitehall. There the Home Secretary, Sidney Estcourt Esquire, was waiting in person to receive him.

The politician's agitated manner caused Conrad Cumlinson, who privately despised all politicians, to surmise instantly that the Home Secretary had made some sort of blunder which he now needed Cumlinson to rectify.

Estcourt brusquely instructed his aides that he was not to be disturbed for any reason, and bore Cumlinson off to his private chambers.

Immediately the door was closed behind them, he stuttered agitatedly, 'There's been an attempt made on the Prince's life, Mr Cumlinson. What are we to do?'

'Are you referring to the Prince Consort or the Prince of Wales, sir?' Cumlinson asked calmly, inwardly enjoying the other man's discomfiture.

'Why, the Prince of Wales, of course,' the politician replied irascibly.

'Might I suggest, sir, that we seat ourselves, and that you lay the facts of the matter before me.' Cumlinson's tone was coldly respectful, yet held a hint of contempt.

Estcourt realised that he himself was displaying an undue lack of control for someone who held such high office. He struggled to calm himself, and they both sat down. After a few moments Estcourt continued.

'The Prince's equerry, Major Teesdale, came directly to me. He's waiting in my drawing room. Although he was not the duty equerry he had remained at the Lodge; a fortunate occurrence in the circumstances. I thought it best that in the first instance I relate to you what he has told me. Apparently it was an ambush . . .'

Cumlinson listened without interruption, his face betraying no reaction other than a judicious consideration of what he was hearing.

Then, when the politician fell silent, he requested that Major Teesdale be brought to join them.

The soldier was tall and fashionably dressed, with a steady, direct gaze.

Cumlinson began to question him.

'What steps have been taken to ensure that the

knowledge of this incident has been kept to as few people as possible?'

'I've ordered everyone in the Prince's household to remain inside the Lodge, and have placed my own orderlies on guard over the dead bodies. The two soldiers have been sequestered, and ordered to say nothing to anyone concerning what has happened. I've also ordered the park rangers to close the park to public access.'

'Excellent!' Cumlinson was pleased. 'Who is ensuring that your orders are obeyed?'

'Mr Gibbs, the Prince's principal tutor. He's a level-headed fellow, for all his pomposity.'

'Have the local police or the Metropolitan been informed?'

Teesdale shook his head. 'Not yet. I judged that Mr Estcourt should be the first to be informed.'

'You judged well, Major Teesdale,' Cumlinson praised. 'And may I congratulate you on your handling of this unhappy incident.'

He looked at Estcourt and nodded, and the politician thanked the soldier and asked him to wait once more in the drawing room.

When Teesdale withdrew, Estcourt questioned anxiously, 'Well, Mr Cumlinson, what's to be done?'

Cumlinson considered his answer carefully before replying. 'Judging from what I've heard this does not appear to be the work of a gang of ordinary criminals. There was obviously no robbery or suchlike intended. And it wasn't some madman acting alone, as were the attacks made on the Queen.

'I think it safe to assume that political malcontents have done this. Very likely to be Irish. I've lately received reports that Irish Americans from the Emmet Monument Association in New York have been travelling to Dublin to meet with Nationalist extremists. There have been whispers that following our recent arrests of members of the Phoenix Society in the west of Ireland, a new secret group is being formed in Dublin. Perhaps this was intended to be their means of demonstrating their abilities to strike against the British.'

'You still haven't told me what's to be done, Mr Cumlinson,' the other man complained plaintively.

A mirthless smile fleetingly quirked Cumlinson's lips. 'Obviously, sir, the news of this attack cannot be kept suppressed for very long. We shall therefore issue our own version of the event for public consumption. I think it advisable, sir, that this attack should be attributed solely to the dead man. We shall state that the authorities believe that he was acting alone. We shall state also that he was a madman, recently released from a private asylum. We can manufacture a false identity for him.'

'But why should we say that?' Estcourt was puzzled. 'Do you have good reason for suggesting this?'

Cumlinson was not accustomed to transient holders of political office, however high that office might be, questioning his professional expertise, or the covert actions he directed to be carried out in the course of his duties. He had become used to being a virtual law unto himself.

This present Home Secretary had only held office for a very brief span of time, and Cumlinson considered him to be a mere neophyte. He decided that this was the moment to assert his own authority, and to claim what he considered to be his right and proper due.

'Sir, my paramount duty is to safeguard the interests of this nation.' His voice was cold and very calm. 'To ensure the safety of the Royal Family, the Government and the Officers of State I need the freedom to act without let or hindrance. If I am obligated to explain and to seek permission for my actions, then a delay in implementing those actions must invariably occur. That delay will inevitably create many difficulties and threaten the success of my operations. I must ask you to permit me to carry out my duties without the necessity of explanation. If you feel unable to do this, then I must respectfully tender to you my immediate resignation.'

The politician's florid face registered shock then indignation. He was about to issue a stinging rebuke, when the memory of a conversation he had recently shared with Lord Derby, the Prime Minister, and the Chancellor of the Exchequer, Benjamin Disraeli, suddenly sprang into his mind. The gist of that conversation had been the necessity of any government's sometimes having to order unlawful actions to be carried out for the good of the country. Those unlawful actions encompassed the entire gamut of biblical sins, and caused much moral doubt and distress to those who were obligated to issue the order. With sardonic humour Disraeli had stated how fortunate their governance was in possessing a man such as Conrad Cumlinson, who had for so long relieved successive incumbents of high office of the obligation to order actions which caused them such moral doubts and distress. A sentiment with which Lord Derby had heartily concurred.

Estcourt was not willing to risk any conflict with his party superiors by forcing a man they valued so highly into resigning. He swallowed the stinging rebuke, forced a smile and told the sparse-bodied, unobtrusive man before him, 'I shall leave it all in your hands, Mr Cumlinson. Naturally I shall fully support whatever course of action you decide upon. You have my complete confidence.'

Cumlinson acknowledged the surrender with a slight bow. 'Thank you, sir. I trust that I shall prove worthy of your confidence.'

Not wishing to create an unnecessary enemy he offered a sop to the politician's pride. 'With your permission, sir, I would like to talk further with Major Teesdale. Might he accompany me now?'

'Why certainly, Mr Cumlinson.' Estcourt felt quite gratified.

'Many thanks, sir. I'll bid you good night then.'

He invited Teesdale to a nearby Chop House and there they ate and drank while they talked, and Cumlinson instructed the soldier in what he wanted done during the night-time hours. They parted on very good terms and went their separate ways.

Conrad Cumlinson took a hackney cab back to Harley Street. His two assistants, Messrs Bush and Craven, were awaiting his return. Cumlinson fully briefed them on the situation, then issued his instructions.

'Mr Bush, there will be a box of perishables delivered here during the night. Have it placed in the cold cellar. Mr Craven, as soon as possible inform the Chief Commissioner that I require the services of Inspector Charles Anderson.'

Cumlinson stopped speaking and began to pace up and down, three steps forwards, halt, turn about; three steps back, halt, turn about; three steps forwards, halt, turn about, and the other men waited patiently, knowing that their superior was mentally formulating his plans.

After fifteen minutes of pacing Cumlinson snapped curtly, 'I want the last reports from America.'

Mr Bush hurried to extract the slender files of paper from a large cabinet and hand them to his superior, who scanned the pages while still pacing.

Several times more Mr Bush was sent hurrying to the cabinet to extract reports from Paris, from Dublin, from various locations in England, Scotland and Wales.

Cumlinson finally came to a halt, and Bush took the files from him and replaced them in the cabinet, then seated himself at his desk, and both assistants took up their pens in readiness to note down Cumlinson's orders in the vast ledgers on the desks before them.

For half an hour Cumlinson talked without pause, and the old-fashioned quill pens scratched rapidly upon the pages. Then Cumlinson returned to his own office.

Mr Craven looked up from his own ledger to smile across at his colleague. 'Sir is in good form, is he not, Mr Bush?'

Mr Bush returned the smile, and agreed with immense satisfaction. 'Indeed he is, Mr Craven. He's in rare good form.'

In his office Conrad Cumlinson was sipping a glass of sweet sherry. The youngest son of a colonial Bishop, Cumlinson had been educated at Eton and Cambridge, and had served as an officer in the Rifle Brigade. He was fanatically patriotic. For him God truly was an Englishman, and the English race were God's annointed Captains of the Earth. Any challenge to England's supremacy he regarded as a personal affront, and he was prepared to destroy any individual or group whom he considered a threat to his country's interests.

Now, as always when faced with a new challenge, he felt exhilarated, and charged with energy.

The hunt was on, and he had unleashed his hounds. Once they had tracked the quarry to its lair, then he would unleash his killer dogs for the final act of destruction.

Chapter Thirteen

In the heart of fashionable London was the wickedly raffish area nicknamed 'Babylon', where the trade in human flesh was on open display at all hours of the day and night. Within a rough quadrilateral of streets enclosed by Piccadilly, Regent Street, the Haymarket, Grosvenor and Bond Streets every conceivable sexual taste could be gratified by those who had the money to pay.

There were wide gradations of quality and price. During the daytime expensive, well-dressed, genteelly conducted girls and women paraded the pavements and arcades. In the evening the theatre saloons and promenades, the hotel bars, the public houses, eating houses, cafés, dance halls, cigar divans, night houses were all thronged by garishly dressed and painted, bold-eyed, coarse-tongued women and girls, and their pimps, panders, bully boys and procurers.

But during the later hours there began an invasion of shabbier, cheaper, more ravaged females, and as night became early morning the most ragged, pathetic and degraded women made their desperate attempts to earn a pittance with which to buy food and shelter.

Emma Carr was one of the daytime promenaders, and she favoured the Burlington Arcade as the place to find her clients. Her delicate looks and petite figure were enhanced by the fashionable crinoline, paletot and dainty bonnet that Rosaleen Calatrava had given to her and, compared to many of the women who prostituted themselves on the streets of London, she looked innocent and childlike – a fact which helped to arouse the interest of potential clients.

Today she plied her trade with a heavy heart, and beneath her gown her body was painfully bruised from the vicious beating Billy Gilligan had inflicted on her the previous night. For nearly a week now his mood had been brutally savage, and his violence against her had increased in frequency and intensity. On the previous Sunday night he had returned to the rooms they rented with his clothing rain-soaked and muddied. He had behaved very strangely, pacing the floor all night, starting nervously at every sound from the street outside. Then early the following morning he had insisted that they find fresh lodgings, and she had trudged miserably after him, her baby crying in her arms, her scant belongings tied in a bundle upon her back, until he had at last secured a terraced cottage to rent in a mean slum quarter of Lambeth.

He had instructed her that she was to tell no one of his whereabouts, or where she was now living, had forbidden her to go anywhere near her only friend, Rosaleen Calatrava, and had warned her that she was not to try to get in touch with the woman in any other way. He had reinforced this warning with blows and threats that he would kill her and her baby if she disobeyed him.

Gilligan had not left the house since they entered it, and spent most of the time in bed, tossing and turning in restless sleep. When he was awake he spent his time getting drunk on the gin she bought for him each day. He kept the baby with him, and all the while she was away from the house, Emma worried and fretted about the child's safety, frightened that its crying would trigger off a violent reaction in her lover.

Now, as she walked the Burlington Arcade, her anxiety for her baby was preoccupying her to the extent that for long stretches of time she was oblivious of the passing crowds, and neglecting potential clients. On the occasions when a man accosted her, she did not even bother to haggle about her fee, absently accepting what he offered. Stoically she endured his abuse of her body in the 'Introducing House' she used close to the Haymarket, and returned to the Burlington Arcade without even speaking.

Emma was completely unconscious of the fact that for some considerable time a red-haired man dressed like a seafarer in a pea jacket, canvas trousers and greasy peaked cap had been closely watching her. He followed her when she went with her customers to the 'Introducing House', waiting until she came out, then trailed her back to the Arcade.

When he had sighted her in the Arcade Detective Sergeant Colum Macrae had blessed his luck, and had pointed her out to the youthful constable with him, who was also wearing seafaring rig.

'Look over there. That little piece in the blue dress. That's Billy Gilligan's mott.'

And he instantly sought for any sign of the man hovering around her. But to his intense disappointment found none.

'Who's Billy Gilligan? What's he done?' the young constable wanted to know.

'Gilligan is a piece of scum that I've been after for years.' There was rancour in Colum Macrae's voice. 'He's done the lot, garrotting, burglary, violent robbery. About three years ago he stabbed a man in a pub brawl. A chap name of Jacob Straw, a decent, hardworking family man; and a good friend of mine, as it happened.

'I arrested Gilligan and he came to trial, but a slimy lawyer got him off by bribing witnesses. Poor old Jacob never fully recovered from his wounds. He couldn't work, fell really sick, and him and his wife and kids ended up in the Poorhouse. Jacob died in there, and his wife and kids are still there today.

'Gilligan dropped from sight after the trial. But he bobbed up again about a year ago. Him and another piece of scum garrotted an old fellow, but while they were stripping him out they were seen by one of our patrols. Gilligan's mate was collared, but Gilligan got away, as usual. He's been lying low since then, but I always knew he'd surface one of these fine days. And now it looks as if he has.'

'How do you know that she's his mott? She looks very clean and respectable – too nice to be a mott.' The young constable was still inexperienced in the ways of the world.

'I know Emma Carr, my lad.' Colum chuckled grimly. 'And don't be fooled by her respectable looks, and sweet, innocent face. She's been on the game ever since she got out of wrapping cloths.' A gleam of sympathy fleeted across his eyes. 'Not that she can be condemned for that. She's just another poor creature who's more to be pitied than blamed. Especially since that bastard Gilligan got his hooks into her. He gives her a hard time of it, I can tell you.'

Colum drew the younger man into a discreet entrance. 'I want to see if Gilligan will show up here.'

The constable looked uneasy. 'But, Sarge, aren't we supposed to be watching that Frenchman? What if he tries to fence the stuff today and we miss it? We'll be in real trouble with the Superintendent then.'

Colum's fiery temper flared. 'Bugger the bloody Frenchman. Collaring Gilligan is more important to me.'

'Yes, but, Sarge . . .' The constable was now very nervous. 'You know what the Superintendent said to you about the importance of this job.'

'The Superintendent is Arse-Licker-in-Chief to the Aristocracy,' Colum hissed with contempt. 'The bloody Countess of Albany gets her fob watch snatched by a bloody French sneak thief, and we're supposed to drop every other case we're working on, just to get it back for her.'

'But the Superintendent told us that if we didn't get it back, we'd be in hot water . . .' The young man appeared near to tears.

Colum softened a little. 'Listen, son, you go and keep watch on the Frenchman. I'm staying here. Go on now. Don't worry about what the Superintendent will say. So long as you follow his orders, he'll have no quarrel with you.' He grinned, and joked, 'And I'll put your protest to me in my report, so you might even end up getting a commendation out of it, for doing your duty in spite of Detective Sergeant Colum Macrae.'

He reached out and patted the troubled man's shoulder, and told him kindly, 'Go on, get after the Frenchman. You won't have any trouble taking him in. He's only got one bloody arm, after all, and I've seen skeletons with more meat on their bones than he's got. A child of three could arrest him.'

Despite his nervousness the young man was reluctant to go. 'I don't want to see you get into any more trouble with the Superintendent though, Sarge.'

'Don't you worry about that.' Colum laughed with real amusement. 'I thrive on getting into trouble with my superior officers. It's all I live for.'

The constable shrugged. 'All right then, Sarge. If that's what you want me to do.'

Colum winked, and gently shoved the other man on his way.

He stayed watching Emma Carr for several hours, until the lamplighters came round with their ladders and slow matches, and she finished her work and took an omnibus across the river to Lambeth.

He followed in a hackney cab, making the cab driver keep some distance behind the bus, and when he saw her alight, he followed suit.

She walked through the mean, shabby streets, past stalls with hoarse-voiced vendors and flaring naphtha lamps, occasionally halting to buy items of food. Then she left the main thoroughfare and turned into a narrower street of old, fetid tenements where ragged, rickety, snot-nosed children played in the filthy, stinking gutters, and slatternly women stood in doorways or poked their frowsty heads out of windows, laughing, talking, disputing in harsh tinny voices, while their rough-looking menfolk lounged, hands in pockets, against the smoke-grimed walls, or close-huddled in groups, barring the way and exuding a suspicious hostility to those who passed by.

Emma Carr entered a tenement doorway, only to

reappear almost immediately and go hurrying towards the garishly decorated public house which stood further along the street.

Colum sauntered along on the opposite side of the road. Once more she reappeared quickly, this time with a dark bottle in each hand.

He knelt and pretended to tie up his bootlace while she hurried back to disappear through the doorway. Then he rose and ran swiftly to the house and knocked on the warped panels of the door.

Emma Carr stared suspiciously at the tall, well-built seafarer with his greasy cap set cockily on his red hair.

'What you want?' Her cockney accent was at variance with her ladylike appearance.

He smiled. 'I'm a friend of Billy's. Can I speak to him?'

She frowned with instant wariness. 'Billy? Billy who?'

'My mate, Billy Gilligan,' he told her and moved closer, trying to look into the room.

Suspicion clouded her features, and suddenly she cried out, 'You're a fuckin' "Jack", ain't you!'

Colum instantly slammed his shoulder against the door and burst through into the small, scantily furnished room, sending her staggering back before him.

She shrieked in fear, and the baby lying in an old basket upon the floor began to howl.

Colum hurled himself up the ladder that led to the bedroom.

The man lying in the bed that was the sole furniture in the bedroom shouted in shock and tried to rise, but before he could throw the covers back from his naked body Colum was on him. The man snatched a broad-bladed knife from beneath the grubby bolster, and Colum punched him hard on the jaw. The man's head rocked but he still gripped the knife. Colum seized his knife arm in a wrestling lock and twisted savagely, forcing the elbow joint until, with an audible crack, it parted. The man screamed in agony, and Colum heaved on the broken arm to drag him bodily from the bed and onto the floor, where he lay half-fainting, alternately groaning and screaming.

Through the broken, rag-stuffed windowpanes the voice of Emma Carr could be heard screeching in the street below.

'Help! Help! There's a fuckin' copper in me house! He's after me 'usband. Help me! Help!'

Other deeper-toned shouts sounded as men came to see what the commotion was about, and Colum muttered ruefully, 'Jesus Christ, that's put the cat among the pigeons.'

From an inner pocket of his pea jacket he pulled out a pair of handcuffs and, bending over the injured man, told him, 'I'm a police officer, Gilligan, and I'm arresting you for the robbery with violence committed on Tadeus Bates.'

From below there now sounded a storm of shouting, and Colum knew that he would have trouble from the gathering crowd. Policemen were regarded as the enemy in this area of the city, and were frequent targets for assault.

He looked about the tiny room and, crossing to the fire grate, tested the strength of its rusted iron bars. Satisfied that they would hold, he snapped one cuff around the injured man's ankle and hauled him across to the grate, to snap the other cuff around the iron bars.

Heavy boots clumped into the room below, and gruff voices bellowed.

'Gerron down 'ere, you blue-bottle bastard, or else we'll come up and get you.'

Colum pulled a lead-loaded cosh from his pocket and, positioning himself to the side of the ladder hole, shouted, 'Come on up, lads. The first one gets a broken skull.'

'Fuckin' saucy bastard! Let me at him!' A coster, brave with drink, came up the ladder, and the next instant went crashing down, his head spurting blood.

'Who wants to be second? Come on now, don't be shy!' Colum jeered in invitation but, behind his façade of reckless defiance, fear was shuddering through him.

'Let's burn the bugger out,' a man bawled, and half a hundred voices took up the cry.

'Burn him out! Burn the bugger out!'

'Jesus Christ, help me! Sweet Jesus, help me!' Colum begged silently, and for a few moments sheer terror threatened to overwhelm his senses. He had seen people burn to death and had a horror of such a fate.

'You can't do that, my 'usband's up there with him! My man's up there!'

Colum breathed a fervent prayer of thanks as he heard Emma Carr shrieking in protest.

Feverishly, he racked his brain for some way out of his deadly predicament. He knew that the mob, inflamed by drink and by the injury done to the coster, would try to lynch him once they got their hands on him.

'Why do you always act like this, you bloody cretin!' he cursed himself bitterly. 'You jump in as if you're a hero, and then find out that you're nothing but a rotten coward. Why do you keep on doing it?'

The men in the room below were now mumbling to each other, and the crowd outside started baying in concert.

'Top the copper! Top the copper! Top the copper!'

The next instant another man attempted to storm up the ladder, wearing an upturned wooden bucket on his head for protection and, despite his ravening fears, Colum almost laughed at the ludicrous sight. Then, as so often before in moments of danger, the survival instinct took control of Colum's mind and body. He seemed suddenly able to think with amazing speed and clarity, and fresh strength pulsed through his frame. Although the man was climbing very fast, yet to Colum's eyes he appeared to be moving almost in slow motion. He waited until the man had stepped onto the floor of the room then palmed both hands and struck upwards at the rim of the bucket, forcing it up and back so that the dangling wire handle bit into the angle between neck and throat. The man emitted a choked bellow and stepped back. His foot met only empty air so that he fell, thudding onto his companions clustering around the ladder bottom, bringing them down into a cursing and shouting tangle of bodies.

Now Colum upended the double bed and jammed it down across the ladder hole, so that anyone mounting up to the room would have to struggle to push the awkward obstacle away.

He looked upwards at the steeply gabled roof beams and, crossing to the edge of the room furthest away from the street, carefully dislodged and lifted a couple of tiles down into the room.

Cautiously he peeped out and down. Below him was a narrow yard which ran the length of the terrace of houses. Across the yard a row of washhouses and privies paralleled the terrace. Beyond lay more rows of houses and yards. He levered his head through the small aperture and looked right and left. To the left, the terrace ended at a street, but to the right it joined another row of terraced houses at a right angle, and the roofs met.

Colum pulled his head back into the room, and heard Emma Carr screeching.

'Am you all right, Billy darlint? Am you still alive, darlint?'

Gilligan's heavily stubbled face was grey with pain, but he managed to shout hoarsely, 'Don't let him take me, Emmy. Don't let him take me!'

'We shan't!' a score of voices promised.

Colum briefly considered his options, trying to work out the various distances to the surrounding police stations and patrol posts.

'The Borough Road,' he decided. 'That's the one.'

He grabbed a ragged piece of blanket from the floor and tore strips from it, which he used to truss up the injured man, ignoring the shrieks of pain and piteous pleas to be let alone. He finished by gagging and blindfolding Gilligan, and then quickly removed more tiles from the hole in the roof and clambered out onto its steep pitch.

Sickening dismay assailed him when he realised that because of its sunless position the roof tiles were slimy with mould.

'I'll not be able to keep a grip, and I'll slip over the edge.'

For a brief moment he hesitated, then inspiration struck, and he kicked in more tiles so that he could mount almost to the top of the roof. He experienced a momentary temptation to peep over the roof ridge at the crowd in the street, but resisted it. Then he carefully lay down at full length, head towards the gable ridge, summoned all his nerve, and rolled rapidly across the roof. The rapidity of his rolling combined with the friction of his clothing to prevent him sliding downwards too quickly, and in scant seconds he had cannoned into the angle where the terraced roofs joined.

The right-angled roof was dry and comparatively free of slimy mould, and he was able to scramble along its length. When he reached the end he moved to guttering level and, trusting his weight to a sagging drainpipe, regained the ground.

He walked straight through the nearest back door, giving a polite greeting to the shocked elderly couple sitting before the fireplace, and was through the house and out onto the street before they could even gather their senses to protest at his appearance.

Then he began to run. Dogs chased, yapping at his heels, and people turned to gape at his headlong passing. He crossed busy roads, ducking beneath horses' heads, twisting away from ironbound wheels, and finally burst through the doors of the police station, shouting out his message before he had even come to a standstill.

'You what?' The bewhiskered desk sergeant stared at the sweating, panting, red-faced man before him with astonishment, and his hand sought for the truncheon which he kept on a ledge at the rear of his tall desk.

'I'm Detective Sergeant Macrae, attached to the Central Division,' Colum repeated gaspingly, impatience boiling within him. 'I've just arrested Billy Gilligan for robbery with violence. He's the one who garrotted the old man in the City Road a year since. I need assistance to go and bring him in.'

'Have you got your warrant card, or any other identity?' the desk sergeant asked, half convinced that he was faced with a madman.

'No, I haven't. I don't carry identity when I'm working.'

'Well, the regulations state very clearly that you must carry identity at all times.' The desk sergeant's plump chins quivered with indignation at this breach of regulations.

'The regulations should also state very clearly that the quickest way to get your throat cut in the places I work in is to be found with identification as a copper.' By now Colum's impatience was turning to anger. 'Look, we can sort out the identification later. Right now I need assistance to fetch Billy Gilligan in.'

'But if you've arrested him, why ain't you brung him along wi' you?' the other man asked reasonably. 'That's what I'd like to have explained.'

'Because there was a hundred bloody people yelling for my blood,' Colum gritted out. 'But I've left him cuffed to a fire grate.'

The desk sergeant's bulbous eyes widened in amazement. 'Cuffed to a fire grate?'

'Yes, to a bloody fire grate,' Colum hissed, and his temper seethed. 'I've left him cuffed to a bloody fire grate in a house in Walnut Tree Street off the Kennington Road in bloody Lambeth. But unless you get me some men to go back with me, he'll be set free, and then he'll scarper. And then I'll have to spend bloody weeks and weeks searching for the bugger again.'

By now a small group of constables had gathered in the Charge Room to listen to what was going on. A door opened and a frock-coated inspector poked his head into the room.

'What's all this disturbance, Sergeant Wilkes?'

'I'm the disturbance, sir.' Colum was now becoming desperate, and he quickly explained what was happening, and that he needed instant assistance.

The inspector shook his head and said disapprovingly, 'This sounds all very irregular to me. You come in here without any means of identification, and give me this cock and bull story . . .'

Driven beyond endurance by the thought that with every minute passing the likelihood of Billy Gilligan's escaping was becoming more of a certainty, Colum interrupted the other man.

'Look, just give me what I'm asking for, will you? We can sort out everything else later. Once we've got Gilligan safely in the cells.'

The inspector scowled warningly. 'I don't like your tone, my lad.'

'I don't care whether you like it or not.' Colum was now past caring. 'Just give me the men, and let me go and fetch my prisoner.'

'But you've got no proof of identity,' the desk sergeant interjected.

'Never mind that now. Just help me to secure Billy Gilligan.' Frustrated almost beyond endurance, he tried a new approach. 'Listen, sir, my division is under the

111

command of Colonel Sir Harry Temple. My station commander is . . .' He went on to rattle off a list of names and ranks, finishing by demanding, '. . . How could I know all this if I am not who and what I claim to be?'

'Why now, that's easy enough to answer,' the inspector scoffed. 'You could have got all this information out of the *Gazette*.'

Colum's frustration finally burst through his control. 'You stupid bloody fool! A dangerous criminal is going to get away because you haven't got a bloody brain in your thick head.'

The inspector's face purpled with rage. 'Lock this maniac up, Sergeant. And then find out who and what he really is. Because I'm damned sure that he's not a policeman . . .'

'And I'm damned sure that you are a policeman,' Colum retorted scathingly. 'But you're one of the block-heads that give the rest of us a bad name. It's no wonder that we are jeered and mocked at when we've got pompous fools like you commanding us.'

The inspector now lost his temper completely and grabbed Colum by his coat collar. 'I'll teach you to bad mouth me, you bugger.'

He hit Colum on the side of his head with the flat of his meaty hand, and Colum brought up his fist and knocked the inspector flat.

The next instant he was submerged in a rush of blue uniforms and knocked flat himself, then was dragged along the floor by his feet, and tumbled roughly into a cell. The door slammed, keys rattled in the lock, and the desk sergeant shouted through the judas hole in the cell door.

'You'll be spending the next couple of years in Millbank, you bloody maniac.'

'Sweet Jesus Christ, what have I done now?' Colum groaned in utter dismay, and painfully picked himself up off the floor . . .

Chapter Fourteen

Detective Inspector Charles Anderson regarded the bedraggled, unshaven, grimy figure standing before his desk. Pursing his lips he shook his head slowly from side to side.

'I don't know, Colum, you never learn, do you?'

Colum Macrae ruefully agreed. 'No, Charlie, I don't, do I?'

Anderson sighed heavily. 'Well, you're finished in the Force, and there's nothing I can do to save your bacon, my friend. You've done this sort of thing too many times before. That bugger you hit is refusing to accept anything less than your being kicked out. And you're the best man I've got, that's the pity of it. You're worth ten of him.'

'What's more the pity is that Billy Gilligan got away as well.' Colum seemed to regret that fact above all else. 'If I could have taken some men back there, I would have had him, Charlie.'

'Listen, Colum, the best advice I can give you is not to wait for the Enquiry Board but to let me have your resignation now. That way you'll avoid being kicked out. Then at least you can apply for one of the colonial forces, or maybe another force in this country. Better to have "resigned" on your record than "expelled".'

Colum nodded, then shrugged. 'Ah well, that's what it

will have to be then, Charlie. I'll write you my letter of resignation straight away.'

'It's for the best,' the older man accepted regretfully.

A trace of bitterness entered Colum's tone. 'There's no justice in it though, Charlie. I was only trying to do my job.'

The older man chuckled mirthlessly. 'There's never been any justice in this world for the likes of us, Colum. And there never will be.'

Later Colum walked aimlessly through the bustling noisy streets, his thoughts bleak. Despite Charlie Anderson's assurance that he would be able to join another police force in Britain or one of the colonies, Colum knew that his record of constant clashes with those in authority over him, both in the army and in the police force, would almost certainly disbar him. Civilian employment he might find, but it could only be menial and badly paid, because he had no trade skills to offer. Despondently he turned his steps towards the small house he rented in Holborn.

'Where have you been? Sleeping with some poxed-up whore? Don't think that you'll share my bed, you dirty whoremaster. And just look at you. You're a bloody tramp. I don't know why you bother to come home at all.'

Greeted by the familiar drunken tirade from his wife Margaret, Colum also wondered for a moment why he ever bothered to come home.

'Are the girls here?' He looked about for his small daughters, Dorcas and Dorry, concern for them causing him to speak more roughly than he intended. 'Where are they?'

His wife's fat face, framed by tangles of greasy, uncombed hair, registered a spiteful pleasure at his obvious anxiety.

'Where are they?' His voice rose, and she sniffed loudly.

'At my mother's.'

Colum looked in disgust at the half-empty gin bottle on the table, and then at the drink-flushed features of his wife. She glared at him, and spat aggressively.

'It's your fault that my nerves are so bad that I have to take a drop of gin to soothe them.'

Knowing the futility of arguing with her when she was in this condition, he merely sighed with resignation, and asked quietly, 'How long have the girls been with your mother?'

'That's for me to know, and for you to find out!' she sneered in drunken satisfaction.

He glanced at the dead ashes in the fireless grate, the unwashed dishes on the table, the general mess of the room and, turning away from her, went back out into the street.

She shrieked after him, 'Yes, you can clear off, you rotten bastard! I should never have wed you. I threw myself away when I wed you, you rotten bastard! . . . Rotten bastard . . . Rotten bastard . . .'

The echoes of her shrieked epithets followed him, and he tried to shut them from his mind.

At his mother-in-law's rooms, some streets away, his two small daughters came rushing to greet him, shouting excitedly, 'Daddy, Daddy, Daddy, Daddy!'

He swung them high, and kissed and cuddled them, and they screamed with enjoyment and struggled against him, as he made playful pretence to scrape his

116

rough bristles against their soft rosy cheeks.

His wife's mother, physically an older, fatter version of Margaret, watched, smiling, as father and daughters showed their joy in each other.

'Have they been good girls, Ma?' Colum asked her with a smile. He was very fond of this old woman. She was good and kind, and she doted on his beloved girls.

She beamed at the tiny identical twins. 'They're always good girls, bless their little hearts.' Concern showed in her eyes. 'You've been home I take it, Col?'

He nodded, then took two sets of small peg-top dolls from his pocket and the children crowed with delight.

'Here you are then. Now that your grandma says you've been good, you can have these.'

For a moment he gently teased them, holding the brightly painted wooden figures just out of their reach, and they stood on tiptoes, and jumped to try to reach the dolls. Then he kissed each girl and gave her her dolls, and they settled on the rug before the cheerily burning fire to play their own games.

'Will you have something to eat, Col? I've some meat pie, and I can cook you some potatoes.'

He shook his head. 'No thanks, Ma. I'm not hungry.' The encounter with his wife had taken his appetite away.

'Can the girls stay with you tonight?' he beseeched.

Quickly she assured him, 'Of course they can. They can stay as long as you want them to. I only wish I could have them here with me all the time, but their mother won't let me.' Tears suddenly brimmed in her eyes. 'Margaret's my own flesh and blood, Col, but she's a bad lot. And she's not a fitting mother to these mites. She takes after her Dad. He was a drunken bad lot as well.'

117

Colum tried to summon a smile. 'Never mind, Ma, the girls have got you and me, haven't they?'

'They have that, Col. They've got us, thanks be to God.'

She made tea and they sat companionably each side of the fireplace, the children playing between them, and talked quietly.

Colum had been orphaned as a baby and for him this old woman was the mother that he had never known. He could talk openly and unguardedly to her in a way he had never been able to talk to his wife. He told her now of what had happened on the previous day, and about his expulsion from the police, and she looked very anxious.

'Oh my God, what will we do now, Col? What will happen to us?'

Colum was her sole financial support also.

'Don't you worry, Ma.' He sought to comfort her. 'We won't starve. I've got a few sovereigns stowed away. And I'll find something else, and soon.'

He spoke with an outer confidence that was at odds with his inner desperation. He knew just how little money he had put by, and how bleak were the prospects of finding work which would pay enough to support them all. But he was grateful that she believed him, and she cheered up at once.

He stayed until the two girls were put to bed, and then said, 'I'd best get back. Margaret should be sleeping by now.' He grinned wryly. 'One bottle normally puts her to sleep these days.'

Momentary anguish showed in the old woman's expression, and she jerked out, 'God forgive me for saying this, but I could wish that Margaret would go to sleep and never wake up. You could find a decent woman then, who'd be a good wife to you, and a good mother to the girls.'

'I've made my own bed, Ma, and I have to lie on it,' he told her bleakly. 'And so long as you're here, then the girls have already got the finest mother anyone could ever have.'

'But I won't be here for ever, will I, Col?' the old woman replied sadly.

'None of us will, Ma.' He rose, crossed to her and kissed her cheek. 'I'll see you tomorrow morning.'

Back at Holborn he found his wife slumped across the table, head on arms, snorting and snoring in drunken sleep. Despite her considerable weight, he lifted her thick, dumpy body and carried her upstairs. He laid her carefully on the bed, covered her with a blanket, and then went back down below.

He sat before the fireless grate in the cold, cheerless room, and buried his face in his hands as the black bitterness of despair suddenly overwhelmed him.

'Oh God, what's going to become of my girls if I can't get work? What's going to happen to my darling girls?'

Chapter Fifteen

The corpse of Sean Gallagher lay upon a trestle table in a cool, dank cellar beneath 50 Harley Street. Conrad Cumlinson and Detective Inspector Charlie Anderson, accompanied by Mr Bush who was carrying the lantern, came to inspect the corpse at three o'clock in the afternoon on the same day that Colum Macrae had left the police force.

Cumlinson and the policeman had known each other for a very long time, and shared a deep and mutual respect for each other's professional expertise. Cumlinson had summoned the inspector to come here today in order to utilise the policeman's uncanny gift for recognition. Anderson was famous in his own circles as a 'Show-Up King'.

Periodically criminals were paraded in front of detectives, so that the detectives could memorise their faces and physical attributes and be given full details of the criminals' offences and *modi operandi*. These parades were known as 'Show Ups'. Charlie Anderson's proud boast was that he never forgot any criminal's face or record once he had seen and studied him or her at a 'Show Up'. It was a boast which he lived up to, and over the years he had achieved some remarkable feats of identification.

At a signal from Cumlinson, Mr Bush pulled the covering sheet off the corpse, revealing it in its nakedness. The first greening patches of decomposition were already patterning the pallid flesh, but the smell was not yet too rancid, causing the three men no actual discomfort.

'Can I take the glim please?' Anderson requested, and Mr Bush handed him the lantern.

The policeman moved around the corpse, studying the features intently, forming an estimation of height and weight and age.

For such a large, corpulent man, Anderson walked lightly on his feet, but the wheezing of his tobacco-and-whisky breath was loud in the silence of the darkly shadowed room.

A full fifteen minutes elapsed before Anderson halted and turned to Conrad Cumlinson. 'His name is Sean Gallagher, sir. He was one of the Young Irelanders who were taken up after the '48 rebellion. Got sentenced to transportation for life. I saw him at a "Show Up" in Millbank Prison in the year '50. He was reported to have escaped from Tasmania with Terence McManus a few years since. It was believed that they made their way to America.'

'Thank you very much, Inspector Anderson. You've done splendidly, as always,' Conrad Cumlinson congratulated warmly. He knew there was no need to press the policeman for any further proof of the dead man's identity. Anderson did not make mistakes.

'Please, Mr Bush.' Cumlinson nodded towards the body, and while the elderly clerk replaced the sheet over the corpse, invited, 'Will you take some refreshment in my office, Inspector?'

'I'd appreciate that highly, sir.' Anderson always enjoyed Cumlinson's fine old whisky.

After they had settled themselves comfortably, tumblers of whisky in their hands, Cumlinson told the other man, 'I had surmised that the attempt on the Prince's life was the work of Irish extremists. Your identification of Gallagher would seem to confirm this . . .' He went on to tell of the reports concerning the new grouping of extremists with Irish-American connections.

Charlie Anderson listened in silence. He had worked for this man on several occasions in the past, both overtly and covertly, and he knew that he was being given this present information for some good reason.

Cumlinson finished his recital, and after refilling both their tumblers, smiled bleakly. 'I have no doubt that you have already understood that I am going to enlist your assistance in this present operation, Inspector.'

Anderson grinned broadly and nodded, as Cumlinson placed his tumbler on the desk and leaned back in his chair, steepling his fingers beneath the fringe of beard on his chin. He appeared to be musing aloud.

'For this operation I need a man who is courageous, highly intelligent, and a gifted actor. He must possess the utmost discretion and be completely trustworthy. Furthermore, he must be able to act on his own initiative, and to act alone, without any aid. Above all else, he must be able to kill without compunction.'

Another bleak smile touched his lips, and he stared into the policeman's eyes. 'Where might I find such a paragon, Inspector? I might add that he will be extremely well rewarded for his work.'

Instantly the thought of Colum Macrae sprang into Anderson's mind. But just as instantly doubt followed.

Cumlinson sensed that the policeman had thought of someone. But knowing his man, he waited for him to speak first.

After some moments Anderson offered diffidently, 'I know a man who might be suited, sir. But I'm not sure about the killing part of it. It's obvious that you need someone who can kill in cold blood. The man I've got in mind could kill in hot blood, indeed he has done so in the past, but I'm not sure about his readiness to act as an assassin.'

Again Cumlinson displayed his acute percipience. 'Perhaps the man you're thinking of is not yet sufficiently motivated to be able to kill in cold blood, Inspector. But in my experience I have found that given sufficient desperation of circumstances, then even the most moral of men are capable of overcoming even the strongest of scruples.'

Anderson's wry grin was an acknowledgement of the other man's sagacity. He pondered briefly, and then offered, 'Is it possible to wait a few weeks, sir? I'm sure that the man I have in mind will be desperate enough by then. And he's the ideal candidate for the position on offer.'

Cumlinson took up his tumbler of whisky. 'We'll drink to that, Inspector.'

And suited his action to his words.

Chapter Sixteen

The uniformed doorkeeper looked the man before him up and down insultingly several times, noting that his clothes, although tidy, were not the expensive garments of a gentleman. Then he demanded aggressively, 'What's your business with Mr Harcus?'

Colum Macrae successfully resisted the urge to reply with equal aggressiveness and informed the man politely, 'I've come about the advertised situation for a clerk.'

The doorkeeper stared suspiciously at the tall, muscular figure before him. 'You don't have the look of a clerk. You look more like a bloody navvy. Wouldn't you be better pushing a shovel instead of a pen?'

Again Colum was sorely tempted to put this jumped-up 'Jack-in-office' to rights. But unhappily mindful of his empty purse and empty stomach, he bit on his tongue.

'Well?' The doorkeeper's sallow features displayed a spiteful pleasure in wielding his petty power.

'Well what?' Colum returned query for query.

The doorkeeper gusted with irritation. 'God love me, what a bloody mawkin you are. I wants to know what experience you've had. Where you was working before and suchlike.'

Colum's hot temper fired, and he snapped curtly,

'That's a matter for the organ grinder to enquire about, not for his monkey.'

'Don't you get saucy with me,' the doorkeeper warned truculently.

Colum fought to control his anger, and to swallow his pride. 'I'm sorry, I don't mean to speak disrespectfully. But I'm in sore need of a position, and it's making me over-impatient.'

Triumph gleamed in the other man's eyes, and he sneered, 'Well, if you're in such need of a position, then you'd ought to be more respectful to them as might be able to help you to find one.'

'Please, can I see Mr Harcus?' Colum requested humbly, and the shame of his humiliation burned through him. But he kept the image of his two small daughters in the forefront of his mind, knowing that it was for their sakes he was enduring this badgering.

The doorkeeper was enjoying himself hugely.

'Where was you working previous?'

'I was in the police force.'

The sallow features displayed shocked surprise. 'A Rozzer? You was a Rozzer?'

Colum nodded.

The other man whistled through his teeth. 'A bleedin' Rozzer, was you? So why ain't you still a Rozzer?'

'I resigned.'

'Resigned?' The doorkeeper scoffed disbelievingly. 'Resigned, you say? Got caught on the bloody fiddle, more like.'

The sallow features suddenly radiated intense hostility, and the narrow-lipped mouth hissed, 'All you bleedin' Rozzers are the same. Taking bribes from rich coves to let them off the hook, and shoving poor ordinary chaps in bloody quod on put-up charges. Get off from here! There's no chance of the likes of you getting to see Mr Harcus.'

He stepped back into the building and slammed shut the heavy door.

Colum stood with his nose only inches from the dark panelling and fury boiled within him, but in company with that fury came the deepest of despair.

His initial impulse was to hammer on the door, but even as he raised his clenched fist to do so, the realisation of the futility of that action swept over him, and he let his hand fall back to his side.

Turning away he trudged on along the street, head down, shoulders bowed, heart filled with the bitterness of yet another failure.

It had been a month since he'd left the police force, and in those few weeks it seemed to Colum that he had endured more humiliation, more worry, more despair than during his entire previous existence. Day after day, hour after hour, he had tramped the streets of London, searching for work, fruitlessly applying for job after job, and meeting only rejection. It had been a salutary experience for Colum to find out that as an ex-policeman he seemed to be regarded as a social pariah. He had long known that the lower classes hated the police, whom they regarded as the arm of oppression. But it had come as a shock to find out how contemptuously many of the middle and upper classes regarded the force. To these people the police were a necessary evil who were needed to keep the 'dangerous classes' in their proper subservient condition, but these prosperous, respectable classes considered policemen to be their social inferiors. In addition they resented the expense of the police force, and challenged its power when it was directed against their own transgressions of the law.

Colum had learned a bitter lesson during these past weeks, which was that an ex-policeman, shorn of his power, was regarded at best with contemptuous disdain and at worst with virulent hatred.

Now, with the shame and anger of this latest humiliation seething in his brain, he tried to think rationally about his predicament. He decided that there was little or no point in pursuing any further the chimera of respectable employment. His scant savings were all but exhausted, and Colum was now facing the inevitable necessity of pawning his own and his family's few possessions if he could not find immediate work. He would have to seek casual labour. Today it was too late, but early tomorrow morning he would go to the docks, the last resort for men like himself, desperate for any type of work. No recommendations or character references were asked for at the docks; the only requirements were bodily strength and the willingness to endure long hours of gruelling labour for scant return in wages. But he had no other choice if he was to put food in his family's stomachs.

A hansom cab trundled past him, its ironbound wheels rattling metallically over the paving blocks. It came to a standstill and a portly, well-dressed man alighted. Colum noted the gold-topped cane in the plump hands, and glimpsed the heavy gold watch chain stretching across the protuberant belly as the man took coins from his pocket to hand to the cab driver. For a brief instant Colum envisaged tracking a man like this one through the streets, and in some quiet corner robbing him.

'Pray God I never become driven to do such a thing.'

But even as he voiced this prayer, he acknowledged bitterly that if it became a choice between seeing his children starve or turning thief, then he would turn thief, even though that way of life filled him with revulsion.

He hurried on past the plump man, feeling guilty at harbouring such thoughts about a man who had done him no harm. But still the realisation that one day he might be driven to such desperate measures in order to feed his children lurked in the recesses of his mind.

Chapter Seventeen

The dawn was dull and overcast and the burgeoning nimbus clouds threatened rain. Colum rose and dressed in a flannel shirt, rough pea jacket, canvas trousers, and heavy hobnailed boots. His wife lay watching him, her fat face sullen.

'I'll need some money,' she told him. 'The rent's due today.'

He opened the wardrobe door and reached inside to feel in the pockets of his Sunday best coat. His searching fingers encountered only emptiness. He frowned angrily and rounded on her.

'Where's it gone?'

'Where's what gone?'

'The money I left in my coat pocket. Where's it gone?'

She pouted. 'How should I know?'

He stood staring at her for a moment, then moved suddenly and thrust his hand beneath the mattress she lay on. He felt the smoothness of the gin bottle, and wrenched it out to brandish it in front of her eyes.

'You took that money and spent it on this muck?' he accused angrily. 'That was the rent and food money. It was all we had left.'

'I never took it. I never took anything. It must have been the kids who took it. It wasn't me,' she blustered indignantly, but the guilt in her eyes was plain to see.

She began to sob noisily, and complain, 'It aren't fair. You always blames me. It aren't fair!'

A sense of hopelessness invaded Colum, driving out his anger, and he shook his head wearily, and told her, 'For God's sake, hold your noise. You'll wake the girls up.'

'Oh yes, the girls!' she flared at him. 'That's all that concerns you, aren't it. The girls! You couldn't give a bugger for me, who's your lawful wedded wife. You only cares about them little bleeders! That's all you cares about! No wonder I needs to take a drop now and again, it's the only bit of comfort I gets.'

She went back to snuffling noisily, burying her face in her hands, and Colum accepted defeat.

'Here, take it.' He placed the bottle of gin by her side, and went to wake up his two daughters.

He forced himself to be cheerful, tickling and joking with them as he dressed them. Then they all went hand-in-hand, chattering gaily, to his mother-in-law's house.

The old woman sighed with sympathy as she opened the door to her visitors and, before Colum could speak, told him, 'Of course I'll look after them. Is Margaret on the drink again?'

He grinned ruefully. 'I should think she's just about got started on it now.' He went on to tell the old woman about the bottle he had found, and that the last of his money had disappeared.

She nodded sadly, but made no comment.

Colum handed her a pocket watch. 'Will you pawn this for me please, Ma. Then use some of the money to buy food for you and the girls.'

Her swollen, arthritic fingers fondled the solid silver watch, and her weak eyes squinted at the inscription engraved upon its inner casing. 'To Ensign Colum Macrae, 7th Regiment of Fusiliers. Presented by his comrades in recognition of his exceptional gallantry at the Battle of Inkerman.'

Tears filled the old woman's eyes. 'Oh, Colum.' She sighed sadly. 'Has it come to this?'

'Yes, Ma, I'm afraid it has.' Momentarily his own sadness showed through, then he once more assumed a cheerfulness he was far from feeling, and told her, 'It needn't stay in Uncle's for ever, Ma. I'm going to get work on the docks today, and earn a fortune.'

He bent to his daughters. 'I'll see you tonight, my sweethearts. You be good girls for Grandma now, and maybe I'll have something nice in my pockets for you when I come back.'

He kissed their soft cheeks in turn, and left them in the loving embrace of the old woman.

He walked eastwards from Holborn through the narrow thoroughfares of the City, quiet now and deserted but for the occasional sleepy nightwatchman or patrolling policeman, but soon those empty streets would begin to fill with the hordes of businessmen, bankers, merchants and clerks whose expertise and shrewd judgements had made this square mile the financial and commercial centre of the world, and the richest city on earth.

The transition from City to Whitechapel was a journey from peaceful opulence to noisy, bustling poverty. The narrow fetid streets of the East End were filled with men, women and children going to their daily toil, and the main roads were choked with every conceivable type of waggon and carriage. Already the shop men, the street vendors and pedlars were crying their wares, beggars were whining and pleading, and displaying their sores and deformities, porters were humping their back-breaking loads like human beasts of burden.

The great London Dock covered more than ninety acres along the river front of the parishes of St George, Shadwell and Wapping, and the teeming swarms dwelling in the jumbled, tumbledown, rancid courts and alleys serviced the mighty wharves and warehouses, loaded and unloaded the cargoes, spent their strength, prostituted their bodies, destroyed their health for little reward. The vast majority earned barely enough to drag out a precarious and hard existence. Although the goods, raw materials and wealth of the world flooded through the great London Dock, precious little of these untold riches accrued to those who worked the hardest.

At the main gate of the Shadwell Docks crowds of men had been assembling since before dawn, and when Colum reached there, the crowd already numbered several hundreds. The men were as disparate a set as could be found in the vast metropolis: old and young, of all races, creeds and colours. Yet they were uniform in their ragged, desperate poverty.

Top-hatted, blue-coated, grey-trousered dock police stood sentinel before the huge gates, keeping the eager masses from entering. Colum moved through the dense crowd but, knowing something of the hiring routine of the docks, did not try to push himself to the head of the waiting throng.

At seven o'clock the rain began to fall in a steady downpour to be greeted by a roar of foul-tongued execrations from the waiting men. But no one sought shelter. Threadbare collars were turned up, ragged coats buttoned to the chin, greasy caps and battered, crumpled hats were pulled low on grimy foreheads, and the men stoically endured the discomfort of water soaking through their clothing and seeping through the holes in their broken shoes and boots.

At seven-thirty there was a sudden stirring through the crowd, and the dock policemen signalled that they could enter. Cheering hoarsely, the crowd swarmed through the gates, rushing towards the line of the 'calling foremen' who were awaiting them.

Colum hurried forward with the rest. He knew that he would have to trust to luck to be picked by any particular foreman, so it did not really matter which grouping he joined. The air was resounding with a cacophony of shouting, wheedling, pleading voices as the men pushed and jostled, jumped up and down and cried out to catch the eye of the foremen.

'It's me, Master Gittings, Tom Court. You promised me some work!'

'Master, I'm a good hand, I am.'

'For the love of God, sor, give me the start!'

'Johnny, Johnny, I'll see you right if you gives me a couple o' days.'

Desperate though he was for work, Colum could not bring himself to shout and beg and plead. His pride was not yet so broken.

The foreman before whom he was standing was a stocky, straight-backed, smartly turned out man with a military bearing. He held an open book in his hands and called out names one by one. The successful supplicants stepped forward with broadly smiling faces, clapping each other on the back in congratulation, as if they had won some wonderful prize.

The foreman repeated one name twice, and no one

stepped forward. The absence of the called man brought a redoubling of frenzied pleas from the unsuccessful and the noise was deafening.

The foreman's hard eyes swept over the jostling, pushing crowd, and locked onto Colum's. He beckoned Colum to him and, when they were standing facing each other, questioned harshly.

'Are you an old soldier?'

'I am,' Colum told him, and could not help but stand taller and straighter.

'What regiment?'

'Seventh Fusiliers.'

'Were you in the Crimea?'

'I was.'

'When?'

'From the landings until the fall of Sebastopol. I saw action at the Alma and at Inkerman, and before Sebastopol. But none at Balaclava.'

The foreman jerked his head. 'I'll give you a day.'

'Many thanks,' Colum told him gratefully, and the man grinned mirthlessly.

'No need for thanks, soldier, the pay don't warrant it.'

He slammed shut his muster book, and a chorus of complaints and groans sounded from the unsuccessful men.

'It ain't fair. That bugger only gives work to them as was bleedin' redcoats like hisself.'

'He should ha' stayed in the fokkin' army, and not come here to mess us about.'

'Miserable bastard!'

'Fokkin' lobster.'

The foreman ignored the insults and protests and led his selected crew deeper into the docks, while the dock police chivvied the rest of the men back out through the gates.

The rain was still falling steadily and the foreman told his crew, 'You're in luck today, boys. You're in the wheel sheds.'

The big fur-capped Negro walking by Colum's side grinned and muttered, 'Have you ever been on the treadmill, mate?'

Colum shook his head. 'No.'

'Well, you're going to have a bellyful of it today. But at least we gets paid for it here, not like in quod.'

They came to the wharf, shadowed by towering warehouses and the forest of masts and smoke-belching funnels. Along the wharf were sheds with monster wheels poking through their roofs, making them resemble the paddle boxes of gigantic steamers. From these massive wheels, cables stretched to the dockside cranes and derricks.

The foreman detailed eight men, including Colum and the Negro, to go into the wheel shed.

'Sammy, you'll give the shout,' the foreman told the Negro, who grinned and lifted his fur cap to disclose a shining, shaven black pate.

'I surely will, Master Gittings. Because it's only us niggers who can sing good, ain't it.'

The foreman grinned back, and told Colum, 'Sammy'll show you the ropes, soldier.'

Inside the gloomy shed it was dank and musty-smelling, but reasonably dry.

The great wheel had a big circular wooden cylinder built around its mighty axle, and this cylinder was lined with wooden battens, with rope handholds attached to them.

'You take hold of them ropes to keep your balance, mate,' Sammy told Colum, 'and you just keeps on tramping.'

The men filed into the wooden cylinder, took hold of the handropes, and Sammy bellowed, 'Ready now, one, two, three, and away.'

The men tramped down on the first batten in unison and with a groaning of wood and metal the huge wheel began to turn.

'Left, right, lef', right, lef', right . . .' Sammy shouted the cadence, and then began to sing in a loud, tuneful voice: 'Ohhh, I seek no more the fine nor gay . . .' and the rest of the crew swung in to join him, '. . . For these do but remind mee . . . How swift the hours did pass away . . .' punctuating the tune with rhythmic stamping of their feet.

At first Colum found the work easy, and even pleasant, and joined in the songs and chants, but soon the gruelling nature of the task displayed itself as loads of varying weights were lifted by the cable, and the tempo of the work increased. Soon his leg muscles began to ache, sweat poured from his body and his breathing became harsh and laboured. The songs and chants ceased and soon all that could be heard were the gasping pants of toiling men driven to the very limits of their physical endurance.

After four hours a halt was called, and the crew came off the wheel and slumped down to rest. A food vendor appeared with slices of bread and dripping and tin mugs of gritty-tasting coffee.

'He'll give you credit 'til you're paid if you ain't got no tin,' Sammy informed Colum.

Colum grinned wearily. 'Tell you the truth, I'm too

136

knackered to eat. I'm not used to this sort of labour.'

The Negro's white teeth flashed in his glistening, sweaty face. 'Bloody mules ain't used to this kind of labour, mate, never mind human souls. Why, even the bloody convicts on the treadmills gets spelled every fifteen minutes. Ain't we lucky to be free men.'

'What happens if a man can't keep it up?' Colum wanted to know. 'Do they give him other work?'

'Give him other work?' The Negro laughed hugely. 'The only other work they'll give you is to carry your sack out of here. Don't drop out if you wants to keep working on the docks, mate. Once you drop out, you never get work again.'

'Come on, let's be having you. Time and tide won't wait for the likes o' you!' The foreman came bawling into the shed and, groaning and grumbling the crew reentered the cylinder and resumed their muscle-straining toil.

Colum's muscles cramped agonisingly, and it was sheer torture for him to keep on moving, but he gritted his teeth and kept going, and gradually the cramps wore off. Despite the aching weariness, he was determined that he would endure as long as, or longer than, anyone else on the crew.

At last the interminable day ground to its end and, light-headed from hunger and tiredness, Colum lined up with the other men to receive the two shillings and sixpence wages for his work.

The foreman handed him the coins, and nodded. 'You did all right today, soldier. I'll give you work whenever I can.'

'Thanks very much.' Colum experienced a warm glow of gratification, and felt proud that he had achieved this small measure of success.

'Will there be work tomorrow?' he enquired eagerly.

Gittings grimaced doubtfully. 'There's been contrary winds all day, and they looks to continue. That'll stop the boats coming up river. So it's not likely that there'll be anything going tomorrow. You'll just have to do what the rest do, and that's to come every morning on spec.'

Acute disappointment clouded Colum's earlier pleasure, and he realised that steady work was just as far removed from him here as it had proven elsewhere.

At the dock gates the men were stopped by the police and made to form a single file, then one by one they were carefully searched to ensure that they had not concealed any stolen articles upon them. Only then were they allowed to leave the docks.

As he trudged back towards his home Colum ached all over his body, and his hunger made him feel weak and giddy. He stopped and bought some sweets for his daughters, and a piece of bread and salt butter for himself, which he tore at ravenously as he walked. The rough food made him feel a little steadier in head and body, and he told himself, 'Well, at least I've got the prospect of work if there's any going. And I'll get used to it in time. I just need to harden up, that's all. I've gone soft lately.'

Then he thought of the meagre amount he had earned that day, and despondency engulfed him. 'I can't maintain my family on that amount a day, even if I was able to get work seven days in the week. It's just not enough for five of us to live on. If Ma came to live with us it would ease things a little bit, as far as rent and the rest, but even then we couldn't live on that amount.'

He decided that he would go first to his own house, and check on the condition of his wife, before he went to fetch his daughters. If she was sodden drunk, as he fully expected her to be, then he would ask his mother-in-law to keep the girls for the night.

When he reached the corner of his street he instantly noticed the hansom cab standing outside his house.

His first thought was that his wife had done herself some sort of injury, and the neighbours had summoned a doctor. He broke into a run, but such was his weariness that he was only able to manage a shambling trot.

The cab driver was lolling sleepily on his seat, and Colum demanded, 'Who have you brought here?'

The man yawned and shrugged. 'Some fat cove, Guv. He didn't gi' me his rank and title.'

Colum went into the house, and found the corpulent Inspector Charles Anderson sitting at the table, smoking a pipe.

'Charlie?' he exclaimed in surprise. 'What brings you here? And where's my missus?'

The fat man jerked his head upwards. 'She's well lushed, Colum. She's snoring away like a good 'un up there. You ought to keep her away from the drink, my lad, she can't handle it.'

Colum nodded tiredly. 'Don't I know it.'

'You've had it rough these last weeks, Colum.' Anderson's shrewd eyes measured the other man. 'I've had an eye kept on you, so don't you try gammoning me that everything in the garden is lovely. Because I know different.'

Colum shrugged, and thankfully slumped down onto a chair to face the inspector across the table. 'I'm sorry

I can't offer you any refreshments, Charlie. But I expect you've already checked on the state of my larder, so you'll appreciate why that's the case.'

The fat man chuckled, and admitted, 'Well, I did take a peep about, Colum. Force of habit. But I might be able to put you in the way of filling those empty shelves. That's why I'm here.'

Hope rose instantly in Colum and he demanded, 'A job? You've got a job for me?'

The other man raised his hands as if to signal halt, and Colum forced himself to be silent.

'There's a possibility of a job for you, Colum, but that's all it is, only a possibility.'

The fat man reached into his inner pocket and brought out a slip of pasteboard, which he handed to Colum.

'You're to report to this address tomorrow morning at eight o'clock, and mind you're smart and clean.'

Colum excitedly scanned the address, and demanded, 'Who do I ask to see, Charlie? What sort of job is it?'

The other man shook his head. 'I can't tell you anything else. Report tomorrow morning at eight sharp.'

He rose suddenly and with surprising speed was opening the door into the street before Colum could even react.

'Eight sharp, Colum, and check your tea caddy.'

With these parting words the door slammed shut and Charles Anderson was gone.

Colum rose slowly, grimacing at the ache in his stiffened joints and, taking the empty wooden tea caddy from the shelf, opened it and peered inside.

Tears brimmed to sting his eyes, and he was forced to

swallow hard to dispel the lump that had instantly risen in his throat.

'Oh, you soft bastard, Charlie!' he muttered aloud. 'You soft, good-hearted bastard!'

Five golden sovereigns lay at the bottom of the caddy.

Chapter Eighteen

Colum Macrae had been waiting for more than five hours in the antechamber of the hallway of number 50 Harley Street. He knew nothing of the functions of this house, but he had realised from the moment of entry that it was a department of Government. His reception by the doorman had been one of rude hostility, and he had been left alone in this tiny room to kick his heels, without explanation or apology.

As he waited, hour after hour, he could not help but brood, and that brooding invoked a mood of bitterness against the authorities who, by punishing him, had also punished his beloved daughters. Yet he was honest enough to accept that the main fault for his present plight lay with himself. He constantly castigated himself with a fierce self-disgust for his own rebellious nature, for not being able to control his fiery temper, for not being able to act humbly towards those set above him in authority, for acting without thought of consequences.

His troubled reverie was interrupted by the appearance of an elderly clerk who ordered peremptorily, 'Come with me.'

Colum's fiery temper had not been improved by the long hours of solitary waiting, and now the rudeness of the clerk added more fuel to the fire. He was seething inwardly as he followed Mr Bush along corridors and up flights of stairs, to the green baize-covered door upon which the clerk tapped gently.

'Enter,' the voice from within ordered.

Mr Bush stood aside, and gestured for Colum to go through the door.

Conrad Cumlinson was ensconced in his capacious black leather-covered chair behind the vast expanse of his black leather-topped desk, hands clasped before his chest, fingers steepled to touch the fringe of whiskers beneath his chin.

Colum marched smartly forwards and came to a crashing halt to stand at rigid attention.

The older man winced at the noise, and said softly, 'Really now, Macrae, all this military etiquette is quite unnecessary, you know. We are neither of us any longer in the army, so I do think that we can dispense with such formalities, although the police make it a practice.'

'As you like, sir, since I'm no longer in the police either.'

Colum's accent was difficult to place with any certainty. It appeared to hold traces of the west of Scotland, or maybe the east of Ireland, or maybe the extreme north-west of England.

Cumlinson frowned slightly and when he answered his tone was acerbic. 'I do not need reminding that you are no longer a serving policeman, Macrae. I have received a full report on your disgraceful behaviour.'

Colum's dour freckled face reddened darkly with angry resentment and almost matched the colour of his reddish chestnut hair. He remained silent until the older man prodded.

'Well, Macrae. I am awaiting your explanation.'

'If you have received a full report, sir, then you will

already know all there is to know. I arrested a wanted man, and sought assistance from a fool. All else followed from that,' Colum informed him grimly.

'Have a care, Macrae. Your manner is verging upon insolence.'

'With respect, sir, my manner is perhaps influenced by the fact that I have been kept waiting in the hallway for several hours without even the courtesy of explanation or apology, and have been spoken to by everyone here as if I were a cur dog.'

'Have you indeed, Macrae. Do you think that you are too important a person to be kept waiting in hallways, or to be addressed brusquely?'

The younger man reacted hotly to the sneering question. 'I think that my lack of importance is the point in question here. I doubt that I would have been kept waiting for so long without explanation or apology, or spoken to as I have been, if I had been in a position of power and influence.'

Cumlinson was secretly pleased to find that this man's spirited pride was undiminished by his misfortunes. A cowed lickspittle would not have suited his purpose. Nevertheless he was accustomed to instant and unquestioning obedience from those beneath him, and did not tolerate being taken to task by anyone, be they subordinate or superior to himself.

'Let me remind you, Macrae, that it is my portion to command, and it is your portion to obey. It is I who decide whether or not you are wasting your time by being kept waiting in hallways, because your time is mine to do with as I please. If you cannot accept that fact, then there is no place for you in this department. And if there is no place for you in this department, then

I will make so bold as to prophesy that you and your dependants will face a very hard and bleak future. Do you understand what I am saying, Macrae?'

Colum's eyes betrayed his shock, as the realisation struck home that he was indeed going to be offered some sort of work by this man. New hope flowered.

'I think I understand, sir.'

Cumlinson silently pondered for some considerable time, then requested, 'Refresh my memory concerning your military service, Macrae. The salient facts will be sufficient.'

'I enlisted as a private soldier in the 7th Fusiliers in 1849. I was promoted to corporal in 1850, and to sergeant in 1854. At the Battle of the Alma my conduct was noticed by my commanding officer, Colonel Lacy Yea, and I was recommended by him for a battlefield commission. Lord Raglan was kind enough to approve this recommendation, and I was gazetted as ensign. After the Battle of Inkerman I gained a lieutenancy without purchase, in the same regiment . . .'

'But then you quarrelled with a fellow officer whilst in the trench lines before Sebastopol and fought a duel with him, causing him severe injury, did you not, Macrae?' Cumlinson broke in on the recital. 'There was considerable sympathy for you among your fellow officers, it being considered that you had acted honourably. Nevertheless you were advised to sell your commission and to leave the army.

'Upon your return to this country you joined the police force here in London, and soon were transferred to the detective force. Shortly after that transfer you gained promotion to detective sergeant. However, your volatile personality has occasioned you difficulties with your superior officers on several occasions, culminating in this latest disgraceful episode.'

Cumlinson's thin lips quirked in what could have been a wintry smile. 'You are a courageous man, possessing high intelligence and resourcefulness. But, alas, you are a maverick! Can it be that you lack the proper respect owed to those whom God has placed above you?'

He lifted his eyebrows as if inviting reply, and Colum answered stiffly.

'I accept that I am not an ideal subordinate, sir. I have never been able to suffer fools gladly, even though God may have placed them in superior positions to myself. And I have never been able to remain silent when my plans have been brought to ruin by the stupidity of those set above me.'

'Exactly so, Macrae.' Cumlinson's wintry smile now held some degree of genuine warmth. 'Exactly so. You are always ready to rebel against authority, Macrae. And that is why I consider you to be ideally suited for the task I am about to offer you.'

Colum's features betrayed an instant of relief, which the older man's shrewd eyes took note of. Cumlinson nodded, and stated quietly, 'Ah yes, Macrae, this employment I am offering is a Godsend to you, is it not? I take it that you are eager to accept?'

He paused expectantly, and Colum answered without hesitation.

'I am indeed, sir. And I am most grateful for this offer.'

The older man nodded in satisfaction. 'I am pleased that you acknowledge your sense of gratitude, Macrae. Now, as to your task. An Irish extremist group has lately been attempting to recruit British soldiers into their ranks. Your primary task is to infiltrate and become a trusted member of that group.'

Again he paused and studied the younger man's features, trying to gauge his reaction. But Colum's expression gave no hint of his inner thoughts, so Cumlinson asked, 'Well?'

Colum registered surprise. 'Well what, sir?'

'Do you consider yourself able to carry out this task?' Cumlinson demanded with a hint of impatience.

'But of course, sir. I'm sure it is what God intends for me to do,' Colum informed him politely.

A smile once more flickered on Cumlinson's lips. 'I see that you possess a sardonic bent of humour, Macrae. I trust that it will serve you well in the work you will be doing from now on. But always remember that sarcasm is the weapon of the inferior mind.'

He fell silent for a brief while, as if carefully considering his next words. Then he asked quietly, 'Are you capable of killing, Macrae?'

Colum was slightly puzzled by the question. 'Every soldier has to be capable of killing the enemy, sir. That is his duty.'

Again the older man appeared to give careful consideration before continuing. 'I am going to impart some secret information to you, Macrae. And I would emphasise that you must never repeat a single word of what I am going to tell you to any living soul . . .' He proceeded to tell Colum about the attempted assassination of the Prince of Wales, and that he considered it had been carried out by the newly formed group of Irish extremists. '. . . We know very little about this new group. We do know that its leader is known to Terence

McCulloch, the leader of the group you are to join.

'This other, newly formed group is the one I want you to track down, Macrae. There may be both men and women in their number. You will identify every single one of them, and when you have succeeded in that, I want you to eliminate them. By fair means or foul, in hot blood or cold. Are you capable of doing this? Think very carefully before you give me the answer to that question, Macrae.'

Now Colum's shock was clearly displayed in his face, and doubt flickered in his eyes. He had killed men before, but they had been enemy soldiers. Also during his police service he had once been forced to kill a man who had attacked him with an axe, in order to save his own life. But these incidents had happened in the heat of conflict. He really did not believe he would be able to bring himself to kill another human being, particularly a woman, in cold blood.

But then the faces of his daughters came into his mind, and he knew that for their sakes, to secure their futures, to save them from the degradation and sufferings of the workhouse, he must steel himself to carry out the previously unthinkable. He must suppress his own morality, in order to save his beloved girls. In his present circumstances moral scruples were a luxury he could not afford. The welfare of his children must be paramount.

'Sir, I must speak truly,' he told Cumlinson. 'Although the thought of killing in cold blood repels me, yet I can and will do it.'

The other man nodded, as if satisfied, and ordered curtly, 'Report to Mr Bush and receive your instructions. I bid you good day.'

*

Late that evening Cumlinson summoned Mr Bush to his office.

'Macrae?' he questioned.

'He has been fully instructed, sir. The operation will be initiated on Friday next. He knows only what it is necessary for him to know.'

'Naturally so, Mr Bush. It's best that he should remain ignorant as to the existence of our informer. That way we have a dual check upon them, since they will be reporting back to us about each other's doings. And if it should become politic to sacrifice one of them, then the other will continue to serve us in happy ignorance of his own expendability.'

Cumlinson extracted his gold hunter watch from its fob and glanced at its ornate face. 'Bless me, how time flies. I am late for my supper. I bid you good night, Mr Bush.'

'Good night, sir.'

Outside in the dark street fog swirled thickly. Cumlinson breathed deeply of the smoky air, as if relishing its sulphurous taste, and he smiled with buoyant satisfaction. In his mind he spoke to the unknown Irish American who had become his prey.

'Welcome to my game, Paddy. It's called "the Spider and the Fly". And I, of course, am the Spider.'

He stepped out jauntily, humming beneath his breath the tune known as 'The Devil among the Tailors'.

Chapter Nineteen

Colum Macrae had moved his wife, mother-in-law and children out of London to a cottage in Reading almost forty miles from the city. If Colum was compromised he did not want to have his children placed in any danger of reprisal, and in this quiet town where no one knew him or them, they would be perfectly secure, no matter what might happen to him.

He rose very early on Friday morning and spoke privately with his mother-in-law.

'I have to go away this morning, Ma, and I don't know for how long I'll be gone. It could be for months. Will you be able to cope with Margaret and the girls?'

'Of course I will,' she snapped indignantly, then asked, 'Where are you going, son? Is it to do with the work that you've found?'

He shook his head. 'I can't tell you anything, Ma, except that I'm employed honestly. So please, don't press me.'

She had been accustomed to Colum disappearing for differing periods when he was a detective, so she accepted his answer without further questions.

'Here.' He handed her a small canvas moneybag. 'There's enough there to keep you all for a month. On the first day of every month after that a gentleman will call on you here, and he will give you more money. That arrangement will continue until I return.'

'What about Margaret? Does she know that you're going away today?'

He grimaced. 'No. She's not interested in my doings, just so long as I keep her supplied with money. I've given her some for her own use, but you're not to give her any of the cash I've given you, or any of the money the gentleman will be paying you. If she wants to drink herself to death, she must earn the money to pay for the gin herself.' He frowned worriedly. 'Do you think you'll be able to handle her, Ma? She can be a handful when she's in drink.'

'I can handle my own daughter, don't you doubt that,' the old woman assured him firmly. 'You need have no worries about the babbies or Margaret while you're away, son, I can take care of all of them.'

He smiled gratefully. 'I know you can, Ma.'

'Shall I wake the girls so that you can say goodbye?'

Sadness clouded his eyes. 'No, leave them to sleep. I've already crept in and kissed them. To tell you the truth, Ma, I don't think that I could bear to leave if I have to tell them goodbye.'

'But they'll be asking after you,' she protested. 'What can I tell them?'

'You can tell them that I've gone to look for a treasure, and that when I come back I'll have a bag full of presents for them.'

She stared thoughtfully at his troubled face, and questioned, 'Is it dangerous, where you're going?'

He shrugged. 'It could prove so, Ma.' Then he forced a smile. 'But you've no need to worry about me. The Devil looks after his own.'

Tears sprang into the old woman's eyes. 'It's God

who'll be looking after you, son, because you're a good man. You're the best man I've ever known.'

He leaned forward and kissed her worn cheeks and she hugged him fondly.

'Take care, son.'

There was a lump in Colum's throat and he felt the sting of tears in his eyes as he walked away from the secluded cottage and turned his footsteps towards the railway station.

At number 50 Harley Street, he entered by the small concealed door at the rear of the house. Mr Bush was awaiting him, and together they went down into a lamp-lit cellar. There, Colum discarded his own clothing and put on greasy, threadbare old clothes, broken boots and a shapeless billycock hat.

Bush examined the taller man's appearance and nodded with satisfaction. 'Yes, that will do. Now, do you recall all your instructions and the information you have been given?'

'I do,' Colum assured him.

'Seamus Slavin is your best mode of entry into McCulloch's group. He is at present engaged upon recruiting duties, and spends a deal of his time at the rendezvous in Westminster. We know that he is actively trying to subvert soldiers, and any others he thinks might be useful to his cause. I would suggest that you keep as near to the truth as is possible when you make his acquaintance.' A wintry smile briefly quirked Bush's thin lips. 'After all, the simple truth concerning your antecedents renders you extremely promising material for rebellion, does it not?'

Colum's lips tightened angrily, but he made no reply.

'Now remember,' Bush went on, 'when you leave this

house, you will not return to it until your assignment is successfully concluded. Your reports and any further instructions we might have for you will be channelled through Abraham Vincent the pawnbroker in Leather Lane, High Holborn. If you should be compromised by McCulloch, or be apprehended by the authorities for any reason, then you must remain silent. We shall do our best for you. But, and I must emphasise that if you should break silence, or betray your connection with us, then we shall deny all knowledge of you, and you will be left to your fate. Is that fully understood?'

Colum nodded grimly. 'It is.'

'Good! Wait here.' Bush turned away and walked out of the cellar room.

Even before his echoing footsteps died away fresh footfalls sounded and one of the dour security staff entered, carrying a lighted lantern.

He signalled to Colum to follow him, and led the way down a steep flight of stone steps, along narrow passages with damp, mildewed walls and down and up further flights of stone steps until they reached a small rusty iron door. The man unlocked this and opened it to disclose an ancient sewerage tunnel stinking of filth and echoing to the squeaking scurrying of dozens of rats.

'Follow this tunnel,' the big man instructed. 'You'll need to feel your way along the right-hand wall. At twenty paces you'll find a hatch set into the wall. Go through the hatch and you'll be in the basement rubbish tip of the Century Hotel. Make sure no one sees you.'

He stood aside to let Colum pass him, and then slammed the iron door shut, plunging Colum into pitch blackness.

Colum stood perfectly stationary, hearing the key

turning in the lock behind him. The foul stench caused him to gag. He blocked his nostrils with one hand, breathing through his mouth to shield himself from the worst of the vile smells, and moved cautiously through the blackness, his outstretched hand feeling along the wet slimy brickwork, his feet carefully testing the ground beneath.

He felt a sense of utter relief when his searching hand met the cold iron hatch set into a small recess in the brickwork. He gently pushed the top-hung hatch open a crack and squinted out. Piles of rubbish stretched before him, and he listened carefully for any sounds. All was silent. In a swift movement he wriggled through the hatch and quietly let it shut behind him. He scrambled across the heaped rubbish and within scant seconds was out among the bustling crowds on the sunlit streets.

The Drum and Bugle public house in Westminster was the aptly named recruiting rendezvous, and from early in the morning until late at night it was a meeting place for the army recruiting sergeants who gathered there to take refreshment, exchange gossip and help their new-found recruits drink away the 'Queen's shilling' before taking them before the local magistrate to be attested and sworn into the army.

Colum walked slowly around the corner and down the street towards the public house on the far corner. He could see a group of army sergeants standing around the entrance door of the public house. They had the brightly ribboned cockades of recruiters pinned to their pillbox forage caps, and he knew that their sharp eyes were examining him as he sauntered towards them. In return he surreptitiously studied their faces, seeking for the man fitting the description of Sergeant Seamus Slavin. He experienced a surge of excitement as he spotted the lantern-jawed features bearing a long ragged scar from the left eye to the chin.

When he came within a few paces of the group a cavalry sergeant with flamboyant mustachios, resplendently uniformed in the blue jacket and cherry-coloured overalls of the 11th Hussars, stepped from the group and spoke to him.

'You look like a man who's down on his luck, my friend. A man who might be needing a good meal and a skinful of beer.'

Colum halted and grinned. 'No offence, friend, but I'm not looking to 'list just now. And if I was lookin' to 'list then I wouldn't be joining the Cherry Pickers, my arse wasn't made to fit a saddle.'

'No offence taken,' the sergeant answered affably, and his eyes measured Colum's erect, muscular figure. 'I'd say that you're an old sweat.'

Colum nodded.

'What regiment.'

'Seventh Fusiliers.'

'Been out long?'

'A couple or three years.'

'Are you giving some thought to re-enlisting?'

'I'm giving it some thought. But like I told you, I won't be riding any horses if I do.'

'Fair enough.' The cavalryman turned away and rejoined the other sergeants. He muttered to them, and the tall, lantern-jawed, scar-faced sergeant wearing the scarlet and blue of the infantry spoke to Colum.

'What's your name, friend?'

'Colum Macrae. What's yours?'

'I'm Sergeant Seamus Slavin, my friend, of Her Majesty's Scots Fusilier Guards. So we've something in common, haven't we? We're both Fusiliers.'

Satisfaction filled Colum. His luck was running well, he had found the man he sought.

'In the Old Seventh, were you?' Slavin grinned.

'That's right.'

Slavin noted the accent but could not place it exactly. 'Is it an Irishman you are?'

'By birth. But I've been over here since I was a babe in arms.'

'Well then, why not step inside and take a jar with a fellow countryman. There's no strings attached to it,' Slavin invited.

Colum frowned, and appeared hesitant to accept, and with hearty jocularity Slavin reassured him.

'Now I've no thought of getting you pissed and slipping you the "shilling", my friend. I wouldn't try to work that dodge on an old soldier like yourself. That's summat we do to the bloody Bog Men and the country Chawbacons. It 'ud be a waste of my time trying to work that dodge on an old soldier like yourself, wouldn't it now. So step in and have a pint for friendship's sake.'

'Well, just so long as you've got it straight that I'm not looking to re-enlist, then I'll take a pint with you,' Colum agreed.

'Then it's after you, sor, be pleased to step up to the bar.' Slavin grinned broadly and gestured for Colum to enter the public house ahead of him. As Colum went inside Slavin winked slyly at his fellow recruiters, and whispered, 'What odds will you give me that I'll not have him listed before Taps is blown?'

They laughingly declined his challenge to wager. They knew him for a sly and artful recruiter who had successfully inveigled or tricked all too many reluctant men into taking the Queen's shilling and joining Her Majesty's army.

Slavin called for two pots of beer, two clay pipes and a twist of tobacco each, and after they were seated, with pipes drawing well and the first gulps of beer inside their bellies, they began to talk, exchanging reminiscences about the Crimean campaign, and discussing the current fighting in India.

Colum made no mention that he had won a battle-field commission to become an officer, but he did let drop that he had until recently been a police detective.

This item of information was received by Slavin with great interest and he began to question Colum about his police experience. Colum answered evasively, and the more Slavin pressed him, the more evasive he became.

The hours passed and the beer flowed freely. Recruiters were allowed generous sums to spend on snaring good recruits.

Colum pretended that he was becoming drunk. He became less evasive in his answers, and began to rail against the unfair treatment he had received from the police force, and to express his bitter resentment against the authorities who had expelled him.

Slavin was thinking hard. If this man Macrae's claim to be an ex-police detective sergeant was the truth, then he might prove to be very useful to Terence McCulloch. Obliquely the sergeant touched on politics, and on the question of Home Rule for Ireland. Colum expressed himself vehemently on that point, proclaiming his hatred for the oppressive English Government, and his belief that Ireland should be a free and independent nation.

Slavin decided that Terence McCulloch should be informed about this promising newfound acquaintance, and be given the chance to have a look at him.

Colum, sensing that his carefully cast bait had been taken, yawned heavily, and slurred, 'Jasus, I'm knackered. I need to get me head down and have a kip.'

'Have you a place to go to?' Slavin wanted to know.

Colum shook his head. 'I've been roughing it for the last couple of weeks. But I'll find some corner or other to crawl into.'

'I might be able to help you there,' Slavin told him.

Colum scowled blearily. 'I told you that I wasn't going to 'list, didn't I? I'm not intending to wake up in the fuckin' barracks tomorrow morning, wondering how I come to be there!'

The other man laughed, and shook his head. 'No, friend, I'm not offering you the shilling. But I've got a mate who keeps a lodging house close by here. I can get you a kip there for tonight.'

Colum shook his head. 'I've no money to pay for any bed.'

'Who mentioned money?' Slavin demanded indignantly. 'I've took a liking to you, Macrae. And if I can't help a fellow countryman when he's down on his luck, then I'm not a true Irishman, am I?'

Colum squinted owlishly at the other man, and demanded suspiciously, 'Hey now, you wouldn't be one of them who has the taste for men's flesh, would you?'

'It's a good job that I like you, Macrae,' Slavin replied evenly, 'or I'd be breaking your face for suggesting such a thing.'

'I'm sorry! Truly I'm sorry! I don't know what made me say such a thing,' Colum apologised contritely. 'It's just that since I've been on my uppers, I've had more than a few bastard she-shirts coming up to me and offering me a bed for the night.'

The soldier laughed grimly. 'Well, you're a fine-looking man, Macrae, just the sort that the she-shirts like.'

'I'm sorry, Sergeant, truly I'm sorry.' Colum kept on apologising, until he drove the other man to address him sharply.

'That's enough now, man. I don't need telling no more that you're sorry. Come on, we'll go and get you fixed up for the night.'

The lodging house was in the same street as the Drum and Bugle, and to Colum's relief appeared some-what cleaner than the normal houses of its type.

Slavin led him through to the large kitchen which was furnished with long tables and benches. Several men, women and children were seated at the tables while others busied themselves at the range preparing vari-ous foodstuffs, and the smells of frying fish, offal and burning fat thickened the smoky, overheated air.

'How's it going, Tim?' Slavin greeted the proprietor, a hulking Kerryman, and winked meaningfully. 'I've got a new pal here who needs a bed. He's one of our own. Colum Macrae is his name.'

The Kerryman grinned, disclosing blackened, broken teeth, and offered his massive hand to Colum. 'Me name's Joseph. Joseph Connors. Any pal of Seamus is welcome here. Take a seat. Could you do with summat to ate?'

'I could, but I've no money,' Colum told him.

'That don't matter.' The huge man went to the cooking range and thrust aside the ragged cluster. One man turned on him threateningly, and Connors casually buffeted him across the head, sending him staggering across the room to collide with and fall over a bench. A woman was frying some fish in an iron skillet and Connors took it from her and brought it to the table to lay it in front of Colum.

'Here, get this down you.'

Colum glanced at the woman, and felt guilty when he saw her haggard, stricken face, but sensing this was some sort of test, he grinned and fell upon the food like a starving man, breaking pieces of the steaming white flesh with his fingers, blowing on it to cool it and stuffing it into his mouth.

His two companions exchanged a long look, an unspoken message passing between them, and they stepped aside and talked for a while in low whispers.

Then Slavin told Colum, 'I'll leave you now, friend. Joseph will look after you.'

'Many thanks,' Colum told him. 'I'll not forget your kindness. I only wish I could repay you for it.'

'Think nothing of it,' Slavin grinned, 'I'll likely see you tomorrow morning.'

Connors seated himself opposite Colum and watched him closely until the fish was all eaten.

Then he invited, 'You'll join me in a dram, Col?'

'I will, and gladly. But I feel bad about taking so much from you without being able to return it.'

'That's enough of that sort of talk.' The huge man mock-scowled. 'You're among friends.'

He gestured with his hand and instantly a bottle was brought to him.

He took a long swig from it, and gasped, 'Jase, but that's the right stuff. Here.'

Colum drank in his turn, and coughed as the fiery spirit burned his throat.

'Isn't that the finest poteen you've ever tasted?' Connors grinned, and Colum was fulsome with his praise.

'Tell me about yourself, Col,' the huge man invited, and Colum talked at length, sticking as near to the truth as he could, but with some very judicious editing.

Connors listened intently, and remained silent until Colum had finished his story. Then he said, 'I take it that you've no love for the bloody English after the way they've treated you.'

Colum shrugged. 'It's not the ordinary English people I hate. They have to sweat and struggle for little or no reward like us. It's their fuckin' Government and upper classes I hate. They've been grinding us down for hundreds of years, and it's time we stopped them doing it.'

The huge man grinned. 'Well spoke, Col. You're a man after me own heart, so you are.' His small eyes gleamed speculatively. 'Tell me now, you look to be a well set up man, can you use your fists?'

Colum tensed warily. 'I can, and me feet and head, and a shillelagh, a blade, and a gun as well.'

'Would you be fussy about who you used them things on?' Connors pressed.

Colum shook his head. 'I used to be fussy, but not any more. Not after what's been done to me.'

'Good.' Connors grinned and proffered the poteen bottle once more.

This time Colum didn't cough when he drank, and the other man was appreciative.

'I'm glad to see that the poteen is agreeable to you, Col. Now I'll show you to your bed, and tomorrow I might have a proposition to put to you.'

'It's work I'm in need of,' Colum told him. 'Not propositions.'

'Well, this proposition might lead to a job for you, Col. But you get some kip now. You look all in.'

He used a tallow candle to light their way upstairs to the very top of the building and showed Colum into a small, windowless cubbyhole, its limited floor space covered by a straw-filled palliasse, which had a couple of blankets and a greasy flock pillow on top of it.

'Here, this will be better for you than kippin' with the others. You'll sleep peaceful here. I'll talk with you tomorrow morning.'

He left the lighted candle with Colum and clumped back downstairs.

Colum lay down on the foul-smelling palliasse, but did not remove boots or clothing, knowing from past experience that in lodging houses of this type thievery and physical assault were all too likely to occur, and that even broken boots and threadbare clothing were marketable.

He was more than satisfied with his progress. Luck had been with him, and he was confident that Slavin and Connors were going to be his means of entry into Terence McCulloch's organisation. His thoughts turned to his daughters, and he pictured their bright, fresh faces in his mind, and promised, 'I'll do whatever I have to do, to keep you from hardship, my darlings.'

His eyes closed sleepily, and then the first bugs found their way to his warm flesh and began to bite. He cursed angrily and scratched hard, but didn't bother to get up, knowing that wherever he laid down his head in this house the fleas and bugs and lice would be waiting in ambush. Eventually, the deadening effect of the copious amount of alcohol that he had drunk came to his aid, and he snored in restless slumber.

Chapter Twenty

A fresh breeze was gusting inshore from across the heaving grey-green sea, and the gulls were crying plaintively as they buffeted their wings against the constantly fluctuating strength of the wind. The blanket-wrapped invalid in the bath chair being pushed by the tall, raw-boned nursing woman, and the heavily veiled widow who walked beside them, attracted no attention on the stone promenade pier at Margate. Invalids and widows were a very common sight in the watering place during the bathing season. The invalids came in the hope that the salt sea breezes would restore their health, the widows to recover from their heartbreak of bereavement, and perhaps hoping to find a new husband to complete the recovery.

'It's damned chilly, let's go back,' Dermot Calatrava grumbled.

Rosaleen lifted her dark veil and smiled down at her brother. 'Let's just go on as far as the lighthouse, I'm enjoying the fresh air. It's a lovely day, isn't it, Theresa?' She appealed to the tall, dour woman, who sniffed disparagingly. 'It's too fine to be sitting indoors.'

'It might be a fine day for the seagulls, but as for meself I'd sooner be sitting by the fire in company with a jug of stout.'

'You go on by yourself, Rosa, and Theresa can take

me back,' Dermot insisted. 'There's no point in curing me of my wounds, only to have me catch my death of cold from this damned wind, is there?'

'All right then. You go on back, and I'll join you presently,' Rosaleen agreed and, bending, she lightly kissed her brother's pale, cold cheek. She paused a moment before straightening to stare at him searchingly. 'Are you really feeling better, Dermot?'

His dark eyes, deeply sunk in his pale thin features, softened as he returned her stare. 'Yes, Rosa, I'm really feeling much better. And if you'll only let me get back into the warm, then I'll be feeling even better than I do now.'

She laughed softly, and fondly watched his chair being wheeled away until it had gone from sight among the perambulating crowds on the pier. She walked on slowly towards the lighthouse on the pier's extremity, and when she reached it halted to gaze out across the choppy, heaving waters of the mighty Thames estuary, thronged now with the shipping of a hundred nations going to and from the Port of London.

Over a month had elapsed since the debacle at Richmond, and for Rosaleen that month had been a time of strain and torment. Fearing that her brother's presence in her house at St John's Wood might be discovered she had brought him down here to the seaside town of Margate where invalids attracted no undue attention and, using an alias, had rented a house in one of the better-class streets close to the shore.

For that first week she had stayed with her brother at all times, nursing him devotedly, snatching brief hours of sleep in an armchair by his bedside. Her devotion had been rewarded by his rapidly returning strength.

At the end of that first week he was able to tell her in detail what had happened in Richmond Park.

He berated both of his accomplices. 'Gallagher deserved what he got, the stupid, clumsy swine. And I'll kill that treacherous bastard Gilligan when I get hold of him. If he'd stood his ground I wouldn't have got this.' Dermot indicated his wounded right leg. 'The damned coward ran and left me to face the soldiers alone. I didn't stand a chance with just my revolver against their carbines.' He paused, and his handsome, drawn features radiated hatred. 'I'll kill that bastard when I see him again.'

Rosaleen shared her brother's hatred of Gilligan, but she realised that her own and her brother's poor planning had contributed to this present situation.

'We've acted like simpletons, Dermot.' She forced him likewise to face that unpalatable fact. 'We gave no thought to what we should do if it all went wrong like it has. We made no plans to deal with this sort of situation.'

But she knew that continued self-recrimination would not serve any good purpose. She must now calmly and rationally plan ahead and salvage whatever could be salvaged from this disaster.

As soon as he was out of danger she left Dermot in the care of Theresa Quinn and returned to London with Thomas Quinn.

There was an unexpected stroke of good fortune awaiting her there. Solomon Montague's financial dealings had necessitated him going from the Midlands directly to Scotland, where he would remain for some weeks to come. He had sent her a loving letter, pressing her to join him in Glasgow, but she had written back to tell him that she was too busy preparing for their forth-coming marriage to be able to join him. His absence meant that every week, as today, she had been able to take the steamer for the six-hour voyage from London to Margate and spend time with Dermot.

There had been many moments during the past month when she had been sorely tempted to take flight from England – to close the house in St John's Wood and simply disappear abroad. But she feared that Dermot was still too weak to risk subjecting him to a rough passage by sea or overland. She had summoned all her fortitude, knowing that above all else she must keep her nerve. Every day that Dermot was able to rest and grow stronger in Margate meant that he would be better able to endure flight abroad should the need arise.

The one salient fact that continually baffled her had been the reaction to the failed attempt on the Prince of Wales's life. Every day she had avidly scanned the news-papers, expecting there to be sensational reports about the event. But there had only been two or three brief paragraphs, and those appeared at long intervals between each other. The main news of the papers fea-tured the successful suppression of the great Sepoy Mutiny in India. The attack on the Prince, according to the brief official communiqués, had been attributed to a madman recently released from a private lunatic asylum. The reports had stated that the madman had hurled a stone in the direction of the Prince's party, and had been pursued. During that pursuit Major Winstanley's horse had fallen and the Major had been thrown from his saddle and killed. On the verge of being captured the madman had suddenly produced a pistol which he had used to commit suicide.

Rosaleen was deeply puzzled by these terse official statements, and could not understand why the authorities were so blatantly lying.

At present her biggest worry was Billy Gilligan. She had sent Thomas Quinn to search for Gilligan. He returned to tell her that the man had disappeared from his lodgings, and that Emma Carr and her baby had disappeared also. Rosaleen's nerve was sorely tested by this information. She did not believe that Gilligan would voluntarily surrender himself to the authorities but she thought it a certainty that, professional criminal that he was, he would inevitably be picked up by the police for committing some offence or other, and that then he might try to bargain his freedom for information.

Again Rosaleen's first impulse was to take flight. But she fought against it.

Only keep your nerve, and all will be well, she told herself over and over again.

In her mind there had formed the conviction that Gilligan must be killed in order to ensure that he could never betray them, so she set Thomas Quinn to scouring the drinking dens and shebeens where criminals gathered in an effort to try to find out Gilligan's whereabouts. But again he had had no success. Gilligan seemed to have disappeared from the face of the earth. She was now considering approaching Terence McCulloch and enlisting his aid in the search for Gilligan, but hesitated to do so, instinct telling her that it was better that McCulloch should know nothing of her. But she was being forced to face the fact that to enlist McCulloch's aid was becoming the lesser of two evils. Without him she had no chance of tracking down Billy Gilligan.

There had been no newspaper references to the attempt on the Prince's life for some weeks now, and Rosaleen was becoming more confident in the belief that she and her brother had got away with that sadly bungled operation. If she could only ensure Gilligan's silence, then all would be well, and the way would be clear for another attempt to strike at their enemies.

The gusting of the wind became stronger, and she was forced to hold down her veil. She turned away from the open sea and began to walk slowly back along the length of the pier.

As she walked she came to the decision that it was time to contact Terence McCulloch. She would return to London the very next day.

Chapter Twenty-one

Terence McCulloch was walking slowly homewards when the heavily veiled woman dressed in widow's weeds called to him from the stationary carriage.

'Your pardon, sir, am I addressing Mr Terence McCulloch?'

He halted and turned to face her and, despite his surprise at being so accosted, his hand automatically moved to lift his top hat in polite salute to a gentlelady. But even as his hand moved his eyes switched from side to side suspiciously, and he noted the hard face of the liveried coachman sitting dourly above him.

'Forgive me for startling you, Mr McCulloch, it was not my intention, I do assure you.' The woman's voice was soft and lilting.

'Are we acquainted, ma'am?' He was tense, fearful of some sort of ambush, and his free hand moved surreptitiously towards the small loaded pistol he carried in the capacious pocket of his topcoat.

'We are not personally known to each other, Mr McCulloch, but we do have a mutual acquaintance in common. Will you allow me to give you a lift to your home?'

He hesitated, curiosity battling with suspicion, and she emitted a soft laugh, and coaxed him. 'Please, Mr

170

McCulloch, I can do you no harm, I am a weak and defenceless woman.'

'What do you want with me, ma'am?' he demanded.

'I wish to discuss a matter of great importance to both of us. We share a common interest, Mr McCulloch. We serve the same cause.'

Still his wary eyes flickered around him, watching to see if anyone was coming towards them, but there were only two maidservants walking away from him, carrying shopping baskets and chattering animatedly together.

'I am quite alone, Mr McCulloch, the carriage is empty but for myself.'

She leaned back from the door window so that he could see into the interior of the vehicle.

'I shall be at your mercy,' she told him.

His hand slipped into his topcoat pocket and his fingers closed upon the small pistol. If treachery were intended, then he was fully prepared to blow her head off.

He stepped to the carriage and entered it, sitting himself on the leather seating to face her.

She raised her gloved hand and rapped on the panelling.

'Walk on,' Thomas Quinn growled, and the bays moved forward, jerking the carriage into motion.

'Who are you, and what do you want with me?' McCulloch demanded.

She lifted the thick black veil up and over her bonnet and he drew a hissing intake of breath as he saw her face.

'I see that you detect the family resemblance, Mr McCulloch.' She smiled with amusement. 'Yes, I am Dermot Calatrava's twin sister. My name is Rosaleen Calatrava.'

A score of questions sprang to his lips, clamouring to be voiced, but he stayed silent. He was far too wise and wily to betray his bafflement at this present situation.

Rosaleen appreciated his silence, recognising McCulloch's shrewdness and self-control in his restrained reaction, and could not help but feel that her brother had perhaps underestimated this man's capabilities.

She decided that she would give him an honest account of what had occurred, but would omit the part she herself had played in the killing of Winstanley. Her own capacity for ruthless action was best kept a secret.

'Mr McCulloch, I am going to tell you a story,' she said quietly. 'I would ask that you stay silent until I have finished. Do you agree?'

He nodded, and she went on to tell him of the bungled attempt on the Prince's life, but blamed Billy Gilligan for the murder of Winstanley.

He sat listening impassively, only fleeting hints of what he was feeling flickering in his eyes. She finished her account just as the carriage came to a halt outside his house.

Her dark eyes fixed intently upon his face, and she waited for him to reply. For long minutes he stayed silent, pondering deeply on what he had been told. At length he asked, 'Do you intend to continue to try and assassinate the Prince?'

'Of course,' she replied firmly. 'And to assassinate all the other oppressors of our nation. I intend to continue this struggle until we have freed Ireland from all foreign tyranny.'

He smiled grimly. He could think of a hundred ways

in which this beautiful woman could be of immense value in the struggle against the hated enemy.

'Am I to take it that you want my assistance in tracking down Billy Gilligan?' he queried.

'Yes, I need your help to do that. I also want us to work together in the future.'

He pursed his lips reflectively. 'And who would be the captain of our band, ma'am?'

She winked coquettishly, and her accents metamorphosed into a lilting brogue. 'Ah now, sor, how could a mere woman like meself even' dare to think of giving orders to a fine man like you.'

He was charmed by her beauty and ironic humour, and he chuckled with genuine amusement. Then sobered abruptly.

'I think that you and I might work together very well. But I have grave doubts concerning your brother. I consider him to be dangerously undisciplined.'

A frown creased her smooth forehead. She hated to hear any criticism of her beloved Dermot. Yet at the same time she accepted that McCulloch had considerable justification for his opinion.

'I'll handle Dermot, Mr McCulloch. You need have no fear on that score.'

Again he pondered deeply for a few minutes, then sighed and nodded.

'So be it, ma'am.' He held out his hand. 'We have an agreement.'

They shook hands and then he told her, 'There is much we must discuss, but before all else I think that Billy Gilligan must be tracked down and disposed of.'

'Do you know the man?' she questioned eagerly.

'I have heard of him. My business interests bring me

into some considerable degree of contact with the criminal classes. I'll have enquiries made immediately. I'll lay him by his heels in short order, you may be sure of that.'

'I am sure of it, Mr McCulloch,' she told him sincerely.

'I need to know more about you, ma'am, if we are to work together. Both your past and present circumstances. I shall also need to be given the names of people known to me who can vouch for you.'

'And will you give me similar information and names concerning yourself?' she challenged.

He nodded gravely. 'Certainly I will. We are going to have to place complete trust in each other. And to do that, we must know virtually all there is to know about each other. I have to leave you now, but I suggest that we meet tomorrow, and we talk at length then.'

This time it was Rosaleen who offered her hand, and told him, 'We have an agreement, Mr McCulloch.'

Chapter Twenty-two

It was in the seventh week following Rosaleen Calatrava's meeting with Terence McCulloch that Solomon Montague returned from Scotland to London. Rosaleen stared at her lover in alarm when he shuffled into her drawing room in St John's Wood, leaning heavily upon a gold-headed walking cane.

'What's the matter, Sol?' She rose and came to him, staring anxiously into his pallid, skull-like features which were beaded with sweat despite the cool freshness of the day.

'I fear that I'm ill, my dear,' he croaked hoarsely. 'I took a giddy turn while I was travelling down on the train.'

She took his arm and led him to a chair, and he slumped down onto it, wheezing for breath.

She hastened to pour some brandy into a glass and handed it to him. 'Here, sip this. It will restore you.'

He coughed and shook his head, then slumped forwards and slowly toppled from the chair.

Even as she crouched to lift him, Rosaleen knew that her lover was dead.

'Oh my God!' She shivered with shock, as she turned him over onto his back. His jaw fell open, and the porcelain false teeth slipped free to protrude grotesquely from his gaping mouth.

'Sol? Sol?' She took his face between her hands and stared into his sightless eyes. 'Oh my God!'

She struggled to control her scattered wits. Death was no stranger to her, it had been a constant companion throughout much of her life. But the sheer suddenness of Solomon Montague's dying had momentarily unnerved her.

She gently lowered his head to the floor and stood up. Her first impulse was to shout for Thomas Quinn to come, but then she paused. She needed a few minutes to gather her senses and to think clearly.

After a while she was able to consider more calmly the possible connotations of Montague's unexpected death. Her protector had gone, and with him her financial security. Her situation had suddenly become parlous. Montague had a son and three married daughters still living. She knew that his existing will left all his wealth and possessions to them. He had promised her that after she married him, then he would change the will in her favour.

Her full lips quirked in a wry grimace. 'I should have insisted that he changed his damned will on the day we became betrothed.'

She thought of her brother Dermot who was still convalescing in Margate. His wound was healing slowly, and he was still weak and lame. It would be many months, perhaps years even, before his vigour might return, and even then he might never fully recover.

'How can I continue to support him? And then there's Theresa and Thomas. And how can I finance our cause any longer?'

She stared down at the dead man lying at her feet, and a fleeting sadness touched her.

'You were good to me, Sol,' she murmured. 'If you had to die, then I'm glad that it came so quickly and easily to you.' She smiled ruefully. 'But I wish to Christ that you'd changed your damned will before you went.'

The temptation to load all that she could into the carriage and just disappear was strong. But she realised that such a course of action would inevitably rebound against her. Montague's children knew of her existence. The old man had told them of his plans to marry her, and that news had caused bitter quarrels between him and his family. If she disappeared now with whatever valuables were in the house then the old man's family might well call in the police and accuse her of thievery. She decided that she would act as a dutiful and caring fiancée should. She would play the part of the grieving, bereaved lover, discreetly of course, and face his son.

She went to the door of the room and called for Thomas Quinn to come to her. When he did so she showed him the dead man.

Quinn only shrugged his massive shoulders and muttered, 'Ah well, it comes to us all. The old fella had a good run, didn't he?'

'Go to Marylebone and find Doctor Reginald Quigley,' Rosaleen instructed. 'He's Sol's doctor. Tell him what's happened and that he's to come here immediately.'

'What about him?' Quinn indicated the corpse. 'Do you want me to shift him upstairs onto the bed and lay him out a bit decent like? He looks like a drunk lying there like that, all twisted up.'

Rosaleen shook her head. 'No, leave him lay. It's best

that the doctor should see him like this. We don't want any suspicions as to how it happened entering the man's mind, do we?'

Quinn's expression was ambiguous as he agreed. 'You're right, Rosa. If I was to lay the old man out on the bed the doctor might be thinking that he'd overexerted himself, mightn't he?'

Sudden anger flared in Rosaleen as she suspected a hidden meaning in Quinn's attitude, and she snapped curtly, 'Or that I'd excited the poor old soul into overexerting himself, Thomas, isn't that what you might be meaning?'

Again the big man only shrugged his shoulders, and replied evenly, 'It's no matter what anybody might be meaning, is it, Rosa? The old fella is still as dead as a door-knocker either way.'

When Quinn had gone on his errand, Rosaleen took a cheroot from the silver box and lit it with a lucifer match. She seated herself on a chair across from the dead man and drew the fragrant smoke deep into her lungs, savouring its aroma and gently exhaling so that it wreathed up around her head. Her thoughts turned to Terence McCulloch.

They had had several meetings during the past seven weeks, but so far nothing concrete had come of them. Despite McCulloch's assurances that he would track down Billy Gilligan, the man had still not been traced. It was as if the earth had swallowed him up.

McCulloch had also proven reluctant to make plans for further assassination attempts against the Royal Family. His answer to Rosaleen's urgings to make such plans was always that they must wait. They must allow time for the abortive attempt to fade from the authorities' memories, until vigilance had relaxed a trifle, and security measures become slack once more.

Rising, Rosaleen went from the room and into the kitchen at the rear of the house. She seated herself at the scrubbed table and the hours slowly passed. When the room darkened she went through the ground floor, lighting the gas lamps, and was in the front hallway when she heard the iron-shod wheels of the carriage crunching up the short driveway to the house.

'You have my deepest sympathy, ma'am. If there is anything that I can do to help you in this tragic hour then you have only to command me.'

Reginald Quigley's demeanour was respectfully solicitous, but inwardly he pleasurably savoured this meeting with the mysterious woman known as Montague's whore. He had been aware of her existence for some while, but this was the first time he had ever met her face to face, and his eager eyes devoured her beauty. 'Where is Mr Montague?'

'He's through here.'

She led him into the drawing room and he followed, noting with appreciation the grace of her carriage.

'Might I suggest that you leave me alone with him, ma'am. It will be less distressful for you,' he urged gently, and she concurred and withdrew.

Quigley was a highly competent physician who had been the Montague family doctor for several years. The old man's sudden death had not come as a surprise to him. His heart had been failing for years, and Quigley had warned him many times against indulging in excess of any description.

He grinned down at the dead face and muttered, 'Now that I've seen your woman, Solomon, I can't say that I blame you for overindulging yourself to the full. She's a beauty.'

He carried out a perfunctory examination of the limp body, and was satisfied that the ailing heart had finally given out. He straightened the limbs and crossed the arms upon the chest, then went in search of Rosaleen Calatrava.

She was seated at the kitchen table, but her dour servant was nowhere to be seen.

'It was his heart, ma'am,' he informed her, 'and I shall report as such to the coroner's office.'

She nodded and thanked him in a quiet voice.

He looked closely at her, and then suggested delicately, 'This tragedy has been a terrible shock for you, ma'am, and I don't doubt has left you both bewildered and distraught. In the circumstances, would you perhaps prefer me to let Mr Montague's family know what has happened?'

She hesitated, and then told him, 'It is difficult for me, Doctor. I became betrothed to Mr Montague only recently, and our betrothal engendered some resentment among his family. At least Mr Montague gave me to understand that such was the case. I do think therefore that it might be less distressing for them to receive this sad news from you, rather than from myself. I would be very grateful if you would render me such a service.'

'I will be honoured to be of service to you, ma'am.' He was charmed by her manner, and could understand why the old man had become so besotted with her. In fact he was already freely admitting to himself that if she were looking for another protector, he would be very happy to put himself forward to fill that position.

'Forgive me for mentioning such a matter at this sad

time, ma'am,' he went on. 'But I feel that Mr Montague should be moved from his present position, perhaps to a chapel of rest? I can arrange it for you, if you wish.'

She smiled sadly.

'My servant will carry Mr Montague up to his own bedroom here, Doctor, and perform the necessary offices. I feel that he would prefer to be beneath a roof that has sheltered him on so many occasions, and in the company of someone who loved him dearly.'

My God, I do believe that she truly cared for the miserable old bastard after all, Quigley thought in surprise, and was touched with a genuine sympathy.

'I'm sure that he would much prefer to remain here, ma'am,' he told her sincerely. 'Now I shall go and inform his family, and tomorrow I shall call on you again, ma'am, to see if there is any further service I may render to you.'

'Thank you very much, Doctor, your kindness is a great comfort to me.'

She rose and offered her hand, and he took it eagerly, fighting against the impulse to caress its soft warmth.

'Until tomorrow then, Doctor.'

'Are you sure that you would not like me to remain with you for a while longer, ma'am?' he offered. 'It would not discommode me, I do assure you.'

'It won't be necessary, thank you, Doctor. I would prefer to be alone with my loved one, and be able to freely vent my grief.'

'Of course, ma'am, of course.' He bowed, and reluctantly took his leave of her.

Thomas Quinn came into the kitchen.

'Do you want me to take the old man upstairs, Rosa?'

'Yes please, Thomas. I'll come with you.'

'There's no need, Rosa. I can do the needful for him.'

She smiled with a genuine tenderness. 'I was fond of the old man, Thomas. He was always very good to me. I'll lay him out myself. It's little enough to do for him.'

Quinn carried the dead man like a baby in his arms, and when he had laid Montague on the bed he and Rosa stripped the clothing from him and carefully washed and carried out the last offices on the corpse.

Before she left the room Rosa said a brief prayer for the old man's soul, and then went back down into the kitchen.

'Fetch out the gin, Thomas,' she told him. 'We'll have an Irish wake for him, even though he was a Jew.'

The couple passed the rest of the night drinking, smoking, singing Irish ballads, and reminiscing about other wake nights they had passed in other places.

When dawn was breaking Thomas Quinn told her, 'Well, Rosa, at least the old fella has been given a good send-off. There's many a poor soul that I can remember who wasn't so lucky. All they got for a wake was people crying with starvation.'

Rosaleen nodded, and her terrible memories flooded over her, threatening momentarily to break her down. But she forced a laugh, and told her companion, 'Let this wake be for them as well then, Thomas. Come now, fill up the glasses and let's have another song . . .'

But behind the façade of gaiety her heart ached with a bitter sadness, and her mind was peopled with the faces of those she had loved and lost.

Chapter Twenty-three

Rosaleen was woken by the thunderous hammering on the front door. She lay for some seconds trying to gather her dazed senses, her head throbbing from the excesses of the previous night. She raised herself up on her elbows and saw that she was still fully clothed.

The clock chimed ten and she realised that she had slept for only a couple of hours.

The hammering on the door was joined by a man's voice, bellowing loudly. Rosaleen scowled and went to the window. She opened the casement and peered down at the man below.

'Who are you?' she called.

He stepped back from the door, and Rosaleen sighed with relief at the cessation of the thunderous impacts. The man was middle-aged, short and squat, and was dressed in full mourning: black frock coat, waistcoat and trousers, a black necktie and gloves, his top hat swathed in black crape and a black crape armband above one elbow.

'Who am I, madam?' he bawled furiously. 'Who am I? You dare to ask who am I?'

Rosaleen reacted angrily to his manner. 'There is death in this house, sir, be good enough to lower your voice.'

He pulled a black-bordered white handkerchief from

his pocket and, lifting his top hat, mopped the sweat that sheened his balding head, then replaced the hat and, scowling, told her in a more moderate tone, 'I know that there is death in this house, madam. I am the bereaved party. I am Samson Montague; and in my carriage there are three more bereaved parties, my sisters. We are the children of Solomon Montague.'

Rosaleen glanced at the roadway beyond the forecourt wall and saw a luxurious closed carriage. The coachman was also wearing funereal mourning, and the horses bearing black plumes on their heads.

'I'll come down and let you in,' she told Samson Montague.

Before she went downstairs she brushed her teeth and sweetened her breath, tidied her hair and dress, then went to see where Thomas Quinn had got to. She could hear his loud snoring through the closed door of his room, and decided to leave him to sleep.

When she opened the front door she found that Samson Montague had been joined by his three sisters, all resembling their brother in build and features, and likewise wearing full mourning: black shawls, black bombazine crinolines, crape-trimmed black bonnets, and jet jewellery.

'Please come in,' Rosaleen invited, and the fattest of the sisters sniffed indignantly.

'Hark to her, inviting us to step inside our own property. She has gall, this one.'

The four swept past Rosaleen and went into the drawing room where the three women seated themselves while Samson Montague went to stand with his back to the fireplace, without removing his hat.

Rosaleen felt her lips tightening with resentment at

their rudeness, but she kept herself leashed in, and followed her unwelcome visitors into the room.

'Would you care to see your father?' she invited the man.

He shook his head. 'There'll be time enough for that presently. After you have left this house.'

'Left this house?' Rosaleen blinked in surprise.

'Exactly so, madam.' He scowled. 'You have no right to be here. So I must ask you to leave immediately.'

'But this is my house, sir, and if you don't act more civilly it will be you who will be leaving here immediately.' There was an edge to her voice, and her dark eyes glittered angrily.

'Hark to her, the shameless hussy,' the fattest of the sisters exclaimed indignantly.

'Get out!' Rosaleen ordered. 'Get out of my house, all of you. And don't return here until you have learned the rudiments of good manners.'

Samson Montague grinned mockingly, and produced a ribbon-bound sheaf of vellum from his pocket which he brandished in her direction.

'This is a copy of our father's last will and testament, madam. There is no mention of the Calatrava name to be found in it.'

'You know my name then,' Rosaleen challenged, 'so why do you not use it?'

'Because I don't choose to, madam,' he snarled at her, and there was hatred in his expression. 'My father disgraced himself, he besmirched the memory of our beloved mother, and soiled our family name by taking up with you.'

'Your father and I were betrothed to each other. There was nothing shameful in our relationship, and we were to be married within days of his return from Scotland.' Rosaleen was now furious, yet she knew that she must take care how she acted towards these people, and to guard her tongue. 'And as for this house, your father gave it to me, there was no need for him to put it in any last will or testament.'

'Oh no, madam, my father did not give you this house. I have taken great care to examine all the deeds of my father's properties, and this house remains in his name. Therefore it is part of his estate, and so has been bequeathed to us, his family, under the terms of his will.'

The black bonnets of the sisters nodded in vigorous unison.

Samson Montague grinned triumphantly into Rosaleen's tense face. 'I've seen you riding like a great lady in your carriage and pair, madam, but let me inform you that you will not ride in such proud state again. This house and everything in it belongs to us. Now, be good enough to leave it. Take your personal trappings and go.'

'And if I refuse, what then?' Rosaleen challenged defiantly.

He bowed mockingly and invited, 'Take a look out of the front door, madam. Knowing the type of woman that you are, I had anticipated some difficulty in removing you from our property, and I've taken measures to deal with it.'

Rosaleen's lips tightened, and she went from the room to do as he had invited.

Standing in the entrance to the short driveway were two blue-coated police constables.

She turned to return to the drawing room, and saw

Thomas Quinn, bleary-eyed, shirt-sleeved and barefoot, coming down the stairs.

'What's up, Rosa? Is someone giving you trouble? I heard the voices.'

For a brief moment she was sorely tempted to unleash the big man onto her unwelcome visitors and have him pitch Samson Montague bodily through the door. Then she sighed, knowing that she could not risk any sort of conflict with the police at this time, and hissed at him, 'Go back upstairs, Thomas. I'll come to you shortly.'

He was reluctant to leave her, fearing that she might be in some sort of danger, but she hissed again, 'Do as I say!'

And with a bad grace he obeyed.

'Well, now that you have seen the constables, madam, I shall allow you two hours to gather your personal belongings and leave this house.'

Montague produced a gold hunter watch and flicked open its casing. 'If you are not gone from here at the end of that time, then I shall order the police to evict you, by force if necessary.'

Once again Rosaleen was forced to battle against the urge to call Thomas Quinn down and have him hurl this arrogant little man bodily through the door. But she was determined not to give Montague the satisfaction of thinking that he had caused her any difficulty or distress by this summary eviction.

She smiled sweetly at him. 'Two hours will be more than sufficient, Mr Montague. Would you care to stand and watch me pack? You can make a list of what I take with me.'

She swung on her heels and went upstairs, calling as

she did so, 'Thomas? Thomas, fetch the trunks down from the attic. We're leaving here.'

As she busied herself in packing away her clothes and belongings Rosaleen thought hard about her next moves. She had a sum of ready money which she had kept for emergencies. It would be sufficient to support herself, her brother and the Quinns for a couple of months – longer if they lived austerely. Her jewellery could be sold also, which should bring enough for a further few months' support.

She smiled mirthlessly. 'It will buy time and enough for me to find another protector.'

Such a prospect was not a pleasant one for her to contemplate: to become the paid whore of yet another rich man, just when she had been confident that she was going to escape back into respectable gentility.

She sent Thomas to bring a hired cab to the house.

When he returned he asked, 'Where are we going, Rosa?'

'We'll join the others in Margate for a while,' she told him.

Samson Montague and his sisters were waiting at the front door to see her leave, expressions of smug triumph on their faces.

Thomas Quinn carried the trunks and portmanteaux out to the waiting cab, and Rosaleen came down the stairs dressed in her widow's weeds, a thick black veil masking her features.

'Just look at her!' the fattest sister exclaimed indignantly. 'Of all the impudence to dress as a respectable widow.'

Rosaleen paused momentarily, lifted her veil and spat full into the sour, pudgy face, then swept out through the door, leaving a shrieking, howling, protesting cacophony behind her.

Her spirits lifted at the sound of the commotion she had caused and she smiled gaily at the dour Thomas Quinn as she took her seat to face him in the cab.

'Let's be off to the seaside then, Thomas, and fill our lungs with fresh air.'

Chapter Twenty-four

'How is he shaping up?' Terence McCulloch stared down from the high window as he asked the question. Keeping his eyes fixed on the traffic-choked, bustling street far below.

'He's a sound man. I've tested him and he's straight and honest,' Joseph Connors asserted. 'I reckon we can trust him.'

'Has he the nerve to do the business?'

Connors shrugged his massive shoulders. 'That's a thing we'll not know until he's put to it, will we, Mr McCulloch? But he's proved well able to handle trouble. I've had a couple of good men try him out, and he's put them on their arses in short order.'

McCulloch turned and ordered, 'Fetch him up here, I'll take a closer look at him.'

It was some minutes before the big man returned, bringing Colum Macrae with him.

When Colum entered the attic room and saw the stranger standing by the window, elation mounted within him. The short, broad figure, the full grey beard, the bald head fitted the description of Terence McCulloch that he had been given by Mr Bush. For two months Colum had worked as Joseph Connors's deputy, here at this lodging house and at other lodging houses in the district. During that time he had known that he was being closely watched, and tested. The fact that McCulloch was here now must mean that Colum had passed those tests, and was on the verge of being invited to join the secret organisation of which McCulloch was known to be a leading figure.

'How do you do, Mr Macrae,' McCulloch greeted pleasantly, and offered his hand.

Colum smiled and shook hands. 'I don't know your name, sir.'

'It's McCulloch, Mr Macrae. My name is Terence McCulloch.' He gestured to the small table and straight-backed wooden chairs that stood in the centre of the room. 'Let's sit down and make ourselves comfortable, Mr Macrae. I'd like to talk with you.'

When they were seated, Joseph Connors remained standing to Colum's rear.

'Mr Connors tells me that you're a straight and honest man, Mr Macrae.'

'I'm glad to hear that he holds a good opinion of me.'

'Oh yes, he holds you in high regard.' McCulloch smiled and nodded, then leaned back in his chair and stroked his beard. 'Mr Connors tells me that you're also a good Irishman.'

'If you mean, am I an Irish patriot, then he is right,' Colum answered levelly.

'Would you be ready to prove that you're a good Irish patriot, Mr Macrae?'

'In what way?' Colum assumed an air of caution.

'By carrying out an action which would help to set Ireland free from the chains that bind her.'

Colum took some time before answering, and then

his reply was ambiguous. 'I would need to be convinced that that action would indeed help to set my country free, Mr McCulloch. And even then I'd have to think hard about it, before I committed myself to action.'

'It would help, I can assure you of that,' McCulloch stated firmly, and then challenged, 'Why do you prevaricate so, Mr Macrae? I thought that you were an Irish patriot. That you were ready and eager to strike a blow against Ireland's oppressors?'

'Go to any taproom in any public house where Irishmen drink, Mr McCulloch, and you'll find Irish patriots who are ready and eager to strike a blow against Ireland's oppressors. The only trouble with them is that when the drink wears off, the courage goes with it, and so no blow is ever struck. I've had my bellyful of blowhard taproom patriots, Mr McCulloch. I'm not one of that breed.'

McCulloch remained silent for some minutes, stroking his beard and appearing to be in deep reflection. Colum too sat in silence, perfectly motionless, waiting patiently.

Finally McCulloch nodded, as if he had reached a satisfactory conclusion.

'Neither are we blowhard taproom patriots, Mr Macrae. Do you know what a Fenian is?'

'Is, or was?' Colum questioned. 'As I remember from my schoolbooks a Fenian was a soldier of the Fianna, the ancient Gaelic war band of the warrior Fiona MacCumhail.'

'Indeed so.' McCulloch appeared delighted at this display of erudition. 'Now, suppose I was to tell you that once again the Fenians are rousing themselves to do battle against the enemies of their land. That in

192

Ireland and in America, and here in England, the warriors of the Fianna are once more organising themselves in readiness to take up arms against the Saxon oppressor. Would you wish to become a part of this organisation, Mr Macrae?'

Again Colum waited for long, long moments before replying quietly, 'If such an organisation is forming and readying itself for the battle, then yes, I would like to become a part of it.'

Terence McCulloch looked directly at Joseph Connors, and raised his eyebrows in silent question.

Connors nodded decisively, and McCulloch fixed his intense stare upon Colum and told him, 'Then you shall become a part of our Fenian Brotherhood, Mr Macrae, but first you must do something to prove your worthiness to join us.'

'What must I do, Mr McCulloch?' Colum asked evenly.

'You must kill a man. A man who is an enemy to our sacred cause.'

Colum pursed his lips, and considered what he had been told. Then he sought confirmation. 'You are telling me that I must murder a man who could be a stranger to me, and who has never done me any wrong. That I must accept your word that he is a danger to the cause of Ireland's liberty?'

McCulloch nodded silently.

Colum folded his arms and bent his head, staring down at the floor for some considerable time.

The other two men exchanged another look, and McCulloch's eyebrows again rose in silent question. Joseph Connors nodded confidently.

Then Colum lifted his head and said quietly, 'I accept

the terms of entry to the Fenian Brotherhood, Mr McCulloch.'

'Very well.' McCulloch rose to his feet. 'Mr Connors will direct you in this matter. I'll say good day, Mr Macrae. I hope that the next time we shall meet, it will be to administer our sacred oath of Brotherhood to you.'

Left alone with Connors, Colum asked him, 'Who is this man that I have to kill?'

'He's a scum!' Connors spat out. 'He should have been knocked on the head on the day he was birthed. We've been looking for him for weeks, and now we've found him.'

'How am I to do the business?'

'However it suits you.'

'Then you'd best give me the details about him, so I can get it done with.'

Connors peered speculatively at Colum, and told him, 'Come to think of it, you being an ex-police Jack, you might have come across this bowsey before. Is the name Billy Gilligan familiar to you?'

The shock of surprise fleeted in Colum's eyes, and the other man caught that flicker and shrewdly surmised, 'You know him, don't you?'

Colum decided to be open about the fact. 'I do indeed. It was through that bastard that I got kicked out of the Force. I've been itching to meet up with him again.'

Connors chuckled knowingly. 'So you won't find it any problem to your conscience to kill the bastard then?'

'It's going to be a pleasure, Joe. A real pleasure,' Colum affirmed grimly, and deep in his inner being realised that he really was anticipating obtaining his revenge on Billy Gilligan with satisfaction. Then he asked, 'Why has he to be killed?'

The huge man paused, as if uncertain about explaining, then shrugged. 'Aghh, it'll do no harm to tell you, now that you're one of us bar the oath-taking, which is a bloody nonsense anyway in my opinion. Oaths don't bind a man to anything unless he has it in his heart to be bound, and if it's in his heart, then he doesn't need to take any bloody oath.'

'About Gilligan?' Colum brought the other man back from his verbal meanderings.

'Yeah, Gilligan. That bowsey. Tell me, was you still in the police when that madman threw a stone at the Prince of Wales in Richmond Park?'

'I was in the process of getting chucked out.'

'Do you know what really happened that day?'

Colum grinned ruefully. 'There were a few rumours floating around. But to tell you the truth, I wasn't really interested. I had troubles enough of my own without bothering about who threw what at the fuckin' Prince.'

'Well I'll tell you what really happened . . .'Connors went on to relate the story of the assassination attempt, as Rosaleen Calatrava had related it to McCulloch, who in his turn had related it to Connors, without divulging the source of his information. McCulloch had kept Rosaleen Calatrava's existence secret to himself.

As Colum listened his excitement heightened and he could hardly believe the good luck that had come to him. His targets were not only being identified for him by Connors, he was even being aided to kill one of them.

'So there were just the three of them in the gang then,

the old one, Sean Gallagher, who was killed; Billy Gilligan; and this fellow who came over from America.'

Connors nodded.

'What's the American's name, and where's he got to now?'

The big man shrugged. 'I don't know.'

'But McCulloch knows?' Colum pressed.

Again the big man shrugged his massive shoulders. 'He's said nothing to me about that. But then, McCulloch is a close-mouthed man. He doesn't even let his right hand know what his left hand is doing.

'I've seen the Yank once meself. He come to one of our meetings at McCulloch's house. To tell you the truth, he didn't sound like a bloody Yank, but more like an Englishman. I thought he was a bloody madman then, and he proved it right enough, didn't he, by trying to kill the Prince. Just between you, me and the gatepost, I said afterwards that we should stay well away from that wee scut. He could bring ruin down on all our heads. And the rest of the lads agreed with me, as well.'

'Perhaps McCulloch will get rid of him?' Colum suggested. 'In fact maybe he's got rid of him already, and by having me kill Billy Gilligan he's just tidying up.'

Connors shook his head. 'I've no idea, and I don't pry into McCulloch's affairs. It's not a healthy thing to do.' His tone took on a warning note. 'And if I was you, my friend, I'd not pry either. Just do as McCulloch says, and ask no questions. That way you'll live a sight longer, and have a happy life.'

Colum realised that he should leave well alone now. He was more than happy to have made the progress he had. The job was turning out to be easier than he had anticipated. One of his targets was already dead; Billy

Gilligan soon would be dead. And this mysterious English-sounding American might already be dead. He smiled inwardly with satisfaction, and asked, 'Where's Gilligan hiding now?'

Connors's black rotted teeth showed in a gleeful grin. 'He's in the same place where he's been for the last three months. That's why we've had trouble finding the bowsey. He's in the Coldbath Fields "steel".'

The 'steel' was the nickname for a House of Correction, a short-term hard-labour prison. The Coldbath Fields 'steel' lay between Clerkenwell and Holborn.

'He got done for hammering some whore. The Peelers wouldn't have bothered lifting him for that if he hadn't threw her through a bloody shop window. It was the shopkeeper who laid the charges against him, and Gilligan got three months for damaging the window,' Connors went on. 'But he's due out this week. Most likely Thursday. Just what that bowsey needed, three months on the "cockchafer". He'll not feel like fuckin' a woman for a good many more months, I'll bet on that.'

Colum could not help but smile grimly. The 'cockchafer' was the convicts' nickname for the dreaded treadmill, and the nickname described one of the unpleasant consequences to prisoners of spending long periods on that apparatus.

'How did you find out where he was?' he asked, but already knew the answer. Terence McCulloch had a wide circle of contacts and informants among the criminal underworld of London.

Connors winked broadly. 'You'd need to be a needle in a haystack to escape Mr McCulloch, Col. And even then, given enough time, McCulloch will find the bloody needle.'

Colum chuckled, and then told the other man, 'I'll be away for a few days from tomorrow morning, Joe. You'll see me again when the job is done.'

Connors nodded. 'Okay. Do you need anything? I've a "barker" you can use.'

Colum shook his head. 'No. A gun is too noisy. I'll do the business quietly.'

'Good luck now.'

Colum's expression was bleak, his eyes cold and ruthless. 'I don't need luck, Joe, and the only good luck that Gilligan can have is to die before he gets out of the "steel".'

Joseph Connors looked into his companion's eyes and, hardened and fearless ruffian though he was, he experienced a sudden frisson of unease at this abrupt metamorphosis in the normally affable and inoffensive man that he had come to know and like during these past weeks. That man had suddenly disappeared, and had been replaced by a stranger – a murderous stranger.

God help you, Gilligan, when this one gets ahold of you, he thought. I'm glad it's not me he's after.

Chapter Twenty-five

From six o'clock each morning, except for the Sabbath day, a small crowd of men, women and children would gather opposite the great iron-studded main gates of the Coldbath Fields House of Correction. The crowd was of all types and ages, ranging from old to babes in arms, well-dressed to ragged, respectable to disreputable.

From half past six to seven the picket gate set into the main gate would open at intervals to allow the released prisoners to step out into freedom and be greeted by those who waited for them.

It was drizzling with rain, and the breeze was chill when Colum arrived at Coldbath Fields just after six o'clock. In his rough clothes, and with his billycock hat pulled low on his forehead, he attracted no attention. To those who might notice him he appeared to be just another labouring man. He took up his station some distance from the crowd, lounging with his back to the wall, half hidden from direct view by a jutting pillar of brick. It was the third morning he had come here to take up his vigil, and today he was rewarded by sighting the face he sought. Emma Carr was in the crowd opposite the gates. She looked bedraggled, her clothing threadbare and soiled, and even at this distance Colum could see the livid streaks of scarring that disfigured and made ugly her once-delicate features. His lips twisted angrily as he surmised that the scars were the result of her brutal lover's last assault on her, when he had hurled her through the shop window.

'And yet here you are again, you stupid woman, coming back to the man who treats you worse than he would treat a dog.'

Colum had long since ceased to marvel at the capacity, the willingness even, of certain women to endure long years of savage abuse from their men. But his initial sympathies for those women had gradually become eroded as he had witnessed them refusing to leave their brutal abusers despite all entreaties and offers of help.

The picket gate opened and a young man dressed in the flash 'slang' fashion favoured by successful thieves, his long 'Newgate Knocker' side whiskers curling low down on his cheeks, stepped through it. A garishly dressed young girl in the crowd whooped joyfully and ran to him, and they hugged and kissed and then swaggered away arm in arm. At frequent intervals the picket gate opened and closed and more men filed out, some with brash bravado, others with a hangdog, furtive air, and were met or not met as the case might be. But time passed and Billy Gilligan did not appear.

Colum frowned as the nearby church clock chimed the quarter and then the hour of seven o'clock, and he wondered why Gilligan had not been released. The crowd had by now virtually all dispersed, but still Emma Carr waited, and then the picket gate opened once more and Billy Gilligan stepped through it. Colum studied his target closely. Gilligan was well dressed; frock coated and top hatted, still swarthily handsome, although pallid from his confinement.

'Billy!' Emma Carr hurried to her lover, her scarred face alight with happiness. 'Are you all right, darlint? Are you all right? Oh it's good to see you. It's so good. I've missed you so much.'

She reached out for him. Gilligan stared down at her contemptuously, and roughly struck aside her seeking hands, demanding curtly, 'Have you got us a place?'

'Yes, darlint,' she told him. 'It's all ready for you.'

'Have you got any push? I need a drink.'

She rummaged in her skirts to produce some coins, which he snatched from her, complaining surlily, 'Is this all you've got? It won't buy enough mecks to get the taste of this hole out of me mouth.'

'I've got some drink in the room for you, Billy,' she assured anxiously. 'And plenty of grub as well.'

'Where's the room?'

'It's in Shoreditch, in one of the courts off Pitfield Street.' She peered anxiously up into his features. 'It's all right there for you, ain't it, darlint? Only you said I was to get a place where you weren't known.'

He nodded grudgingly. 'Right then, let's go.'

Colum followed discreetly behind the couple as they walked side by side eastwards.

At the door of a public house Gilligan halted and snarled at Emma, 'You wait here for me.'

'Don't you want me to come inside for a drink with you, Billy?' she asked in surprise.

He pointed at the livid scars on her face, and sneered cruelly, 'That fuckin' mess 'ud put any man off his drink. I'll need a few gins inside me before I can stand having you close by.'

Her sallowed skin flushed red, and she retorted with a flash of spirit, 'It's you who made my face what it is.'

'Don't take that tone with me,' he growled threateningly. 'Whatever I give you, you deserved it.'

'Why? I'd done nothing wrong. You'd no call to serve me so bad.'

'Shut your mouth,' he ordered, 'and wait here.'

He pushed through the door into the smoky noise beyond, leaving her standing miserably in the drizzling rain. She buried her face in her hands and slumped against the wall, her shoulders heaving with her bitter sobs.

Colum patiently watched and waited.

It was more than an hour before Gilligan reappeared and the couple moved on eastwards once again. The same scene was repeated several more times during their journey, Gilligan going into a pub alone, Emma waiting outside for him, and it took several hours to traverse the mile and a half between Coldbath Fields and Shoreditch.

By the time they reached the court where Emma had her room, Gilligan was drunk and staggering.

Colum had spent the time steeling himself for what was to come. To kill a man in cold blood was completely alien to his nature, but as he saw how Gilligan was treating Emma Carr, and looked at the livid disfigurations on her features, Colum's resolution hardened.

Now he was eager to get it done and over with. He decided that it would be a matter of seeing the opportunity and taking it. His fingers touched the handle of the thin-bladed sheath knife in his pocket.

'If possible I'll take him from behind. One upward thrust between his ribs and into his heart will do it.'

Self-revulsion momentarily swept over him. 'Is this what I've become? A coward who strikes from behind.'

He deliberately forced himself to picture the faces of his beloved daughters, and to think of what might happen to them should he fail on this assignment. It's the life of a piece of worthless scum like Billy Gilligan against their future wellbeing, he told himself. I'll do what I must.

Gilligan and Emma Carr disappeared from his view down a long covered entryway, and he walked slowly past it, peeping surreptitiously along its darkened length. He could see shadowy figures moving in its gloom, and realised that there were people sheltering within it from the rain, which had now become heavier.

He tugged his hat lower to hide his features and with the high collar of his coat turned up he likewise pushed into the fetid, dank shelter.

The acrid stench of filthy human bodies filled his nostrils, mingling with the stink of excrement, urine and rotting rubbish.

He was aware that feral eyes, already accustomed to the gloom, were studying him, and he readied himself for possible attack. His own eyes rapidly adjusted and he was able to distinguish the bearded features that thrust close to his own.

'Give us a couple o'·coppers, mate. I ain't had a bite to ate all day,' the vagrant demanded aggressively, and his foul breath gusted into Colum's nostrils.

Colum could now see other shadowed figures moving towards him from further along the covered entryway, and experience told him that he must immediately establish his dominance over the situation if he was to pass through in pursuit of his quarry.

He slipped his knife from its sheath, then shot his free hand out and grasped the vagrant's throat in a choking grip. Giving vent to a maniacal laugh, he held the knife blade inches from the other man's eyes. 'I was about to ask you the same thing, Chavey.' Again he laughed like a madman. 'Give us a couple o' coppers mate, I ain't had a bite to ate all day.'

There was an instant shuffling of retreating feet, and he heard a man shout, 'Gerrout from here, he's a fuckin' loony!'

Colum's grip tightened harder on the vagrant's throat. The man's mouth gaped and he emitted choked, squealing wheezes as he fought to draw breath.

Colum laughed into his bulging eyes. 'You're no fuckin' use to me, you fuckin' pauper. You mean, tight-arsed bastard. You ain't got a penny piece to bless yourself with, have you. Gerrout on it.'

He bodily heaved the man away, kicking his legs from under him, and the vagrant fell heavily to the filthy ground, his hands scrabbling at his injured throat, dragging in air with a strangled, harsh rasping.

Colum laughed again and stalked on along the entry, deeper into the gloom, calling out in a high-pitched voice, 'Who's got a copper to spare me? Who's got a penny for the Guy? Who's got a penny for the Guy?'

And the denizens of the entryway scrambled from his path and let him pass freely.

The entry debouched into a long, narrow, curving alleyway lined with high-walled tenement blocks that swarmed with noisy life.

Colum replaced his knife in its sheath before leaving the covered entry and then went on. Some curious eyes noted him, but he was not accosted or challenged as he walked the full length of the alley, and found that it was a cul-de-sac with no other entry to the outer world other than the one he had come through.

His next task was to find the room where Emma Carr lived. He could not risk asking openly but he knew that in the enclosed little worlds of the courts, gossip was constantly exchanged about the inhabitants, and the best place to hear gossip was in the social gathering places. He had noticed two drinking dens on the ground floors of the tenements he had passed, and now he entered the nearest of the pair.

The noise hushed at his entrance, and the rough-looking men and slatternly women who were drinking there regarded him closely. But he looked too big and tough to be an easy prey, and too shabbily dressed to be worth cultivating for his wealth, so after a few moments the talk and laughter and disputes resumed and he was ignored. He ordered a tumbler of gin from the server behind the makeshift counter, took his drink and went to sit on one of the rough benches with which the single room was furnished. From here he listened to the talk of his fellow customers.

A young woman with a mass of frizzled hair and sporting a badly swollen black eye came into the den, and was greeted by her friends with raucous laughter and gibes.

'That'll larn you to pick on a little 'un!'

'One punch and the war was over!'

'Have you only just come round, Aggie?'

The newcomer swore horribly, and vowed, 'You mark what I say, I'll have that scar-faced little bleeder afore she's much older.'

Colum's attention was caught by the mention of scars.

'Not now you won't, Aggie. Her's just fetched a bloke home with her. And he looks a bit tasty as well.'

'I don't give a bugger,' Aggie affirmed vehemently. 'She can fetch the bloody Brigade o' Guards home with her, but it won't stop me paying her out for this.'

She pointed at her damaged eye, and went on aggrievedly, 'I wouldn't have cared if she'd hit me fair and square, but she copped me when I wasn't looking.'

A chorus of jeers greeted this statement.

'Who're you on about?' a man questioned.

'That little wench wi' the scarred face. Her who lives on the third landing back at old Kenly's place.'

'What happened wi' her and Aggie then?' the man sought to know.

'They had a dust-up the other night. And the little wench went fuckin' mad. She can fight like Tom Cribb, I'll tell you, for all her's so small. She didn't half give Aggie a pasting.'

'What's her name?'

'I dunno.'

'Is she on the game?'

'If her is it must be wi' the bloody lamps not lit. Her face 'ud put a man off his shaggin'. He 'udden't be able to keep a hard on looking at it.'

There was an outburst of laughter as another man put in, 'Don't talk daft. You don't look at the mantelpiece when you'm poking the fire, does you? I'd crawl over my old woman to get to the little wench any time, never mind her bloody face being scarred, her cunny's still in the right place, ain't it?'

'Well, you won't be getting into her cunny tonight, Tommy. Not now she's brought a bloke back with her.'

206

Colum had heard sufficient to convince him that he had found where his target was located. It would be a simple matter to find old Kenly's tenement, and the room at the back on the third floor. He would wait until night fell, and then he would make his strike. He rose and went to the counter and ordered another gin, then returned to his seat and sat sipping the fiery spirit, waiting for the hours to pass.

'You're hurtin' me, darlint! You're hurtin'! Don't be so rough. Please . . .' Emma Carr moaned in pain as her lover's hands cruelly mauled her naked flesh.

He enjoyed her pleas, and twisted her small breasts and bit savagely on her nipples until she squealed in agony, then entered her, pounding violently down upon her frailness, grunting and panting obscenities, until orgasm shuddered through him and his sexual energies were spent.

Almost instantly he rolled off her and brutally shoved her away. 'Gerron out of it and give me room to lie,' he ordered, and silently she rose from the bed and began to dress, wincing with the pain that throbbed in her abused breasts.

He turned on his side and was soon snoring loudly. When she heard him, Emma Carr's demeanour changed. Her eyes glittered like those of a deranged woman, and she stood staring down at the sleeping man, and began to whisper to him, the words tumbling in rapid hisses from her lips.

'You never even bothered to ask about my babby, did you, you rotten bastard. You wasn't interested enough to even ask me where she was. All you could think about was getting drunk and shagging me. Getting drunk and hurting me, that's all you was interested in doing, wasn't it? You never said a single word about my babby. About my darlint little daughter. Well, I'll tell you about her, shall I, you bad, rotten bastard. When you chucked me into that window, and hurt me so bad that I had to be took to the hospital, they took my babby into the foundlings' asylum, and when I come out from the hospital and went to get her again, they told me that she was dead and buried.

'Did you hear that, Billy Gilligan? They told me that my babby was dead and in her grave. The poor little soul had died while I was in that bloody hospital, not able to care for her because I was near to death meself. That's what killed my babby. She died because I wasn't there to care for her. Because you'd put me into the hospital, you rotten bastard. My darlint babby is dead because of you. You killed her. You murdered her. And now I'm going to pay you out for murdering my poor babby. You dirty, evil bastard. That's why I've brung you back here. Just to pay you out for what you did to my poor, helpless babby.'

The sleeping man snorted and swallowed hard then rolled onto his back, his jaw hanging slack, his mouth wide open.

Emma Carr moved backwards, keeping her glittering, deranged stare fixed on the snoring man.

'Just stay like that,' she hissed. 'Just stay like that for a minute.'

From the bottom of the wall cupboard she lifted a wide-mouthed earthenware jug covered with a thick cloth. Smiling, she advanced towards the bed, holding the jug between her hands.

'Here's another little drink for you, darlint.' She emitted a high-pitched giggle, flicked away the cloth covering, and carefully poured the jug's contents onto Gilligan's face and into his gaping mouth. The sulphuric acid hissed and smoked as it bit into the flesh, and Gilligan's face blistered and bubbled.

He vented a terrible scream and jerked upright, arms flailing. Emma Carr's eyes bulged in her chalk-white, livid-scarred face as she laughed with an insane joy, and the joyous pealing laughter mingled with the terrible screams in an unholy chorus.

Colum was still sitting in the drinking den when a woman poked her frowsty head through the doorway and shouted, 'Come and see this. There's bleedin' murder going on at old Kenly's.'

Her excited words caused an immediate exodus, and Colum joined in the general rush through the door and along the alleyway.

A clamorous crowd was seething around the door of the tenement and as Colum pushed through he saw two men emerge, dragging the maniacally laughing Emma Carr by her arms.

'She's off her head. She's gone bloody loony.'

They told eager questioners, 'She's done for her bloke. Chucked bloody vitriol all over him; it's nigh on ate his bloody face away.'

'Is he dead?'

'Not yet, more pity for the poor bastard! But he'll not last long. It's got down his throat and everywhere. It's ate his eyes out. The poor bastard is suffering terrible. But he'll not last long.'

'Get the evil cow!' The black-eyed Aggie, drunk and screaming, hurled herself at the laughing Emma Carr, her fingers crooked to rend and tear. But the men who were clustered around Emma Carr buffeted the would-be attacker back.

'Leave her be, she's bloody loony. She'll have to be put in the madhouse, the poor little cow don't know what she's done.'

They dragged Emma Carr along the alley, and then another group of men came out of the tenement carrying a blanket on which the naked body of Billy Gilligan writhed.

Colum saw the black-charred, red-streaked, unrecognisable head of the man in the blanket and knew that he must confirm the identity. He pushed through the crowd, disregarding the curses of protest his rough passage evoked, and bent over the naked body, the sickening stench of burned flesh assailing him. He lifted the man's arm and turned it until he could see the crude tattoo on the inner biceps. It depicted an Irish harp with the initials 'W.G.' intertwined above it. Colum had seen that particular tattoo before. He knew now for certain that it was Billy Gilligan who was dying in that blanket. He let the arm fall and merged back into the crowd as it followed the dying man through the long entryway and out onto the main thoroughfare. Once there Colum slipped away.

As he walked through the murky streets back towards the lodging house in Westminster, he marvelled at what had happened. The bitter irony of the situation evoked a sardonic humour in him.

I'm getting paid to kill these buggers, and the work is being done for me. Two down and one to go, and I've yet to lift my hand against any of them.

All I need to do now is to find Dermot Calatrava, and

then it will be over with, and I can go home to my kids. But the way my luck is running, I wouldn't be at all surprised to find out that McCulloch has already done for Calatrava.

Chapter Twenty-six

Terence McCulloch had anticipated this meeting with Rosaleen Calatrava with some relish. He greeted her at the front door of his house and smilingly told her, 'I have good news for you, Miss Calatrava.'

He led her into his shabbily furnished parlour and once she was seated announced, 'Your brother is safe now, Miss Calatrava. Billy Gilligan is dead, and his unfortunate woman in a mental asylum.'

He went on to tell her how Gilligan had met his death, but emphasised that his own men had been poised to kill Gilligan.

Rosaleen felt concern for the tragic Emma Carr, but her overwhelming emotion was relief that her beloved brother was out of danger.

'Thank God for that. I'm very grateful to you, Mr McCulloch. We are in your debt. Poor Emma was her own biggest enemy.'

'How is your brother's state of health?'

'Much improved. But I fear that his wound has left him somewhat lamed and he tires quickly.'

'Will you return to London now that there is no danger for your brother?'

She hesitated before replying, 'I haven't sufficient funds at present to set up house in London.'

He nodded understandingly. 'Of course. The untimely

death of Solomon Montague must have adversely affected your financial situation.'

'It did,' she admitted frankly.

He smiled at her. 'Forgive me for speaking bluntly, Miss Calatrava. But with your beauty and attainments it would be easy for you to find another protector. Is that your intention?'

She returned his smile, but her eyes were cold. 'I am giving the matter some thought. But to speak bluntly, Mr McCulloch, I do not really enjoy being the paid whore of rich old men. I was hoping that you could perhaps suggest some alternative way in which I could earn my keep.'

He nodded. 'I've been considering how best we might work together to further our cause, Miss Calatrava, and I have a project in mind.' He paused and grimaced ruefully. 'But that project would entail you using your charms to ensnare a man.'

'Why not speak plain, Mr McCulloch,' she told him evenly. 'When you say "using my charms", you really mean playing the whore, do you not?'

His expression hardened. 'There are many different types of weapons, Miss Calatrava. Your looks and your body and your brain are weapons which can be utilised to gain objectives. To play the whore in your nation's service is as praiseworthy as to take up the pike and storm an enemy's barricades.' He smiled bleakly. 'And in many instances is a much more effective way of gaining victory.'

'Tell me what it is you have in mind,' she demanded.

'Edward Firthallan, the Earl of Kendrick.' He noted the instant recognition in her expression, and nodded. 'I see that you know of that gentleman.'

213

Her voice throbbed with contempt. 'He's nothing but a filthy gombeen man. He's been responsible for the ruin of hundreds of our people during the Famine, and the deaths of many can be laid at his door.'

'Just so,' McCulloch agreed. 'And it's high time that he was made to pay the price for it.'

'You want him dead?' she asked.

'No, I want him compromised. He is of more use to us alive. I want to have a hold over him. You know that he's married to Lord Macarry's daughter, don't you? Firthallan has no money of his own, his father-in-law holds the purse strings, and if his wife was to become alienated from him, then he'd be a ruined man. Macarry only tolerates him for the sake of his daughter.'

Rosaleen's agile mind had already divined McCulloch's intentions. Not for the first time doubts as to his motivations and personal probity were aroused in her.

'You want me to become Firthallan's mistress, don't you? And then you can blackmail him for your own ends.'

He frowned. 'Not for my own ends. I will blackmail him for the furtherance of our cause.'

She frowned back. 'There's some might say that you would be dishonouring our cause by using such methods.'

'Nonsense,' he blustered. 'The end justifies the means.'

'How will having a hold over him further our cause, Mr McCulloch?'

His voice became hard and authoritative. 'Let me remind you that I command this organisation, Miss Calatrava. I do not explain or discuss unless I wish to do so. Let me remind you also that without my aid your brother would still be in peril from Billy Gilligan.' He paused for a moment, then added meaningly, 'I act as your brother's shield. The Authorities would give a great deal to know the identity of the man who tried to assassinate the Prince of Wales, and who was responsible for the murder of Major Henry Winstanley.'

'It was Gilligan who killed Winstanley,' Rosaleen protested.

'In the eyes of the law your brother is equally culpable. Keep that always in the forefront of your mind.'

The sudden awareness of how completely she had placed her brother's and her own safety into this man's hands struck sickeningly through Rosaleen. Dear God, how could I have been so damned stupid?

'I shall take a house for you here in London, and supply your financial needs.' McCulloch was talking as if the matter was decided. 'Edward Firthallan has an eye for a pretty woman, and I shall make sure that you come to his attention. As soon as you have taken him into your bed, then I shall decide the best way in which to compromise him.'

Rosaleen could not help but challenge, 'And if I do not choose to take Firthallan into my bed, Mr McCulloch, what then?'

'Then your brother will very soon find himself dangling at the end of a rope, Miss Calatrava. Flight will not save him. The arm of the British Government is a long one, and no country would give him sanctuary.'

'America would,' she declared with a confidence she was far from feeling.

'You are talking nonsense,' he scoffed contemptuously. 'America would not risk trouble with England just for the sake of a single rebel Irishman.'

She made no reply, knowing that any further argument would be futile.

'Return here in a week's time, Miss Calatrava,' he instructed. 'I shall have everything arranged for you by then.'

She nodded in silent acquiescence, and he showed her to the door, then stood watching her walk away, a contemptuous smile hovering on his lips.

Rosaleen was furious with herself, and a fierce hatred for McCulloch was burgeoning in her mind.

I should have seen this coming, she told herself over and over again. I should have known that the bastard would try and use me in this way. That he'd force me to prostitute myself for him. He claims to act as my friend, but in reality he's my enemy.

Then a colder logic intervened. Don't waste your energies ranting and raving, girl. Of course McCulloch is going to use you in this way. After all, that's what you are, isn't it, a common whore. That's what all men see you as. And even if you'd married Old Solomon, men would still have regarded you as a whore.

A cooler resolve assumed dominance.

At present I've no choice in the matter but to go along with McCulloch's plans for me. I've Dermot to think about, haven't I?

Although she had told McCulloch that her brother was recovering his health, the real fact was that while his body was healing, his mental state was causing her increasing concern. He was drinking very heavily, and in drink his temper was becoming increasingly volatile and violent. She was beginning to fear that his mind was unstable, and that there were times when madness hovered dangerously near.

All right, McCulloch, she decided grimly. I'll do what you want. I'll get Firthallan into my bed. But I'll be watching for any chance I have to turn the situation to my own advantage. And when I get that chance, then you'd best look to yourself, because I'll hang you high.

She turned her thoughts towards Edward Firthallan, Earl of Kendrick. The Firthallan family had been a part of the Anglo-Irish ascendancy for centuries, and had once been a power in the land. But profligacy and ill-judged financial speculations had lost them their lands and wealth, and it was only the marriage of Edward Firthallan to the daughter of the mighty Lord Macarry that had saved the Firthallan dynasty.

Edward Firthallan had gained himself a reputation for ruthless cruelty during the terrible years of the Famine, by his heartless treatment of his father-in-law's tenantry on the vast Macarry estates in the west of Ireland, and there were many in high society who hated and despised him for what he had done. But because of his father-in-law's wealth he could still exercise some considerable political influence in the corridors of Government.

Despite her feelings about McCulloch, Rosaleen was forced to admit that the man was shrewd and far-seeing. If he could obtain a hold over Firthallan, then there were many advantages to be gained for the cause of Ireland's freedom.

Her deeply engrained pragmatism surfaced, and she smiled with a bitter resignation. 'I just hope that Firthallan isn't too physically repulsive for me to stomach, and that he takes a bath occasionally . . .'

Chapter Twenty-seven

The great circular reading room of the British Museum, its cast-iron shelves lined with a million books towering up to the base of the high-domed roof, evoked a feeling of awed amazement in Rosaleen Calatrava when she entered, accompanied by Terence McCulloch. She had never seen so many books in her life.

The couple stood for a few moments looking across the long straight rows of contiguous reading desks where men and women sat silently poring over manuscripts and volumes.

McCulloch's eyes glinted with satisfaction, and he touched Rosaleen's elbow and whispered in her ear. 'See there, at the end of the fourth row. That's your man.'

Rosaleen stared with interest at the seated man. Edward Firthallan was middle-aged, with a shock of thick grey hair, and clean-shaven. His features were pale and thin and with his pince-nez perched on the end of his long nose, he resembled a timid pedant rather than the savage, ruthless destroyer his reputation had led her to envisage.

McCulloch slipped an embossed card and a piece of notepaper into her hand. 'You know what to do?'

She nodded and, satisfied, he turned and left her.

She approached a small square desk set apart from the rest, where a small, bespectacled librarian was busily writing in a ledger, his quill pen scratching across the page.

He looked up and frowned interrogatively at her, and she handed him the card and the slip of paper on which some book titles had been written.

He peered at the card, nodded and handed it back to her, then gestured with his hand towards the reading desks, and mouthed, 'Where?'

She indicated the vacant seats by Edward Firthallan, and the librarian nodded.

Rosaleen went to the seats and took the one next to Firthallan. He glanced sideways at her, and then turned his head to look fully into her face.

She placed her small, rolled parasol on the side of her desk, then folded her hands on her lap and sat demurely, head bowed, well aware that at frequent intervals he was stealing admiring looks at her.

The librarian brought her the books she had requested, and she began to study them. After some time she decided to make her next move. With her elbow she pushed one of her books so that it fell on the floor between them.

Instantly Firthallan bent to pick it up, reading its title, and then presenting it to her with a smile. 'We share a common interest in the Ancient Greeks, I see, ma'am,' he whispered.

'Do we, sir?' she whispered in return, and smiled brilliantly at him as she took back the fallen book.

During the next hour she sensed his gaze upon her many times, and occasionally she would peep at him and allow her eyes to meet his, so that he began to believe that she was perhaps as taken with him as he was with her.

When she judged the time was right, she rose and began to gather her books together, feigning difficulty in handling both them and her parasol.

'Please, ma'am, allow me to help you,' he whispered, and when she frowned slightly in demurral he insisted, and finally she accepted with a grateful smile.

Once the librarian had received her books, she smiled once more at Firthallan and began to walk slowly towards the entrance doors.

She was well aware that he hurried to return his own books and to follow her, and once outside the main building she halted and stood on the pavement, looking about her and frowning as if something was troubling her.

'Forgive me, ma'am, I've no wish to intrude upon you, but are you in some sort of difficulty?'

When she faced him, he lifted his top hat and bowed. 'Allow me to introduce myself, ma'am. My name is Edward Firthallan.'

'Sir,' she acknowledged.

'Might I have the honour of knowing your name, ma'am?'

She paused as if uncertain, and he bowed again. 'I do assure you, ma'am, I mean you no disrespect in approaching you in this manner and without formal introduction. Only you do appear as if something is troubling you, and I only wish to be of service to you, if you will be so kind as to permit me that honour.'

After a further pause, she told him, 'My name is Farquar, sir. Mrs Farquar.' She looked about her, and then clucked her tongue in annoyance. 'It's my carriage, sir. I gave orders that I was to be met here at this hour and, as you can see, it has not come.'

'Then please permit me to place my carriage at your disposal, Mrs Farquar.' He lifted his arm, and from the row of parked vehicles further along the roadway an opulent four-horsed carriage with a liveried coachman and two liveried footmen instantly started towards him.

She shook her head, and refused sharply. 'Oh no, sir, I could not. It would not be proper. We are strangers, sir.'

'You misunderstand me, Mrs Farquar,' he informed her gravely. 'I do not propose that we should share the carriage. I shall remain here to await its return while you journey to your destination. Please, Mrs Farquar, please do permit me to render you this small service.'

She frowned, then smiled. 'Well, I must admit time is pressing upon me, and I do have an engagement to fulfil. Many thanks, sir, I accept your kind offer. But I can't allow you to remain here while I make use of your carriage. I am confident that I shall be perfectly safe in sharing your carriage with you.'

As they travelled towards the house in Holloway that McCulloch had provided for her they talked animatedly together. She let slip that she was the widow of a rich merchant, and he admitted to being the Earl of Kendrick. To her own great surprise she found that she was at ease in his company, and she was forced to remind herself continually that this charming and erudite new companion was the same man who had turned starving, diseased people out of their wretched homesteads to die by the roadside.

Before she left the carriage he had elicited from her the fact that she would be at the Reading Room on the following afternoon. And they parted with the

221

unspoken, smiling understanding that they would be meeting again.

'Well? Have you hooked our fish?' McCulloch was waiting for her inside the house.

She nodded with absolute assurance.

'Good girl,' he congratulated.

'Listen, Mr McCulloch, I want to bring my brother to live with me here.'

He shook his head. 'That wouldn't be a good thing. Not just now, at any rate. It's better he stays in Margate for the time being.'

'But I need him here with me,' she insisted.

'You can have him here when I say so,' he told her sharply. 'Now let's hear no more about it.'

Sullenly she accepted defeat, but promised McCulloch silently, You might have it all your own way now, but my turn will come.

After McCulloch had left she lit a cheroot and paced up and down, her thoughts troubled and her mood apprehensive.

When she had told Dermot that she was returning to London, and that he must remain in Margate, he had thrown a violent tantrum, ranting and raving, smashing ornaments and furniture, and verbally abusing her. Fearful of what might happen while she was away from him, she had left both of the Quinns down in Margate to care for him, and had returned to London alone, staying in this house alone also since her return.

Theresa Quinn had come up to see her on a couple of occasions to report on Dermot's condition, and those reports had not been reassuring. Dermot was daily becoming more volatile and violent, his drinking now

222

virtually out of control, and Theresa Quinn had hinted that it might be best to have him placed in a more secure situation, where he could not come and go as he pleased. It was a week since the woman's last visit, and Rosaleen was becoming increasingly anxious with each succeeding day. She was desperate for news, and spent the empty hours listening for the knock on the door which would signal Theresa's arrival.

At this moment she was sorely tempted to take the steamer and go to Margate herself, but the thought of McCulloch's reaction should she do so held her back. She was not physically afraid of the man, but she was terrified of provoking him in case he should carry out his threat to inform on Dermot. She had seen enough of McCulloch by now to realise that he wielded far more power than anyone could suppose; he had many contacts and much influence. She was coming to believe that he enjoyed the protection of powerful figures in high circles, and that this rendered him secure against most threats.

But if he should ever harm my Dermot, then all his protection won't save him, she vowed passionately, because I'll kill him myself, no matter who might try to prevent me.

She went to bed but, tormented by a sense of foreboding, it was several hours before she drifted into uneasy sleep.

Gravel rattling against her window roused her late the next morning, and when she peered out she exclaimed in shocked surprise. Her brother was standing below.

She hurried downstairs to let him in, and questioned anxiously, 'What are you doing here?'

His thin face was deathly pale, and his eyes deep sunk.

Fear shivered through her. 'For the love of God, Dermot, has something happened? Where are the Quinns?'

'Still stinking in their bed, I shouldn't wonder. That's all they're good for.'

'What's happened?' she demanded again, and he smiled savagely.

'It's what's going to happen that matters, Rosa.'

'For God's sake, tell me what's going on!' she urged frantically.

'I'm sick and tired of doing nothing. It's time to strike again.'

She shook her head. 'You're not well enough to think about doing that. You must wait until you're completely recovered.'

'I can walk well enough, see.' He paced up and down the room with rapid, limping steps. 'And I'm getting stronger by the day, Rosa.'

'But we've nothing planned,' she protested.

'You may have nothing planned, but I have.' His eyes glittered fanatically. 'I've done nothing else but plan while I've been recovering from this damned wound. And I've a plan that will put the fear of God into thousands.'

He reached out and briefly grasped her hands in his, squeezing her fingers painfully hard in his excitement.

'That fellow Guy Fawkes had the right idea when he tried to blow up the Parliament. We could put the fear of God into the English by making explosions. By blowing up things.'

'Blow up things?' Rosaleen's fears for her brother

fuelled her anger, causing her to react furiously. 'Have you really gone out of your head, you bloody idiot? Do you really think that you're going to be able to run around carrying barrels of gunpowder and setting fuses to them? You damned stupid fool!'

'Don't be so quick to call me a fool, Rosa,' Dermot admonished grimly. 'Here, take a look at this.'

He proffered a sheet of notepaper and she snatched it from him.

It was a list of names and addresses in different parts of the country. She shrugged in bafflement.

'What are these?'

'They're factories and mills, Rosa,' he told her, and with his finger pointed to a particular address. 'See this one in Birmingham. That's Phillips and Pursalls.'

'So?' she queried.

'Phillips and Pursalls make percussion caps, Rosa.'

Understanding dawned, and she gasped in shock. 'Oh, dear God.'

Dermot nodded. 'You have it now, don't you, Rosa? You can see what I intend. Every name on this list is either a gun powder mill or a factory making armaments which holds stores of powder and explosive materials. All that I'll need to use to blow them up is a lighted match.'

Rosaleen's imagination pictured the carnage that massive explosions could create, and horror invaded her. 'Hundreds of ordinary, innocent people could be killed and maimed,' she muttered. 'That's never been my intention. My war is against the British ruling classes; the rich and the powerful, not the poor and powerless.'

Dermot's expression was implacable. 'There's always

225

a sight more poor than rich who get killed in a war, Rosa. I'm only doing what has to be done. God knows we haven't gained any victories for the cause up to now, have we? At least I'm going to be letting these English bastards know that we're still fighting them.'

'This is more like murdering than fighting,' Rosaleen rejoined.

Her brother looked stonily at her troubled face. 'Have you forgotten our own kin that were murdered, Rosa? Have you forgotten how it felt to carry your own murdered baby at your breast? They're crying from the grave for vengeance. And we'll be cursed through eternity if we fail them.'

His harsh words once again resurrected the terrible memories in Rosaleen's mind and, slowly and inexorably, the deeply engrained hatreds once more asserted their dominance. The sudden attack of conscience that had assailed her weakened and receded. If the battle demanded the lives of the poor and powerless, then so be it. She would answer to God for her actions when death claimed her, and until then she would do whatever the cause asked of her.

'We'll have to take care, Dermot.'

'Don't we always have to take care,' he scoffed. 'Tell me something that I don't know.'

She was fighting an inner battle with herself. She wanted to tell Dermot how she had called on Terence McCulloch for help in disposing of Gilligan, and that by doing so she had placed them both in his power. But she was afraid of her brother's reaction when he learned of this unpalatable fact. She was equally afraid of his reaction when he found out that McCulloch was forcing her to play the whore with Edward Firthallan.

Dermot sensed her inner battle, and he questioned anxiously, 'What is it, sweetheart? There's something that you're holding back from me, isn't there?'

She sighed heavily, then hardened herself, and slowly told him all that had occurred while he had been convalescing in Margate.

To her surprise he listened without interruption, and when she was finished he stayed silent for long minutes, his face set hard.

'Well?' she felt driven to ask at last.

'It seems as though McCulloch holds the whip hand over us,' he muttered. 'He leaves me no choice, does he? I'll have to kill him.'

'No!' she told him vehemently.

'Why not? It will only take one bullet.' He appeared very calm, his tone one of quiet reasonableness, and Rosa experienced a frisson of uneasy dread. There was an emanation radiating from her brother which she could sense clearly; an emanation which she feared betokened madness.

'I don't want you to go anywhere near McCulloch,' she told him firmly. 'Be ruled by me in this. I want him dead as much as you do, but think for a moment, will you, Dermot. McCulloch hasn't survived by being a fool. I'm sure that there are many such as us who want him dead. I'm equally sure that a good number have tried to kill him before now. He must have known when he told me that he'd inform on you that I would tell you about it. It's almost as if he were baiting a trap for you, Dermot, which he is hoping you will fall into. He's hoping that you'll take the bait, and try to kill him in order to silence him. Just think about it, will you. Think! Why should he risk you killing him unless he is

227

fully prepared and guarded against it? Think, honey! Think!'

She saw her words take effect. Dermot was thinking hard.

After a time he asked, 'Then what shall we do, Rosa?'

'We'll play his game. I shall pretend that you're still ill in Margate, and I'll go along with his plan for Edward Firthallan. In the meantime, you can put your new plan into operation, while I shall be watching for the opportunity to turn the tables on McCulloch.'

Dermot shook his head. 'I'm not happy with this, Rosa.'

'Happy or not, you will do as I say,' she insisted forcibly. 'You can use Thomas Quinn to help you cause these explosions, but let Theresa stay in the rooms at Margate. Then if McCulloch sends someone to check on your whereabouts she can tell the necessary stories.'

It was her turn to grip his hands between her own and squeeze hard in emphasis. 'You must do as I say in this matter, Dermot. You must! It's the only way!'

Reluctantly he acquiesced.

Chapter Twenty-eight

Christmas had come and gone and the new year of 1860 was well advanced. For Colum Macrae the past months had been a time of increasing frustration, and now as he waited in the rear room of Abraham Vincent's pawnshop he toyed with the idea of requesting that he be relieved of his present assignment.

The door opened and the sparse figure of Mr Bush entered the room carrying a leather document case in his hand. The newcomer wasted no time in irrelevant courtesies.

'We are concerned about your lack of progress, Macrae,' he stated curtly. 'We expected that you would have successfully completed your assigned task some time ago. What is the problem? Why the delay?'

Colum accepted the criticism without resentment. He could understand his employers' attitude towards his apparent failure.

'Frankly, Mr Bush, although I have tried to gain the full trust and confidence of McCulloch, he has not seen fit to confide all his secrets to me. I am no nearer identifying the third member of the group who attacked the Prince, the man from America, than when I first began. I'm not even sure he is still in this country or indeed whether he is alive or dead.'

The other man nodded judiciously. 'Yes, McCulloch

is an uncommonly close-mouthed and cunning individual, I'll grant you, but surely there are other means of ascertaining the third man's identity and whereabouts?'

'I could always torture McCulloch until he tells me,' Colum offered sarcastically, and then was shocked by the other man's reply.

'It may well come to that, Macrae.'

'What?' Colum jerked out.

Bush opened his case and extracted a sheaf of papers from which he proceeded to read aloud in a flat, emotionless tone. 'October last, five persons killed in an explosion at Woolwich Powder Mills. October last, explosion at Birmingham of Phillips and Pursalls percussion cap factory, twenty-one workmen killed, eighteen injured. November last, explosion at Chatham Dockyard in powder magazine, no lives lost, three men injured. December last, explosion at Bury Powder Mills, twelve lives lost, thirty-two injured.'

Bush rammed the sheaf of paper back into his case and continued quietly, 'There have been further explosions during this year, resulting in considerable loss of life and damage to property. Although all of the explosions have been attributed to carelessness or misadventure, we have grounds for believing that they are in fact deliberate outrages perpetrated by Irish extremists. Have you any comment to make?'

'Nothing leads me to believe that McCulloch's group is responsible for any of the explosions, Mr Bush. You have seen my reports. The group holds regular meetings, all of which I have attended, and they talk and argue, and agree on nothing and decide on nothing. They spend much time and effort in trying to recruit new members to the Fenian Brotherhood, and have managed to suborn a handful of Irish soldiers from the various regiments of the London garrison. But that appears to be the sum total of their achievements.

'Terence McCulloch declares himself to be whole-heartedly committed to the Fenian movement, but appears to spend the major part of his time and effort in advancing his own financial interests. He's got his fingers into many pies, Mr Bush, and a lot of those pies are of a criminal nature, but I don't think he's involved with these explosions.'

'We know that already, Macrae,' the older man snapped pettishly. 'We believe that the explosions are the work of the American, the third man among the Prince's attackers.'

'How can you know that?' Colum questioned.

'A sentry at the Chatham Dockyard spotted and challenged a man who was running from the scene of the explosion. The man's description matches the American. Also, prior to the explosion at the percussion cap factory in Birmingham, a man of the same description was noticed behaving in a suspicious manner in the factory environs. Sightings at some of the other locations have also been reported, but with a less exact description. However, we are satisfied that it is the same man who is responsible for all these outrages.' Bush frowned severely. 'Mr Cumlinson has expressly instructed me to inform you that failure on your part to speedily eliminate this man, and any new confederates he may have acquired, will be viewed very unfavourably by the department, and may well result in, shall I say, unhappy repercussions in regard to your future prospects.'

This open threat provoked an angry reaction from

Colum. 'I don't need any threats to make me do my duty!' he retorted sharply. 'And if Mr Cumlinson is not satisfied with my work, then perhaps he'd best dismiss me, and find someone else to take my place.'

The other man was not at all disconcerted by this defiant challenge. He merely pointed out quietly, 'That is easily done, if it becomes necessary, Macrae. What is not easily done, however, is to ensure your daughters' future wellbeing. If you remain in our service, then whatever might befall you, your daughters will always be safeguarded by the department. Their future prospects will be bright. However, if you leave our service, or are dismissed from it, I fear then that their future prospects will become bleak in the extreme.'

He allowed Colum to digest his words, and then asked, 'Well, Macrae? What am I to report to Mr Cumlinson?'

Colum thought of his beloved girls, and knew that he had no real choice. 'You may report to Mr Cumlinson, that I shall exert all my endeavours to do my duty.'

For the first time since he had come into the room the older man allowed some warmth to enter his tone.

'You have chosen wisely, Macrae.'

'There is something I need to know, Mr Bush.'

'Yes, what is that?'

'I believe that Terence McCulloch knows the present whereabouts of the American. But to get that information from him, I may have to use extreme measures. Am I authorised to do so?'

Bush chuckled, and the sound was like the final throat-rattle of a dying man. 'All measures and no measures are authorised, Macrae. But at present it is best that McCulloch is not harmed. You must endeavour to extract the necessary information from him by guile, not force. That is, until you receive instructions to the contrary. And now I bid you good day, Macrae.'

Colum emerged into the chill, foggy air of Leather Lane, and was shocked to hear his name called.

'Hello, Colum. What brings you so far from home?'

He spun round to find himself staring into the bulbous lenses of Thomas Docherty's spectacles. For a couple of moments he remained silently staring at the neatly dressed, stoop-shouldered clerk, a fellow member of McCulloch's Fenian Circle. Colum was considering the possibility that McCulloch had set the man to follow and spy on him, but it was impossible to detect any expression in Docherty's eyes, distorted as they were by the spectacle lenses.

He forced a smile and greeted the man heartily. 'Hello yourself, Tommy. You've discovered my secret source of the "Readies". I usually have to pay a call on Uncle at this time of the week.'

'And there was me thinking that McCulloch paid you a small fortune. I can hardly believe that you need to pop your valuables.' There was a sly, questioning edge in Docherty's voice. 'It just goes to show how wrong a man can be, doesn't it?'

'I'm only the assistant deputy in his lodging houses, Tommy, not his bloody partner,' Colum laughed. Then asked, 'And yourself, what brings you up here? I thought you worked in Clerkenwell.'

'I do.' The other man tapped the side of his nose with his ink-stained forefinger. 'I'm the same as yourself, my friend. I usually have to call and see Uncle about this time of the week.'

He opened his other hand to show a heavy silver

watch chain. 'This was my old Da's, God rest him. But when he give it to me he never thought that it would be spending more time in Uncle's drawers than across my belly. If he'd thought that, he'd have given it to me brother.'

'Ah well, I'll have to be getting back,' Colum told him.

'Wait on a minute. I'll just pop this chain, and then I'll walk with you a bit of the way.'

Colum's instincts were warning him that this meeting was not fortuitous, but had been deliberately engineered by the other man.

But if that's the case, he thought, he must have been watching me. How else could he have known I was here today?

Colum had made no attempt to hide his regular visits to the pawnshop from Joseph Connors who, being a frequent user of pawnshops himself, accepted the practice as a normal part of life. But as far as Colum had been aware no one else in McCulloch's circle knew that Colum came to this particular shop.

Within a couple of minutes Docherty came out of the pawnshop jingling some coins in his hand.

'How about a livener, Colum?' he invited. 'A couple of jars would go down very well, wouldn't they?'

The invitation strengthened Colum's suspicion that this meeting was no accident. He agreed to the suggestion and they entered the first public house that they came to. After ordering a pint of beer and a measure of whisky each, they moved to sit at a table in the corner of the room.

For a while they chatted aimlessly, but Colum sensed that the other man was tense and anxious. Finally he decided to probe the clerk, and asked quietly, 'You seem to be a bit on edge, Tommy. Is there something troubling you?'

The man stared full at him and stuttered nervously, 'There is something troubling me, Colum. I'm convinced that there is an informer among us.'

Colum's heart pounded, and he feared that his shock might have betrayed itself.

'I don't rightly know what to do about it, Colum,' Docherty continued, speaking rapidly, his fingers drumming nervously upon the table. 'You see, I've no concrete proof to lay out on the table, so to speak. But I'm convinced that I've found out a traitor in our Circle.'

'Why are you telling me?' Colum demanded. 'Why not go direct to Mr McCulloch?'

'I've been watching you for weeks now, Colum. That's why I was able to follow you today. I've listened to you speak at our, meetings, and I know that you're a clever man, and have a lot of experience about such things, being an ex-police jack. That's why I'm wanting your advice.'

Colum's initial shock lessened, and his brain began to work coolly.

'Who is he, this informer?'

'It's Seamus Slavin.'

'Slavin?' Colum did not have to feign surprise, it was a genuine reaction. 'The sergeant? I can't believe it! From what I've been told about him he's been a member of McCulloch's Circle ever since it was formed. He's recruited more members than anybody else. It was him who recruited me.'

'Just so,' Docherty agreed eagerly. 'So now do you

see my problem, Colum? How can I tell McCulloch that his most trusted man is an informer? A traitor to the cause. And I haven't got any proof other than my own word on it. McCulloch isn't overfond of me anyway, and if I go to him with a story about his most trusted man being an informer, he'd likely blow my head off. He's had men killed for less before now, I can tell you. So what would you advise?'

'How do you know that Slavin is a traitor?' Colum queried. 'How did you find him out?'

Docherty touched the side of his nose with his forefinger. 'I have my methods, Colum.' His eyes blinked rapidly behind the bulbous lenses. 'Well now, what do you think I should do?'

Colum was in something of a quandary. If Seamus Slavin was an informer, then that meant that Colum and he were in a sense on the same side. It was possible that Slavin was in fact a Government agent, who had been infiltrated into the Fenian Brotherhood by the Authorities. It would not be the first time that different Government and police departments had had their agents working on the same investigation, unknown to each other.

Colum knew that should McCulloch accept the truth of what Docherty was alleging, then Slavin would be killed. But before being killed he would undoubtedly be tortured to force him to reveal all that he knew. In the worst possible scenario, Slavin might indeed be a Government agent and he might also have knowledge that another agent, namely Colum himself, had been infiltrated into McCulloch's group. To give himself time to think he questioned Docherty.

'If you haven't proof to put before Mr McCulloch,

then how are you going to convince him that Slavin is an informer?'

The other man drew in breath with a wetly sucking sound. 'Ahh now, when I spoke of concrete proof, I meant that I'd no documentary evidence. But I've seen enough to know that I'm right.'

'Then you'd best tell me what it is you've seen, Tommy, and let me form an opinion on it.'

'I was down in a pub close by Wellington Barracks a couple of weeks since, just having a quiet jar, and who should come in but Seamus Slavin. Well, I was about to give him a shout, but then another fella came in behind him, and the pair of them went into a back room. This other man was a respectable-looking gentleman, if you know what I mean. Dressed like a clerk, he'd be about sixty years old, to my reckoning. I couldn't help but wonder what such a respectable-looking old fella was doing with a redcoat. To tell the truth I thought at first he might be one of them perverts. There's an awful lot of them that hangs about the pubs by the barracks to pick up the Guardsmen.'

'I wouldn't have taken Slavin to be a she-shirt,' Colum objected.

'Nor me neither. That's what made me so suspicious as to who the old fella was,' Docherty agreed, and lapsed into silence as he took off his spectacles and wiped the lenses on a bit of rag, his red-sore, watery eyes looking preternaturally small without their glass shields.

It seemed an age before he replaced his spectacles, and Colum waited tensely, struggling against the desire to urge him to continue speaking.

'Anyway, I went outside the pub and took up a

vantage point to see what might happen. Well, Slavin came out first and went off towards the barracks. Then a bit later on this other fella came out, and I followed him. He went to a house up in Harley Street there.'

Apprehension dried Colum's mouth, and to cover it he forced himself to laugh. 'He must be a doctor treating Seamus for the "clap".'

Docherty did not smile.

'Oh no, I don't think that the fella is a doctor, Colum. You see, I talked to a few of the servants living at the other houses, and they told me that the house, number 50 it is, isn't like a normal family house. Nobody seems to know the name of the party who lives there, for one thing. And they only see men going in and out of it. Never any ladies. And another funny thing about that house is that there aren't any females in service there. Only men. Now that's very strange, isn't it, Colum. I mean, who ever heard of men doing the work of kitchen maids and parlourmaids?'

Colum shrugged and with assumed carelessness offered, 'Then perhaps it's some sort of business premises, Tommy?'

'Exactly!' Docherty exclaimed excitedly. 'But what sort of business? I had a word with the postman who delivers to Harley Street, and he told me that he doesn't very often make any deliveries to number 50. Now any proper business would have loads of letters and parcels delivered, wouldn't it?'

By now real alarm was pulsing through Colum's mind, and he was inwardly cursing this cunning little man who had seemingly unearthed the secret of number 50 Harley Street.

He shook his head, as if uncertain. 'It doesn't seem to

prove that Slavin is an informer, Tommy. I admit that the house doesn't sound like a normal family house, but there could be a dozen explanations for that. And a dozen innocent reasons for Slavin meeting with the old man. He could be an old officer that Slavin has business of some sort with.' He forced himself to chuckle amusedly. 'Perhaps the house is a sort of retirement home for decayed officers, and Slavin is being offered a job as the bloody parlourmaid there for after he leaves the army.'

The other man frowned. 'This is no joking matter, Colum. If Slavin is an informer it could end with us all getting our necks stretched for treason.'

The harsh realisation that Docherty presented a real threat to himself was staring Colum in the face. If he went to McCulloch with this story, then Colum was uneasily aware that McCulloch might well be able to uncover the true purpose of number 50 Harley Street. The man had so many contacts in all sorts of unlikely places, that it was all too likely he would be able to ferret out the information.

By now Colum was being forced to consider silencing Docherty for good. The thought of murdering the man was abhorrent to him. After all, Docherty had done him no harm, and had always shown friendship to him. But it was beginning to seem that Colum had no other choice but to silence him. Then he thought of a way in which he might be able to gain some time.

'I'll tell you what, Tommy,' he offered. 'I've still got a lot of contacts in the police. Especially with the jacks. Give me a couple of days or so to make some enquiries myself about this house in Harley Street. If I find out something then we can both go to McCulloch. He'll listen to two of us, before he'll take heed of one. There'll be less chance of getting our heads blown off, as well.'

Docherty sighed with relief. 'Will you do that, Colum?' he demanded eagerly. 'Will you see what you can find out about that house?'

'I've just said I would, haven't I?' Colum assured him. 'Now, if you'll take my advice you'll say nothing about this to anybody. Don't breathe a word about it until I've had a chance to find out what I can.'

'There's me hand on it!' Docherty held out his ink-stained fingers, and they shook hands as if sealing a bargain.

'Now, I've got to go,' Colum told him. 'Meet me here in this pub two nights from now, we'll say at around nine. And hopefully I'll have some news for you then.'

'God bless you, Colum. You're a great man,' Docherty beamed at him. 'A true friend.'

Colum experienced an odd sense of guilt as he heard these sentiments expressed so sincerely by the other man. But as soon as he went out into the chill night air that sense of guilt abruptly disappeared as the imperative necessity of planning how he might safeguard himself took priority over all else.

He considered whether Docherty might have been directed to act as an *agent provocateur* by McCulloch, to test his, Colum's, loyalty to the Fenians, and to McCulloch personally. He knew that McCulloch was cunning enough to do such a thing. If that was the case, then number 50 Harley Street was hopelessly compromised.

Colum knew that whatever the case was he must get a report to Cumlinson with the greatest urgency, to let him know that Docherty at least was dangerously close to uncovering the secret of the house, and there was a possibility that others also were privy to Docherty's suspicions.

If Docherty was acting alone, and was truthful in what he had told Colum, then it might be safest to kill him.

Colum's head ached with the endless permutations and possibilities of the situation, and many hours would elapse before he came to a decision on what action to take.

Chapter Twenty-nine

Despite the lateness of the hour the rear door of 50 Harley Street was opened within seconds of Colum's first tug on the bell pull.

Two of the burly custodians were in the passageway, both armed with revolvers, and even as the door was opening a third man came from the shadows behind Colum, also carrying a revolver in his hand.

'It's all right, Larkins,' the senior man, Simpkins, said as he saw Colum's face in the shaft of gaslight. 'I know him.'

The third man melted back into the shadows and Simpkins jerked his head. 'Step inside.'

'I have to see Mr Cumlinson straight away. It's urgent,' Colum stated.

'I hope it is, for your sake,' the big man growled in rustic accents. 'You'm breaking with procedure, coming here like this.'

'Just get me to Cumlinson,' Colum snapped.

'Wait here with him,' Simpkins told his companion, and disappeared through the door at the end of the passage.

After a few minutes, during which Colum waited impatiently under the dour stare of his silent guard, Simpkins came back.

'Follow me.'

Conrad Cumlinson was standing before his vast black leather-topped desk when Colum was ushered into his office. He was dressed in his usual sombre clothing and, despite its being the small hours of the early morning, he betrayed no trace of weariness.

'You are in breach of your procedural orders, Macrae,' he snapped coldly. 'You had better have good reason for this disobedience.'

Colum flushed with resentment. His nerves had been strained to the utmost during the past hours and he was well aware that he was in breach of his orders.

'I've good reason for coming here like this, sir.'

'Let me hear it.'

Colum gave him a full account of all that had passed between himself and Docherty. Cumlinson's thin features betrayed no emotion other than intent attention to what he was hearing.

'. . . and so, sir, I judged the situation to be so urgent that I could not afford to waste time in sending you my report through the Leather Lane location,' Colum finished, and fell silent.

Cumlinson nodded brusquely. 'I trust you took care to make certain that you were not followed here?'

'Of course, sir.'

'Sit down, Macrae.' Cumlinson indicated a chair standing against one wall, and as Colum obeyed he began to pace up and down, his head bent low.

It was fifteen minutes before he came to a standstill, and spoke to Colum once more.

'You will go to Terence McCulloch and tell him that through the medium of your late superior officer in the police force, namely Detective Inspector Charles Anderson, you have discovered that this house does indeed harbour a secret department of the Government. That Anderson could not tell you the purpose of that secret department, but that it was rumoured in official circles to be involved with the surveillance of political subversives. Do you understand your orders?'

Colum stared at the other man in absolute amazement. 'Then Docherty is right, sir! Seamus Slavin is an informer!'

A wintry smile touched Cumlinson's thin lips. 'I think it would be more correct if you were to use the past tense, Macrae.'

'Do you want me to warn Slavin that he is discovered, sir?'

'I have not ordered so, Macrae.' The older man frowned. 'Just do what you have been instructed to do. Nothing more, and nothing less.'

'But if I go to McCulloch without warning Slavin, then he's a dead man.'

'Whether Slavin lives or dies is no concern of yours, Macrae. Now, I want you to go to McCulloch as soon as you can. The earlier the better. That will be all.'

'But, sir . . .' Still Colum was driven to protest, but Cumlinson cut him short.

'I said, that will be all, Macrae. Just do your duty.'

He lifted the small handbell from his desk and rang it, and instantly the senior orderly responded from the other side of the door where he had been waiting.

'Show Macrae out, Simpkins, and then have Mr Bush come to me.'

'Very good, sir.'

When Mr Bush came to his superior's office, Cumlinson was seated at his desk, sipping a glass of sherry.

'Ah, there you are, Mr Bush. We shall be moving to the Charing Cross location as soon as possible.'

'Very well, sir, I'll issue the necessary orders immediately. Is there anything else, sir?'

'Yes, remove Seamus Slavin from the Muster Roll, will you?'

'Do you wish me to enter any reason for the removal in the records, sir?'

Cumlinson pondered briefly, and then shook his head. 'No, that won't be necessary, thank you, Mr Bush.'

As he followed the burly figure of Simpkins downstairs and along the passageways Colum was increasingly troubled by what Cumlinson had ordered him to do. He knew that a sentence of death and, perhaps even worse, an extended period of torture before death intervened had just been passed on Seamus Slavin. Although Cumlinson had not admitted openly that Slavin was one of his informers, it was glaringly apparent to Colum, and he was appalled that Cumlinson could so casually use a man and then throw him to the wolves without any hesitation, and without even a word of regret or commiseration for the man's destruction.

When Simpkins was unlocking the back door, Colum's heated feelings burst from him.

'Cumlinson has just told me to stand by and watch a man be murdered, without even trying to save him. What's worse, I'm to bring that murder about.'

The burly man straightened and regarded Colum curiously. 'You was in the Crimea, warn't you?'

'Yes, I was.' Colum nodded.

'So was I. We saw enough of our comrades sent to

245

their deaths there, didn't we? Why should what happens to one man bother you?'

The question caused Colum to consider his own reactions. 'Well, in the Crimea we were all facing death, weren't we?' he replied thoughtfully. 'And it was just luck who lived and who died. But we all fought for each other there, didn't we? But this is different. I mean, this man is being deliberately sacrificed, as I see it.'

'And warn't we deliberately sacrificed when we tried to storm the Redan without sufficient numbers?' Simpkins demanded. 'Or when the bloody Commissariat left us to starve and freeze to death in the soddin' trenches, or be shipped to Scutari Hospital and left there, lying in our own filth to die?'

Simpkins's dour features twisted in a grimace of disgust. 'Us rankers have always been counted as expendable. And that's what we still am, expendable, just like this man is! Take a tip from me, my friend, you just worry about your own skin, and don't give another thought to what's going to happen to him. Because if he was in your place and you in his, he wouldn't give a fuck about what was happening to you.'

He opened the door and ushered Colum through it. 'Take care,' he grunted, and the door closed, leaving Colum standing in the darkness.

Chapter Thirty

There were nearly twenty men crammed into the room above the stables, and the clumping of their booted feet on the wooden flooring caused the horses in the stalls below to become restless, whinnying and tossing their heads, and stamping their hooves spasmodically.

Three smoking oil lamps cast their light down upon the men, and the room was close and foul with the stench of unwashed bodies and stale breath.

Terence McCulloch entered and took his stance by the door, flanked by Joseph Connors and Colum. Thomas Docherty stood to one side of the trio, constantly licking his lips and swallowing hard, his head twitching agitatedly.

'Let's have some quiet now,' McCulloch ordered, and the humming of voices died down to a silence broken only by occasional coughs and sneezes.

McCulloch's grim gaze passed across the faces in front of him. On some faces he dwelt for long moments, until the man would become uncertain and smile nervously or grimace or look away. Their leader's grim air created an atmosphere of foreboding, and tension heightened in the room.

There were several redcoats among the crowd, soldiers from the London garrison, and McCulloch's gaze kept on returning to these men. Finally he spoke, and the tension had risen so high that a gusting of relieved sighs greeted his words.

'I've called this meeting for a special purpose. To demonstrate to all of you that treachery will always be found out, and punished.'

Guarded looks were exchanged, and heads shaken as men immediately began to wonder and to suspect.

'We have an informer among us. A traitor who would sell his comrades. But let this be a lesson to all of you. We always find out who is trying to betray us.' McCulloch paused for a moment, then barked the order, 'Step forward, Seamus Slavin.'

Shock and fear paled the sergeant's ruddy features.

'Step forward, you dirty bastard!' McCulloch hissed with hatred in his eyes.

Slavin took a grip upon himself, and came forward, loudly protesting, 'I'm no informer! I'm no traitor! Show me the man who accuses me and I'll tear his fuckin', lying tongue out of his head.'

'Stand there, Slavin,' McCulloch shouted, pointing to a spot in front of the crowd, then he jerked his head at Joseph Connors, and the huge man moved to stand watchfully by Slavin's side, his bulk making the tall, robust soldier appear physically smaller and diminished.

'Step forward, Thomas Docherty,' McCulloch ordered, and the clerk took a hesitant pace to his front, the lamplight flashing on his thick lenses as his head twitched agitatedly.

'Tell us what you know, Docherty,' McCulloch instructed.

The man stuttered out his story, and then stepped back.

'What do you say to that, Slavin?' McCulloch demanded.

'I say that Docherty is a fuckin' eejit who has got this all wrong,' the sergeant asserted heatedly.

'Do you deny meeting the man from Harley Street?' McCulloch questioned.

'No, of course I don't. I've met the man from Harley Street a good many times,' Slavin admitted freely, then lied fluently, 'I've known that man for nigh on twenty years. He was my Company Commander. His name is George Freedom, and he left the army about four years ago. Check with the *Gazette* and the *Army List* if you don't believe me.'

'Well, I have to admit that you'd be a fool to lie about a thing that's so easily checked.' McCulloch's tone suddenly altered, and became almost friendly. 'And this house in Harley Street, does he live there?'

'He has rooms there, but he lives in Cumberland. His family has land up there.' Slavin was gaining confidence as he noted the encouraging change in McCulloch's tone. 'That's why I was meeting with him, Mr McCulloch, because he's concerned about his land in Cumberland. He reckons that the agent he has now is no use, and is cheating him. He wants me to leave the army and to go and work for him. Take the place of the agent he has now.'

'So, it looks like Thomas Docherty was jumping to the wrong conclusions.' McCulloch smiled grimly. 'Is that what you're telling me, Seamus Slavin? That Thomas Docherty, being the fool that he is, has got it all wrong?'

'I am indeed, Mr McCulloch. Docherty is a sneaky, four-eyed bastard who hasn't got the sense of a fly. He's got it all wrong, Mr McCulloch. I'm no informer. I'm no traitor. And as soon as this is over and done with,

I'm going to shove Mr Thomas Docherty's scabby head right up his fuckin' arsehole.'

'And Colum Macrae? Will you shove his head up his arsehole, as well?' McCulloch enquired silkily.

'Why, what do you mean?' Slavin's eyes were wary. 'Is he telling lies about me as well?'

'You'd best hear what he has to say first, and then form your own judgement,' McCulloch replied, and signalled to Colum to step forward.

Colum's stomach was churning, and he felt a sickening sense of shame about what he was about to do. Steeling himself to meet Slavin's furious glare, he looked the man full in the eyes and stated in a loud, firm voice, 'You're a filthy traitor to Ireland and the Fenian Brotherhood, Seamus Slavin. The house in Harley Street is a Government office, and the men there are agents of the British Crown. They spy on people they suspect of being political enemies of the British State.'

There was a growling outburst of execration from the crowd, and ugly threats and hating eyes focused on Seamus Slavin.

The sergeant was a brave man, and kept his head. 'I don't know why you should tell these lies, Macrae,' he responded accusingly. 'I know that Docherty is a sneaking, lying bastard, who delights in getting better men than him into trouble. But I took you for a straight, honest man. Have you been got at in some way by Docherty? Is that why you're doing this? Has he a hold over you?'

If Colum had not known for certain that Slavin was an informer, he would have been hard put to doubt the sincerity of the man, and he could not help but admire the cool courage with which Slavin was confronting his perilous situation.

'Save your breath, Slavin,' McCulloch snapped curtly. 'I am satisfied as to your guilt.'

He paused, then barked out, 'Take him, Joseph.'

Connors moved with lightning speed to lock the soldier's arms behind him and bring him crashing face downwards onto the floor. His massive body crushed the breath out of Slavin and, despite the latter's fierce struggling, held him powerless.

McCulloch moved to stand above Slavin and, drawing back his heavy boot, kicked the unprotected head one, two, three, four times, breaking bones, tearing flesh, bringing blood spurting. Slavin shouted out in agony, until his cries were stifled by McCulloch ramming a piece of rag into his gaping mouth.

'Tie the bastard up,' McCulloch ordered, and willing hands fetched ropes and trussed Slavin so that he could hardly move. He lay on his back, his eyes for the first time filled with terror.

'Now we'll find out just how much you've told your friends,' McCulloch hissed, and told Connors, 'Go to work on the bastard, Joseph. And the rest of you watch, and learn from this.'

For more than three hours Slavin was tortured mercilessly, with fire and steel, until he was reduced to a moaning wreckage of charred and bloody flesh.

Colum watched with horror, his heart sick, his stomach heaving, a terrible guilt rending him.

Slavin told his torturers virtually nothing, for he knew virtually nothing. He had been recruited as an informer by that same elderly man, who had struck up a conversation with him in a public house. The man had told him that he, Slavin, was known to be recruiting soldiers into the Fenian Brotherhood, and that unless he co-operated, he would be arrested and charged with treason, which was a hanging offence. Afterwards he had regularly met that same elderly man who had received his reports from him, and had paid him. Slavin could not even tell them his elderly paymaster's name. The reports were merely lists of the names of those in the Circle, and accounts of what they talked about at their meetings.

Once McCulloch was satisfied that he had extracted all the information he could, he told the subdued and fearful men in the room, 'We have nothing to fear. The elderly man, this piece of shit's paymaster, is in my employ. I used him to test Slavin's loyalty. Slavin failed that test.'

Colum felt a physical shock course through him as he heard this information. If it were true, then he himself must be in mortal danger.

'No, it can't be true,' he told himself desperately. 'But if it isn't true, then why is McCulloch acting so coolly about it?'

Bafflement swept over him.

'Soldiers are shot,' McCulloch was continuing, 'murderers are hanged. But for traitors and informers there's only one suitable way of execution. The way that we get rid of cur dogs.'

He took a long thin piece of cord from his pocket, wrapped its ends around his hands, slipped it over Slavin's head and expertly garrotted the half-conscious man.

Slavin's body jerked and his heels drummed the floor in his death throes, and the cold sweat of horror streamed down Colum's face.

A curious moaning sound came from the watching

crowd, and several men turned their faces away, while others retched and vomited.

When Slavin was limp and still in death, McCulloch ordered Connors and Colum, 'There's a big shit heap in the laystall in the yard. Bury the bastard in that for the time being. That's the only grave that shit like him deserves to rest in.'

Connors heaved the dead man over his shoulder as if he were weightless and carried him down to the yard with Colum following behind. They used long-handled shovels to dig out a hole in the great steaming heap of manure, and then heaved Slavin into it and covered him over.

Connors told Colum, 'You did well. McCulloch was pleased with you, I could tell.'

Colum fought to appear cool and uncaring. 'One way is as good as another to get rid of a treacherous bastard like Slavin. We should have made him suffer longer before we killed him. I need to take a piss. You go on up, I'll not be a minute.'

As soon as he was alone, Colum bent and vomited, retching and heaving until his stomach was voided and only bitter bile came to his mouth. Then, reluctantly, he went back upstairs to join the others.

McCulloch declared the meeting to be at an end, and in ones and twos the crowd dispersed. Their manner was subdued and thoughtful, many of them made worried and fearful by this demonstration of how deadly dangerous their involvement with the Fenian Brotherhood could be.

When only Connors and Colum remained in the room McCulloch told them, 'You did well, both of you. Here.' He handed each of them a small leather bag of

253

sovereigns. 'Go and enjoy yourselves. Eat, drink and be merry.'

They thanked him and turned to leave, but he held Colum back for a moment. He smiled and clapped him on the shoulder.

'Well, at least Seamus Slavin did one good thing for the Cause. He recruited you, Colum. Now tomorrow you're to go to Shibco the tailor in Marsden Street. Tell him that he is to make you a good-quality suit of clothing, and completely rig you out from head to toe, and charge the bill to my account.'

He chuckled at Colum's startled expression.

'Now that you've proven your loyalty to me, I'm going to utilise your services in other ways, Colum. I've a special job that I want you to do for me. Report to me at my house in ten days' time. I want to see you dressed like a gentleman when you come. So impress upon Shibco that the quality and workmanship must be as good as he can make it.'

Again he clapped Colum on his shoulder in a friendly gesture. 'Be off with you now, and have a good time.'

Colum went to join Connors, but he knew that he would have no good time. He was racked with shame, guilt and self-disgust.

I don't believe that there is a drink that's ever been brewed that can wash the taste of what I've done this night out of my mouth, he thought with hopeless despair. Judas was paid thirty pieces of silver as blood money. My blood money is the price of a suit of new clothes.

Chapter Thirty-one

Kitty Wainright didn't knock on the door before entering Rosaleen Calatrava's drawing room in the house in Holloway.

'Haven't I told you a hundred times to knock before you come in here?' Rosaleen scolded angrily. She disliked this woman whom Terence McCulloch had insisted she have as her housekeeper. Rosaleen preferred to think of Kitty Wainright as her jailer, knowing that the woman had been placed here to keep a close watch on her.

Wainright scowled sullenly. Although McCulloch had told her nothing of Rosaleen's antecedents she could plainly see the family resemblance to the man who had so savagely assaulted her, and accordingly she returned Rosaleen's dislike of her in full measure.

'Mr McCulloch's come to see you,' she announced, then turned and flounced out of the room.

When McCulloch came in Rosaleen stared curiously at the tall, well-dressed, red-haired man who accompanied him.

Colum Macrae regarded this beautiful woman with an equal curiosity. McCulloch had told him nothing about her, except that she was one of his employees. He had no idea why he had been brought here, but knowing McCulloch's methods he guessed that this woman was somehow involved with the special job that McCulloch had promised him the previous week.

McCulloch wasted no time in polite formalities. 'When is Firthallan calling on you again?'

'Tomorrow evening,' she told him.

McCulloch turned to Colum. 'Edward Firthallan, Earl of Kendrick, do you know of him?'

Colum shook his head, and McCulloch went on to fill him in on Firthallan's details, then informed him bluntly, 'This woman is his mistress. She goes by the name of Farquar, Mrs Rosaleen Farquar. You are to play the part of her husband, Captain Robert Farquar.'

Both Colum and Rosaleen stared at him in shock, and he smiled mirthlessly.

'Firthallan has had his fun with Rosaleen, and now he must pay the price for it.'

It was Rosaleen who was the first to react. 'But Firthallan believes me to be a widow. You told me to tell him that.'

'Just so,' McCulloch agreed equably. 'I know that Firthallan has an eye for a pretty woman, but he's a cautious bastard. He wouldn't risk bedding a married piece in case he got caught at it. But a widow is a different kettle of fish. And you're not the first married woman to tell lies about her state if she saw a chance to have an adventure with a rich man. An adventure which could gain her some financial advantage.' His tone became sneering. 'And you have gained some financial advantage, haven't you, Rosaleen? Kitty Wainright has told me how very generous Firthallan's been to you.'

The sneer stung Rosaleen to snap back heatedly, 'If you force me to play the whore, McCulloch, then you can't begrudge me a whore's wages, can you?'

He frowned at her, and warned, 'Don't take that tone with me, lady, you've too much to lose if I should take it amiss.'

She flushed, and looked down at the floor, biting her full lips, and Colum wondered what it was that McCulloch held over her.

Satisfied that he had cowed her, McCulloch went on, 'Now listen very carefully to me, both of you. Firthallan is no fool. He'll not fall for the badger game so easy. I know for a fact that it has been tried on him before, and has failed. So you'll need to act the part of husband and wife very well to convince him that you are indeed so.'

He took a large envelope from his inner pocket. 'In here you'll find all the details about your wedding and previous life together. I've arranged to have the necessary entries made into the church register, and the named priest will confirm that he wed you when Firthallan has enquiries made. I'll take specimen signatures from both of you now so that they can be copied into the register. Have you pen and paper here, Rosaleen?'

'In there.' She nodded towards the bureau.

'Do them now then,' McCulloch ordered, and they both complied, signing the names of Robert and Rosaleen Farquar on a sheet of notepaper.

McCulloch blew fine drying powder onto the wet ink, folded the paper and stowed it away. Then he told them, 'I'm going to leave you to get to know each other. Remember what I said, you have to play the part well enough to leave no doubts in Firthallan's mind that you are indeed man and wife.' He smiled with a hint of salaciousness. 'I've no objection to you consummating your

257

relationship, because you might well have to answer questions concerning each other, and confirm that you have an intimate knowledge of each other's bodies and sexual habits.'

He frowned and became very serious. 'I'm not joking about that. Firthallan will more than likely employ lawyers and enquiry agents, to check and double-check, and you must be able to convince them. So I want you to spend the next few days getting to know each other well, and studying the details of your new identities.'

He paused expectantly, and Colum nodded.

'We'll do whatever has to be done.'

After a couple of moments Rosaleen also reluctantly concurred.

'Good!' McCulloch seemed satisfied. 'Then I'll say goodbye for the present.'

He left immediately.

Rosaleen and Colum looked at each other with embarrassment, and for some moments there was a strained silence. Then Colum held out his hand.

'My name is Colum Macrae. If we are to work together, then let us try to be friends. I can assure you that I shall behave towards you with the utmost respect, Mrs Farquar.'

She stared searchingly at him, trying to ascertain his sincerity. Then, satisfied with what she saw in his eyes, she took his hand and shook it firmly. 'My name isn't really Farquar,' she told him. 'It's Calatrava. Rosaleen Calatrava. And I've never been married. I was betrothed once.' Sadness touched her dark eyes. 'But he died before our wedding could take place.'

'I've never done anything like this before,' Colum smiled ruefully, 'and I'm not sure that I like it. But I don't have any choice other than to do as McCulloch bids me.'

She returned his smile. 'Myself likewise, Mr Macrae. It was not of my choosing to become a whore, and it is most certainly not of my choosing to act the black-mailer.'

Her open description of herself as a whore paradoxically evoked respect in Colum. He admired her honesty, and lack of hypocrisy. As a soldier and as a detective he had met and known many whores, and had at times purchased the services they offered. He did not despise or condemn women who sold their bodies. He knew that it was cruel necessity and harsh misfortune that forced so many of them to do so.

'Shall we take a look at what McCulloch has concocted for us?' he suggested, and she readily agreed.

They sat down side by side at the table and as he opened the large envelope and extracted its contents he became aware of her scented fragrance and the delicate small white hands that joined with his own in spreading out the sheets of paper before them.

As he studied the closely written notes Colum began to marvel at McCulloch's cunning and thoroughness in preparation. The man had created biographies for the couple and, as explained in the notes, had used real people as his sources. There had been a man named Robert Farquar, born in Sunderland, whose family had been wiped out during the cholera epidemic of 1832. The man had served in the army as a captain and, following the Crimean War, had emigrated to America, where he had since disappeared.

For Rosaleen likewise McCulloch had based her story on an actual woman, in this case born in Dublin, whose family had been drowned when an emigrant ship had been lost in a storm in mid-Atlantic. Rosaleen's alter ego had been one of the survivors, but her fate after rescue was unknown. The fact of her survival was however recorded in the records of the shipping company in Liverpool.

In both the man and woman's cases, their dates of birth were registered in the records of the respective parishes in both cities.

Rosaleen was forced to a grudging admiration for McCulloch's expertise, and she voiced this sentiment to Colum, who wryly agreed with her.

During the days that followed their meeting Colum came to Rosaleen's house every afternoon, and time went quickly as they pored over the notes, committing them to memory and testing each other at frequent intervals about their false identities. Colum recognised that Rosaleen possessed a quick and agile brain, and a sense of humour that meshed easily with his own. As the days passed he also became uneasily conscious of the attraction her physical beauty had for him.

For her part Rosaleen experienced an increasing sense of rapport with this stranger, and was forced to acknowledge her regret that they had not met in other times, other places, other circumstances.

They would frequently take a break from studying and Rosaleen would go to the kitchen and prepare some refreshments for them, bringing tea and cake back with her on a tray. Afterwards she would invariably light up a cheroot and lean back on the chaise longue to enjoy it, and Colum was secretly enchanted by this daring display of glamorous decadence.

They soon became completely at ease with each

other, and exchanged small jokes and laughter, bantering as if they had been close friends for many years.

Although Colum was all too well aware of the essential squalidity of what they were preparing to do, yet that fact had somehow retreated into the innermost recesses of his mind, and as he joked and laughed with this beautiful dark-haired woman he felt like a young boy experiencing the first heady joys of dawning love.

Harsh reality came jarring back one early evening when Rosaleen informed him, 'It's tonight that you have to confront Firthallan. McCulloch came to see me this morning to tell me that he's got everything prepared.'

Kitty Wainright came rushing in to warn Rosaleen, 'Firthallan's carriage is outside!'

'Oh, my God! He wasn't due to come until later. He mustn't see you here now. It'll ruin everything. Quick, go to the kitchen and wait there.' The bell jangled in the hallway, and Rosaleen urged, 'Go, quickly'.

As soon as Colum was hidden in the rear of the house Kitty Wainright let the visitor in and showed him to the drawing room.

Edward Firthallan had always been a man who appreciated pretty women, but had never known what it was to love and desire a single woman. Having the woman he knew as Rosaleen Farquar as his mistress had changed that. He was utterly besotted with her, and begrudged every hour that he must spend apart from her. Yet he was still careful to keep their relationship a close secret. He had no desire to risk losing the patronage of his father-in-law, Lord Macarry, knowing that should that happen he would become a nonentity in the privileged and powerful circles he moved in.

Sexually he was a greedy lover, and since he had not been able to visit Rosaleen for several nights he was hungry to possess her voluptuous body again.

As soon as Kitty Wainright had left the room Firthallan pulled Rosaleen to him and kissed her passionately.

'Come, let's go upstairs,' he urged.

'But it's not yet quite past nine o'clock,' she protested. 'I thought that we might have supper first.'

'Be damned to supper! It's not food that I want. Come.' He gripped her arm and pulled her with him.

'They're up in the bedroom,' Kitty Wainright told Colum. 'We'll give 'em a bit of time to get stuck into it, and then we'll go and spoil the fun. He's a randy bastard, Firthallan is. He fucks her all night long. She's earning her pay with him, right enough. There's some mornings that she can hardly stir out of the bed, he's been at it so much. I don't know where the bastard gets his energy from. To look at him you wouldn't think he'd got a good screw in him.'

Colum felt jealousy rising against this man whom he had never seen, and resentment at Rosaleen Calatrava for prostituting herself. He castigated himself savagely. You bloody fool, she's nothing to you. Why should you care what she does, or who she does it with?

The woman's shrewd gaze caught the flash of fury in his eyes, and she told herself, This bugger has the fancy for that bitch himself. Look at how he's raging inside.

Spitefully she twisted the figurative knife. 'Of course, them lords and toffs can't be satisfied with a simple fuck, can they? They likes the women to do all sorts of things to them, and them do the same to the women. I'll tell you straight, I wouldn't let any man do to me the filthy things that Firthallan does to her, and makes her do to him.'

He could not stop himself reacting sharply to this tormenting baiting. 'Hold your tongue! I'm here to do a job, not listen to your nonsense.'

'Oh, aren't we hoity-toity then. What are you, a bloody Methodist or something? Too pure to hear what goes on in a bedroom?' she sneered, and inwardly savoured his angry reaction.

He stayed sullenly silent, but could not stop his vivid imagination picturing a myriad degrading sexual acts taking place in the room above, and he found himself dreading what scene he might be confronted with when he burst in upon the couple.

Over the years Rosaleen had learned the art of detaching her mind from her body. She had learned how to give her flesh to a man, yet not her spiritual self. She had slowly and grimly trained herself to regard her body as only a fleshly machine that her mind inhabited, a machine that she utilised to serve her own purposes, just as she might use a pen to write with, or a pot to cook with.

This hard-learned skill had served her well, and up to now she had been able to endure the physical demands of Edward Firthallan with equanimity.

But tonight, as he eagerly undressed her, and she felt his hot wet mouth sucking her nipples, his hands caressing the soft skin of her buttocks and thighs she discovered to her dismay that she was unable to detach herself from what he was doing to her. When he parted her thighs and entered her she wanted to push him away, and his gasps and grunts of pleasure filled her with an unbidden anger that he should be so enjoying using her. She experienced a sudden sickening self-disgust, and a bitter shame savagely assailed her. Try as she could, she was unable to excuse or rationalise her position. She was a whore and nothing could change that.

The thrusting of Firthallan's hips quickened and his grunts metamorphosed into a long-drawn-out, panting moan. In her mind she begged desperately, 'Please let it finish! Oh, please God, let it be done with.'

As he collapsed upon her, and his harsh panting quietened, he began to murmur endearments into her ear. His words of love, which previously she would have taken as tribute to her power over him, now perversely infuriated her, and she bit on her lips to stop herself screaming at him to stop, to leave her alone, to go from her and from this room and this house.

He sensed that something was wrong, and he levered his body upwards, withdrawing from her, and asking anxiously, 'What's the matter, my darling? Did I hurt you?'

She fought to control her rampaging emotions, knowing that the only way to resolve this situation, to gain freedom from this sexual bondage, was to continue with the prearranged plan. To remain here until Colum Macrae should come.

Colum Macrae! The visual image of his red hair and hard-etched features had been with her constantly since their first meeting.

'Rosaleen? What's the matter?' Firthallan was now kneeling on the bed, bending over her, his eyes peering anxiously at her face. 'Why won't you answer me? Rosaleen, what is it?'

'I don't want Colum to see me like this.' The realisation thundered in her mind.

'Don't want who to see you?' Firthallan demanded in bafflement, and Rosaleen stared at him in dismayed confusion, as she realised that she had unwittingly given voice to her thoughts.

She saw the suspicion dawning in Firthallan's expression, as he demanded again, 'What are you saying? Who don't you want to see you like this?' He hurled the questions at her like missiles.

She made no answer, and rose from the bed and hurriedly began to dress, trying frantically to gather her scattered wits.

Firthallan came to stand in front of her, badgering her remorselessly.

'Tell me, Rosaleen. Why are you behaving like this? Who is it that you were referring to?'

Faces rapidly juxtaposed themselves in her mind's eye: Dermot, Terence McCulloch, Colum Macrae. She dared not fail now. She knew that if she did then Terence McCulloch would wreak a terrible vengeance. He would do as he had threatened and inform on Dermot, of that she was certain. Her gaze sought the wall clock. It lacked only a couple of minutes to the hour of ten o'clock. Surely Colum Macrae must confront them soon.

'I feel so guilty, Edward. I should have told you the truth,' she muttered.

An alarm bell sounded in Firthallan's brain. Besotted with her though he was, his paramount concern was always his own welfare. 'The truth? The truth about what?' His expression was already guarded.

'The truth about myself,' she muttered.

265

Firthallan became agitated and he shouted into her downcast face, 'I think that you had better tell me that truth now, madam, or it might go hard with you.'

Colum was coming up the stairs with Kitty Wainright at his heels when he heard Firthallan shouting. He mounted the final stairs in two bounds and came bursting through the door of the bedroom, and saw the half-clothed woman and the naked man.

Edward Firthallan cried out in alarm, and the situation threatened to dissolve into complete farce as he snatched up the sheets from the bed in an effort to hide his nakedness.

Colum followed McCulloch's instructions.

'Do you see this, Mrs Wainright?'

'I do indeed, Captain Farquar, and I'll swear to it in the courts.'

Firthallan was badly frightened and when Colum stepped menacingly towards him he cowered back and lifted the sheets up in front of his face to shield himself.

Colum tore the flimsy shield away and Firthallan flinched and cried out.

'I could kill you for what you're doing with my wife,' Colum growled savagely. 'But instead I'll content myself with ruining you. Now get out before I lose control of myself.'

Shaking with fear, Firthallan snatched up his clothes and ran from the room.

Within a few moments the trio in the bedroom heard the sound of the door slamming as he made his panic-stricken exit from the house, and it was now that the grim humour of the situation struck fully home to Colum. His eyes met Rosaleen's, and he saw that the humour had struck her also, and the pair of them

266

grinned at each other and dissolved into helpless laughter.

In the early hours of the morning Terence McCulloch came to the house. He listened in silence to their three separate accounts of what had happened. Then he told them, 'You'll continue to play your parts for the time being. You'll stay here, Colum, and you, Rosa, and act like man and wife. So will you stay, Kitty.'

'For how long do we have to continue with this play-acting?' Rosaleen wanted to know.

'Until I tell you to stop,' McCulloch answered, then ordered, 'Give me the letters and notes sent to you by Firthallan.'

She took a flat box from a hiding place beneath her dressing table and gave it to McCulloch. He quickly scanned through the letters and notes in the box, and sneered, 'If he did all the things to you that he's proposing to do in these letters, then you earned your wages the hard way. The man's perverted.'

Rosaleen's eyes met Colum's and she coloured hotly in embarrassment.

'These will serve admirably,' McCulloch smiled when he had finished scanning the letters. 'Firthallan will curse the day that he ever put pen to paper.'

Then he turned to Colum and handed him an embossed card. 'On Thursday morning you will go to this lawyer, and consult with him as to what suits you can bring against Edward Firthallan. Give him instructions to initiate proceedings.'

Colum frowned doubtfully. 'But surely, if I have to go to the courts then there is a real danger of my being recognised?'

'It'll not come to that,' McCulloch stated confidently. 'I'll crack Firthallan in days. Now remember, all of you, play your parts well.'

'Have I got to drudge for the both of them?' Kitty Wainright demanded indignantly. 'Because if that's the case, then I'll need some help.'

'You can bring Old Betty in to do the donkey work, but she's not to sleep here,' McCulloch conceded. 'And make sure that she believes that the Farquars are a true married pair.'

When he had left them, Kitty Wainright disappeared to her own room, and Colum and Rosaleen faced each other with some degree of awkwardness.

'Don't be concerned that I'm expecting to share your bed in order to convince Old Betty that we're married,' Colum smiled. 'But we'll have to act free and easy around each other when she's in the house.'

Privately he was wondering how frustrating he would find his celibacy when living in intimate proximity with a woman to whom he found himself so strongly attracted.

Rosaleen was grateful that he should respect her in this way. She also was wondering how she would feel, living so intimately with this man. She found him both physically and mentally attractive, but more disturbing than this was the way he was already affecting her emotions. When she talked and laughed with him, she was able to forget that in the eyes of the world she was a paid whore. Then a word or a sentence would bring her cruelly back into confrontation with what she was, and shame would cut deeply into her. It was this sense of shame that troubled her so badly. She did not experience it in the company of other men, but when she was with

Colum Macrae it was an emotion hovering constantly in readiness to strike and wound.

When he had gone to the bedroom next door to her own, Rosaleen sat down at her dressing table, and gazed into the mirror.

'Do you think that you might be falling in love with Colum Macrae?' she asked her reflection. 'Because that would be a very foolish thing for you to do.'

And she fancied that her reflection answered, 'But how can you not fall in love with him, if it is already fated that you should do so?'

'But I'm a paid whore. And that is what he knows me as. Men don't fall in love with whores.'

'Now isn't that a foolish thing to say? Men fall in love with women all the time, and when they fall in love it doesn't matter to them what the woman is, or has been.'

She frowned at her reflection. 'It would matter to Colum Macrae, wouldn't it?'

And her reflection smiled, and told her, 'Well, that's something that you'll just have to wait to find out, won't you . . .'

Chapter Thirty-two

The old man shuffled across the courtyard and the beam of his bull's-eye lantern skittered across the rain-slick cobbles.

Crouched in the shadowed doorway the two men watched him approach and tensed themselves in readiness to spring.

As he drew abreast of their hiding place he was shaken by a fit of coughing, and he spat out great gobs of phlegm, then shuffled on, groaning and complaining audibly.

The hidden men relaxed and resumed their efforts to force the lock of the iron door which guarded the gunpowder store. The crowbar gouged deep streaks into the metal surrounds but the lock held despite the combined strength of the two men heaving against it

'It's no use, Dermot,' Thomas Quinn panted. 'We'll need a key for this one.'

'Then we'll get a key,' Dermot Calatrava hissed. 'That old bastard will know where it's kept.'

Quinn scowled doubtfully. 'We'd be foolish to risk it. If he kicks up a racket it could bring others to see what's up.'

'Then we'll just have to make certain that he doesn't kick up a racket, won't we?' A tangible aura of savage aggression radiated from the smaller man. 'Come on.'

He led the way, keeping in the shadows, following the faint sounds of the watchman's frequent bouts of racking coughing and spluttering.

'There he is.' Dermot halted as he saw the flickering beam of the lantern. 'If we go across there, we can cut him off.'

He pointed to the black bulk of a neighbouring building, and the pair stealthily moved to it.

'Bloody rotten job this is,' Jesse Baden grumbled hoarsely to himself. 'Bloody stinking rotten job. I oughter be in me bed, not traipsing around this bloody rotten place night arter night. A man o' my age deserves to be having a bit o' peace and quiet of a night. I oughtn't to be traipsin' around this bloody place. And where's that bloody cow got to wi' me beer? That's what I'd like to know. Where's her got to? Her should have brought it hours since. I'll rattle her bleedin' bones when her comes, I'll tell you. I'll give her what for.'

Phlegm clotted in his rotting lungs and he stopped to cough and spit and groan yet again.

A heavy weight cannoned against him, and a hand smothered his yell of fright. As he was brought tumbling to the ground the lantern flew from his hand, arched in the air and smashed down on the cobbles and the flaming oil bubbled across the ground, spreading wide and flaring before dying with a smoking hissing.

The small child staring from his bedroom window saw the light shoot high, fall and then flame wide, and his eyes widened in fearful delight.

'Mammy, Mammy!' Crying out at the top of his voice he went scurrying past the bed where his sleeping brothers lay and across the landing to his parents' room. 'Mammy, Mammy, a star just fell into the yard. Mammy, Mammy!'

The woman awoke, and the sound of her child's shrill cries brought her to quick wakefulness.

'What is it, Petey? What's the matter?'

'A star just fell into the yard. A star just fell into the yard. It was on fire, Mammy. The star was on fire.'

'Fire?' The dreaded word galvanised her. 'Arnold, wake up!' She pummelled the snoring man by her side. 'There's a fire! Arnold, there's a fire! Wake up!'

'Fire!' The cry pierced his sleep-dulled senses and he was instantly alert. 'Where? How bad is it?'

'Petey says it's in the yard,' his wife told him, and her face was pale with fear. Her constant nightmare had finally come true. There was fire in the powder mills that her husband managed. 'Oh God, we'll all be killed!' she suddenly shrieked in terror. 'We'll all be blown to smithereens.'

The child, infected by his mother's fear, also began to cry, and from the bedroom across the landing the voices of his brothers, roused by this sudden commotion, added to the noise.

'Shurrup!' Arnold Harbot bellowed and, fearing his wrath more than the prospect of an explosion, the family hushed.

The man tugged on his trousers and ordered his small son, 'Now you show me where this fire is.'

The child led him to the window and pointed down into the courtyard. 'It was down there, Pa. Down there.'

The man squinted into the darkness. 'Well there's nothing there now, Petey. Are you sure that you saw it?'

'Yes, Pa, I saw it. It jumped up and fell down and

272

then it ran along the ground. It was all on fire, Pa,' the child told him solemnly.

Arnold Harbot was a strict, but fair father. He knew that his son was a truthful child, and he accepted that if the child said he had seen something on fire, then he had done so.

'All right, son, you get back into bed now, and all of you go to sleep.'

He went back to his own room and pulled on his boots, telling his frightened wife, 'There's nothing to be seen. But I'll go and check it out anyway. Old Jesse might have done something odd with his lantern, the drunken old fool.'

'I aren't got any keys. The master keeps 'em all in the big house,' Jesse Baden moaned piteously. 'Harbot's got all the keys. I aren't got never a one. Gerrof me, I can't breathe.'

'Where's Harbot?' Dermot demanded. He was kneeling astride the old man's chest, compressing the frail ribcage with his weight.

'In the big house. Over there by the gates.' His words were mumbled and almost unintelligible.

'Where?' Dermot squeezed the sticklike neck until the old man choked for air.

'Over there, t'other side o' the yard,' the old man wheezed.

'That'll be it. On the left-hand side there.' Thomas Quinn pointed to the house which adjoined the main structure of the mills.

'Right, let's go and get the keys,' Dermot ordered.

'What about him?' Quinn asked.

'We'll leave him here.'

273

'But he'll raise the alarm if we leave him here,' Quinn objected.

Dermot laughed softly. 'No he won't.'

He took a thin stiletto dagger from his pocket and thrust it through the old man's right eye, twisting his wrist to rotate the point in rapid circles.

Jesse Baden was dead almost instantly.

'Jasus!' Thomas Quinn gasped in awed shock.

Dermot withdrew the thin blade, wiped it on the dead man's coat, and ordered, 'Come on.'

He ran limping across the yard towards the house and after a final glance at the old man, Thomas Quinn followed.

Arnold Harbot closed his front door just as the shadowy, limping figure was coming up the short path of the house.

He peered and questioned, 'Is that you, Jesse?' and in the next moment was slammed back against the door with the sharp point of the knife blade digging into his throat.

'The keys! Where are they?' his assailant's voice hissed venomously into his ear.

'In my hand,' Arnold Harbot gasped, unnerved by this totally unexpected assault.

As he spoke he saw another dark, shadowed figure join his assailant.

'Who else is in the house?' the voice hissed.

The instinctive desire to protect his family was now paramount in Arnold Harbot's mind. 'Nobody. My family have gone away on a visit.'

'Where are the servants?'

'There's only the one here, the cook. The maids have gone with my family.'

'Go and fetch the cook,' Dermot ordered Quinn, but the big man flatly refused.

'For the love o' God, man, have sense! We don't need any fuckin' cook. We can't waste any more time. Let's get the job done with before anybody else shows up.'

For a brief instant a white heat of fury swept over Dermot at this challenge to his authority. But then cooler reason prevailed, and he realised that the other man was right. They needed no other hostage now they had possession of the keys.

He shifted his grip to the prisoner's hair, and keeping the knife point digging into the soft roll of flesh beneath Harbot's chin, forced the man to walk in front of him back to the powder store.

Megan Baden kept her shawl pulled tight around her head as shelter against the cold night air. She carried the jug of beer in her hands, and fought against the desire to drink from it, knowing from past experience that if her husband found the measure short he would beat her unmercifully.

She passed the horses' drinking trough at the bottom of the hill on which the powder mill was situated and briefly considered whether she could risk taking a drink of ale and topping the jug up with water. Again past experience dissuaded her. The last time she had done that she had lost two front teeth to her husband's fist.

'It aren't fair,' she pitied herself. 'If ever a poor soul suffered then that poor soul is me. I should never have married that mean bad bugger. Me Mam was right about him. He 'udden't give a blind man the time not even if he was wearing two watches, tight bastard that he is.'

She climbed the steep hill, and was wheezing heavily

by the time she reached the mill gates. She leaned against the wall to recover her breath, peering through the fretted ornamental ironwork of the gates into the courtyard. She blinked, and stared hard. Although she was old and decrepit her eyesight was still keen and sharp, and she could clearly distinguish the three men crossing the courtyard and see that they were not walking normally. The man in front seemed to be held by the man with him.

The cloud cover was pierced momentarily by a shaft of moonlight, and in that brief instant Megan Baden recognised Arnold Harbot as the leading figure. The brief light also revealed another object on the ground beyond the three men.

Excitement coursed through the old woman. 'There's summat going on here.'

She carefully placed the jug of beer against the base of the wall, and watched closely. As soon as the men disappeared inside the powder store she scurried into the courtyard and went to the object that was lying on the ground. One look told her all that she wished to know. Her hated husband was dead and, judging by the bloody socket of his right eye, he had been murdered.

The old woman had lived long and hard, and was no stranger to violent deaths. The discovery of her husband did not panic her or cause her to lose her wits; quite the opposite in fact. She felt a fierce exultation as she stared down at his upturned face.

'You've got what you deserve at long last, you wicked old bugger,' she told him, then her sense of self-preservation took over. She scurried back through the main gate, and took a long drink from the beer jug.

'Ahh, that's better,' she breathed in satisfaction, and

wiped her mouth with her ragged sleeve. 'Now what's to be done?'

She took another gulp of beer, wiped her mouth again, and decided. 'I might get a reward if I fetch the Peelers. Them fellas with Harbot must ha' done my old man in.'

She carefully hid the beer jug behind a pile of rubbish and then scurried back down the hill, her shawl flapping around and her skirts billowing.

Inside the powder store it was pitch black, and Dermot demanded, 'Where's the light?'

'Just here.' The manager was eager to co-operate, fearing that unless he did so he would die.

'You'll have to let go of me,' Harbot said. 'I won't be able to strike a light otherwise.'

Dermot released his grip but kept the knife point pressed into the back of the manager's neck.

There was the small flaring explosion of a lucifer match being ignited and then the soft mellow glow of an oil lamp drove back the engulfing blackness.

The lamp was set in an alcove and had a thick glass window between itself and the inner room where the gunpowder was kept, so that there was no danger of contact between flame and explosive.

Harbot unlocked the inner door and pushed it wide. By now his ordeal was starting to affect him strongly, and his body was trembling visibly, while sweat beaded on his forehead. He stared at his two captors with frightened eyes.

'Take whatever you want,' he begged, 'I won't say anything about it to anyone. Just take what you want and go. Please, go.'

Dermot vented a roar of laughter, and then smacked the manager lightly across the cheek, and admonished, 'Now you're insulting us by calling us thieves. We're not thieves. We haven't come here to steal anything. We're soldiers. And we are here in the service of our nation.'

Harbot shook his head in utter bewilderment, and Dermot requested Thomas Quinn, 'Hand me the bar, will you please, Thomas.'

He hefted the crowbar in his right hand, lifted it high and smashed it down across Harbot's head.

The manager emitted a faint cry, then slowly crumpled to the floor.

Dermot stared down at his inert body and remarked with distaste, 'I don't like the cut of this fellow at all, you know, Thomas. He's not a gentleman. I can smell the sweat of him.'

Quinn's dour features betrayed nothing, but in his mind he was fast becoming convinced that Dermot Calatrava had finally gone completely insane.

From around his waist Dermot uncoiled the long length of slowmatch.

'Break open a couple of kegs of powder, please, Thomas, and spread it around. Make sure that you reach all the areas. I'll work out what length of slowmatch is needful.' He chuckled amusedly. 'It would be ironic if I didn't allow enough length to give us time to get clear, wouldn't it? As the poet says, we'd be hoist with our own petard.'

It took only a short time to lay the slowmatch as he wanted it, and by then Thomas Quinn had finished his task.

'We'll have a full half hour to get clear, Thomas.' Dermot struck a lucifer match and lit the end of the

278

incendiary cord. It spluttered and smouldered, and the bright red glow travelled slowly along the cord towards the inner storeroom.

Outside, Dermot locked the iron door, and hurled the key into the darkness, smiling at his companion. 'That will make sure that nobody can put the fire out, won't it?'

They moved towards the main gates and had passed through them when a stentorian bellow shattered the silence.

'Stand fast in the Queen's name!'

Two police constables and a police sergeant came running at them, wielding wooden truncheons.

Dermot whipped out his revolver and coolly waited until the policemen were only scant yards away, then aimed and fired.

Even as the explosions sounded Thomas Quinn's pistol barked, and two of the policemen staggered and dropped. The third, young and burly, kept coming and his truncheon flailed wildly at Quinn's head, thudding into bone, and the big man cried out in pain and stumbled backwards. Dermot aimed and fired again, and his bullet impacted into the side of the policeman's skull, and he spun round and fell.

'Are you all right?' he demanded of Quinn.

The man was groaning, slumped half-dazed against the wall, his hands clapped to the long gash on his head from which blood was streaming.

Dermot looked down at the fallen bodies. Two were still alive, one moaning softly, the other trying to rise to his feet. Dermot stepped to the nearer of the two, put the muzzle of his gun behind the man's ear, and pulled the trigger. Then did the same to the other.

By now lights were being lit in the adjoining terraces of houses, windows being raised and voices calling.

Dermot stared hard at Thomas Quinn. The big man's face was masked with blood, his clothing likewise. Dermot knew that dawn was close, and he also knew that with Quinn bleeding as he was and his clothing bloodied, they would attract attention in their passage through the city streets. He looked about him, and saw that men and women were already coming from their houses, and knew that in only minutes a hue and cry would spread throughout the city.

He faced his companion. 'I'm really sorry, Thomas. But I've no other choice. You'll have to stay here. They'll capture both of us else.'

He levelled his pistol and shot Quinn in the middle of his forehead. Then ran away from the gathering crowd and into the maze of mean streets. He rounded the first corner and ducked into an entryway. He stripped off his cloak and bundled his top hat into its folds then threw it further up the entry. He heard the howling pursuit coming rapidly nearer and the feet pounding on the cobblestones, and as the crowd hurtled past the entry mouth he came running from it and joined in with the mass, his mouth wide, howling in concert with the rest of them.

Chapter Thirty-three

When Dermot Calatrava got off the night train at Margate station he bore little resemblance to the dandy who had left the town a week before. His face was grimy and gaunt with weariness, his clothing travel-stained.

Although the news of the Nottingham outrage had been transmitted to London by the electric telegraph, it had yet to be printed in the newspapers or spread wide by word of mouth, and Dermot was confident that it would be hours or even days before it became public knowledge.

Yet still he acted with caution. He carefully reconnoitred the environs of his rented house, trying to establish if there was anyone watching the building. It seemed to be all clear.

There was a light in the downstairs window and he moved stealthily to peep through the grimy panes. He saw Theresa Quinn sitting at the table, a bottle of gin and a half-filled glass in front of her. He tapped on the window, and she instantly came to it.

'Is it all clear, Theresa?' he called softly.

'Come round to the back door,' she told him.

When he came through the door she questioned, 'Where's Quinn?'

'He's dead,' he told her bluntly. 'The Peelers were waiting in ambush for us when we came out of the mill.

One of them shot Thomas in the head. But I killed him, and two others with him. I'm truly sorry for your loss, Theresa. He was a good man.'

She shrugged uncaringly. 'He was a good man for the Cause, Master Dermot, but he was a bad husband to me. All I ever got from him was harsh words and batterings. I'll not be grieving for him.'

She looked closely at the young man. 'You look all done in. Take a drink while I get you some food.'

Her calmness steadied his jangling nerves, and after she had drawn the curtains he sat at the table and drank straight from the bottle, gasping as the cheap raw spirit stung his throat.

She put a cold joint of beef, a loaf of bread and lump of salt butter before him and he fell upon the food with voracious hunger, cutting slices of meat and cramming them into his mouth, together with the bread and butter, and frequently swigging from the gin bottle.

When his agonising pangs of hunger had been assuaged he asked her, 'Has anything happened here? Have you had word from Rosa?'

She shook her head.

'We'll need to move from here straight away,' he told her. 'There'll be a hue and cry raised and rewards offered for our capture.'

'But no one knows us here, who'd suspect us?' she objected.

'McCulloch knows we're here.' He scowled. 'I don't trust him to keep his mouth shut if there's money to be gained by turning us in.'

'All right.' She accepted unquestioningly. 'I'll get our stuff packed.'

Despite his weariness Dermot went to the wash house

and by candlelight he stripped off and bathed in cold water drawn from the handpump, sluicing his body repeatedly until the grime and sweat were cleansed from his flesh. Then he went to his bedroom and, throwing himself down on top of the bed, fell into the snoring sleep of utter exhaustion, until woken by Theresa Quinn a couple of hours later.

By dawn they were on the paddle steamer bound for London.

Chapter Thirty-four

Colum shaved and dressed with care before going downstairs. He had come to anticipate with pleasure the first daily sight of Rosaleen Calatrava sitting opposite him across the breakfast table. For two weeks now the couple had been playing the roles of husband and wife, and for Colum it had been one of the happiest, albeit most sexually frustrating, periods of his life. It seemed to him that every day he discovered some new facet of Rosaleen's character which could delight him, and he was forced to admit to himself that he was infatuated with her.

When he entered the dining room she looked up from where she was sitting and smiled in welcome. She was very fresh and beautiful in her plain white gown, her long black hair netted in a snood hanging down her back, her complexion and red lips devoid of any cosmetic artifices.

Kitty Wainright brought in a platter of eggs and bacon, and the newspaper. And Rosaleen poured him coffee and added cream and sugar to his taste.

Colum revelled in this feminine attention. Such contented domesticity was a new experience for him. During his marriage the meal table had for the most part constituted a battleground verbally fought across by him and his wife.

For Rosaleen also the past two weeks had been something of a revelation. She had found in this red-haired man someone whom she was coming to believe she could happily share her life with. He was a companion with whom she could talk and laugh easily, and she had developed an admiration for his intelligence and wide experience of life. There was one aspect of him which she appreciated above all else, and that was the simple fact that he treated her always with respect. There had been many moments when she had seen in his eyes the desire he felt for her, but he had never by word or gesture made any sexual advances towards her, and after the long years of being treated as a sexual plaything by men, she valued this respect he showed towards her above all else. She was beginning to hope that their relationship could develop into a union that could endure for a lifetime. And she was tentatively allowing herself to begin to believe that her long years of shame had come to an end, that from this time on a new life was starting for her, a life in which she could regain her self-respect and put behind her everything that had gone before.

Colum glanced at the newspaper before beginning to eat, and a paragraph heading caught his attention. It was a report of the murder of three policemen and the carnage of an explosion in Nottingham. He frowned as he read the brief account, and instantly surmised that this outrage was the work of the American. He knew that Conrad Cumlinson would be furious at this fresh evidence of his, Colum's, failure to achieve any worthwhile result in the hunt for the American, and he felt a frisson of anxiety at what his formidable employer might now do.

Rosaleen noted his worried frown and enquired, 'Is anything the matter, Colum?'

Colum wished with all his heart that he could be honest with her; that he could tell her the truth about himself. Instead he merely replied, 'I was just feeling sorry for these poor people in Nottingham.'

He handed her the newspaper, and indicated the report.

'Oh my God!' Rosaleen gasped as fear clutched her heart.

Colum was surprised at her reaction, and she instantly realised that her unguarded exclamation might cause him to wonder at it.

'It's such a terrible thing. It appals me,' she told him, and he was touched at this evidence of her gentle heart.

'I'm sorry it distresses you so,' he sympathised.

She really was feeling distress, and desperately worried about Dermot. She knew without any shred of doubt that this explosion and the killings of the policemen were his work. What was causing her the greatest concern was the identity of the dead man who, the report stated, was believed to be one of the perpetrators of the explosion. It must be either Dermot or Thomas Quinn. But which one?

She knew that she must be alone, or otherwise she would betray herself. Brutality and indifference she could cope with, but Colum Macrae's tender concern for her threatened to break down her defences, and she was terrified that she would give way to the almost overwhelming urge to confide in him, and seek comfort in his arms.

She forced a smile. 'I have to go back to my room, Colum.'

'Why? Are you feeling ill?' he begged to know.

She shook her head. 'We women have certain problems that occur from time to time. It's a normal thing, and nothing for you to worry about. But I must have some privacy for a while.'

At the mention of 'women's problems' he nodded in understanding and forbore to press her further. 'Of course, my dear, I understand. We'll talk later.'

She smiled gratefully and then hurried to her own room. Her worry about Dermot intensified and she felt near to panic.

I mustn't give way to it. I must keep calm, I must keep calm, she reiterated over and over again, and the sheer repetition seemed to have a steadying effect. The first thing I must do is to find out who the dead man is. I should go and see Theresa.

She dismissed that idea almost instantly. If the woman knew anything, then she would undoubtedly come straight here. The mere fact of her absence was evidence that she knew nothing.

McCulloch, she thought. He could probably find out who the dead man is. He's got contacts everywhere.

But she was afraid to go to McCulloch. She did not trust the man. As far as she knew he had as yet no inkling that Dermot was responsible for the series of explosions and the resulting deaths and injuries. She was very uncertain as to how McCulloch would react if she told him that it was her brother who was carrying out these attacks.

She paced up and down her room, trying to decide on a course of action, and the hours painfully wore away. She felt that her nerves were becoming shredded, and what was far worse, she feared that a net was inexorably closing around her from which she would never break free.

Time and time again her thoughts were drawn to the innocent victims of the explosions, and though she tried to harden her heart and count them as necessary casualties of a just and holy war, she was unable to do so, and guilt gnawed at her. Then she thought of her own dead loved ones, and her misery intensified unbearably.

'Why, God? Why? Why do you let such things happen?' she challenged, and anguished sobs burst from her.

At that moment, Colum passed Rosaleen's door on the way to his own room and heard her terrible grief. Impulsively he went in to her.

She was standing by the side of the bed, her face buried in her hands, her shoulders heaving uncontrollably.

'Oh, my love.' Seeking only to comfort her he went and took her in his arms, cradling her gently against his chest, his hand stroking her hair.

Like a child seeking solace she clutched at him, nestling her face into the hollow of his neck, and they remained close-locked until her sobbing eased and slowly she calmed.

She looked up into his face and saw his concern, and the loving warmth of his eyes, and for the first time since she was a small child she felt totally safe, totally protected.

Their lips tenderly touched, and tasted, and she knew that she wanted this man as her lover. She wanted to give herself body and soul into his keeping.

Desire was pulsing through Colum, yet it was not a desire to take, but rather to give. To give her his loving, to give her delight and pleasure, to cherish and protect her, to share his life with her.

'I love you, Rosa,' he told her sincerely. 'And your troubles are my troubles. Tell me what's upsetting you so. Let me share it with you and perhaps I can do something to ease your grief.'

The urge to confess, to tell him everything clamoured within her. But she could not give way to it. She could never betray her beloved brother, not even to this man whom she knew now without any shred of doubt that she was in love with.

'It's nothing that anyone can help me with, my dear,' she told him. 'So please don't press me further.'

He frowned worriedly. He knew that he must leave her for a while, that he must go immediately to the pawnbroker's in Leather Lane and find out what Conrad Cumlinson now required from him, after this outrage in Nottingham.

'Listen, honey, I have to go out for a while. We'll talk about this when I come back. I'll not be long.'

He kissed her and they stayed locked in a gentle, loving embrace for long, long seconds, and then she pushed him away from her.

'Hurry back, sweetheart,' she whispered tenderly.

Chapter Thirty-five

For some years Terence McCulloch had had an arrangement with a clerk in the receiving room of the Central Electric Telegraph Office. McCulloch paid the man well to pass on to him any confidential messages received over the wire which might concern events that were currently of interest to McCulloch. This advance news service was of great utility to McCulloch, enabling him to profit by being in possession of information before it became general public knowledge. One series of events which had been of great interest to McCulloch was the explosions in the powder mills and factories. He had seen the reports telegraphed to the police and Government offices, and he had realised that the explosions were not accidents, but deliberate. McCulloch strongly suspected that Dermot Calatrava was involved with these explosions. When the reports about the Nottingham outrage came over the wires the clerk hastened to bring copies to McCulloch.

He studied the detailed accounts thoroughly, then sent for Joseph Connors and despatched him to Margate to check on the whereabouts of Calatrava.

'If he's not there, but there's someone in the house, do you want me to get it out of them where he is?' Connors asked.

'Yes, I must know where he is.'

McCulloch then sent for Thomas Docherty and issued instructions that he was to keep a watch on the house in Holloway, and carefully note anyone entering or leaving who was not a part of the present household. If he saw the American, then he was to report that sighting instantly to McCulloch.

'The American?' Docherty showed surprise. 'Do you mean the one who came to talk to us about killing the Royal Family?'

McCulloch made no answer and the silence lengthened while he pondered, and Docherty twitched and fidgeted and sweated nervously.

McCulloch reluctantly decided that he must divulge a secret shared up until now only with Joseph Connors. To McCulloch secrets were treasures to be hoarded and cherished. They were potent weapons to be used against enemies. Secrets were both his armour and his armoury, and it was only when he had no other course of action open to him that he disclosed any of them.

He fixed Docherty with a threatening scowl and told him, 'Listen carefully. What I am going to tell you must go no further than ourselves . . .' He went on to explain the relationship between the American and the woman in the house in Holloway. Then he dismissed the man with a further warning to keep his mouth tight closed about what he had learned.

When he was alone again, he sat and thought deeply about the disturbing situation that had unexpectedly risen to confront him.

Terence McCulloch had for a decade been playing a very devious game. Once he had been a true Irish patriot, and in the abortive rebellion of 1848 he had played a major role. But that fiasco had cost him dearly.

He had lost everything and had been reduced to beggary, and those who had once cheered him for his patriotism turned from him and spurned him. That experience had embittered him, and had changed him from an idealistic patriot into a ruthless and utterly cynical self-server. His present involvement with the Irish revolutionary movement was purely to serve his own ends. It gave him access to money supplied by the American-Irish, and enabled him to wield a degree of power over elements amongst the expatriate Irish in this country.

He knew that the British Secret Service had penetrated the various Irish revolutionary groupings, including his own, and that they also had informers placed in the American Fenian Circles.

He also knew the factor that influenced the British authorities to leave him alone. Through his proprietorship of male and female brothels he had accrued knowledge and documentary evidence concerning the sexual practices of certain high-ranking politicians and other prominent members of the British ruling establishment. Those men, knowing what he knew about them and terrified that he would reveal all, were forced to exert their protective influence on his behalf.

But McCulloch was well aware that that unwilling protection was of finite quality. His leadership of a Fenian Circle could be winked at only so long as that Circle remained merely a focal point for would-be revolutionaries, and did not represent any actual physical threat to law and order.

McCulloch was confident that should the members of his Fenian Circle begin to put into action their hotheaded threats of armed rebellion, then the Authorities would move swiftly and ruthlessly against him and them, and his present protection would avail him nothing. Scandal was, after all, much easier to survive than armed attack.

This was why McCulloch regarded Dermot Calatrava as a serious problem. He was afraid that the man's deadly attacks would provoke the Authorities into a ruthless response which would bring about his own ruin. But he was not yet sure in his own mind about how to deal with Dermot Calatrava. The man had been recommended by the Americans, which meant that he was highly regarded by them. If McCulloch was to have him killed, it might well cause considerable ill feeling between himself and the Americans, and a consequent loss of American money.

'Damn you, Calatrava, you've put me between a rock and a hard place,' McCulloch murmured grimly.

His thoughts turned to Rosaleen Calatrava, and he gave grudging acknowledgement to her cunning. She's a sly bitch, that one. She had me believing her tales of how crippled and weak her brother was. Still, I don't want to lose her if it can be avoided. She did a great job for me with Firthallan. I've a couple of other likely prospects lined up for her already. It would be a great pity to lose her now.

He had already approached Firthallan and intimated to the man that he could prevent Captain Robert Farquar from continuing with his legal suit, and Firthallan had readily agreed to pay the very large sums of money that that prevention would require.

How can I keep the woman working for me, and still rid myself of her brother? wondered McCulloch.

He brooded through the long hours, as night's

darkness closed around the smoking chimneys of the city.

Joseph Connors returned from Margate soon after dawn.

'Now, Joseph, what have you got to tell me?' McCulloch growled. 'What have you found out?'

'The house is empty, Mr McCulloch. I got in through a window and checked it all out. They've done a runner all right. I made a few enquiries and found the cabman who took them and their luggage to the steamer stage. From the description it was Dermot Calatrava and that serving woman, Quinn.'

McCulloch swore softly. 'So it was Tom Quinn who was killed, and that mad bastard is out there somewhere. But where? How do we find him?

'If we don't stop his gallop very, very soon, he'll bring ruin down on all of us. We could all find ourselves kicking our heels on a gallows tree, or at best making the trip to Van Diemen's Land.' He paused to let that unpleasant fact sink fully home, and Joseph Connors raised his hand in the air, like a schoolboy seeking permission from his teacher.

'Yes, Joseph?' McCulloch permitted.

'We've got Colum Macrae placed with the sister, Mr McCulloch. Surely you've only got to warn him what's happening, and he'll be able to find out where Calatrava is? And there's Kitty Wainright as well.'

McCulloch's breath wheezed as he chuckled mirthlessly. 'Ahh well now, Joseph, you know that Kitty Wainright can't be relied on any more. The drink has her brain puddled. I only gave her the job at Holloway for charity's sake. And what you haven't considered is

294

how trustworthy Colum Macrae is at this moment in time. You see it's my opinion that he's fallen head over heels in love with the whore.

'When a man's in love, Joseph, he has a tendency to do foolish things, and to forget where his best interest lies. So I don't think that we can entirely rely on Mr Macrae to be with us, should it come to a choice between Rosaleen Calatrava and ourselves.'

Connors nodded in grim acceptance.

'So now, Joseph,' McCulloch's good temper appeared to have returned in full measure, as he smiled broadly, 'I think that the solution to our problem is really very simple. We first of all find out from Rosaleen Calatrava if she knows her brother's whereabouts, and then we pay him a visit. If she doesn't know, then we simply set a trap for Dermot Calatrava, and we use her as the bait. Either way, we'll have him.'

Within the hour McCulloch arrived at the house in Holloway. Colum Macrae had gone out on his errand to Leather Lane, and Rosaleen was sitting alone in the drawing room.

McCulloch's shrewd eyes studied the drawn-looking face of the young woman. He saw the newspaper with its account of the Nottingham outrage on her lap, and he became absolutely certain that she had been aware of her brother's part in the series of attacks on the factories and power mills, culminating in Nottingham.

He decided he would not waste time fencing with her. 'I can ease your mind about your brother, Rosaleen. He's still alive and well. It was Thomas Quinn who was killed.'

She gasped and physically started, and McCulloch

nodded and lied, 'Oh yes, my dear, I've known all along what Dermot was getting up to, blowing up these factories and powder mills all around the country. What I can't understand is why you should have tried to keep it secret from me? We're on the same side, aren't we?'

He gave her no chance to answer, he wanted to keep her mentally off balance.

'Anyway, the thing we have to do now is to decide what's to be done about this present mess. There'll be a hue and cry after Dermot the like of which has never been seen before in this country. Every man, woman and child's hand will be raised against him.

'He's gone from the house in Margate, and Theresa Quinn's gone with him. We've got to get him out of the country and back to America. So you'd best tell me where he is now, and we can start to get things organised.'

She shook her head, and her face was deathly pale. 'I don't know where he is. I didn't even know whether he was alive or dead until you just told me.'

'Oh he's alive all right, you may be sure of that.' McCulloch believed her when she denied knowing her brother's whereabouts, but he remained confident that Dermot Calatrava would contact his sister, and sooner rather than later.

'Listen, my dear, I'm sure that your brother will make contact with you very soon.' His tone was kindly and concerned. 'When he does, you must inform me straight away so that we can organise Dermot's escape.' He smiled. 'In the meantime you must not worry about him. He's a very capable young man, and far too intelligent to let himself be caught by the police. And together we shall insure that the Government agents do not catch him either.'

Rosaleen's relief at being told that her brother was still alive momentarily overshadowed her dislike and distrust of this man. She was able to smile at him as she readily assented to his request, with no intention of complying with it.

'I'll let you know the very moment I hear from Dermot, Mr McCulloch. And I thank you from the bottom of my heart for coming here to let me know that he is alive and well.'

When McCulloch had gone, Rosaleen could conceal her joy no longer, and a beaming smile lit up her face. Her only regret was that she could not share her good news with Colum when he returned.

'But I can do something to share my happiness with him,' she told herself, and smiled roguishly.

Colum's visit to Leather Lane was fruitless. He was merely told that no new instructions had been received for him and that he was to report back in a week's time. If something came up before then that required any action on his part, he would be contacted at the house in Holloway.

Colum was relieved that at least Conrad Cumlinson had not dismissed him from service. He hurried eagerly back to Holloway, anxious to see if Rosaleen was feeling more cheerful.

He went to the drawing room, found it empty and called out for Rosaleen.

Kitty Wainright came scowling at his shout.

'She's in her room. She said would you go up to see her when you came back.'

Colum ran upstairs and found Rosaleen standing by her bedside, wearing her peignoir, her long black hair flowing loose about her shoulders. She smiled as he entered and held out her arms. He went to her and kissed her hungrily.

'Are you feeling better, honey?'

She smiled radiantly and answered simply, 'I want you, sweetheart. Let's not remain apart any longer.'

Without haste they put aside their clothes, constantly kissing and caressing, and when naked stood for long, long moments glorying in the sight of each other's bodies. Then they sank down upon the bed and gave themselves to each other with passionate joy.

Chapter Thirty-six

The total death toll at Nottingham was three police-men and nine civilians. Nineteen others had been injured, and there was no way that the outrage could be glossed over as having occurred by mischance. A nation-wide hue and cry was raised for the perpetrators.

Conrad Cumlinson was under immense pressure to bring the criminals to justice. He travelled to Nottingham himself to interview Megan Baden and other eyewitnesses to the shooting of the policemen and Thomas Quinn.

He had Thomas Quinn's corpse, which no one in Nottingham had been able to identify, brought to his new offices close to Charing Cross. Then summoned Detective Inspector Charlie Anderson to view the dead man.

The two men went down to the cool basement where the corpse lay on a table covered in a sheet, and Cumlinson stripped the sheet back.

Charlie Anderson peered closely at Quinn's battered features, then shook his head. 'No, sir. He's not known to me.'

Cumlinson grimaced in disappointment. 'That's a great pity, Inspector. I tell you frankly, I was pinning my hopes on your identification.'

'You believe the perpetrator of the Nottingham

explosion is the same man as has blown up the other mills and factories, do you then, sir?'

'I do, Inspector. The man we know as the American. It bears his hallmark. It would seem that he's abandoned his ambitions to assassinate the Queen's son, and instead is concentrating on blowing up her subjects.'

'I'm surprised that Macrae hasn't ferreted him out by now. He got to Billy Gilligan in short order.'

'Yes,' Cumlinson replied tersely. 'And he seems to have gained a considerable degree of trust from Terence McCulloch. But McCulloch hasn't yet led him to the American.'

'I suppose you've already considered bringing McCulloch in, sir,' Anderson offered diffidently.

'It's a question of relative values, Inspector, as you well appreciate.

'Terence Aloysius McCulloch is a remarkable man. I have over the years come to know a great deal about him. He enjoys the protection of some very powerful individuals in this country. He has amassed information concerning those individuals' secret peccadillos, and should anything untoward happen to McCulloch, or in the event of his untimely death, he has made it plain that that information will then become public knowledge. The resulting scandal could create immense unrest throughout the country, destroy political careers and bring great families to ruination.

'Therefore the situation must become desperate in the extreme before I would be permitted to take action against McCulloch. Of course, the man is aware that he is virtually untouchable, and acts accordingly.

'However, this situation is not without certain advantages to myself. By leaving McCulloch untouched I am able to constantly evaluate the progress of the Fenian Brotherhood in the furtherance of their aims.

'I've had an informer, Seamus Slavin, in his group almost since it was first formed. Recently I was forced to jettison Slavin, but with Macrae *in situ* it did not affect our intelligence gathering. I'd very much like to have things remain as they are for as long as possible. But . . .' he pursed his lips judiciously, 'it may well become necessary to force McCulloch to divulge the identity of the American if these outrages continue. I'm already being subjected to immense pressure from the Prime Minister and the Home Secretary to do whatever must be done to apprehend those who are responsible for these explosions. However, I shall let Macrae continue with his efforts for a little longer, before I take other action. I've no wish to risk my own career at this stage by damaging McCulloch, and so being held as the man responsible for the deluge of scandal that would result.'

Anderson peered at the dead man, and bent to examine the stiffened hands more closely, using his fingers to probe and knead the cold flesh.

He turned his attention to the face. 'We might still be able to identify this fellow, sir.'

Hope flared in Cumlinson's expression.

'I'm of the opinion that he's been a pug, sir. A pugilist. If you take his hands, then they feel as if they've been broke more than once, and his knuckles are all misshapen. And he's got the dense flesh around his eye sockets that the prizefighter develops as a result of being clouted there so many times. You can't go by his nose being broken, because that can happen in a score of ways, but with his hands and his eyebrows like they are,

I'm confident that he's been a professional pugilist.

'I know an old man who's always been a great follower of "the fancy". He's seen every pug who's ever stepped into the ring these past fifty years, and he can recite their histories. With your permission, sir, I'd like to bring the old man with me to have a look at this one.'

'Bring him immediately, Inspector.' Cumlinson had cheered up considerably, and he vouchsafed his companion a wintry smile. 'What would I do without you, Inspector?'

'What would you indeed, sir,' the Inspector grinned.

Within hours Anderson returned in company with the old man.

'It's Tom Quinn!' the old man declared positively.

'Are you sure?' Cumlinson demanded, and the old man waxed indignant.

'O' course I'm bloody well sure! I saw him fight Isaac Poulson at Stratford in the spring of fifty-three. Poulson had the mastery of him in twenty-seven rounds. He was game enough, was Tom Quinn, but he hadn't got the science to match the top men.'

'Have you any knowledge of where he's lived, and what he's been doing recently?' Cumlinson urged. 'Think hard, man, you'll be well rewarded for any information you can give me.'

The old man scratched his head and pondered for some time. 'Well now, as I recollect I did hear as how Tom Quinn had been seen in the Strand a few months since, driving a carriage and pair. He was in livery, so he must have been in service. But I can't tell you any more than that.'

'Who was it who gave you this information?' Cumlinson pressed.

'Benny Gibbs. He's the crossing sweeper by Johnson's Chop House. He used to be a good pug in his day. He knew Tom Quinn well.'

'Very well.' Cumlinson gave the old man several gold sovereigns, and instructed, 'You are to forget what you've seen here today.'

The old man was quick with fervent assurances. 'Oh, I will, sir. You've no call to fret about that. I've forgot already.'

'Make sure that you have,' Charlie Anderson warned, 'because I'll soon find out if you open your mouth.'

When the old man had gone, Charlie Anderson offered, 'Do you want me to have a word with this Benny Gibbs, sir? He might be able to tell us something more.'

Cumlinson nodded. 'Yes, if you please, Inspector.' He stared down at the waxlike features of the dead man, and mused aloud, 'It might well be that through Thomas Quinn here, we've found a pathway to the American.'

Chapter Thirty-seven

The Strand streamed with traffic, the iron-rimmed wheels and iron-shod hooves creating a clangourous uproar on the stone setts of the roadway. Horses constantly defecated and the steaming manure was trodden and scattered and crushed to form an odorous ankle-deep carpeting.

The ragged, burly man wielded the big besom broom with a furious haste, clearing a path through the filth for the polished boots of his customer to tread on. When the broom and the polished boots reached the opposite pavement a coin changed hands.

'Thank you, sir. God bless you!' The coin was secreted among the rags and the hoarse voice bellowed, 'Who wants to cross? Who wants to cross? Do you want to cross, sir?'

'No, Benny, I want a word with you, that's all. I'll pay you well for it.' Charlie Anderson held a gold sovereign between his finger and thumb and showed it to the ragged man. 'And if that word is to my liking, there might be another o' these for you.'

Benny Gibbs's eyes were bloodshot with gin, his face a wreckage of thick-ridged scar tissue, and his nose a flattened smear of shapeless flesh. But those bloodshot eyes were alert and knowing. 'You'll be a jack, you will.'

'I will indeed, Benny,' Anderson agreed pleasantly.

'Now you tell me what you can about the last time you saw Thomas Quinn. The Tom Quinn who was one of the fancy, like you.'

Benny Gibbs answered with quick readiness. 'A few months ago, it was. He was driving a carriage and pair, dressed in good livery. His people warn't short of a few bob, I should say, the horseflesh was prime. Matching bays they was. He parked the carriage over there, just down from Johnson's Chop House, and he went and had a couple o' words with the doorman at the Chop House. Then he started to go back to the carriage.

'I hailed him, and he didn't look very pleased about it neither. But fair play, he stopped and he give me the time o' day, and a couple of bob, and said he couldn't stay to talk because he was on urgent business. And that was it really.'

He reached out his filthy hand and the policeman dropped the sovereign into it.

Benny Gibbs's toothless gums showed in a sly grin. 'There's summat else I just recalled, as well.'

'What's that?' Anderson wanted to know.

The other man rubbed his fingers together. 'Another word, another sov, warn't that what you told me?'

Anderson scowled. 'No, Benny. What I told you was that if the word was to my liking there would be another sovereign. So don't you try being a fly cove with me, my lad, or you'll be seeing the inside of the steel in double-quick time.' His voice hardened threateningly. 'Come on. Spit it out.'

Benny Gibbs was not disconcerted by this abrupt change of attitude. His toothless gums bared again as he chortled admiringly.

'My oath, you'm a bit of a tartar, ain't you just. Well

now, like I told you, Tom Quinn went back to the carriage, and a widow lady gets out and they both goes back towards the Chop House, and the widow lady has a word with one of the waiters. Then the widow lady goes back to the carriage and arter a few minutes a gentleman comes out from the Chop House and Tom Quinn speaks to him, and they both goes to the carriage and the gentleman gets into it to keep the widow lady company, and Tom Quinn drives it off.

'He aren't been gone but a half hour when he drives the carriage back here and the gentleman gets out. The gentleman looks bloody awful, as if he's just been struck by fuckin' lightning. He looks pig-sick, I'll tell you.'

Charlie Anderson's agile brain was racing. The instincts honed by years of man hunting were sensing that he had struck lucky.

He gave the crossing-sweeper the second sovereign, and then produced a third.

Benny Gibbs's bloodshot eyes glistened with delight. This was becoming one of the best days he had known for many, many years.

'Now then, Benny, this gentleman, might you be knowing his name?'

'He's one of my regular customers, because he crosses here often to go to Johnson's Chop House. His name is Smyth-Prescott – the Reverend Smyth-Prescott. And he's a chaplain to the Royal Family.'

Pure elation surged through Charlie Anderson as an absolute certainty burgeoned in his mind that somehow this meeting between Thomas Quinn, the widow lady and the Reverend Smyth-Prescott had a direct connection with the attempted assassination of the Prince of Wales in Richmond Park.

Charlie Anderson grinned. 'Here, I really like the word you've given me.'

He pressed not one, but three more golden sovereigns into Gibbs's filthy hand, and they parted as two very happy men.

Within hours Charlie Anderson had sought out the Reverend Smyth-Prescott, and was closeted with him for a long-drawn-out and strictly confidential interview.

Chapter Thirty-eight

Conrad Cumlinson listened closely to Charlie Anderson's detailed account of his interview with the Reverend Smyth-Prescott. The cleric had proven to be an easy target for the wily Anderson, who had bluffed him into believing that he knew far more than he actually did. Smyth-Prescott had broken down completely and had confessed the whole sordid story of his perversions and resulting blackmail by the mysterious widow woman.

Cumlinson's thin lips twisted with a contemptuous disgust, and not for the first time he asked himself why he had devoted his life to defending a nation whose ruling classes were so riddled with degeneracy and corruption.

'So, Inspector, this was how the American obtained the necessary information to be able to plan his assassination attempt against the Prince.

'This woman – Smyth-Prescott describes her as a lady in manners, speech and dress? Have you any ideas about who she may be, Inspector?'

Anderson's fleshy features betrayed just a hint of smugness. 'Well, sir, after I'd talked with Benny Gibbs I gave some thought to the description he'd given me of the carriage and pair she was riding in. Benny said that the horseflesh was prime. Two matching bays, that must have cost a fortune. He said the whole rig reeked of money. So I put a man on making enquiries around the horse dealers and auctioneers. There was a matching pair of bays that was sold about eighteen months ago by Jesse Beaumont, who's got the stables down Bleeker Mews in Bayswater. Fine beasts they were, and there was a lot of interest in them at the time; bidding went very high, very high indeed. It was Solomon Montague who bought them.'

'The financier?' Cumlinson interjected.

'That's him, sir. Died some time since.'

Cumlinson's quick mind was already moving ahead of the story. 'Did he have a mistress? Was it for her that he bought the bays?'

The Inspector grinned appreciatively. 'You've got it, sir. His family was very disapproving of her. I've talked with Montague's son, and he thinks that she's an adventuress. Apparently the old man was on the verge of marrying her when he died. And the family soon sent her off packing after his death.'

'And this mistress, you think that she is the widow lady who blackmailed Smyth-Prescott?' Cumlinson sought confirmation of his own conjectures.

Anderson nodded. 'I think it's very probable that they're one and the same woman, sir.'

'Have you discovered anything about her? And do you know her present whereabouts.'

'She called herself Rosaleen Calatrava, but I've not been able to find out very much about her, sir. From all accounts she is a very good-looking woman in her late twenties. Very Mediterranean in colouring, like an Italian or a Spaniard perhaps. But a mystery otherwise. And I've no idea as to her present whereabouts, sir. Oh, and there's one other thing that Montague's son told me. Apparently this Rosaleen Calatrava has a brother, but the son couldn't tell me anything about him. I wonder if the American could be her brother, sir?'

Cumlinson abruptly rose to his feet and began to pace up and down.

Anderson, knowing the idiosyncrasies of his employer, stood and waited.

At last Cumlinson stopped pacing and faced the policeman. 'From what Smyth-Prescott has confessed, it would seem to be certain that the American is working with a woman. We will assume that this woman is Rosaleen Calatrava. That being the case I think that we may assume that there is a strong probability that the American is indeed her brother.

'She is the woman who is currently masquerading as Mrs Rosaleen Farquar; the woman who is living in the same house as, and undoubtedly sharing the bed of Colum Macrae.'

Cumlinson's eyes radiated an icy fury. 'Macrae appears to have switched his allegiance, Inspector.'

'I can't believe that, sir,' Anderson protested.

'Macrae himself has reported that McCulloch has been using him and the woman to play-act a married couple, a Captain and Mrs Robert Farquar, to work the "badger game" against Edward Firthallan, Earl of Kendrick. Do you seriously doubt that living in such close concert as he has been doing with this woman, Macrae has not discovered that she is involved with the American? And that she also has a brother? He would have to be the stupidest man in Christendom to fail to find out these things, and to draw conclusions from them. And I know that he is definitely not a stupid man.'

310

'I can't believe that Colum Macrae has turned traitor, sir,' Anderson asserted doggedly. 'I've known him for years. He's an honest and loyal man. I'd stake my life on him. If he hasn't reported the connection between the Calatrava woman and the American, then it'll be because he knows of none.'

Cumlinson's respect for the sagacity of the policeman inclined him to give credence to what he claimed.

Once more he began to pace up and down the room, his mind working rapidly. No matter how he approached this problem, whatever route he took, it was becoming clear in his mind that a quick solution necessitated his taking a personally unpalatable course of action.

'Inspector, I want you to arrange a meeting between Terence McCulloch and myself. Treat it as a matter of urgency.'

'Very well, sir.'

'And, Inspector, because of your high opinion of Macrae I shall take no action against him at this stage. He may continue in his present role. But he must know nothing –' he repeated the word with emphasis, 'nothing, concerning any arrangements that shall be made between ourselves and Terence McCulloch. Is that fully understood?'

'Yes, sir.'

Chapter Thirty-nine

The physical consummation, and the acknowledgement of their shared love, was proving to be a mixed blessing to both Rosaleen and Colum. The ecstasies of passion were followed by the torments of guilt. Each was deceiving the other, and each experienced great unhappiness in that knowledge.

Rosaleen longed to tell her lover about Dermot, and to share with him all her secrets. But she dare not. Colum was increasingly troubled by his own deception, and several times he was on the verge of confessing all to her. But he feared not only her reaction but also his daughters' welfare should he betray his true role and so deliberately abort his mission.

So they continued to act out their separate roles, and were able to find a bitter-sweet happiness together.

Almost two weeks had passed since the Nottingham outrage and Rosaleen was very worried. Dermot still had not contacted her. But she drew a degree of comfort that there had been no reports of any arrests in the newspapers, and like all stale news the outrage seemed to be all but forgotten.

This morning she awoke and turned to cuddle against Colum's warm body. He was sleeping soundly and, loth to wake him, she quietly slipped from the bed.

She crossed to the window which overlooked the roadway and, tweeking the edge of the curtain aside, peered out.

People were passing by on their way to work, mostly sombrely clad, top-hatted clerks, with here and there a roughly clad labouring man and several women. A coal cart was delivering bags of fuel to her neighbour's house, and a peak-capped young coster came rattling by, his pony cart loaded high with fruit and vegetables. He himself was standing up on the shafts, balancing cockily, showing off his skill.

Rosa could not help but smile. 'God, he's a slang cove, isn't he just.'

A little further along from her house there was a section of the roadway which was partitioned off by planked hoardings. Navvies worked within the hoardings but no one was able to see what they were doing and the progress of their work seemed to be dismally slow. At night a watchman guarded the site.

A ragged, shuffling tramp, his head hidden in a shawl of sacking, caught her attention, and she frowned uneasily. Something about him disturbed her. She stared hard and then her heart pounded. The tramp was limping!

She drew the curtain fully aside and opened the casement, bending to peer eagerly at the oncoming figure.

Dermot Calatrava saw his sister in the open window and he quickened his pace. He halted directly in front of the window and leaned against the wall as if he were stopping to draw breath. Then he looked up at her.

He lifted his hands and pleaded, 'Give us a bit o' bread, ma'am. I'm starving hungry.'

Rosa thought that she would explode with joy as she

met her brother's eyes in the filthy stubbled mask that was his face.

'Wait there. I'll bring you something,' she called.

Through an eyehole in the hoarding a man wearing navvy's rig was watching the tramp intently.

Rosaleen rushed out to the gate with a loaf of bread in her hands, her eyes shining with joy, her smile radiant.

The watching navvy told himself, 'That's no stranger she's greeting. Not the way she's smiling at him.'

Dermot gave his sister no chance to voice the questions she longed to ask.

'Say nothing, only listen well,' he hissed. 'Get together all the money and valuables that you can, and meet me at the old place in Liverpool. Everything is arranged for us to take passage to America. The ship sails tomorrow night.'

Before she could reply he had shuffled off quickly down the road, leaving her standing staring wildly after him.

The hidden watcher was in a quandary. There should have been another man with him, but he had not yet arrived. They had strict instructions to maintain a constant watch on the house, but if the American appeared one of them was to follow him and discover his hiding place, while the other reported immediately to Terence McCulloch. The watcher was not sure that the tramp was the American, but if he was and the watcher failed to find out where he was hiding, then McCulloch's wrath would be a terrible thing to face.

The woman had smiled so happily. She would never greet a tramp like that. The watcher decided that he would follow the tramp.

Rosaleen took no heed of the navvy who came out from behind the hoardings and walked rapidly past her on the opposite side of the road.

The import of Dermot's words struck fully home to her. 'Tomorrow night. The ship sails tomorrow night. I'll have to move quickly.'

She experienced a confusion of conflicting emotions: joy that Dermot was safe and well, relief that they were going to escape from this country, concern about Colum.

Not for an instant did she question the fact that she would be accompanying her brother to America. She loved Colum Macrae, but her bond with Dermot was far deeper and more powerful than any other love. She and Dermot were two halves of a whole. They were united indissolubly, they were soulmates.

'Could Colum come with us?' She dismissed that idea almost instantly. Dermot would never permit it. 'Colum could join me in America. Once Dermot and I are settled there, he could come out to join me.'

This notion she clutched eagerly to her. She would have time to accustom Dermot to the fact that she loved Colum Macrae and that he loved her. That they would be married and live in honourable union. The more she considered it, the more feasible it seemed. She knew that Dermot hated the men for whom she had been a paid whore. But he would come to like and respect Colum in time, she was sure of that. He would be content because he would see how happy she was with Colum.

Now she frowned worriedly. How was she going to tell Colum that she was leaving him, that they must part for a while? She went back into the house and stood in the hallway, trying to think and plan calmly.

There was a movement behind her, and strong arms enfolded her gently, warm lips nuzzled the side of her neck.

'What on earth are you up to?' Colum chuckled fondly.

'I gave some bread to a poor old tramp,' she told him.

Colum grimaced doubtfully. 'You shouldn't encourage them, sweetheart. Once the word spreads that you're an easy touch, they'll come swarming around and you'll not get a moment's peace from them.'

She kissed him on the lips and teased, 'Don't be such a Scrooge. Now go back to bed and wait for me. Go on now, I have to have a drink of water.'

She went to the kitchen and drew water from the handpump. While she sipped its musty coldness a plan formulated in her mind. She was saddened that she must cause worry and hurt to Colum, but she promised herself that she would make it all up to him once he was able to join her in America.

Meanwhile, upstairs Colum was lying in bed, waiting for Rosaleen to come back to him. He grimaced as he remembered that this afternoon he was due to report to Leather Lane. He wished with a fierce longing that all this play-acting could be over and done with and that he could be living in honest union with Rosaleen and his daughters. Despite the joy he had found with Rosaleen, he still missed his children dreadfully.

'Oh God, please let all this come to an end soon,' he prayed fervently. 'Let me live with Rosa and my children as an honest man, and be done with all this deception.'

When Rosaleen rejoined him in bed, he teased her jokingly.

'You were so long in coming up that I thought the tramp had come back and you'd run away with him.'

A momentary flickering in Rosaleen's eyes betrayed her shock as, for an instant, she feared that somehow or other Colum had discovered the truth.

Colum saw that flicker in her eyes, and mistaking it for an enjoyment of his teasing went on, 'Something tells me that there are things going on here which I know nothing about, and I feel that I should know of them.'

Without conscious volition Rosaleen suddenly felt words trembling on her lips, and she was on the very verge of telling him everything. Horrified by her impulse, she became aggressive and she snapped, 'Don't say such things, even in jest. Perhaps there are things going on in your life that I should know of?'

Her attitude gave Colum pause for thought, and he knew that he should leave this dangerous ground without delay.

He grinned wryly at Rosaleen's tense face. 'Is it our first quarrel that we're nearing, honey?'

His sally eased the strained atmosphere that had sprung up between them uninvited.

'I hope not. There'll be time enough for quarrels when we're an old married couple.'

She had spoken without thinking, and the words created an emotional tumult for Colum. He felt joy that she had unconsciously voiced her expectation that she would wed him, yet despair followed close on his joy as he faced the fact that as long as his wife lived, then he would never be free to marry this beautiful woman. Divorce was not an option for people at his level of society; only his wife's death could set him free.

Rosaleen kissed him tenderly, and his heart welled over with the love he felt for her.

Downstairs the jangling of a bell announced that breakfast was ready, and Rosaleen said teasingly, 'I think Kitty's got the breakfast on the table, sweetheart. You'd best go down there before it gets cold.'

Colum chuckled huskily as desire tightened his throat. 'I think that breakfast can wait. I much prefer to eat it cold today.'

He kissed her passionately and drew her gently down beneath him.

Chapter Forty

As Dermot Calatrava shuffled along the Seven Sisters Road he was well aware of the navvy some twenty yards behind him on the opposite side of the road. He had tested the man by taking a winding and apparently haphazard route, and now he was satisfied that he was being trailed. He had not approached his sister's house without making careful and lengthy reconnaissances of the environs, both by day and by night. He had suspected that the hoardings were being used as an observation point and now it was proven.

'If it's the police who're watching, then they must have found out the connection between Rosa and myself,' Dermot puzzled. 'But how could they have done that? Could McCulloch have betrayed me?'

Murderous fury pulsated at the thought.

He led his pursuer towards the wide expanse of Hampstead Heath, just over a mile distant, and when he reached there, followed a path which led through a stretch of dense woodland. In the concealment of the trees he took a slender-bladed knife from his boot and hid in some shrubs overlooking the pathway.

The navvy came cautiously along the path and Dermot allowed him to take a single pace past his hiding place before springing his trap.

The navvy went sprawling face forwards as Dermot

cannoned into him, and then cried out in terror as he felt the knife against his throat.

'Who put you to watch the house?' Dermot snarled. 'Speak out if you want to live.'

He slid the sharp-edged steel over the flesh so that it sliced in and blood spurted.

'No! Don't kill me! Please don't kill me!' the man begged piteously. 'I'll tell you!'

'Who was it?'

'It was McCulloch. Terence McCulloch.'

'Who were you told to watch for?'

'The American.'

'Why does McCulloch want the American?'

'I don't know! I swear to God, I don't know!'

'How many of you are watching?'

'There's two of us by day, and two others by night. We was told that one of us must follow the American, and the other report to McCulloch straight away.' The terrified man was babbling in a desperate attempt to save himself. 'Pat never showed up this morning. I've been on me own there.'

'What time do the night men come on?'

'At six, we change over at six.'

Dermot wrenched the head back fully and slit the windpipe and the man died in a gurgling rush of bubbling blood.

Dermot dragged the still-twitching body deep into the undergrowth, and efficiently kicked dead leaves and dirt to hide the bloodied ground.

He slid the knife back into his boot top.

'McCulloch's done some sort of deal with the police!'

Dermot was certain of it, and his first impulse was to go in search of Terence McCulloch and extract a bloody revenge. But then he thought of Rosaleen.

'I have to make sure that she gets away. But I'll need to find out if that other bastard is watching the house.'

Pat Gillen was wondering where his mate had got to. His head was thick from the drink he had taken the previous night, and he was getting tired of standing looking through this spyhole.

'I know I was late meself, but he should have stayed here until I come instead of sloping off somewheres. I wonder if he's gone to get a gargle?'

'Mr McCulloch'll go mad if he finds out that we're missing out on the job. Jasus, me head is sore, and I'm thirsty. I could drink horse piss, so I could.'

So engrossed was he in his catalogue of woes that he was completely unaware of the figure who had sneaked into the enclosure behind him, and the deadly blow from the steel blade of the shovel killed him instantly.

'We're needing a bag of spuds,' Kitty Wainright told Old Betty.

The other woman sniggered to herself. 'Another bottle o' gin more likely, that's what you'm needing, you drunken cow.'

'Come on, get your shawl on, I'm not mauling meself around carrying it,' Kitty Wainright ordered.

Old Betty sullenly did as she was bid, and the two women set out from the house on their errand.

'Are you sure you're feeling all right?' Colum was troubled by Rosaleen's wan face and preoccupied air. 'You don't seem to be your usual self this morning.'

Rosaleen forced herself to feign a happiness that she

was very far from feeling. 'I'm fine, really I am,' she smiled. 'Didn't I prove that to you earlier?'

He chuckled fondly, remembering their early-morning lovemaking. 'Indeed you did.'

'What time do you have to go out?' she wanted to know.

'That's about the tenth time you've asked me that,' he chided jokingly. 'Your memory is getting very bad. For the eleventh time of telling, I need to leave here at about two o'clock. But I shouldn't be long away.'

'All right, I'll try to remember it this time.' She kept the beaming smile on her face, but her heart was heavy as the time of parting drew inexorably nearer. It was saddening her increasingly, as the hours passed, that she must leave him in this underhand manner. But she accepted that she had no choice in the matter. It must be done. But she was wishing with all her heart that there could have been some other way.

She intended to take only a small carpet bag of toilette necessities, her money and jewels, and leave everything else behind. She would also leave Colum a note promising that she would get in touch with him as soon as she was able to do so, and assuring him of her love.

A noise sounded in the passageway outside the door, and Colum looked up from the book he was reading. 'What's that?'

Rosaleen shrugged. 'It'll be one of the women.'

Colum shook his head. 'No, they've both gone out. I saw them go past the window not two minutes since.'

'Then it will be the cat.' She experienced a sudden foreboding, and snapped, 'Just leave it.'

He grimaced questioningly at her. 'How can it be the

cat? We haven't got one. I'll just take a look.'

He got to his feet and opened the door, to be confronted by a filthy, bearded tramp wielding a shovel blade in his hand.

Colum took a crashing blow to the side of his head and staggered backwards. Another blow sent him to the floor and his senses blacked out.

'No, Dermot, don't kill him! Please don't kill him!' Rosaleen screamed.

Dermot stared at his sister, and her face was chalk-white with horror. She shook her head wildly, begging him, 'No, please, no!'

With the shovel blade still poised for the killing slash, Dermot glared down at the unconscious figure sprawled beneath him, and back at his sister's agonised features.

'No, I beg you, Dermot, no!'

Reluctantly he lowered the shovel blade.

'We must get away from here now,' he urged. 'Make haste and get your bag, McCulloch has sold us out to the Peelers.'

Still she hesitated, staring anxiously down at Colum's bleeding head.

'I'll not kill him,' Dermot promised. 'He'll have nothing more than a sore head when he wakes up. Now move, or you'll put me on the gallows!'

The reminder of the deadly peril facing her brother galvanised her, and she ran to obey.

She was back within scant minutes, her eyes seeking Colum. She saw his chest rising and falling and tried to reassure herself that he was not seriously injured.

Dermot pushed her bodily from the room, and to the back door of the house.

'Go to the railway station and get the Liverpool train.

We'll travel separately, and meet up at Mother Sweeney's lodging house. Go now, for the love of God, or you'll get me hung.'

'Swear to me that you'll not kill that man,' she demanded, and Dermot saw her stubborn expression and promised.

'I'll not touch him.'

Still she made no move, and in exasperation he swore. 'Be damned to you for a stupid woman! I'll go before you, then you'll see that I'm not harming him.'

He went from the house and after a couple of moments she followed, keeping him in sight as they hurried towards the centre of the city, and not losing him until he disappeared among the crowds of the vast railway station.

She purchased her ticket and took a seat in the Ladies' Waiting Room until the train should leave.

Tears ran down her pale cheeks as she thought of Colum, and in her heart she knew that she had lost him for ever. Anguish tore her at the mental vision of him lying bleeding. But she knew that no matter how she might grieve for the loss of her lover, the bond of union she shared with her brother would always be paramount. Dermot and she were one soul, and could never be spiritually divided.

Other travellers in the waiting room looked at the weeping woman with sympathetic eyes, but refrained from intruding upon her distress. Weeping women were an all too common sight in the railway stations of this vast metropolis.

Chapter Forty-one

The pain in Colum Macrae's heavily bandaged skull was a stabbing ache, but he found it easier to bear than his mental pain and anger. Through long grinding days and sleepless nights he had lain in this bed reliving the events of the past weeks, and savagely castigating himself for his own stupidity. In his feelings for Rosaleen love and hate were inextricably mingled, each emotion striving to eject the other as if locked in bitter conflict. Over and over again he cursed her treachery, and over and over again he relived their moments of passion and tenderness.

Colum had only had one visitor since his arrival here in the infirmary. Mr Bush had come several times to interrogate him, and had confirmed that it was the American who had been his attacker, and that Rosaleen was the American's accomplice.

This was all the dry, spare old man would reveal. Colum, racked by bitterness and jealousy, spent endless hours tormenting himself about the couple, convinced that they were lovers.

'How are you feeling, Col?'

Colum opened his eyes to see Charlie Anderson standing at the foot of the narrow bed.

Anderson looked around the tiny, bleak room which

contained only a washstand and the bed, then grinned bluffly at Colum.

'It's a jolly room you've got here, aren't it, Col.'

Colum scowled. 'I don't need the jokes, Charlie. I know that you've come to tell me what a bloody fool I've been, and that my services are no longer required, so just tell me and go.'

The Inspector's jovial grin did not falter. 'I don't think that you're a fool, my lad. You're not the first bloke to be bamboozled by a good-looking woman, and you'll certainly not be the last. Just be thankful that you got out of it alive.'

'The American is her lover, isn't he?' Colum's expression was a mirror of his bitter chagrin.

'If they are, then they're committing incest, Col. Because from what we know they're brother and sister. The American's name is Dermot Calatrava. It seems likely that they're twins.'

Colum experienced a poignant relief when he heard this. At least he had the cold comfort of knowing that she had not betrayed him by taking him into her bed while still sexually loving another man.

Charlie Anderson moved to sit on the side of the bed and, leaning towards Colum, said in a low voice, 'We're pretty certain that they took passage on a Collins Line steamship about nine days since. So they'll be landing in America in a day or two.'

Anderson was feeling very guilty about his friend Colum Macrae and it was that sense of guilt which now impelled him to confess.

'We found out the connection between the American and Rosaleen Calatrava before this happened to you. But I couldn't warn you about it.'

'What?' Colum could hardly believe what he was hearing. 'You knew, and you didn't warn me? What sort of a bloody friend are you, Charlie?'

'A bloody good friend,' Anderson retorted indignantly. 'The reason you weren't warned was because Cumlinson believed that you had turned traitor.'

'Me, a traitor?' For an instant Colum wondered if this might all be a dream, a nightmare.

'That's right, a traitor. Because you'd been living with that woman for weeks, and you reported nothing about any connection between the two of them. And you'd been in McCulloch's circle for bloody months, and hadn't found out a thing about the American. No wonder Cumlinson suspected you.'

Colum was forced to admit to himself that the other man had a strong point. He had failed in his task, and failed miserably.

Anderson hesitated, then went on, 'I'll tell you the full story, but you must keep what I say to yourself.'

Colum nodded agreement, and his friend continued on, 'Cumlinson made a bargain with Terence McCulloch. I don't know the exact details because it was settled between the two of them in private. But as a result of it, McCulloch sold out the Calatravas to us. He was going to tell us Dermot Calatrava's whereabouts as soon as he could find it out, and then we were going to take the brother and the sister. But the Calatravas proved too fly for both us and McCulloch, didn't they? And two of McCulloch's men got killed into the bargain.'

'We even cheat on each other in this bloody game, don't we, Charlie?' Colum interjected disgustedly. 'If you had warned me what was going on, I could have been ready for Dermot Calatrava.'

327

'How could I warn you,' Anderson objected forcefully, 'with Cumlinson believing that you'd turned your coat? It was only me sticking up for you that saved your bacon, my lad.'

Colum's hand rose to touch his thick bandages, and he said ruefully, 'I nearly ended up as bacon anyway, didn't I, Charlie? Still, it's all over and done with now, isn't it, and I'm unemployed again.'

Anderson shook his head. 'No you're not. Just as soon as you're up to it, you and me are going to Yankee Land.'

Colum stared in amazement, and Anderson laughed hoarsely at his expression.

'No need to gawp like a bloody chawbacon, my lad. It's only because Cumlinson reckons that he hasn't had his money's worth out of you yet.' Then he sobered, and explained. 'The situation has changed, Col. It's not a question of secretly disposing of the Calatravas any more. They've made our lords and masters look like incompetent fools, and that can't be allowed to happen. It might make other people think that they can do the same thing. So Cumlinson wants the Calatravas to be fetched back here and put on public trial, to demonstrate to the world that nobody can ever escape from British justice.'

He paused to allow Colum to absorb what he had been told, then went on. 'Now the doctor here tells me that you're recovered enough to be discharged today. So you go home and spend some time with your kids, and get your full strength back. You'll be needing it when we get to Yankee Land. The bloody Fenians are thicker on the ground there than ants are.'

When his friend had gone Colum lay pleasurably

anticipating seeing his beloved children. However, the virtual certainty that at some time in the future he would once again be coming face to face with Rosaleen Calatrava disturbed him greatly. He was both dreading and at the same time longing for the moment to come when he would see her once again . . .

Chapter Forty-two

New York, August 1860

The heat was oppressive and no breath of cooling breeze entered through the small open window at which Rosaleen Calatrava was sitting.

From the street five storeys below there came a constant clamour of noise which by day or night never quietened, but only varied in volume, as did the myriad stenches which permeated the air like a malignant miasma.

Theresa Quinn stirred restlessly in the bed which virtually filled the cramped room, and Rosaleen instantly rose and bent over her, smiling reassuringly into the haggard, fever-flushed face of the sick woman.

'Dermot will be here with your medicine very soon, Theresa. Would you like a drink of water?'

The woman nodded, and Rosaleen dipped a tin mug into the bucket beneath the window and helped the other woman to sit up while she drank. Then she rearranged the coverlet and the coarse sheet and tried to soften the hard-packed lumps of the flock pillows, before settling the woman back.

'I hate this cursed country, Rosa,' the sick woman croaked venomously. 'I wish we'd never come here.'

'Would you sooner be in an English jail?' Rosaleen's

sense of guilt at bringing the woman here caused her to react pettishly to the complaint.

'I'd sooner be in me grave than spend the rest of me life here. It's a wicked, rotten place,' Theresa Quinn whined tearfully.

Rosaleen's pettishness dissolved, and she sighed despondently, but made no answer. She turned back to the window and poked her head through the narrow casement.

The slums of the Lower East Side surrounded her. Jerry-built six-storeyed tenements, interspersed with tumbledown clapboard houses, stretched to each side and before her, the buildings crammed together so that sunlight could only touch the upper storeys, and the fresh air was staled by the pullulating, seething foulness of the narrow streets.

She gazed down at the swarming scene below. In this slum the immigrant poor herded densely together, sharing one thing in common, their abysmal poverty. Irish, Spanish, Germans, Italians, French, British, Slavic Jews, blacks, orientals; men, women and children of all nations, all creeds, all colours, come to this fabled New World filled with hopes and dreams of a better life.

Rosaleen pitied them. For every individual whose dreams came to fruition, there were a thousand who found only bitter disillusion. The New York streets were not paved with gold; the Americans did not welcome these strangers into their midst. The political organisations of Whigs, Republicans, Nativists, Know Nothings actively resented the immigrants, and in particular the Irish Catholic immigrants. Rosaleen had experienced at first hand the constant rejections when she applied for employment, the advertisements for workers that stated,

331

'No Irish need apply'. She was as deeply disenchanted as Theresa Quinn with America and the Americans.

And we're the lucky ones, she thought wryly. At least we've only got the three of us in these two rooms. In almost every other apartment in this street there are two or more families sharing the same space.

But that relative good fortune was fast ebbing. Rosaleen's money and the jewellery had now all but gone, and the real prospect of eviction and actual starvation was looming perilously closer with each succeeding day.

To add to her concerns, Dermot was showing increasing signs of mental instability, his moods fluctuating wildly between deep depression and manic high spirits. He was drinking heavily, and Rosaleen worried about where the money for that drink was coming from. She had none to spare, all her money went on rent and food for the three of them. Yet frequently Dermot would disappear for several days at a time, and come back reeling drunk, filthy in body and clothing, and sprawl for hours cursing the Fenian Brotherhood, the British, the Americans, until mercifully he would slump unconscious and sleep for many hours. Then he would wake sick and ill, his hands trembling uncontrollably, and a period of recuperation would follow, during which he would be like his old self until the poison of alcohol and drugs had cleared from his system, and then the cycle would begin again.

At this time Dermot was in a recuperative stage, and Rosaleen was profoundly thankful for it. She was beginning to fear that her own nerves and endurance were becoming stretched dangerously near to breaking point.

She heard Dermot's footsteps on the rickety wooden

staircase and when he came in she greeted him with a smile.

He handed her the bottle of green-coloured medicine and she quickly dosed Theresa Quinn. She knew that the medicine was a mixture containing laudanum, and although she strongly doubted its efficacy, at least it enabled the sick woman to sleep for many hours and so, hopefully, would aid her recovery to strength and health.

Dermot seated himself on the stool by the window and stared out moodily.

'I saw John O'Mahoney down in Broadway this morning. He saw me coming and went into a shop to avoid me.' The young man scowled murderously. 'Yellow-gutted bastard that he is. It's all McCulloch's doing, you know, Rosa. It's him that's turned them all against me.'

Rosaleen made no reply, knowing the futility of arguing or discussing with him when he was in this mood.

When they had first arrived in New York her brother had been greeted as a returning hero by the Fenian circles in the city. He was the hero who had struck back against the hated ancient enemy with his deadly attacks on powder mills and arms factories, and his killing of their policemen.

But then Terence McCulloch had sent word to John O'Mahoney, John Mitchell, Michael Doheny and other American-Irish Fenian leaders that Dermot Calatrava had murdered two of his men and was not to be trusted; he was a madman who was a liability to their cause. And because Terence McCulloch was known and trusted by the Fenian leadership, they had believed what he told them and turned against Dermot Calatrava. The young man had found himself shunned, expelled from the Fenian Brotherhood, and treated like a pariah.

'Can you give me a couple of dollars, Rosa?' he asked.

'What's it for?' she demanded sharply. 'I've no money to give you for drink, Dermot. I don't have enough for next week's rent even.'

'For God's sake, will you stop whining!' he bellowed and jumped to his feet, eyes blazing with fury. 'All I'm asking for is a couple of measly dollars! A couple of measly dollars!'

She faced him, unafraid. 'And I'm telling you that I haven't got two dollars to give you for drink. You give me nothing for food or rent.'

'You mean-souled bitch. You sound like a bloody gombeen man!' He cursed her, as he roughly pushed her aside and stormed out of the room.

Sick at heart she sank down on the bed, and Theresa Quinn snorted in sleep and tossed about.

'There now, lie quiet . . . Lie quiet, everything is all right,' Rosa murmured soothingly, and stroked the woman's sweaty forehead. 'I'm going to get us out of here, Theresa. Before it destroys us all.'

For some time now she had been considering a course of action she had previously shrunk from putting into effect as it filled her with self-disgust and loathing. But now she knew that she faced a stark choice – either to stay here on the Lower East Side and see Dermot destroy himself, Theresa Quinn slowly die from illness, and herself sink into the very pits of degradation, or to use the most potent weapons she had, her brains and beauty, to free them all from hunger and want.

She ran downstairs to the street and from a

stationer's shop she purchased pen, ink, paper and envelope. Back in the room she considered her words very carefully and then began to write . . .

She re-read the short letter carefully, and waved the sheet of paper to dry the ink. Then she addressed the envelope:

'Dirk van Riesdal Esquire,
c/o The Board of Brokers,
Wall Street.'

She went next to the nearest postal office and despatched the letter, then walked through the bustling streets, praying silently that all would be well. Because this was truly her last hope.

At two in the afternoon on the following day Rosaleen dressed herself carefully. She wore black widow's weeds, but without the heavy veil.

Dermot had not reappeared since their clash of the previous day, and Rosaleen told Theresa, 'If Dermot comes back while I'm away, tell him that he must wait for me here. Tell him that it's important. I must see him.'

She hurried through the mean alleyways and came out onto the Bowery. To continue across the Bowery and onto Broadway would have meant having to walk through the district known as the Five Points, notorious as the most degraded and dangerous quarter of the city. It was a region of rancid, crooked streets and alleys and filthy courts that bore names like Murderer's Alley, Cow Bay and Hell Lane. Respectable New Yorkers gave it a wide berth, and even the police never entered unless in numbers and armed.

Rosaleen chose the lesser of two evils and turned northwards along the Bowery. The Bowery was a broad avenue running from Chatham Square to East Fourth Street, and it too was infested by thugs, criminals, vagrants, and the helpless and hopeless poor. It was lined with gin mills, dance halls, brothels, pawnbrokers, taverns and a myriad of old-clothes and second-hand-goods shops and stale-food shops catering to the desperate needs of poverty. Pigs rooted in the heaps of garbage and fought with the starving dogs and cats for the stinking, rotting delicacies, while hordes of ragged, barefoot children shrieked and fought and begged and pilfered.

As Rosaleen pushed through the thronging crowds she heard snatches of a score of different tongues, and whenever she heard English it seemed to be flavoured with the Irish brogue.

She neared one street corner and noted with trepidation a group of men lounging there. They were wearing inordinately long black frock coats and tall black beaver hats. Their trousers were vivid, bell-bottomed checks, and all had garishly coloured neckerchiefs around their high collars. Every one of them favoured Imperial goatees and thick moustaches. Their dress proclaimed them to be 'Bowery Boys', members of one of the most notorious hoodlum gangs that dominated the slums and mean streets of the city. Each gang strove for mastery of territory, battling with each other and with the police in savage warfare to gain that dominance.

Despite the fact that the 'Bowery Boys' were Irish-Americans, and so her own countrymen, Rosaleen despised and feared them, and she made a precarious crossing of the road, dodging to avoid the carts and waggons that streamed along it.

She changed direction again, traversing streets of shabby tenements and brownstone houses, and came out on Broadway. It was a startling transition from poverty to luxury, from hopelessness to hopefulness, from abject failure to glittering success. The pavements were crowded with well-dressed men and elegantly clothed women. The shops and hotels that stretched as far as the eye could see were sumptuous emporiums crammed with the best that money could buy; palaces of taste and leisure where every whim could be catered to. Money was the absolute ruler here, and those who possessed that commodity were treated as monarchs.

The traffic was a raging torrent, and to try to cross against it was to risk life and limb. But here and there peak-capped, blue frock-coated, brass-buttoned policemen would periodically step forwards and momentarily halt that torrent to allow groups of pedestrians to scurry across the roadway.

Rosa waited for one of the gaudily painted, thirty-seater omnibuses drawn by two teams of panting horses which competed for trade along the opulent streets and avenues of the city. When one arrived she took her seat and travelled on to her destination.

The Metropolitan Hotel was a massive brownstone structure occupying an entire block front on Broadway and Prince Street.

Inside the building Rosaleen went up the wide stairway to the 'Sky Parlour', a long room where unescorted ladies could take tea and look down through the huge windows at the fashionable promenade below.

An obsequious waiter hurried to greet her the moment she stepped through the doors of the Sky Parlour.

'Is madam expected? Can I show madam to a table?'

Rosaleen looked left and right along the extended room, her eyes flicking rapidly from table to table, where fashionably dressed women sat in chattering conclaves, and only the occasional male was to be seen. Then she smiled with relief as she saw the tall, fair-haired man hurrying towards her.

'Thank you,' she told the waiter. 'I am expected.'

'Rosaleen, it's so good to see you again.' Dirk van Riesdal's fine white teeth gleamed in a delighted smile, and his blue eyes radiated happiness. 'You don't know how happy it makes me.'

He led her to his table in the most exclusive section of the room, and instantly waiters hovered around them.

'What will you take?' the young man questioned.

Despite the hunger gnawing her stomach, Rosa told him, 'Just tea, thank you.'

Now that she was face to face with the young man, she was unhappy. She felt squalid in her intentions. She still loved and desperately missed Colum Macrae, and yet she had come here with the intention of ensnaring this young man as her protector and financial support. She had come to bargain her body for money. She regarded herself with disgust at this moment. Once again she was nothing more than a prostitute.

For an instant she felt the urge to hurry away. But then the iron came back into her soul. If she, her brother and Theresa Quinn were to survive in this harsh, merciless city, then she must go through with her plans, and ruthlessly put aside any scruples and hope of self-respect. These were luxuries she had long since found to be far too expensive for her ever to afford.

She smiled warmly at the young man, and reached

across the table to take his hand. 'It's wonderful to be with you again, Dirk,' she told him huskily. 'You can't know how much I've longed for this moment . . .'

'Why didn't you write to me the moment Montague died?' he asked her. 'I was informed of his death almost immediately because of our joint business interests. I waited so eagerly to hear from you.'

She lowered her eyes demurely. 'And what would you have thought of me if I had?'

'I would have thought that you were as attracted to me as I am to you,' he asserted.

Suddenly a wave of self-disgust swept over Rosaleen, and she knew that she could no longer continue to enact this elaborate charade. She decided that she would be brutally honest with him. At least, as brutally honest as would still ensure Dermot's, Theresa's and her own safety.

'Let us be frank with each other, Dirk.' She met his gaze fully. 'I was Solomon Montague's mistress because he gave me financial security. When he decided that he wanted to marry me, his family was appalled. They regarded me as being an adventuress.'

She shrugged her shapely shoulders. 'I can accept that judgement, but in my own defence I must point out that it was a question of needs must when the Devil drives. And I did become fond of Solomon, and I was faithful to him during our relationship.

'When he died his family evicted me from the house and sent me packing.' She chuckled ruefully. 'I can't say that I blame them for doing that. I loathed them as much as they loathed me.'

He tried to say something, but she told him sharply, 'No! Hear me out, please.'

'Very well.' He acquiesced gracefully, and she smiled in gratitude, then went on.

'I am here in America in company with my brother and our maidservant, who is also our dear friend and companion. They are both unwell, and now that my money is all but gone I must find an income sufficient to care for the three of us.

'I am looking for a new protector. It will be easy enough for me to find one. After all, I have a great deal to offer a man. But if I must act as a paid whore again, then I would greatly prefer that the man is someone that I can like and respect, and feel some physical warmth for.

'I like and respect you, Dirk, and I find you very attractive physically. So, I am offering myself to you as a mistress. And as your mistress, I shall expect you to behave generously and kindly towards me and to treat me with respect. If you feel that you do not wish to enter such a relationship, then please tell me now, and allow us to part as friends.'

He erupted with such a peal of delighted laughter that people at the surrounding tables looked at him and smiled to see his pleasure.

'Oh my dearest Rosa,' he leaned across and took both her hands in his own, 'you have made me the happiest man in this city. I accept your proposition, and let me assure you that in me you will find a gentle, generous, kindly and adoring lover.'

She returned the pressure of his fingers. 'And in me, Dirk, you will find a faithful and loving friend. I shall do nothing to hurt or deceive you as your mistress. And I shall not demand that you lavish gifts upon me. Let us be true and gentle with each other, and then if and when the time comes for us to part, we shall have nothing to reproach each other with, and only good memories of each other.'

'It's a bargain.' He grinned like a mischievous school-boy. 'And let us make haste to seal it, my dear. I want you with me tonight.'

She shook her head. 'No, it's not possible. I have to tell my brother what I intend doing. And I must take care of Theresa.'

'Where are you living now?' he questioned urgently.

'In a slum tenement on the Lower East Side,' she told him frankly.

'I shall engage a suite of rooms for you all here at the Metropolitan. And send you in my carriage to collect your friend Theresa and your brother this very day. You will live here until we can find a suitable house for you. You and I will begin searching for that tomorrow.'

He allowed her no time to protest. 'Come, time is wasting, and here in New York, time is money and money is the God that all the city worships. So I'll not listen to any excuses. Come now.'

He rose to his feet and drew her up with him, and together they went hand in hand from the long room.

Chapter Forty-three

To Rosaleen's great surprise Dermot accepted the news that she was to become Dirk van Riesdal's mistress very calmly. Within days of their moving into the Metropolitan Hotel they moved yet again into a luxurious house on Twenty-third Street between Lexington and Fourth Avenues, a district that had been developed as a residential enclave of wealth and privilege during the past decade.

Rosaleen now experienced how the rich lived in New York, and it was a heady experience. Dirk provided her with servants, and a carriage and fine horseflesh. He opened an account for her at the famous department store of A.T. Stewart, a marble palace six storeys high and a block long which employed two hundred clerks and daily sold tens of thousands of dollars' worth of luxury goods.

Rosaleen spent days at a time wandering through its lofty halls and, urged on by her adoring lover, bought gowns from Paris, fine woollens and cambrics from England, Brussels carpets, French laces, Lyon silks, cashmere and paisley shawls, and always Dirk wanted to give her more, and she would protest and have to feign anger to make him stop his urgings.

He frequently took her to the opera at the magnificent Academy of Music on Fourteenth Street, and afterwards they would dine at Delmonico's, the most exclusive restaurant in the city. On Sundays they would take the carriage and drive out to the Croton Reservoir, the favourite picnic spot and promenade of fashionable New Yorkers. The reservoir's high walls resembled an ancient Egyptian temple, and the broad promenade atop the walls afforded superb views southwards over the city, east and west across the Hudson and East Rivers and northwards traversing the rolling country- side that stretched to the villages of Harlem, Yorkville and Manhattanville.

At night Dirk would make ardent love to her in her scented bedroom, and because he was so kind and gentle and generous, she tried her best to give him plea- sure, but she was unable to stop her thoughts straying to Colum Macrae, and though the bitter regrets and mourning for his loss whelmed over her, she wept only in her heart, and kept a smile upon her face for Dirk.

Theresa Quinn stolidly accepted her change of for- tune without any outward manifestations of delight. But at times Rosa would come upon her unawares and find her singing to herself, and so knew that her old friend had found some degree of contentment.

Dermot continued to drink. Disappearing for days on end, returning sick and fevered, half out of his mind from the effects of alcohol and opium. Then he would stay at home, recuperating like an invalid, until he had recovered sufficiently to start the vicious cycle of debauchery once again.

Rosaleen could make no impression upon him and finally decided that what could not be cured must be endured. She prayed to God every night that her beloved brother would come to his senses. But even as she prayed she doubted the efficacy of any prayers to alter him. She could only wait and persevere in her love in the hope that someday he himself would come to realise that he was destroying his life.

And so, as September drew to its close, Rosaleen took stock of her life.

'I've known suffering and heartbreak and degradation. I love and yearn still for Colum. Dermot is my cross to bear. Yet I have a life here that millions of women would envy. I've been blessed with tremendous good fortune, and I must never, not for one instant, allow myself to forget that.'

Chapter Forty-four

London

In the first week of September Conrad Cumlinson summoned Charlie Anderson and Colum Macrae to receive their detailed instructions.

He sat frowning behind his vast black-topped desk as the two men entered his office and stood before him.

'Now, gentlemen, as you must know, the Prince of Wales is currently engaged on an official state visit to Canada. Following the completion of that tour he will then briefly visit some locations in the United States, culminating in a visit to New York. President Buchanan wrote personally to Her Majesty to issue this invitation and Her Majesty, seeking to foster good relations between ourselves and the Americans, graciously accepted on the Prince's behalf. Naturally the American Government has given the fullest assurances as to the Prince's safety while he is on their soil. Nevertheless I am of the opinion that it is imperative we secure the Calatravas into our custody before the Prince goes to the United States. We know from our own unhappy experiences with them that the Calatravas are extremely cunning and dangerous.' He looked meaningfully at Colum, and Colum felt a sharp embarrassment.

'Our agents in New York report that Dermot Calatrava has recently been expelled from the Fenian Brotherhood, but is believed still to be in the city. His sister and her companion, Theresa Quinn, appear to have dropped from sight.

'I have been assured that the New York Police Department will co-operate with us in securing the three of them. However, gentlemen, I have to tell you that, judging from my previous dealings with that department, I cannot guarantee the quality of that co-operation. The New York police are notoriously corrupt, and are used as tools by the political parties dominant in the city. So you must exercise your own judgement in how far you feel you can trust and rely on the officers that you may come into contact with.

'Before you contact the New York police you will meet the man named in this document. It also contains the necessary instructions for that meeting.' He passed a folded sheet of notepaper to Charlie Anderson. 'Memorise then destroy this, Inspector.'

He leaned back in his chair and steepled his fingers beneath his chin.

'It is imperative that the Calatravas are brought back here to stand trial, gentlemen. The nation demands that the Nottingham outrage is publicly avenged. You, Macrae, are being given the opportunity to make amendment for your previous failures. Make sure that you do so, because any further failure will cost you very dearly. And now I'll wish you both good luck and god speed. That will be all, gentlemen.'

Outside the building Colum chuckled ruefully. 'Do you think he was trying to tell me something, Charlie?'

The Inspector roared with laughter. 'I think he did

tell you something, Col. Come on, we'll miss our train else.'

They were in Liverpool by nightfall, and by the following nightfall were at sea on a Cunard steamship bound for New York.

Chapter Forty-five

New York

The man whom Colum and Charlie Anderson had been instructed to meet before making contact with the New York Police Department was named Thomas Doyle. He was an influential figure in Irish-American circles, and a member in good standing of the Fenian Brotherhood. He was also a British spy.

Doyle met them in a bar room at the newly built Fifth Avenue Hotel facing Madison Square. He was a short, plump man who laughed easily and exuded an air of good-natured bonhomie. He had prospered as a merchant and wore a lot of jewellery.

Doyle's eyes twinkled merrily as he drank whisky and quaffed oysters. He chuckled as he told them, 'You've come to the right shop, gentlemen, but the goods that you're wanting to purchase are temporarily out of stock. I'm not able to tell you where Dermot Calatrava can be found at this moment. He and the two women had rooms in a tenement on the Lower East Side, but they flitted from there and no one knows where they went to. He's seen occasionally in the bars downtown, and he was sighted several times down in Greene Street, the last time only a few days since, so he probably uses the houses there pretty frequently.'

'Houses? You mean brothels, I take it?' Colum sought clarification, and Doyle laughed and confirmed. 'That's the only sort of houses that can be found in Greene Street, sir.'

Colum felt both a jealous anger and poignant heartache as the thought struck him that the reason for Dermot Calatrava being in Greene Street could possibly mean that Rosaleen was working as a prostitute in one of the brothels there.

'Calatrava's expulsion from the Fenians, was it McCulloch's doing?' Charlie Anderson wanted to know.

'Yes, he sent reports about Calatrava killing his men, but even if he hadn't sent those reports Calatrava would still have been expelled. The younger members of the movement are greatly admiring of what Calatrava did in England and were talking of him as a possible new leader of the Brotherhood. The existing leadership couldn't risk that happening, it would be too much of a threat to their own interests. So they got rid of him. I think they would like to have had him disposed of permanently, but that would have created an uproar because he's seen as a hero by a good many of the more hot-headed members.'

Doyle paused, and then offered reflectively, 'I had some personal contact with him and I'm convinced that he's a madman. He kept on telling everybody that he was going to strike a blow against the English that would make the whole world sit up and take notice of him.'

'Did he ever talk about the Prince of Wales being in Canada?'

'Oh, yes. He said many times that someone ought to go up to Canada and shoot the Prince. But the leadership quashed that idea very flat. There's too much anti-Irish prejudice here in North America already, and if an Irishman was to kill the Prince while he was on American or Canadian soil then there's no doubt that the American Government would take very strong action indeed against the Fenians. The upper classes and the ruling establishment in this country love Royalty, for all their caterwauling about the tyranny of George the Third.'

Colum and Charlie Anderson exchanged a look and saw that they shared the same thought. Dermot Calatrava would find it extremely difficult to get to the Prince while that young man was touring Canada. The Canadian authorities had taken very great care to protect him from possible assassination, and it was almost a certainty that anyone who tried to hurt or kill the Prince would not survive that attempt. But here in the United States it might prove to be a different state of affairs. Dermot Calatrava would be on familiar ground and might well find a way to get at the Prince. There were Irish-Americans in the police and in the military forces which would be detailed to guard the Prince and his party, and it might be that Dermot Calatrava had someone among their number who would be ready and eager to help him.

After parting from Doyle they discussed at great length their options in pursuing the Calatravas and decided that unless the New York Police Department could come up with a better suggestion, then the most promising line of enquiry lay through the brothels of Greene Street.

Chapter Forty-six

The headquarters of the New York Metropolitan Police was an elegant marble building numbered 300 Mulberry Street.

The office of the Chief of the Detective Department contrasted poorly with the grandiose façade of the building. It was shabby, badly furnished and cramped, and the office anteroom where his force of detectives had their base was even shabbier, more ill furnished and almost as cramped.

When Charlie Anderson and Colum were led into the anteroom the dozen or so men in there, dressed in a wide variety of civilian garb, were straddling chairs, lying on benches, lounging against walls, talking, smoking, chewing tobacco and constantly expectorating with unerring aim into the profusion of spittoons which seemed to be the most plentiful components of the room's furnishings.

Curious eyes examined the two newcomers as their guide tapped on the Chief's door and ushered them inside.

'It's the Limeys, Cap'n,' the guide announced.

Captain John S. Young rose from his desk and advanced to meet them with an outstretched hand. He was a stocky, heavily built man whose sandy head appeared disproportionately larger than his body.

'Good morning, gentlemen, I've been expecting you.' His voice was unwelcoming, and his blue eyes cold as he measured his visitors.

When they had all introduced themselves he invited, 'Please, sit down.' He gestured towards two battered leather-covered chairs, then returned to his own seat behind the equally battered desk.

'Superintendent Kennedy has instructed me to give you any aid within my power, gentlemen, and I shall do so. But I must make it very plain that the New York Police Department is very protective of its jurisdiction, and will not tolerate any attempts to usurp its powers. Any proposed arrests must be carried out by my own officers. You are merely guests here, gentlemen, and have no power or authority to detain anyone.'

'That is perfectly understood, Captain,' Charlie Anderson replied diplomatically. 'And I appreciate your kindness in giving us your help.'

Young briefly scanned some papers before him. 'According to this report you are in search of a brother and sister named Dermot and Rosaleen Calatrava, and their servant, a Theresa Quinn, who are alleged to have committed several murders back in England, including the murders of three police officers.'

'That is so,' Anderson agreed gravely.

Young frowned. 'I have to tell you, Inspector Anderson, that these people are not known to us. We have no record of them on file.' He glanced again at the papers. 'Now, it says here that they took ship for this country almost three months past. Which means that they could have travelled on, and be anywhere in the world by now. So what makes you think that they could still be here in America, and specifically this city?'

Charlie Anderson answered carefully. 'Dermot Calatrava is a member of the Fenian Brotherhood, an organisation you undoubtedly know of, Captain. Just a week before we set sail for New York another member of the Fenian Brotherhood, who was wanted for criminal offences committed in England some years previously, returned to England from this country. Shortly after landing he was recognised by a police officer and arrested. During questioning he told us that he had spoken to Dermot Calatrava here in New York on the very day that he himself had taken the boat to England.'

Young smiled doubtingly and gibed sarcastically, 'Now that's what I'd call a really miraculous coincidence, Inspector. Of course there are some in this department who might think that the British have got spies over here who report back to your Government. However, we'll let that lie.' His voice hardened. 'I know of this Fenian Brotherhood. Speaking as a policeman, I have to say that I consider the Irish immigration to this country to be a curse on us. As a group they cause more trouble than any other nationality of immigrant. For every native-born American we arrest for criminal offences in this city, we arrest five Irish.

'I accept that there are decent, hardworking, God-fearing individual Irish, but the vast majority that have come here in the past decade are ignorant, dirty, drunken rowdies, and I don't like them.'

Colum felt like pointing out to Captain Young that his strictures against the Irish could be directed with equal justification against large segments of any nationality on earth, and that he considered him to be a bigot. But he knew that he couldn't afford to antagonise the man, and so held his tongue.

Young chuckled dismissively. 'I have to say, gentlemen, that in my opinion you're looking for three needles in a haystack. There are almost a million people living in this city, and that makes it a very big haystack to search through.'

Charlie Anderson smiled. 'Well now, Captain, I should say that London is an even bigger haystack, and I've managed to find a good many needles there in my time.'

'I take your point, Inspector,' the Captain conceded. 'But keep it in mind that London is your native haystack, and that New York is not.'

The mutual antipathy between the three was now tangible, even if veiled.

'I've detailed a man to help you, as I've been instructed to do. His name is Ezra Bolton, and he'll come to your hotel if you leave the address with the desk sergeant downstairs,' Young told them. 'But like I said, I think that you're looking for needles in a haystack. Good day to you, gentlemen.'

Chapter Forty-seven

Detective Ezra Bolton came to the hotel room where Colum and Charlie Anderson were staying later that morning. In his mid-thirties, he was tall and willowy, and weak-chinned with the clear, fresh complexion of a child. He spoke with a nasal New England twang and was fashionably dressed in frock coat, tall beaver hat, pristine white starched linen and yellow kid gloves on his small hands. His posture and gestures suggested effeminacy.

His very first words prejudiced both Colum and Charlie in his favour as, with a beaming smile, he greeted them. 'Welcome to New York, gentlemen, you've been given me to help you because that sour bastard John Young doesn't like me and reckons that I'm not worth a damn as a detective. Young considers me to be the spoiled son of a rich and privileged family, and he's correct in that assumption. I've always been spoiled rotten by my rich and privileged family. But he can't get rid of me because my Uncle Linus is the Commissioner of Police, and it doesn't matter a damn how many times I mess up, my Uncle Linus won't have a word said against me. My Uncle Linus truly believes that the sun shines from my rectum.'

Bolton was carrying a small carpet bag and he opened it and produced a bottle of whisky. 'I propose that we have a few drinks and get to know each other, gentlemen.'

By the time the bottle was empty there was a burgeoning friendship between the two Britons and the American. As they discussed what they were to do to trace the Calatravas, Ezra Bolton proved to be quick-witted and highly intelligent. He asked perceptive questions, and his comments on what they told him were well reasoned and shrewd.

'Before we go asking questions in Greene Street it will be to our advantage to go to see someone that I know. We could get our throats cut otherwise.'

They left the hotel and travelled on a white-topped 'Yellow Bird' omnibus until they reached the lower end of Broadway. They left the omnibus there and Ezra Bolton informed them, 'I'm now going to take you to the headquarters of the rulers of the Five Points. The rulers are called the "Dead Rabbits", and they're the nastiest, meanest rabbits that you'll ever get to see.'

Of all the slums in New York, the Five Points was the worst. A mere stone's throw from smart, wealthy Broadway, the Five Points alleys and streets lay deep in filth. Beneath the tumbledown tenements and houses were deep, rat-infested cellars without windows or ventilation, lined by bunks where for ten cents a night anyone might lay their head. On every block there were a dozen or more 'grog shops' which sold cheap rot-gut liquor. Ragged barefoot children swarmed everywhere, scuffling with the pigs amongst the rotting garbage, collecting cinders and rags.

'Hot corn! Hot corn! Here's your nice hot corn, smoking hot, straight from the pot!' Young girls stood on every street corner selling hot corn and crying their

356

wares in shrill voices. 'Hot corn! Hot corn, smoking hot, straight from the pot!'

The three well-dressed strangers attracted much interest as they plunged deeper into the foul streets, heading for the centre of the Five Points where a massive old brewery dominated an open space of rubbish-strewn land. Many of the roughs considered robbing the three, but on looking closer decided that the two men walking at either side of the effeminate dandy were too big and tough to tackle without the cover of darkness. For their part the three men walked close together and kept their hands on the revolvers in their coat pockets.

The Old Brewery was the headquarters of the Dead Rabbits gang and it was here that Isaiah Rynder came to issue his orders. He was a Tammany Hall politician who at one time had held the office of United States Marshal in New York, a cunning, highly intelligent man, well fitted to the savage battle of survival in this ruthless city.

As they neared the Old Brewery Ezra Bolton told the two Britons something about the internecine warfare that went on continuously between the New York slum gangs.

'The Dead Rabbits and the Bowery Boys are bitter enemies, because the Dead Rabbits are native-born Americans, and the Bowery Boys are Irish. There are other gangs in the city, like the Black Snakes, American Demons and the Plug Uglies and others, but the Dead Rabbits and the Bowery Boys are the largest and the toughest. They're both controlled and used by the city politicians, and all of the Volunteer Fire Brigades are manned by gang members. Nearly every time there's a fire in this damned city the brigades fight with each other to see who's going to put it out. And by the time

357

the fight has finished, the damn building has more than likely burned down.'

They reached the Old Brewery and were stopped from entering by scowling, rough-looking men who openly wielded knives and guns. One of these sentinels knew Ezra Bolton, and demanded, 'Who are these two you brung with you, Mr Bolton?'

'They're from England and we've got business with Mr Rynder.'

'He ain't here.'

'Is George Brooks here?'

'Yeah.'

'Then I'll see him.' Bolton stepped forward and pushed past the sentinels, and with some slight trepidation Colum and Charlie Anderson followed.

George Brooks was a mature, grizzled-haired man, well dressed and favoured the ubiquitous yellow kid gloves on his hands. He greeted Ezra Bolton in a friendly manner, and the pair withdrew into an inner room for a short while where Bolton's business with him was completed to their mutual satisfaction.

As they walked back towards Broadway Ezra Bolton explained the arrangement he had made with Brooks. 'Greene Street is Dead Rabbits territory. The brothels are controlled by their leaders. No one would talk to us or answer any questions without the leaders' say-so.' He produced a curiously shaped metal token from his pocket. 'This is the talisman that will unlock lips, gentlemen. It's George Brooks's seal of approval. If anyone doubts that we have his permission, then I just show them this, and their doubts are vanquished. Then if they themselves choose to do so, we might get a few answers to our questions.'

'Is Brooks doing this as a favour to you?' Colum asked.

The American laughed and told him, 'He's doing it for money, Mr Macrae. Fifty dollars, which you gentlemen will have to reimburse me, since I have just paid him out of my own pocket.'

By day the shabby red-brick houses that lined both sides of Greene Street gave it the appearance of respectable, albeit decaying, gentility but when night fell Greene Street throbbed into garish life because almost every house along its entire length was a brothel. The lower end of the street catered to the sailors whose ships docked along the Hudson River and here, interspersed with the brothels, there were dancing saloons where men and women could drink and carouse all night long. The girls who flocked to these dance saloons were the roughest drabs of the city, and in the constantly erupting brawls would fight as savagely as any man.

As the street progressed northwards towards Clinton Place so the quality of the brothels improved, and their prices increased accordingly. Each establishment advertised itself with a huge red gaslit globe above the front door on which was etched, in blazing white characters, the name of the brothel or its proprietor.

As Ezra Bolton conducted Colum and Charlie Anderson along the street that night he pointed out the names, and related anecdotes and histories to his companions. 'The Forget-me-not', 'Sinbad the Sailor', 'Lizzie's', 'The Gem', 'The Black Crook', each shuttered house yielded its crop of stories.

Almost at the top of the street, ranged with the most select brothels, was 'Flora's', and it was here that Ezra Bolton told them, 'This is the best place to start making enquiries, gentlemen. Flora gets to know practically everything that happens down here, and she's always ready to help me, for a price of course. I recommend potential clients to her establishment.'

Hard eyes scrutinised them through a door flap before the door was opened to Bolton's knocking.

'Is it business or pleasure you're wanting, Mr Bolton?' the burly, broken-nosed doorman asked politely.

Bolton turned to Colum and Anderson. 'How about it, gentlemen? Would you care to sample the merchandise before we get down to business? Flora's girls are the freshest goods on the street. I don't mind admitting that I often take my pleasure here myself.'

'Only because you don't have to pay for it here, Ezra.' The woman who came towards them was middle-aged, but still handsome and firm-bodied. She was dressed with great elegance in an expensive ballgown with a décolletage that displayed her rounded breasts to full advantage.

'Flora, how are you?' Bolton greeted her like an old and dear friend. 'I've brought two gentlemen from England to see you, Flora. George Brooks has told me to impress upon you that any help that you can give them will be much appreciated by him personally.'

He discreetly showed her the token.

'Mr Brooks knows that I'm always more than willing to help him in any way that I can, Ezra.' She smiled, displaying small white teeth, and Colum could not help but think that she was a very desirable woman, even though she had long passed her first flush of youth.

'You're most welcome here, gentlemen,' she told the Britons, and led the three men to her own private room, an opulently furnished salon at the rear of the house. There she insisted on pouring them huge tumblers of whisky, pressed cigars upon them and seated them before asking, 'What is it you want to know?'

'We're interested in a man named Dermot Calatrava, ma'am,' Charlie Anderson informed her. 'And we wondered if you might know him, and if so, where we might be able to find him?'

'Dermot Calatrava?' the woman mused. 'Yes, his name rings a bell with me. But let me check my files, so I can be certain that he's the one I have in my mind.'

'That's very kind of you, ma'am.' Charlie Anderson smiled, and all three men rose politely as she left the room.

'Flora is a first-class businesswoman,' Bolton said admiringly. 'She vets her clients very carefully. There's never any ructions in this house. Whenever she admits a new client she gets her girls to pump him for all they're worth, and then Flora keeps a record of what the girls tell her about him. She's got a better dossier on the men who come here than we've got on the convicts in the Tombs. Of course, there are those in the Police Department who are unkind enough to suggest that Flora might be indulging herself in a little blackmail now and again. But so long as she keeps me happy, I'm not going to believe such scurrilous accusations against her.' He winked slyly.

Flora returned, carrying a large leather-bound ledger, and seating herself she opened it on her lap. After some checking she found the page she sought.

'Dermot Calatrava. Is this what he looks like?' She read out a physical description. 'About five feet six inches in height. Slim build. Dark eyes and hair. Looks to be in his late twenties, or early thirties. A dandy in his dress.'

'That's him.' Charlie Anderson nodded.

'There's not much more than that to tell you,' Flora said with apparent regret. 'He likes blonde women with fair skin and plump build. He drinks very heavily, and indulges in opium, and sometimes when he's real drunk he rants and raves about the English. He doesn't like them at all. A few weeks ago he told one of the girls that he had come into a lot of money, and that he was living in a mansion down on Twenty-third Street between Lexington and Fourth Avenue.'

Colum and Anderson exchanged an excited glance.

'How often does he come here, ma'am?' Colum enquired.

She frowned severely. 'He doesn't come at all these days. He got rough with one of the girls the last time he was here, and I've banned him from ever coming here again. I will not tolerate anyone, not if it was the president himself, ill treating any of my girls.'

'Have you heard where he might be found these days?' Bolton asked.

She shook her head. 'Naturally I spread the word among my acquaintances about what he'd done here, so he is no longer welcome at any of the better-class establishments on this street. But like any other business, gentlemen, there are some unscrupulous people who would make no objection to whatever he did to the poor girls in their employ, just so long as he made financial recompense to them for any damage to the goods on offer. So it's very likely that he is patronising one of the houses in the lower portion of the street. They are not people to whom I speak, gentlemen, so I really can't tell you who uses their houses.'

'But I'm sure that you could find out, couldn't you, Flora?' Bolton entreated. 'I would count that as a real favour.'

She chuckled throatily. 'Come back and see me tomorrow night, Ezra.'

When the three men were making their way back towards Broadway Ezra Bolton said, 'I suggest we take the omnibus back up town to Twenty-third Street, gentlemen.'

They journeyed on the bus as far as Madison Square and then strolled along Twenty-third Street. As they passed the towering brownstone mansions Colum's emotions became increasingly confused. If Dermot Calatrava was indeed living in one of these magnificent houses then it must be because Rosaleen had acquired yet another wealthy protector. He stared up at the sumptuous façades and his heartbeat quickened. Rosaleen could be gazing out of one of these glittering windows at this very moment. Jealousy, anger, yearning and heartache swirled in maelstrom in Colum's mind, and apprehension tightened his throat as he wondered what his reaction might be if he was now to come face to face with Rosaleen.

As they progressed along the street Ezra Bolton identified the tenants of each house: Gracies, Rhinelanders, Astors, it was a litany of wealth and power; van Riesdal, Jones, Cornell, Jerome, Mathieson, Hensberg and many other names redolent of riches.

Bolton was scathing in his comments about these members of New York's greatest families. 'Most of these people are cheats, liars and hypocrites, and some of them are downright thieves. Half of them will go broke before the year is out, and be back in the gutter where they originated from. I've known dozens in this city who made their fortunes in a hurry, then lost those same fortunes in an even bigger hurry. This city doesn't show any mercy to losers.'

'Assuming he actually is here, how difficult will it be to find out which house Dermot Calatrava is living in?' Colum asked.

'I don't anticipate it being difficult,' Bolton said confidently. 'But after we've discovered that, then we shall have a problem.'

'What do you mean?' Charlie Anderson frowned. 'When we find out where he is, we just go in and arrest him. I don't see that as a problem. I've collared tougher men than Calatrava.'

'It's not a question of toughness,' Bolton explained, 'but of protection. We don't yet know who Calatrava is living with and what the relationship with his host might be. Maybe he's being kept by a woman, or indeed a man, who will protect him. These people are members of the families who run this city and control its politics. We have to tread very softly when dealing with them. It's no use rushing in to arrest Calatrava only to see him set free again because one of these people here has exercised their influence with the Police Department.'

'But you told us that your uncle is the Commissioner of Police,' Colum challenged. 'Surely he'd not release a murdering bastard like Calatrava.'

Bolton winked slyly. 'My Uncle Linus is as corrupt as everybody else when needs be, and although my family is rich, we're paupers compared to these people on Twenty-third Street.' He laughed sardonically. 'The pen may be mightier than the sword, gentlemen, but here in

New York the dollar is mightier than the pen and the sword put together.'

'So what do we do?' Colum's fiery temper roused. 'Do we let Calatrava go scot-free because some rich bastard says that we should?'

'Oh no, I'm not about to do that.' Bolton was not disconcerted by Colum's angry reaction. And he smiled easily. 'But before we do anything else, I am going to see a man who knows more about the skeletons in the cupboards of this city than any other man breathing. I'll have a talk with him before we go any further in this matter.'

'And who is this man?' Charlie Anderson enquired.

'His name is Brown,' Bolton told him. 'Isaac Brown.'

Chapter Forty-eight

To a stranger's eye Isaac Brown resembled nothing more than a dressed-up cab driver. He was big and bulky, with a protuberant belly and a brick-red face, and he walked with a swaggering gait. But Isaac Brown was not a cab driver; he was the sexton of Grace Church, the most fashionable and exclusive house of worship in the entire city.

To be married or buried within Grace Church's walls was considered the ultimate accolade to one's social standing. Only the highest echelons of high society could ever attain such an honour.

Isaac Brown was the most famous man connected with New York high life and for many years had been accepted as the arbiter of who was and was not socially eligible. If a society hostess decided to hold a function, she would send for Isaac Brown. He would examine her guest list and dictate, in the most courteous manner, who should be included or excluded. He would decide in which rooms of the mansion the musicians were to perform, the caterers were to serve refreshments, which florists and confectioners were to be engaged. For his most august clientele he would graciously consent to supervise the function in person, and throughout the event he would be present, ordering the servants, greeting the guests, directing the carriages, making sure that everything ran smoothly.

His speciality was funerals. The laying out of the corpse, the position of the coffin, the arrangement of the furniture and lighting, the hanging of the drapery, the volume of crape, the decoration of the hearse, number of horses, quality of plumes and banners, in all these aspects he was acknowledged to be the very finest and most artistic presenter of a funeral in the entire country.

Isaac Brown considered it to be only his just deserts therefore when one afternoon a group of New York's most august and distinguished citizens summoned him to their private rooms at the Merchants' Bank to ask his advice.

He felt a gratified pride as he looked around at his hosts, Peter Cooper, John Jacob Astor III, Hamilton Fish and John A. King. They were men of immense wealth, national power and importance; the very apex of high society.

They invited Isaac Brown to take wine and refreshment, and chatted about inconsequential matters for some minutes, and then conveyed him into an inner sanctum with sound-proofed walls and doors.

Peter Cooper acted as spokesman. 'Now, Mr Brown, what we are going to impart to you must remain confidential for a time.'

With a lordly inclination of his huge head Isaac Brown indicated his understanding and absolute probity of discretion.

'President Buchanan wrote to Her Majesty Queen Victoria some time ago with an invitation, which Her Majesty graciously accepted, for her eldest son to pay a visit to the United States, following his tour of British North America.

'Our city is to be honoured by the presence of His Royal Highness, Edward, Prince of Wales, and those of us assembled here are the Committee of Hospitality for that occasion.

'After consultation with the British Ambassador, Lord Lyons, the Duke of Newcastle and Major-General the Honourable Robert Bruce we have decided that we shall hold a ball in the Prince's honour. A Grand Ball that will be the most glittering and lavish entertainment that this city has ever witnessed.'

Isaac Brown was visibly impressed, and inwardly prayed fervently that the committee would ask him to select the guest list and arrange the ball. But with consummate self-control he allowed none of his inner excitement to show.

'May I say, sir, that the idea of holding a ball is one of genius,' he congratulated fulsomely. 'According to reports His Royal Highness had professed himself to be thoroughly bored with banquets and stuffy receptions. I must say that, in my humble opinion, the prospect of a ball will absolutely delight His Royal Highness.'

'Perhaps, Mr Brown, perhaps.'

Peter Cooper did not receive Brown's compliment with any great relish. He had wanted to hold a banquet for the Prince, because he had strong moral scruples about the frivolity and sinfulness of wanton dancing, and it was only because of the insistence of the Prince's entourage that yet another banquet was the last thing the Prince would enjoy, and their suggestion that a ball would be preferable, that the Committee had unwillingly decided that this would be the offered entertainment.

'The Committee would greatly appreciate your assistance in selecting the guest list for the ball, Mr Brown, and of course any other assistance that you are able to offer in making the necessary arrangements for the event itself.'

Isaac Brown sobbed his thanks inwardly. Outwardly he majestically inclined his great head in calm acceptance, and informed the Committee in measured tones, 'If my humble talents can in any way be of help to you, gentlemen, then I regard it as my privilege to place them at your disposal . . . Ask of me whatever you will, I stand ready to serve you.'

Chapter Forty-nine

'The Prince of Wales is coming to New York. There is to be a ball, the most magnificent ball that's ever been held in this city . . . In this country . . . Only the very best people are to be invited.'

The news spread like wildfire around the city, and a frantic, ever-increasing demand for invitations began.

The rumour that Isaac Brown was the arbiter of who should attend the Prince's ball was also spreading fast, and although Isaac Brown continually and firmly denied that he had any influence over who was selected to receive invitations, still the rumour persisted, and strengthened and flourished.

Grace Church was besieged; every pew was packed, and disappointed supplicants massed outside the church doors hoping for the chance of a word with Isaac Brown.

On Brown's advice the Committee drew up a list of four hundred gentlemen. Upon the payment of seventy dollars each, these privileged men would be entitled in their turn to issue ten invitations each, of which three must be allocated to ladies. Again following Brown's advice, the Committee ruled that the names of all prospective recipients of an invitation must be submitted to the Committee in advance, to enable them to judge the individual's suitability to attend.

Dirk van Riesdal was one of the four hundred selected gentlemen, and he hurried to tell Rosaleen his good news.

She was sitting with Dermot in the morning room when Dirk arrived. Dermot was recuperating from his last bout of debauchery and he was lying on a chaise longue, his face pale and haggard, his hands still trembling, his nerves jangled and stretched dangerously near to breaking point.

'I've been selected, my dear. I am to be one of the four hundred,' Dirk announced proudly.

'One of which four hundred?' she enquired with a smile.

'Why, the four hundred that have been chosen to invite guests to the Prince of Wales's ball. Isn't it an honour?'

To his surprise she took it coolly, and made no reply.

With some chagrin he protested, 'I thought you would be excited, my dear. The whole of New York society is begging for entrance. It's the most prestigious event for the past decade.'

It was Dermot who answered, showing animation for the first time since Dirk had entered the room. 'When is the ball to take place, Dirk?'

'On the evening of October the twelfth, at the Academy of Music. The Prince is to attend under the pseudonym Baron Renfrew. My regiment, the Seventh, is to mount the Guard of Honour.'

'Are you to command the Guard, Dirk, you're a very experienced soldier, after all?' Dermot's tone was that of friendly interest, but Rosaleen frowned slightly as she recognised the sneer in his dark eyes.

'Good Lord, no.' Dirk was not aware that he was

being baited, and he answered with heartfelt disappointment. 'I'm not senior enough in rank for that, worse luck. I'd have been proud to do so. It's a great honour for the regiment to be selected to provide the guard.'

'Well, now that you are one of the chosen ones, does that entitle you to take a companion to the ball?' Dermot asked.

'It entitles me to invite ten other people, of which three must be ladies,' Dirk informed him. 'So you two had best begin to prepare yourselves for the ball. You must recover your strength, Dermot, and you, my dearest Rosaleen, must go to the finest dressmaker you can find and order her to make a ballgown that is fit for a queen.'

He beamed at Rosaleen, and although his news had greatly disturbed her, she managed to feign a delight that she was far from feeling.

Satisfied that he had made her happy, the young man told her, 'I really do have to go, my father is waiting for me at the bank. We have to meet a very important depositor. I'll see you tonight, my dear. Goodbye, Dermot.'

As the door closed behind the young man Dermot grinned exultantly at his sister, and hissed, 'There is a God in heaven after all, Rosa.' His dark eyes glittered with hatred. 'The Prince of Wales is coming here, to New York, and we are to go to his ball. We'll have our chance there.'

Fear shivered through Rosaleen and she shook her head in dismay. 'No, Dermot. No more. All that is over and done with. We have a new life here. I want no more trouble.'

'I want no more trouble,' he mocked her sneeringly. 'Have you sold your soul, as well as your body?'

She reacted furiously to his cruel gibe. 'My body earns the money that you live on, and my soul is still my own. There's never a day passes that I don't bitterly regret that we ever started on this murderous path. It's brought nothing but grief and suffering to innocent people.'

'And what about the grief and suffering of our own people?' he challenged. 'What about their right to freedom?'

'What about it?' she flung the challenge back at him. 'You've brought death and destruction to innocent people, and has it gained any freedom for anyone? Has it lessened the grief and suffering of our own people by one iota?'

'Don't take the high moral tone with me,' he snarled. 'You've killed as well.'

Her face paled and there was distress in her eyes. 'Oh yes, I've killed. You've no need to remind me of that. There's never a day goes by that I don't curse that day, and beg God for forgiveness.'

He saw her distress and his manner softened. 'Rosa, you killed that man because he was going to kill me. There's no sin in that. It was his life, or ours.'

'That's as may be. But I don't want any more killing, Dermot. I'm sick of it all; of all the posturings and braggings of the windbags who claim that they're fighting to free our nation. Men like D'Arcy McGee and Meagher and Corcoran who are only lining their own pockets with the money that they trick from poor, simple Irishmen who believe that it's going to be spent to further the cause.' She was trembling with the force of her emotions. 'Look at how they turned against you. How they took the word of a man who we know to be a self-serving hypocrite, and gave you no chance to speak out in your own defence before condemning you. You blame McCulloch for what he did, but I blame equally these men here who believed him because it suited them. That's why they turned against you, Dermot. And you must now abandon the struggle, because it has no chance of succeeding while those men remain the leaders of the Fenians.'

Her voice took on a pleading quality. 'For my sake, if not for your own, Dermot, forget about the cause, and the Fenian Brotherhood, and all the wrongs that England has inflicted on Ireland. Live your own life for a change. You can do well here. Dirk is ready and willing to help you to better your condition in life. You can marry and have children, and live happily. It's all here waiting for you. You only have to accept what is being offered freely to you.'

For some time Dermot had suspected that his sister had lost her appetite for the struggle. He realised now that his suspicions had been justified, and his unstable mind suddenly exploded in fury. Jumping up from the chaise longue, he screamed at her, 'Why have you turned against me? Why have you joined forces with my enemies?'

She was badly shocked by his sudden outburst and, as she stared at him, horror filled her. His eyes were glaring with madness.

'I haven't turned against you,' she protested frantically. 'I could never turn against you. You are my brother. I love you above all else in this world. I could never turn against you.'

374

'You lying bitch!' he screamed. 'You lying, treacherous bitch! You want to betray, don't you? Well, so be it. I'll do it alone. I'll show the world what Dermot Calatrava is made of. And after I've killed their Prince, then I'll take command of the Irish Patriot Armies and lead them against the English. I'll smash England into ruin. Nobody can stop me. Nobody, nobody, *nobody* . . .'

As he screamed the word over and over again he began to strut about the room, smashing his fists against the furniture and mirrors and ornaments, and blood spattered from the torn flesh of his hands. 'Nobody, nobody, nobody, nobody.'

She ran to him and tried to hold him in her arms, begging him, 'Calm down, honey. Please, calm down.'

He smashed his fist against the side of her head, knocking her half senseless, and she staggered from the impact of the blow and cannoned into a small table, bringing it crashing with her to the floor.

'Nobody, nobody, nobody, nobody, nobody, nobody . . .' His demented screams filled the air, and the window panes shattered under his blows.

Theresa Quinn came running into the room and on her heels came the male servants.

Still dazed Rosaleen dragged herself to her feet. 'Help me to hold him,' she shouted. 'He'll kill himself if we don't hold him.'

The two women and the three servants hurled themselves at the demented man and under their combined weight he was forced down, biting, punching, kicking, until his limbs were pinioned to the floor. He strained against them, his body heaving and writhing, and then his eyelids fluttered rapidly and his eyes rolled upwards in his head until only the whites showed. His body slumped and he fainted away.

Panting tearfully, Rosaleen looked around at the wreckage in the room and made a difficult decision.

'Go and get ropes,' she ordered one of the servants. 'He'll need to be tied up until I can get a doctor to examine him.'

Theresa Quinn was well accustomed to men's drunken violence.

'Ach now, it was only the drink sent him off like this.' She offered rough comfort. 'Sure, didn't Thomas Quinn break up the house regular as clockwork every Saturday night after he'd been on the poteen. When Dermot wakes up he'll be fine. It was only the drink he'd taken that set him off. Men are like that when they've the drink in them. He'll be fine when he wakes up.'

'I pray to God he will be, Theresa,' Rosaleen muttered with fervent hope, but in her heart she feared that her beloved brother would not be all right when he recovered consciousness. She knew that he had not taken a drink of alcohol or smoked opium for several days. Rosaleen was dreading that his outburst signalled a descent into madness.

Chapter Fifty

'I think we're being gammoned, Charlie.' Colum Macrae stared moodily out of the window of their shared hotel room at the rain which was lashing the street outside.

His friend frowned. 'You can't say that, Colum.'

Colum swung to face him. 'It's been two weeks now that we've been waiting for Bolton to bring us news. I didn't come to America to sit on my arse all day in a bloody hotel room. I can do that in England.'

'He's kept in touch,' Charlie Anderson pointed out.

'Oh yes, he's kept in touch all right,' Colum exclaimed angrily. 'Every two days we get a message from him telling us that his investigations are proceeding. We should have got to Calatrava by now. Bolton's had more than enough time to find out if and where he is in Twenty-third Street.'

The older man regarded Colum speculatively. 'Are you feeling all right, Col? You're very edgy today.'

Colum sighed heavily. 'I'm sorry, Charlie, it's just that all this waiting around unnerves me. And another thing is bothering me. It's the ninth of October today, and the Prince is due to arrive here on the eleventh. What's Cumlinson going to do to us if we haven't got the Calatravas tucked up safely before then?'

There was a knock on the door and Colum opened it to find Ezra Bolton standing there.

'Thank Christ it's you, Ezra. Have you got any news for us?' he questioned eagerly. 'Have you located Calatrava?'

The American's youthful features were uneasy. 'Listen, you've both of you got to come to headquarters right away. Captain Young wants to speak with you urgently.'

Colum regarded him curiously, sensing that something was wrong. 'What is it, Ezra? What's happened?'

'Well, I've found the Calatravas and Theresa Quinn. Isaac Brown checked the guest lists for the ball and told me that the woman, Rosaleen Calatrava, was living in the van Riesdal house on Twenty-third Street.'

'That's great news, Ezra,' Anderson encouraged.

But Bolton shook his head unhappily. 'No, don't cheer. Just come and see Captain Young. He won't tell me what he wants to say to you, but I don't think it will be anything to make you happy.'

He refused to say another word, and the two Britons accompanied him to Mulberry Street in a strained silence.

Captain John S. Young was frowning grimly when he invited them to take a seat in his office.

'I'll come straight to the point, gentlemen. Detective Bolton has located the Calatravas. They're living in a house on Twenty-third Street which is owned by a man named Dirk van Riesdal.'

'That's good work,' Charlie Anderson congratulated. 'When will you be making the arrests?'

Now the Captain's unease became plain to see as he shook his over-large sandy-coloured head. 'We won't be making any arrests, gentlemen. Not at this time, anyway.'

He lifted his hand as if to forestall any protests from his listeners. 'Let me explain the situation, gentlemen. It seems that Dirk van Riesdal and the woman, Rosaleen Calatrava, are intimately acquainted. She is his mistress, and from all accounts he is infatuated with her. Now the van Riesdal family carries a lot of weight in this city. Hendrick van Riesdal, Dirk's father, is one of the leading bankers and a big wheel on Wall Street. He has immense power and influence in political circles. Both the Commissioner and the Chief of Police have advised me that at this time it is impolitic to do anything which might upset the old man. If we arrest the woman or her brother there will be a deal of public interest aroused because of the woman's relationship with Dirk van Riesdal. That public interest would be viewed with great disfavour by old Hendrick. So it's been decided by the Commissioner and the Chief to let sleeping dogs lie, for the time being at any rate.

'The Calatravas are to be left alone, gentlemen. And the Commissioner feels that it would be for the best if you both returned to England as soon as possible.'

Even though he had been expecting it, the confirmation that Rosaleen was living with a new protector still caused a sharp pang of anguished jealousy to strike through Colum. Hot anger burgeoned in the wake of that anguished jealousy. 'She was playing me for a fool all along,' he concluded, and the lust for revenge whelmed over him. 'We can make the arrests ourselves,' he stated.

Young frowned warningly. 'You have no powers of arrest in this country, Mr Macrae. And any such action

379

on your part would mean that we should be forced to take you yourself into custody.'

'So you are prepared to let a murderer go scot-free, just because it might embarrass the van Riesdal family?' Colum accused hotly.

'Shut up, Colum,' Charlie Anderson ordered sharply. His fleshy features betrayed his own anger but he kept himself under firm control, and told Young, 'I can understand the difficulty of your position, Captain Young, but the Calatravas have committed very serious criminal offences. Surely, if the van Riesdal family were informed of what the Calatravas have done, then they would not wish to shelter them.'

'As I understand it, the Calatravas and the Quinn woman are merely suspects,' Young pointed out. 'They are not fugitives. What cast-iron proof can you give me now that they are indeed guilty of what you claim?'

'Theresa Quinn's husband was one of the perpetrators of the Nottingham outrage. We have his corpse as proof,' Anderson argued.

'Proof that *he* was there, Inspector. But what proof do you have that either of the Calatravas were involved, or Theresa Quinn?'

'We know that they are involved.' Charlie Anderson's fleshy features were flushed with anger, but he kept his voice low and controlled. 'Listen, Captain Young, I'm talking to you as one policeman to another; not as some shyster lawyer seeking to fudge issues. We are absolutely certain that Dermot Calatrava was responsible for Nottingham and all the other explosions around the country. We are also certain that he was responsible for the attempted assassination of the Prince of Wales and the murder of Major Winstanley in Richmond Park.

Now, Captain, I don't doubt that you are an honest man and a good policeman, and it is as one good policeman to another that I'm appealing to you not to allow these murderers to go free.'

For the first time since their arrival John Young betrayed signs of embarrassment. He was an honest man and a good policeman, and he could appreciate the intense and angry frustration that the men before him were experiencing. His tone became apologetic.

'Believe me, Inspector Anderson, I am powerless to do anything else other than obey my instructions. I am as unhappy as you are about this. But there is nothing at all that I can do to alter the situation.'

Colum was about to speak out again. He knew that angry words would not change anything, but his fiery temper impelled him to say what he thought. Then he saw the warning scowl that Charlie Anderson directed at him and, rather than involve the Inspector in further futile dispute, he kept silent.

They parted from Young with formal politeness and returned to their hotel. An hour after their return Ezra Bolton came to see them.

'My orders are to keep an eye on you until you take the boat back to England. Captain Young is worried that you might be tempted to take the law into your own hands and snatch Calatrava.' He grimaced with disgust. 'I don't like it any more than you do. It makes me very angry to think that that murdering hound is going to get away with what he's done. But the police here are controlled by the politicians. And we all know what politics is. A dirty game played by even dirtier people.

'Captain Young has asked me to tell you that a

steamboat called the *City of Glasgow* is sailing for Liverpool tomorrow morning. It's docked at South Street. He's arranging with its master for you to take passage on it. He wants you to know that there's nothing personal in this. He's just following orders.'

Colum and Charlie Anderson exchanged a wry grimace.

'Well, I'll leave you to do your packing,' Bolton told them, and added apologetically, 'If you go out of this room, there'll be a couple of our men going behind you. And they'll be on watch outside your door through the night. I'm really sorry about this.'

'That's all right, Ezra,' Charlie Anderson assured him. 'We know that you're only following orders.'

When they were alone Colum demanded, 'Surely there's something that we can do, Charlie? What about if we go to the consul here, and ask him to make a protest?'

Anderson shook his head. 'It won't serve, Col, because nothing has been proven against the Calatravas in any court of law. They're still only suspects, strictly speaking.'

Although Colum had not relished the idea of disposing of Dermot Calatrava in a necessarily cold-blooded execution, the knowledge that the man was to escape punishment for his terrible crimes made him fiercely angry.

'We can't just go back home with our tails between our legs, Charlie, and leave that murdering bastard laughing at us.'

The older man was deeply preoccupied, and Colum scolded, 'Are you listening to me, Charlie? We've got to think of some way of slipping me out of here.'

'And what will you do then?'

'I'll go to the house at Twenty-third Street and put paid to Calatrava. Then I'll head for Canada.'

'What if he's not at the house? What then?' Anderson countered doubtfully. 'He could be anywhere.'

Colum thought for a moment, then his voice rang with conviction as he declared: 'I know where he's certain to be, Charlie. Doyle told us about how Calatrava was saying that someone should go to Canada and shoot the Prince. And how he was always bragging that he was going to strike a blow against the English that would set the whole world talking. Well, that's what he's going to do. He's going to shoot the Prince when he arrives here in New York.'

Anderson shook his head dismissively. 'He'll not get the chance. Ezra told us about the measures being taken to keep Prince Eddie safe. The entire police department and half the army is going to be on guard.'

'But what measures will be taken at the ball?' Colum challenged. 'Oh, there'll be plenty of guards outside, but how many will be inside? There are going to be four thousand people there, Charlie; the cream of New York society. They're above suspicion, aren't they? And they'll be milling around, all of them trying to get close to the Prince, and when he's dancing they'll be within inches of him with no guards in between them to shield him.

'Dermot Calatrava will make his try at the ball, Charlie, I'll stake my life on it.'

Anderson grinned mirthlessly. 'And how do you propose to gain entrance to the ball, Col? You're not Cinderella. There's no fairy godmother going to give you an entrance ticket! Not to mention the fact that there are two detectives standing outside our door, who'll be walking on our heels whenever we leave this room.'

Colum went to the large window and opened it to thrust his head out. He craned and twisted, closely examining the walls beneath, to the sides and above.

'You're not thinking of jumping, are you, Col?' Anderson gibed. 'Perhaps I should have told you before that we're on the sixth floor. It's a bloody long drop to the ground.'

Colum drew his head in and closed the window, then stated confidently, 'I can climb down, Charlie. I'll need to make a rope from the sheets, and then swing to the side. There's a drainpipe let into the wall about five yards to the left. If I can swing to that, then the rest will be easy.'

Anderson realised that his friend was deadly serious and the sarcasm disappeared from his tone. 'What do you want me to do?'

'Well, obviously you'll have to pull the sheets back in. And if Bolton comes checking then cover for me in some way or other. I need all the time I can get, Charlie, to sort out how I'm going to reach Calatrava.'

He glanced back out of the window. 'As soon as it gets dark I'll go. So let's make a start at getting the sheets roped up.'

Charlie Anderson shook his head doubtfully. 'I'm not sure about this, Colum. I know Cumlinson told you that failure to arrest the Calatravas would mean trouble for you, but he's a reasonable man. When I explain to him what happened here, then he'll not hold this failure against you. He won't blame you.'

Visual images surfaced in Colum's mind: images of the shattered, bloody bodies left behind by Dermot

384

Calatrava; images of Rosaleen; images of the filthy
tramp who had chopped him down and left him for
dead; and as those images swirled before him, so the
iron entered Colum's soul.

'I'm not doing this for Cumlinson any more, Charlie,'
he muttered grimly. 'Now I'm doing it for myself . . .'

Chapter Fifty-one

The climb down the side of the wall was far easier than Colum had expected; the inlet for the drainpipe was wide and enabled him to get a firm grip of the pipe. As soon as he was on the ground he waved to Anderson and then hurried towards Twenty-third Street. He was carrying his loaded revolver in a shoulder holster beneath his coat, and had several rounds of ammunition in his pocket. He knew that he must strike quickly because his escape from the hotel might be discovered at any moment, and when that happened he was sure that the police would immediately mount guard over the van Riesdal house.

Twenty-third Street was quiet in comparison to the downtown districts, and only a solitary carriage and a handful of pedestrians were travelling along its length as Colum reached it. Some of the opulent houses blazed with lights but the van Riesdal house had only a light showing through a single upper window and Colum frowned to see this. Perhaps only a caretaker was there and the Calatravas had gone elsewhere. He walked slowly past the house, trying to formulate a plan of action. He knew that he could not loiter in this vicinity for long without attracting unwelcome attention, as the wealthy districts employed nightwatchmen to patrol the environs and guard against the depredations of the criminals that infested the city. But he must be certain that Dermot Calatrava was inside that house before he dared risk entering it.

The possibility that Rosaleen might be so close caused him considerable disquiet. He knew that he still cared deeply for her, no matter how badly she had used him, and he accepted the fact that he could never bring himself to harm her physically. But he was grimly determined that Dermot Calatrava was going to die, no matter how that might grieve Rosaleen.

He turned and retraced his footsteps. As a carriage and pair overtook him he turned to watch its progress. Colum's heart pounded with excitement as he saw the horses turn towards the entrance to the van Riesdal house, and he broke into a run as he realised that the carriage was going to stop there.

The Negro driver got down and went to the horses' heads and Colum slowed his pace to see if anyone would alight from the carriage. Then, realising it was empty, he approached the driver. 'You're Mr Calatrava's servant, aren't you?'

The man shook his head. 'No, suh. I'm Mr Dirk van Riesdal's servant.'

'But Mr Calatrava and Miss Calatrava live in this house, don't they?' Colum's tone was deliberately authoritarian.

'Yes, suh, they do live here, but they ain't here at present. They's gone away for a while.'

'Where?' Colum demanded. 'I've important business with Mr Calatrava. I must speak to him urgently.'

The coachman was hesitant. He had been given strict instructions by Dirk van Riesdal not to tell anyone that Dermot Calatrava had been admitted to a mental asylum. He took the easy way of evasion.

'They's coming back here for the Prince's ball, suh. But I don't know exactly when they's coming.'

'Well, that was the business I had with Mr Calatrava. I was to confirm that he is coming to the ball.'

'Oh yes, suh, Miss Calatrava and Mr Calatrava both will be going as Mr Dirk's guests.'

'Good.' Colum smiled. 'Many thanks for your help.' He slipped the man some coins.

'Thank you, suh.' The man grinned happily, and offered, 'Does you want me to tell Mr Calatrava that you was asking after him, suh?'

'No, that won't be necessary,' Colum answered off-handedly. 'I'm not known to him by name, I'm only the errand boy sent to check that people have received their invitations.'

'Yes, suh. Thank you, suh.'

As he walked back towards Madison Square Colum decided that the Prince's ball would offer him the best opportunity of coming to grips with Dermot Calatrava. How to gain entrance to that glittering assembly he would have to decide on the night. Until then he would blend into the city's teeming masses and patiently bide his time.

Chapter Fifty-two

The exclusive private mental asylum was situated near to the village of Yorkville and was secluded from the neighbouring farmhouses by the extensive woodland surrounding it. The Calatravas and Theresa Quinn had been staying here for several days while Dermot received treatment from one of the foremost medical alienist practitioners in the country, Doctor Claude Schultz, who specialised in treating the wealthy mentally ill.

'How is Dermot today, my dear?' Dirk van Riesdal asked as he came into the room where Rosaleen was sitting.

'He's quiet and peaceful. Theresa is with him. Doctor Schultz was with him for two hours this afternoon and he says that Dermot is well on the road to complete recovery. All he needs is rest and loving companionship.' There was happy relief in her face as she jumped to her feet and came to hug the young man.

'Oh, Dirk, you've been so kind and understanding about this. I'll never be able to thank you enough.'

He kissed her tenderly and his eyes were loving. 'Do you think Dermot is recovered sufficiently to come to the ball with us tonight? Perhaps it will do him good to enjoy himself just for one night. Would you like me to have a word with Schultz about taking Dermot back with us now, for this night only?'

'Oh no!' she said hastily. 'No, he must have complete quiet at this stage in his treatment. Doctor Schultz was most insistent on that point.'

'But he'll be so disappointed at missing the chance to attend the greatest ball the city has ever known,' Dirk coaxed. 'And it would be a chance to introduce him to some beautiful girls, all eminently marriageable.'

'No, Dirk, I can't risk any chance of having Dermot become overexcited until he has made a complete recovery. And that is a matter for Doctor Schultz to decide, not for you or I.'

'Oh well, if you say so.' He seemed genuinely disappointed. 'Anyway, I'll go up and say hello to him now, shall I?'

'Yes, that would please him greatly.' Rosaleen smiled. 'And would you ask Theresa to come down and see me.'

He kissed her again, and told her, 'I'll be so happy when you move back to Twenty-third Street, my dear. The house seems like an empty desert without you.'

As the door closed behind him Rosaleen's smile became a worried frown. In her heart of hearts she feared that her brother would never make a complete recovery. He had been quiet and docile these last few days, and pleasant-mannered, but there had been fleeting moments as she sat and talked to him when the eerily frightening sensation came over her that it was not her beloved Dermot sitting before her but some evil alien entity that had taken possession of Dermot's body. It was nothing he said or did, rather something lurking in the depths of his dark eyes which sent shivers of fearful horror through her.

'Dear God, let it be only my silly fancies that make me feel so,' she prayed desperately now.

When Theresa Quinn appeared Rosaleen instructed her, 'Now don't leave him alone until he's sound asleep. Give him a double dose of sleeping draught tonight. I'm worried that with him knowing I'm not here, he'll become restless and disturbed.'

'For Jasus' sake, Rosa, will you give over fussing,' the woman snorted impatiently. 'I don't know why you're fretting yourself so. Dermot's nearly well again, and it was only the drink that sent him over the top in the first place. Now he's dried out, he's as right as rain.'

When Rosaleen went upstairs herself to her brother's room, she was forced to admit that she was worrying unnecessarily. He was sitting with a book in his hands, absorbed in reading.

He smiled warmly at her as she came in, and told her, 'Now you be sure and enjoy yourself at the ball, Rosa, and have a few drinks for me as well.'

She smiled fondly down at him. This time spent in the hospital had wiped the ravages of debauchery from his face, and tonight he was looking smooth-complexioned and youthful, and his cheeks held a hint of healthy colour.

'And another thing,' he chuckled. 'If you get the chance, I want you to stamp as hard as you can on the Prince's toes, and tell him it was from me, with my compliments.'

She laughed with genuine amusement, happy to see him so light-hearted and apparently content, and when she kissed him good night and went downstairs to join her waiting lover, she felt her heart lighten. Everything was going to be all right, she knew it was. Her lovely Dermot was becoming his old self once again.

*

Dermot continued to sit quietly, absorbed in his reading, and Theresa Quinn went to her own room to sneak a drink from the whisky bottle she kept hidden there against the strict rules of the establishment.

Dermot's eyes traversed the printed lines, and his fingers periodically turned the pages, but his brain was not absorbing the words before him. Instead it was occupied with a fevered self-communion. The insanity that had for so long been dormant, only breaking out for brief forays, was now in full dominance. For him now his sister and Theresa Quinn were deadly enemies who had betrayed him and were keeping him imprisoned here; keeping him from his sacred mission. Every man's hand was raised against him but he was going to prove to them all that he was their superior in all things. Gleefully he congratulated himself on the way that he had fooled them all. He had lulled them into a feeling of security. And now that they had relaxed their constant vigilance, he would make his move. He would break out from this prison and, evading all their attempts to stop him, he would return to New York and there, in the very midst of his enemies, he would strike down the arch-enemy, the heir to the throne of England, Edward, Prince of Wales.

He closed his book and went to the window to stare at the surrounding woodlands, the trees now gloomed by the deepening dusk. The time to act had come. His rooms were in a small wing of the main building, joined to it by a covered walkway. All the windows were covered by iron grilles and to escape he needed to take the walkway into the main building and then exit from the guarded front entrance. At this hour the side doors were locked and barred and to break those doors open would make too much noise, bringing the attendants to investigate.

Dermot smiled contemptuously. How foolish his jailers were to believe that such measures could keep him imprisoned. His hand went to his pocket and he fondled the small empty bottle which was concealed there. It had contained laudanum, and that laudanum was now mixed with the rot-gut whisky in the bottle that that cretinous Theresa believed she had successfully kept hidden from prying eyes.

Dermot knew why she went to her room at the same time every evening. It was to gulp whisky down her throat. He pulled his gold pocket watch out of its fob and glanced at its ornate face. Yes, she would be snoring like a pig by now. It was time to go and make sure that she could not raise any alarm at his escape.

Theresa Quinn was slumped over the table in her room, snoring loudly, the whisky bottle lying on its side on the floor beside her. Dermot crossed to her and checked how deeply unconscious she was. Then he went into the room his sister used and carefully selected some clothing and a bonnet which he packed into a large carpet bag. Humming a lively tune he returned to Theresa Quinn's room.

'Goodbye, Theresa, you treacherous bitch.' He smiled and smashed the lighted lamp he was carrying onto the floor. The kerosene spread in a flaming pool and Dermot stood watching the flames take hold of the wooden boarding and furnishings. He walked down the corridor to the door which led into the walkway and waited there with the carpet bag in his hand.

The fire had taken hold and the thick smoke was billowing out into the corridor. Dermot waited until he was enveloped in its choking fumes then, coughing and spluttering, he opened the door and ran down the walkway, bellowing, 'Fire! Fire! Fire!'

The watchman who guarded the front entrance came hurrying to investigate, and Dermot collided with him.

'It's all on fire, and Mrs Quinn is trapped in there!' Dermot screamed, and bundled the man with him into the main vestibule, leaving the door to the walkway wide open so that the smoke poured through it.

'Get help! Quick, man, get help! Fire! Fire! Fire!'

The commotion brought other patients and attendants from their rooms and, as the smoke poured down the walkway and into the main building, panic erupted and shrieking patients milled wildly around while their attendants tried vainly to calm them.

'Get everybody outside,' Dermot bawled. 'We'll all be killed! Get everybody out, we'll all be killed. We'll all be killed!'

The front entrance was unlocked and flung open and the shrieking mob fought to get through it. Brutally Dermot buffeted people aside, using his carpet bag like a club, and emerged into the cold darkness. Then he calmly walked away from the building and the cacophonous maelstrom he had created.

Chapter Fifty-three

Three hundred thousand people had lined Broadway in the dusk to greet the arrival of the Prince of Wales. As the six-horsed carriage had passed they had cheered wildly and waved and, in their midst, Colum could not help but feel a sense of pride that it was a British Prince being so enthusiastically received.

Colum had also been in the vast crowd that crammed the roads that night to see the torchlight parade of the Fire Department pass in review before the Fifth Avenue Hotel in honour of the Prince. And again he was in the crowds that greeted the Prince at New York University the following day. Even while acknowledging the fruitlessness of doing so, Colum constantly searched the faces around him for any sign of Rosaleen Calatrava. He knew that he must find her in order to locate her brother, since the only sight he had ever had of Dermot Calatrava was that brief glimpse of wild, dark eyes in a filthy, thick-stubbled face.

At eight o'clock that evening the first guests began to arrive at the Academy of Music, and once again Colum was amongst the packed crowds of onlookers, eagerly staring at each group that alighted from the stream of carriages disgorging their passengers before the sumptuous edifice. Soldiers of the Seventh Regiment were on guard, and uniformed policemen swarmed everywhere, their eyes constantly scanning the masses of onlookers, alert for any sign of threat towards the Prince.

As time passed the crowds grew impatient at seeing the elegantly clad gentlemen in their black swallow-tailed evening dress, and their magnificently gowned, bejewelled and coiffured women, and began to chant for the Prince.

At nine o'clock a deputation of gentlemen arrived at the Fifth Avenue Hotel to escort the Prince to the ball. At the very moment that the Prince and his escort emerged from the hotel to be greeted by a roaring of cheers, Rosaleen Calatrava and Dirk van Riesdal arrived at the Academy of Music.

Colum saw her step from the carriage, and his heart thudded painfully. A feeling of utter desolation enveloped him at the sight of her beauty, now lost to him, and a fierce yearning to hold her in his arms once more, and hear her soft words of love took hold.

Get a grip on yourself, you bloody fool, he berated himself angrily. She's not your woman, and never was. She's your enemy. You're free of her now, and you must regard her only as an enemy to be hated.

But deep within his being he knew that he could never really hate her and that rather than his enemy, she was his heartbreak.

Anxiously he sought Dermot Calatrava, but Rosaleen's tall, blond companion was the only other person to alight from the closed carriage.

In the crowd only yards away from Colum, Dermot Calatrava stood staring with hate-filled eyes at his sister. Dermot was wearing the dress and deep-poked bonnet he had stolen from his sister's room at the Asylum, and he had a shawl wrapped around the lower part of his face.

Rosaleen and Dirk van Riesdal entered the decorated entrance and Colum felt a sharp pang as she disappeared from his sight.

From further along the road cheering sounded and the word travelled with lightning speed through the crowds that the Prince was coming.

Dermot Calatrava hefted his carpet bag higher and reached into its depths with one hand. His fingers found the revolver and tightened around its butt.

The carriage bearing the Prince and his escorts came nearer and nearer and the crowd grew more and more excited. Storms of cheers erupted as the Prince's carriage came to a halt outside the Academy, and the guard of the Seventh Regiment presented arms. Dermot Calatrava began to force his way through the close-packed bodies hemming him in; he needed to get closer before he could be sure of hitting his target. He felt exultant. He was within scant yards and split seconds of glory. He could see the smooth epicene features and bulging eyes of the Prince with crystal clarity. One more yard, one more push, and he would be able to shoot. He started to lift the revolver from the bag and, at that moment, the lines of police charged against the encroaching crowds to clear space for the Royal party. The crowd surged and eddied and Dermot found his arms crushed tight to his sides. Unable to free them he was swept backwards and forwards, trapped in the crowd like a piece of flotsam in a tidal wave. His shawl fell from his face and he found himself staring into startled blue eyes only inches from his own.

He felt a shock of recognition.

I know you, he thought. But from where, and when?

Colum's eyes locked with the dark eyes before him and for a brief instant he feared he was hallucinating; that they were Rosaleen's eyes staring into his own. Then he knew where he had seen this face before. He knew he was staring at Dermot Calatrava.

The police heaved at the crowd, and the dense-packed mass of bodies whirlpooled and changed standings, and Colum and Dermot Calatrava were carried helplessly away from each other. Colum fought desperately to keep the bonneted Calatrava in view but it was a hopeless task.

It was only as his shock of recognition ebbed that he fully realised what he had seen. The bastard is disguised as a woman.

Dermot Calatrava cursed bitterly at his lost opportunity to strike down the Prince. But he was not going to give up now. He was going to find a way to get into the Academy and make his kill. He stopped struggling against the mass and let himself be propelled to its outer edges, and once there broke free.

A dark alleyway between two tall buildings loomed before him and he ducked into it, hiding in its gloom while he thought what to do. His mind's eye pictured the man with the startled blue eyes who had been swept past him in the crowd but he still could not remember where or when he had seen those eyes before. He dismissed the man from his mind as being of no importance, and instead began to concentrate on how to gain access to the ball.

'I can take the risk of going as myself. I can go back to van Riesdal's house, change my clothing and simply walk through the front entrance of the Academy. Nobody here can possibly know yet what's happened at Yorkville. The place is probably still burning.'

He was wearing his own clothing beneath the dress, and it took only seconds to strip off the disguise. Then he began to run through the alleys, angling towards Twenty-third Street.

Meanwhile, in the crowd Colum was desperately searching for the disguised man. 'It is him. It is Dermot Calatrava.' The certainty thundered in his brain.

The ball opened with the 'Quadrille d'Honneur' and then continued with lively, lilting waltzes. Miss Fanny Butler, Miss Fish, Miss Hamilton, the chosen beauties danced one after another with the Prince and between each dance those young lovelies who had not been fortunate enough to have been pre-selected as a Royal dancing partner pressed close about the young man who, being notoriously sexually predatory, gloried in the proximity of so much nubile female flesh.

At one end of the vast hall, now crowded to suffocation, a new supper room had been constructed, entered by one stage door and exited by another. Prominent citizens stood guard at these doors, admitting fifty people in at a time to partake of refreshment. There was a raised dais at one end of this new room where the Royal party was seated and served. A massive horseshoe-shaped table ran entirely around the room and behind it liveried retainers, standing virtually elbow to elbow, poured champagne and piled plates high with delicacies for the guests.

The success of the ball was fulfilling all expectations and would be remembered – everybody present was in agreement on this point – for years to come as the most lavish, splendid and brilliant event ever staged in this city.

As Rosaleen waltzed with Dirk she let herself surrender completely to the music and for the first time in many weeks she gave herself wholeheartedly over to pleasure.

Colum searched for almost three hours and finally accepted that Dermot Calatrava had disappeared.

'Perhaps he's abandoned any idea of shooting the Prince,' Colum mused, but could not bring himself to believe it. On the contrary the premonition persisted and strengthened as the hours passed that Dermot Calatrava was going to make an attempt this night, and that he would somehow or other gain access to the Academy to do so.

'I have to get inside there myself. That's where I'll find Calatrava. He'll be near to his sister, I'm sure of it. But how do I get inside?'

The entrance was closely guarded by policemen, soldiers and the stewards who possessed the lists of accredited guests. He began to walk around the outside of the huge building.

'There are bound to be windows opened to let some of the heat escape. Perhaps I can climb through one of them?' He smiled with rueful humour. 'I should have been a monkey, not a policeman.' Then instantly he corrected himself. 'But I'm not a policeman any more, am I?'

To his dismay he found that there had been sentries posted all around the building, and so although there were indeed opened windows high up on the walls, there was no chance of him climbing up to them without being seen.

A cab drew up outside the Academy and the dandified figure of Dermot Calatrava got out. He strolled into the front entrance, passing between the clusters of watchful policemen and soldiers, and one of the stewards challenged him: 'Do you have an invitation, sir?'

'I do indeed.' Dermot smiled, but his body was tense and he was ready to snatch his revolver from its hiding place beneath his armpit and use it should any attempt be made to take him into custody.

'Your name, sir?'

'Calatrava, Dermot Calatrava. I am a guest of Mr Dirk van Riesdal.'

He noted that a tall, bulky-figured man with a brick-red face who was standing talking with another steward turned to look at the mention of his name.

'Excuse me, sir.' Isaac Brown moved to block Dermot's progress. 'You're Mr Dermot Calatrava, the guest of Mr Dirk van Riesdal?'

'I am.' Dermot tried to keep the casual smile on his face, but in his disordered mind he was already sensing grave danger, and like a cornered wild beast was readying himself to strike out.

When he had heard the young man's name Isaac Brown had instantly recalled the detective who had been asking questions about him some weeks previously. Ezra Bolton had been very evasive about the reasons for his enquiries, but Brown knew that those reasons were pressing ones.

Tonight had proven to be a major triumph for Brown, and he did not want any untoward incidents to mar it now. He felt very uncertain about this young man before him, and was extremely reluctant to allow him entrance to the ball. He smiled diplomatically and asked, 'Might I enquire, Mr Calatrava, why you have come here at such a late hour? The invitation expressly stated that all guests were advised to attend before nine o'clock when the Prince would arrive here.'

'I was held up,' Dermot answered, and then bluffed, 'Look, if there is any difficulty about my late entrance, then I suggest that you send for Mr Dirk van Riesdal, because it is upon his private business that I've been engaged. I should imagine that he will be very unhappy that you have further detained me from joining him in this manner.'

The bluff worked. Isaac Brown did not want to offend the scion of one of the most powerful families in the city.

He bowed majestically. 'Enjoy the ball, Mr Calatrava.'

'Thank you, I fully intend to do just that.' Dermot smiled and made his way up the wide staircase.

Outside the front entrance the crowds of spectators had thinned to a mere scattering, and Colum eyed them disconsolately. Then a carriage drove up at breakneck speed and halted in a stamping, spark-flying flurry of hooves and jingling of harness.

The policemen and soldiers guarding the entrance swarmed around the carriage, shouting angrily at its driver, and Colum experienced a rush of adrenaline when he saw who that driver was – the Negro coachman of Dirk van Riesdal. The man was hatless, and there was blood streaming down his face. He jumped down from the seat and was immediately engulfed by the guards. Colum could hear him shouting wildly.

'I's got to see Mr Dirk. I's got to talk to Mr Dirk!'

Colum pushed into the men milling around the coachman.

A police sergeant was shouting, 'Just quieten down, Sambo. Are you drunk or just plain crazy?'

The Negro tried to break free of the hands restraining him. 'Let me pass. I's got to see Mr Dirk. I's got to tell him what's happened.'

The sergeant laughed jeeringly. 'What's happened is that this nigger has gone crazy.'

'No, I ain't crazy,' the Negro bawled furiously. 'I's got to tell Mr Dirk about Mr Dermot. He's gone inside there. He's acting crazy. He nigh on killed me.'

'Then that makes two of you acting crazy,' the sergeant mocked, and told the policemen with him, 'You'd best take this black bastard down to the station. We don't want any of the guests to see him, it might upset them.'

Colum had heard enough. He turned away and ran into the entrance. Immediately more guards converged on him, but he told them, 'Wait, I'm on police business.' He called to the small group of stewards, 'Have you admitted a guest named Dermot Calatrava within the past half hour or so?'

Isaac Brown frowned and came to stand directly in front of Colum. 'Why do you ask?'

'Because if you have admitted him, then the Prince is in mortal danger. Calatrava intends to kill him!'

Isaac Brown flinched as though he had been struck. 'Oh my God,' he exclaimed. Then recovered himself and challenged Colum. 'Who are you, and how can you

403

prove that this is not some stupid hoax?'

His eyes examined Colum's bedraggled appearance and doubt appeared in his expression.

Colum was on the verge of angrily berating the man, but managed to hold his fiery temper in check. Hot words would not convince anyone that he was telling the truth. He sought frantically for some means of convincing this man, and inspiration came.

'Tell me, sir, do you know a gentleman named Isaac Brown? Is he present here?'

Brown's lips twitched, and he replied, 'I am Isaac Brown, young man. So if this is a hoax, you have already been caught out in it.'

'Hear me out, Mr Brown,' Colum almost pleaded. 'Detective Ezra Bolton came to see you some time past, did he not? And he made enquiries concerning Dermot Calatrava.'

Brown nodded, but said nothing.

'My name is Colum Macrae, I am a British police officer, and together with my colleague, Detective Inspector Charles Anderson, I have been working with Detective Ezra Bolton in the pursuit of Calatrava. Please, Mr Brown, I beg you to believe me. If Calatrava is inside this building, then the Prince of Wales is in mortal danger.'

Brown was a highly intelligent and worldly wise man, and he could recognise truth when he heard it.

He swung to his fellow stewards and demanded, 'Can any of you identify the man we admitted named Dermot Calatrava?'

A couple of them doubtfully affirmed that they might be able to do so.

'And you can identify him, of course, Mr Macrae?'

'Definitely.'

Brown beckoned to the soldiers and policemen. 'You two, come with me, you and you and you go with these gentlemen. And you go with this gentleman here.

'The man we're seeking is highly dangerous, but you must not create any undue excitement among the guests. Any panic in such a crowd in this confined area could cause havoc. Move quietly and discreetly and when you sight the man, Calatrava, close in on him and remove him from the ballroom as quickly and with as little disturbance as possible. Let's go, gentlemen.'

Moving with surprising agility for a man of his age and bulk he led the search party upstairs and into the vast auditorium where four thousand men and women were creating a swirling, seething kaleidoscope of colour and movement.

Once through the main doors the party split into its smaller groups which began their urgent search.

Colum did not plunge immediately into the crowd. Instead he stood to one side of the doors and carefully examined the great room. There were four boxes stacked in two pairs on each side next to the proscenium arch, and then two tiered balconies running around the walls. The boxes and balconies were crowded as densely as the floor itself, and Colum experienced a moment of doubt. This was again a question of searching for a needle in a haystack. But this haystack contained a focal point which Dermot Calatrava must be near.

Colum asked a man standing by him, 'Where is the Prince?'

'I believe he's gone back into the Supper Room with the Committee members.'

'Where's the Supper Room?' Colum questioned and,

for the first time, the man looked at him and frowned doubtfully as he saw Colum's bedraggled clothing.

'Down there.' The man gestured vaguely towards the end of the room where the proscenium arch flaunted its masses of flags and bunting.

'Thank you.' Colum nodded and moved through the crowd towards the arch.

'I'm sorry, but I cannot admit you,' the distinguished-looking gentleman who guarded the door to the Supper Room told Dermot Calatrava. 'Only the Committee members and their families are allowed inside for the moment. They are being presented to the Prince.'

'How long will it be before I can be admitted?' Dermot asked politely.

'Not too long, I shouldn't imagine.' The man winked salaciously. 'From what I've seen of him tonight, the Prince enjoys the attentions of young women much more than the attentions of the Committee. I think that he'll be out just as soon as he can be and dancing with some lucky girl.'

Dermot smiled, then moved away from the stage door and effaced himself under the balconies' arcade behind the lines of people who were watching the dancers. He felt godlike now. That it was inevitable he would be killed or captured himself as soon as he shot the Prince caused him not the slightest concern. What he was about to do would elevate him to join the Immortals of Ireland's history. Wherever Irish patriots gathered together, then his name would be known and his deeds talked of. Songs and poems would be written about him and future generations of his nation would hold him in awe and reverence. He laughed aloud as sudden intense joy overwhelmed him, and some of the people standing in front of him glanced back over their shoulders, staring at him with distaste as he laughed and muttered to himself.

He was still muttering to himself and smiling when Colum found him.

Colum drew his revolver from his pocket and kept it concealed down by his side as he moved cautiously forwards, altering his angle of approach so that he would come up to the rear of his quarry.

The doors of the Supper Room were flung wide open and the Prince was framed in them, flanked by members of the Committee.

Someone in the crowd bellowed in a stentorian voice: 'Three cheers for Eddie, the Prince of New York!'

There was a roar of laughter at this sally and a deafening thunder of cheering. The crowd surged *en masse* towards the Prince, leaving Dermot Calatrava standing alone in the shadowed arcade at their rear. Colum moved quickly and came up directly behind Dermot Calatrava just as the young man was starting to move forwards.

Colum gripped the other man's arm with his left hand, and rammed the muzzle of his revolver deep into Calatrava's side.

Dermot turned his head, and when he saw the blue eyes only inches from his own, smiled pleasantly as if he had recognised an old friend. Colum's breath caught in his throat. The lucent dark eyes were gleaming with insanity. And in that instant Calatrava's hand swept inside his coat, and Colum pulled the trigger.

The muffled sound of the shot was drowned in the thunder of cheering, and all eyes and attention were centred on the Prince.

Colum wrestled the dying man back against the wall, and let his body slump onto a chair. He watched the life ebb from the dark eyes, then sat down beside the dead man.

He felt utterly drained of strength, and he bowed his head, closed his eyes and remained in that posture until the touch of Isaac Brown's hand upon his shoulder roused him.

He lifted his head and saw that he was blocked in by a solid wall of stewards that shielded him and his dead companion from view.

Within scant seconds the dead man and Colum were taken out through a small side door. The Prince, completely unaware that anything was amiss, began to dance, and the gaiety rose to fresh heights.

In the cellars beneath the Academy Isaac Brown issued low-voiced instructions to the men carrying the body of Dermot Calatrava, and they moved off along a shadowed corridor, leaving Colum and Brown alone.

Brown stared hard at the younger man for several seconds, and then said quietly, 'I don't wish to know your name, young man, or anything whatsoever about you. I feel that there are things going on here which would do me no service to discover. But you have my deepest gratitude for what you have done here tonight. If knowledge of this incident were to become widely spread then it could prove to be a severe embarrassment to a great many important people in this city, and indeed in this country. I think that it would be for the best if knowledge of it could be restricted to as few people as possible. Do you agree?'

Colum was bone weary and heart sick of the entire affair. He wanted only to leave this city and return to his own country, and above all else to his children.

He nodded.

'Are you in need of any financial assistance?' Brown enquired.

Colum shook his head.

'Might I offer a suggestion?' Brown took Colum's continued silence for assent. 'I think it would be best if you sailed for your own country from some port other than New York. Baltimore, perhaps.'

'I'll do that,' Colum told him.

'I'll say goodbye then, sir, and I wish you God speed and a safe arrival home.'

They shook hands briefly.

'If you take that flight of steps you will come out at the side of the building. Go to your left and you'll easily find Broadway.'

Colum wearily climbed the stone steps and went out into the cold night. He halted for a few moments, and the mental image of Rosaleen Calatrava flooded into his mind. He thought of the grief she would suffer when she discovered her brother was dead, and his own heart saddened for her.

'She'll survive it though, I've no doubt of that. Rosaleen will survive.'

He sighed heavily, and walked slowly away . . .

Other best selling Warner titles available by mail:

☐	Tildy 2: Poorhouse Woman	Sara Fraser	£4.99
☐	Tildy 3: Nursing Woman	Sara Fraser	£4.99
☐	Tildy 4: Pointing Woman	Sara Fraser	£4.99
☐	Tildy 5: Radical Woman	Sara Fraser	£4.99
☐	Tildy 6: Gang Woman	Sara Fraser	£4.99
☐	Tildy 7: Widow Woman	Sara Fraser	£4.99
☐	Tildy 8: Invincible Woman	Sara Fraser	£4.99
☐	The Imperialists	Sara Fraser	£5.99

The prices shown above are correct at time of going to press. However, the publishers reserve the right to increase prices on covers from those previously advertised, without further notice.

W

WARNER BOOKS

WARNER BOOKS
Cash Sales Department, P.O. Box 11, Falmouth, Cornwall, TR10 9EN
Tel: +44 (0) 1326 372400, Fax: +44 (0) 1326 374888
Email: books@barni.avel.co.uk

POST AND PACKING:
Payments can be made as follows: cheque, postal order (payable to Warner Books) or by credit cards. Do not send cash or currency.

All UK Orders	**FREE OF CHARGE**
EC & Overseas	25% of order value

Name (Block letters) ....

Address ....

....

Post/zip code: ....

☐ Please keep me in touch with future Warner publications

☐ I enclose my remittance £ ....

☐ I wish to pay by Visa/Access/Mastercard/Eurocard

Card Expiry Date | | | | |